CHARLIE IS MY DARLING

Mollie Hardwick

Coward, McCann & Geoghegan, Inc.
New York

First American Edition 1977

SBN: 698-10867-1

Library of Congress Cataloging in Publication Data

Hardwick, Mollie.
  Charlie is my darling.

  1. Jacobite Rebellion, 1745-1746—Fiction.
2. Charles Edward, the Young Pretender, 1720-1788—
Fiction. I. Title.
PZ4.H266Ch   1978   [PR6058.A6732]   823'.9'14
ISBN 0-698-10867-1   77-22839

Printed in the United States of America

Book One

The Star

1

Dorothy Beaumont stepped back and surveyed the dining-table. It was almost too beautiful to use, that expanse of snowy Irish linen bearing the silver cutlery and glasses of sparkling crystal. A shaft of June sunlight touched the pieces, striking diamonds from their facets. It lay warmly over the white candles in their silver branches and found the tender curves of bud and petal in the centrepiece of flowers which she had arranged herself: white roses shading from a bright white to a delicate, almost green tinge. They stood in a silver bowl, a fine two-handled piece that bore the Beaumont arms.

It was a charming blazon, she thought, compared with some of the grotesqueries displayed by other noble families. A crowned falcon in a leafy bower formed the crest; before him the arms, a rising sun shining upon a mountain peak; the supporters 'two angels proper, hair and wings or, under-robe sanguine, upper robe azure'. Beneath, on a scroll, was the family motto: *Un je serverai*. Viscount Gainsford, her father-in-law, was living abroad. That was why the family silver and so many other fine things were here, in Dove House, Richmond.

She sat down on a prim, immaculately polished chair and looked round the room, feeling dwarfed by its size though she was well-grown. Later, for the dinner-party, she would change into all her splendour, but this afternoon she was wearing her day-gown of pink dimity, fashionably full and square at the hips, a plain corset-bodice trimmed with bow-knots confining, unnecessarily, her slender waist. She touched one of the knots, smiling, remembering how her father had liked to tease her for her fondness for ribbons.

'Whom Simplicetta loves the town would know:
Mark well her knots, and name the happy beau.'

He would have had to praise the matronliness of her lace cap, perched on hair brown as a young thrush's plumage, swept simply back from her face with its green-grey eyes, tip-tilted nose and wide, sweet mouth, and coiled, one long lock escaping to lie on a neck as white as the roses gracing the table. Did the Gainsford ladies, disposed grandly round the walls in heavy carved frames, look down their aristocratic noses at the scholar's daughter who had been so fortunate as to inherit their goods and chattels through marriage to their descendant, the Honourable Lyndon Beaumont? She hardly cared if they did. They, poor things, were dead, and she was alive and twenty years old, and it was the year 1745, a year that Lyndon said would be the most glorious Britain had ever known.

She moved to one of the windows that looked on to Richmond Green. Lyndon was out there playing cricket. He was quite willing to play in a motley team made up from their own servants and the townsmen, aristocrat though he was. His wife smiled to see him tearing along the pitch as though he were still the schoolboy he looked, flushed and laughing, his unpowdered brown hair flying loose from its ribbon. He must always be active, whether riding, dancing all night, or at play as now he was; and other men were amazed to see him throw down a hand of cards at his club after only one game, too impatient to sit staring at hearts and spades. Sometimes Dorothy, used to a quiet life before her marriage, would feel tired out by the effort to keep pace with him, and he would call her Dolly Dawdle or Mother Bunch and tell her she was getting fat and lazy with good living. It was like having a boisterous young brother as well as a husband. Dorothy thanked Heaven they were so pleasant together, when she thought of some of their acquaintances, alternately yawning and snapping at one another.

It had been so different in the dark, creaky-timbered old house in Red Lion Square, Holborn, where mice pattered, squeaked and unwrapped eternal parcels behind the wainscotting, and the lean cats of London which William Hogarth painted wailed amorously among the twisted chimneypots. It had not been all their own; in the basement and ground floor rooms lived a landlady whose sour cooking smells wafted up into their parlour, and whose sharp voice was sometimes raised loudly enough to splinter the old panelling.

The Vyners were not poor, but they were certainly not rich. Dr Alured Vyner was a deeply learned and cultured scholar with some kind of stipend – Dorothy had never quite understood what – paid to him by his old University of Oxford. He had taken paying pupils as boarders, and they were, in general, none-too-bright youths being crammed with knowledge which they would never have dreamed of pursuing on their own account. Dr Vyner, who had once had leanings towards the Church but had been hampered by immovably stubborn views on the Doctrine of Transsubstantiation, was particularly good with those being prepared for the ministry. The youths were kind to the neat child who sometimes opened the door to them, and was allowed to sit on the floor of her father's study with her own books while he tutored them. They would bring her comfits, or give her a penny for herself; one brought her a bird in a cage, a poor linnet which died within three days, causing the tender-hearted Vyner household bitter distress.

They had been very happy while Mama was alive; Mama who was small and gentle, and who had been born Anna Nairne, daughter of a good Scottish family. She had tried so hard to breed companions for Dorothy, but with the last one, which would have been another daughter, she had died of childbed fever. Dorothy wished the babies had never been visited on them, for they were very content as a family of three, and perfectly good company for each other. Mama had an endless repertoire of old Scots ballads which she sang to her spinet, and Papa knew, and delighted to tell, story after story from the classics to his child, 'My little Ariel, my attendant sprite,' with her eager pointed face turned up to his, and her large eyes wide with interest. Never one for dolls, Dorothy's passion was for these stories, and for her mother's songs of knights and ladies. At night she would send herself to sleep by imagining herself straying in a great, dark forest, not in the least frightening, such as she had seen in pictures, where the most beautiful and uncommon people and creatures would appear to entertain her. She remembered, when she was very small indeed, pleading to her father for 'a 'tory', and his Jovian laughter.

'Well asked, well asked, girl, for art thou not a Tory child, of true blue breed, born to serve the Blood Royal?'

It had been many years before she knew what a Tory was, or learned that the Whigs, who held the whip-hand of Government, according to Papa were a set of vile sneaking canting knaves led by the Prime Minister, Sir Robert Walpole. Even then she was not very clear about it until the day when, just before her ninth birthday, she was taken to Whitehall to watch a procession going to the Abbey. Her father told her that the short stout man in the old-fashioned bag-wig, who gestured curtly to the crowds from the windows of the State Coach with an expression on his red face which suggested that he would rather have been elsewhere, was the Hanoverian usurper, German George II, whose father had kept the British crown from the head of the rightful monarch, King James. Dorothy was surprised; he looked very unlike her idea of royalty, with his cross looks and plain coat and cocked hat.

'I was not yet born when they turned the noble Stuarts off the throne in '88,' said Dr Vyner. 'And this set of coarse-brained, coarse-mouthed rascals have ruled us ever since, to the eternal shame of Britannia, God bless her.'

'Where is King James now?' Dorothy asked.

Her father looked glum. 'In Rome, child, in Rome. With his sons, Prince Charles and Prince Henry. Far from his kingdom. Exiled, a wanderer, as was Odysseus of old.'

'Why does he not return, Papa?'

'He did essay it, thirty years ago, but the bid was a lamentable failure, thanks to a pack of great cowardly lords who left him in the lurch, and bequeathed us' – he said in ringing tones as the State Coach drew near to them – 'a fat, guzzling, whoring person of depraved mind and low tastes.'

Dorothy knew what whoring meant (in George II's London it was impossible not to know) and so, it appeared, did the crowd around them, who were muttering and shaking their fists at Papa so menacingly that she took his hand and pulled at it, frightened. He looked down at her with the kind smile that was so much more suited to him than his ravings.

'There, there, small Gift of God, my Dorothea. Now we have seen the beast, let's go walk in Hyde Park.'

Soon afterwards her mother died, and from that day her father seemed to lose interest in the defects of the monarchy, and in everything else but herself and his precious books. His study was already crammed, from floor to smoke-darkened ceiling, but still he brought home more: beautiful volumes bound in green and scarlet calf with gold lettering, or shabby things lacking their spines, dog-eared and shedding pages. Dorothy, who as she grew up took her mother's place as housekeeper, began to dread the arrival of yet further piles of books, to be heaped up on the floor, smelling musty and sometimes containing horrible small white insects which scuttered out when she took a duster to the volumes.

She knew that long after she was in bed he would sit there, his churchwarden pipe alight and a grog-jug keeping warm on the hob, spectacles slipping down the bridge of his high nose, his eyes red with reading. She was glad of those nights when company came, even though no entertainment came with it for her. Three or four gentlemen, much of her father's age, would arrive cloaked and bearing lanterns to light them through the dark uneven streets, sometimes with a servant for protection. They would make their way upstairs, speaking courteously to her on the way, and when their number was complete there would be the murmur of voices from the study, talking, talking, with now and then a raised tone or a laugh. Going up with refreshment for them she would catch a phrase here and there: '. . . extensive French preparations . . . every confidence . . . already reached the coast . . . the Young Gentleman . . . Lord Traquair sent over . . .'

When they were gone, and she went to clear the table, she knew that she would find there the wine-glasses Papa usually kept in the corner cupboard, which would be locked after they had been washed and returned to it. They were of an unusual pattern, having a globule of water imprisoned at the base of the stem, and a white rose engraved on the bowl.

Sometimes Dorothy forced herself to hope that Papa would be fortunate enough to find a second wife, a homely body who would nurse him in illness. Often now he would appear short of breath as he climbed the stairs, and Dorothy occasionally saw him put a hand to his shoulder as though it hurt him.

But Dr Vyner never met any ladies – and, thought Dorothy ruefully, would probably not take a second look at one unless she were bound in vellum with gilt edges.

She was all the more astonished when, one winter day in 1744, a servant called with a letter. Her father read it and passed it across the table to her. It contained a few lines written in a dashing but unmistakably feminine hand.

> Lady Primrose, being out of her late Mourning, begs
> Dr Vyner's company and that of his Family at a small Levee:
> Cards and Music.

Then followed the date, an evening a week hence, and the address, a house in Essex Street, the Strand.

Dorothy looked up at him sharply. '*You*, Papa? Bidden to a levee?'

'And why not, pray?' He returned to the plate of boiled fowl at which he had been picking and turned over a page of the book propped against the teapot.

'Indeed, why not. But Papa . . . Papa! You are covering that page with gravy. Do stop reading and listen to me. What does this lady mean by begging your family's company?'

'Why, that she hopes for yours, child. I know of no others of my family.' He gazed round the room amiably, as if expecting to see a troupe of relatives appear, all eager for the levee.

'Oh very civil. But – what shall I wear?'

'Wear?' He had returned to his book and the congealing fowl. 'Your best gown, I should imagine.'

Dorothy sighed in exasperation. 'I *have* no best gown, only the stuff one I wear to church, and it's as old as – as Methuselah.'

'Then make one,' he suggested placidly.

Dorothy bit back a very natural enquiry as to where the money was to come from. He had no idea how little she had to manage on. He never noticed that they ate only the cheapest cuts of meat, that his daughter used all her ingenuity to make poor food taste better, or that the still-growing girl wore clothes that had ceased to fit her. His small stipend barely paid their rent, and she knew that whenever he went out without mentioning his destination, and gave her a few guineas on his return, he had been visiting his stockbroker, selling more of his few shares. She would say nothing to him about money.

Inspiration came to her. 'The lute-string gown! To be sure it's meant for summer wear, but if I wrap well . . . there's a tear in the sacque but it will mend. The chemise!' she remembered with horror. 'There was a hole burnt clean through it from the iron. Oh, what shall I do?'

'Ribands, my dear, ribands,' suggested her father, practical for once. 'Beauty's banners, Cupid's bonds.'

And ribands, it proved, were the answer, for a generous row of them – made from a couple of yards bought cheaply because of a flaw in the silk – disguised the ugly burn. When they set out for the levee, arm-in-arm, she was full of pleasant anticipation, thinking how few social occasions there had been in her life: only visits to the homes of girls she had grown up with, her schoolmates at the Academy for Young Ladies in Lamb's Conduit Street, stiff suppers at the house of a legal friend of Dr Vyner's, a trip to Oxford, a month staying at Richmond with her disagreeable Uncle and Aunt Petworth because she had been ill and the river air was recommended for health. So little gaiety (not that she had ever asked for it), and now this grand occasion. Her father had told her that Lady Primrose was a High Tory, exceedingly fond of company, widowed a few years ago, with a wide circle of acquaintance.

'Why have we not called on her before?' Dorothy enquired.

He shrugged. 'I supposed myself too dull a dog to warrant her ladyship's attentions. Perhaps she lacks variety in her friends and has remembered my ugly phiz to set off the others'.'

'Your phiz is a very handsome one.' She kissed his nose. Something in the glance he directed at her held a hint that his reason for accepting Lady Primrose's invitation was not entirely the frivolous one he had given her.

Now they were approaching the door, in a press of carriages at the foot of Essex Street, in front of a fine tall house ablaze with lighted windows. The unmistakable dank smell of the Thames came up from Essex Stairs a few yards away, where bobbing lights indicated the presence of watermen bringing new guests in their little craft. Others were strolling up to the flambeaux-lit door, ladies shrouded under bunchy French hoods, gentlemen hidden under swirling roquelaures, moving up the broad stairs and between the tall columns that flanked them. They looked strange and grand, like the gallants and ladies who walked in St James's and on the green side of Piccadilly. Dorothy moved closer to her father, feeling shabby.

Then, in a flash it seemed, considering the crowd, they were inside the house, in a noble marble-paved hall, under a ceiling painted with garlands. Going up a wide crimson-carpeted staircase, they were greeted effusively by a small lady in very smart black with white edgings and ribands, who said that she was Lady Primrose and was transported with delight to see them. She was neither old nor young – in her late thirties, perhaps – neither pretty nor plain, but with a face full of liveliness and an excited, musical Irish voice. The double drawing-room into which the Vyners were shown was imposing indeed, elegantly panelled and lit by more candles than Dorothy had ever seen at one time. It too was populated with glittering creatures: gentlemen in long, elegant coats of velvet or satin, patterned with embroidered flowers and fastened with jewelled buttons, silver buckles shining on their high-heeled shoes, walking and talking with ladies in wide hoop-skirts and a great show of bosom, and everyone's hair powdered. Even Dr Vyner had covered his greying locks with the sticky white floury stuff which Dorothy hated. It felt gritty and made the scalp itch, and spread itself unbecomingly on the shoulders; but it certainly looked elegant on these people, almost as if they were made of spun sugar and should have melted in the drifting rain on Essex Stairs.

Lady Primrose led her from one person to another, introducing her in a flurry of chatter. 'May I present . . . so charming, not out of the schoolroom, I think, eh, child? The Marquis of . . . Lady . . .

Mrs Deborah . . .', names that went in at one ear and out at the other. Dorothy smiled, and bobbed, and murmured, and eventually settled down beside her father at one of the little card-tables dotted about for the playing of ombre, whist, loo or piquet. They were soon joined by a couple less finely feathered than most, to their relief, with whom they played a rubber in amity. They were waited on by servants bearing wine and comfits, but the lady waved a second glass of wine away.

'No, indeed.' She turned to Dorothy. 'There will be more before long, at supper, when one *must* drink, and I vow it goes to my head shockingly.'

Dorothy followed her example, and was glad, for supper, to which they were bidden surprisingly soon, was lavish, and the servants most pressing with their offerings of wine. Dr Vyner was growing vivacious, for him. He had left her side and was talking with this man and that, nodding or shaking his head. Dorothy began to realise that the evening would be spent largely in talk. Everybody seemed to have a great deal to say, and the buzz was such that it was difficult to make out sentences clearly, but she felt an undercurrent of excitement in the assembly, some knowledge or topic they had in common which had brought them all together.

She must have looked forlorn – so much younger than the others and standing apart. Lady Primrose bounded out of a knot of people and seized her hand.

'Child, you are alone. You have nothing to eat and drink. Come now, you must be entertained.'

Dorothy protested as she was led back to the tables. 'No, indeed, ma'am, I am very well. It is just that I know nobody here but my father. I am happy to look on.'

Her hostess regarded her with a look of puzzlement, then led her to a window-seat and sat down beside her.

'I'd have thought all of us here tonight had much to say to each other since the great news came.'

'News, ma'am?'

Lady Primrose's enquiring eyebrows shot up almost to her widow's peak, and her eyes were comically round.

'Do you mean you've not heard? Your Papa has not told you? No, stuff and nonsense, I'll not believe it.' She shook her head vigorously, her long earrings flashing.

'Indeed, ma'am, I hope I don't seem too stupid, but Papa and I – we talk mostly of – of domestic things. Not much of general affairs.'

'Then,' said Lady Primrose, briskly tapping Dorothy's arm with her fan, 'I must tell you myself that news has just come of the Young Gentleman's firm resolve to leave Paris, sail to Scotland, and after making himself master of that country to seat himself upon the British Throne.'

She leaned back to watch the effect of her revelation, which was considerable. Dorothy was well aware that the Young Gentleman was none other than Prince Charles Edward, eldest son of King James, and rightful Prince of Wales. She felt a wave of resentment that her father had not confided in her on a matter of such importance. Did he not trust her, or did he think she had no interest in anything above sewing and tidying his books? Lady Primrose seemed to guess her feelings, for she said gently:

'It may be your Papa meant to surprise you tonight with the great tidings. After all, one must be careful what one says. Here we are all friends, all of the Brotherhood of the Blackbird.'

She looked up, with devotion in her eyes, at the painting over the fireplace; a half-length of a man in court armour and ermine, the flowing curls of his wig squarely framing a long, pensive face with a melancholy droop to the full lips and night-dark eyes below heavy brows. James Stuart, the Chevalier de St George, King James the Third of England and Eighth of Scotland: the Blackbird in Jacobite code language, a failed man whose only hope was his eldest son. Dorothy recognised his face from a yellowed print that hung in her father's study, one in which he wore the Ribbon and Order and pointed to a shadowy crown.

'I wish Prince Charles well,' she said slowly. 'May his enterprise succeed better than . . .'

'That disaster in '15, and the other two. It will indeed, child, under such a leader as our Prince, so gallant, so martial, of such majesty . . .'

She had drifted away into a group of guests, leaving Dorothy alone, looking up at the picture.

It was thus that Lyndon Beaumont saw her: very slender, young and fresh-faced among so much powder, paint and padding. The heat of the room had warmed her cheeks to a deep rose, but the neck and bosom revealed by the soft lace fichu were pearly white. Lyndon took her in at a glance, from the shoes with buckles of plain cut steel, not of silver, to the hopefully bunched ribbons of her bodice, and the single flower in her hair, dressed low in ringlets tonight. He stared and stared, until she felt his gaze and turned to meet it. She had already noticed him – a young man whose rather loud voice and hearty laugh made him conspicuous among people who tended to chatter or whisper, and whose high healthy colour was in sharp contrast to the pale London faces around him. She turned sharply away from his bold stare, and was moving away, when she found him at her side.

'There is to be dancing in the next room, miss,' he said, pleasantly, not at all in the insolent manner she had expected. 'Will it please you to stand up with me?'

Flustered but not displeased, she said that she would, and took the arm he offered. The little group of musicians were playing a Handel minuet, and as they danced, sometimes at arm's length, sometimes close, he made her laugh with the story of how the musician Heidegger had been fooled by a waggish duke. For when Heidegger was entertaining the Usurper to a music party, the duke had caused another man to wear a wax mask in his likeness and, in it, to order the band to play 'Over the Water to Charlie' instead of 'God Save the King'.

As they danced she realised that she had never had a man for partner before. He was not much taller than herself, but his hand-clasp was more like a grip and his step so firm that even in that stately measure she was almost pulled along behind him.

In three dances, and the breathing-time between, they learned much about each other. He told her of his father, Lord Gainsford, who had discreetly gone abroad when enquiries about his activities in the 'Fifteen became too searching, and who now lived in Rome near the King. He had visited his father when making the Grand Tour, and had been graciously received by His Majesty.

She told him of her quiet life, the housekeeping and the books.

'I hope you're not a bluestocking,' he said sharply. 'I can't abide 'em. I'd rather have the Learned Pig at Saltero s Coffee-house than a bookish woman.'

'I'm not the least of one, sir,' she said, laughing again. 'My father is the only scholar of the family.'

'But you read books?'

'Of course. I wish there were more written for females. I have read *Pamela* and now have nothing else to occupy me for the winter.'

Someone bumped between them, and when they met again he asked her in his abrupt way, 'Will you present me to your father?'

At the end of the piece she led him to where Dr Vyner, looking flushed and relaxed, was sitting on a gilded chair. Introductions were made; then, oblivious of her, the two men began to talk politics in terms that were beyond her. She sat down, conscious of a mixture of tiredness and excitement which was not at all unpleasant. People were beginning to drift away, the musicians were packing up their instruments, Lady Primrose was embracing departing guests at the door. Dorothy touched her father's arm.

'I think we should be going.'

Lyndon broke off in mid-sentence and bowed as they said their farewells. Then suddenly, before they could move away, he stepped into Dr Vyner's path.

'May I call upon you, sir?'

As they walked slowly home through the now foggy streets, over the slimy cobbles, Dorothy said, 'Why did you not tell me, Papa, about Lady Primrose and – the Brotherhood? Was I too young? You *could* have trusted me.'

He turned fog-misted spectacles towards her. 'I know, I know. It was not that. I'm a little flown with wine, forgive me. I find it hard to summon my thoughts. If your mother had lived . . . but you were all I had. I dared not risk you. Now we're all confident, but at one time it seemed as though to befriend Them might mean the end of everything. Spies were everywhere, after the 'Fifteen, but now they're lulled into thinking the Cause is finished, after the French king dropped it this year. There have been wars with Spain, Prussia, now France . . . They think little of what may be brewing elsewhere. But you, child . . . if you'd been a boy it might have been otherwise. What can a maid do in war? Forgive me.'

She squeezed his arm, tucked under hers. 'I always forgive you.'

As they turned the corner into the Square he said, 'That was an extraordinary young man, Mr Beaumont. Extraordinary, but pleasing. Yes, pleasing. I hope I didn't do wrong in saying he might call.'

'I think you did very right, Papa,' said Dorothy.

Two days later Lyndon appeared on their doorstep, with a nosegay of flowers for Dorothy and a pound of highly superior snuff from Freybourg and Tryer's for Dr Vyner. The following day he arrived in a coach to drive them wherever they might wish to go; and as it was a Sunday afternoon they drove to Islington to a tea-garden. To Dorothy his company was like high summer in the midst of winter, his youth a lodestone to her own. His impetuosity, his unpredictability and his burning enthusiasm delighted her. The Gainsford town house in Grosvenor Square seemed to her a Moorish palace of splendours, though it was more or less shut up, with sheets over the furniture and bags over the chandeliers, only Lyndon's chambers being occupied, occasionally, for he preferred to live in the country, at Dove House in Richmond, Surrey. The misted mirrors she passed in the Grosvenor Square house told her the same story as her own modest looking-glass – she was pretty and desired.

Within a month he asked her to marry him. He was not a man to delay in great matters. At first pale, then red (for it had all seemed too good to be true), she put her hand simply into his and said, 'Yes, sir, willingly.'

That same evening they told Dr Vyner (whose permission had, of course, been previously given, for Lyndon was punctilious). He gave them his most cordial blessing, which Dorothy knew he meant. Nobody mentioned that he would now be alone, and Dorothy began to plan what she would do for him after the marriage. He should leave the dark old house for a bright cheerful room in their home, with bookshelves ready-made, and so many candles that his eyesight would never be tried again. As she was planning it, Lyndon put down his glass of celebratory claret.

'Sir, I have news. The Gentlemen for Managing the King's Affairs in Scotland have got word to the Brotherhood. There is the highest hope of an invasion.'

Dr Vyner bowed his head. 'Lord, now lettest Thou Thy servant depart in peace,' he said.

When Lyndon had gone and the room was quiet after his breezy presence, Dorothy sat on a footstool by the fire at her father's knee.

'Are you truly happy, Papa? Truly pleased?'

He put his hand on her hair, warm and silky in the glow from the low fire.

'Truly happy, child. But he will take you on hard roads, on stony ways. He has a Holy Grail before him, and such knights have never made easy company. Would you bear logs for him, Miranda?'

She knew *The Tempest*, the story of the young girl on the enchanted island, who had never set eyes on a man until a prince was washed ashore. Perhaps it appeared like that to her father, this swift betrothal. She smiled up at him. 'I am very strong,' she answered.

Next morning, when she went to call him to breakfast, he was lying half out of the bed, one hand touching the floor, his nightcap askew, a look of peace on his face as though he were visited by a pleasant dream. But he was quite dead; from a failure of the heart, the doctor said.

So it was that their wedding was a very quiet one, at the Church of St George, Bloomsbury (which her father would not have approved of at all, since the spire was topped with a figure of the late Elector of Hanover). Lyndon had said that she must set aside the usual mourning year, unprotected in the world as she was. Besides, he was impatient for his bride.

The house in Grosvenor Square was shut up again, and instead of going abroad on honeymoon they drove down into Surrey, to Dove House, which was to be their home.

2

Before the dinner-party on that June evening, six months after their marriage, Dorothy was obliged to go and take tea with her Aunt Petworth. It was not an uplifting prospect, but, as she said to Lyndon, 'They're bound to hear of our having company, and fly into a tiz at not being asked, so I must go and spin them a tale of what an odd, dull set of people are coming, then they will feel they're missing nothing.'

'Mr Johnson is odd, certainly,' said Lyndon. 'But dull, never. As to Mrs Johnson, I fail to see your aunt and her as bosom companions. Or your aunt and Lady Primrose, come to that. However, tell her what you please. Rather you than me,' and he went off, whistling, to talk to the head gardener about vegetables.

Dorothy sighed. It was such a beautiful afternoon, and Dove House, spruced up for festival, preened itself in the new furnishings Lyndon had ordered for his bride's homecoming: carpets from the East, crimson Turkey or delicate pastel colours; bed-hangings where parrots and other tropic birds pecked among pomegranates and leaves; rich wallpaper of Chinese design, on which mandarins in gold hats walked stiffly beside moon-faced ladies. Nothing, Lyndon said, was too good for Doll, and it had been a mouldy old place before.

With a last look back at the tall, double-fronted house whose bricks were the colour of fading red roses, she set off on foot.

The Petworths lived almost at the summit of Richmond Hill, their windows commanding the famous view from the Terrace, a superb prospect of fields, woodland, mansions, bridge and river. People came from miles off to see it, and no wonder. But very few of them called on the Petworths, who were not noted for their hospitality. Ozias Petworth had made a fortune in the African slave trade, from which he was now retired, and like many who have improved their circumstances grudged the spending of an unnecessary penny. The

22

servant who opened the door to Dorothy was a down-at-heel man of unpolished manners, and the house met her with a whiff of stale food.

Aunt Sybil Petworth, who was the elder sister of Dr Vyner, had changed into her afternoon finery for her niece's visit, and had as usual rouged her cheeks and blackened her eyebrows. Her thickly curled blonde wig gave an illusion of youth at a distance, but closer approach made it clear that she would never see sixty again, and was frankly hard-featured.

Her mouth turned down with disappointment as Dorothy entered alone.

'You've not brought Mr Beaumont?' she asked.

Dorothy bent and kissed a dry cheek smelling faintly of orris-powder. 'No, Aunt, if you'll excuse him. He begged me to say he had pressing business.' She knew that the wearing of the best wig and the brightest cosmetics was in compliment to an expected male visitor.

Mrs Petworth snorted. 'Connected with your fine London company, I take it? You don't take much thought of your late father, with all this giving of routs and levees. Scarcely decent I call it.'

'It is neither a rout nor a levee, Aunt,' Dorothy said patiently. 'Just two or three friends from London: very sober, quiet people whom you would not find at all interesting. And you know Papa would not have wished me to stay in mourning for ever. He was very clear-headed about such things.'

'Ha! I seem to recall he mourned your mother long enough.'

Dorothy flushed, wishing, not for the first time, that her only relatives did not also live in Richmond.

'How is Uncle Petworth?' she asked, and the conversation turned to the usual topics of ailments, stocks and shares, the wickedness of servants and the rising cost of living. Dorothy nodded and smiled, putting in a word here and there, longing for the arrival of tea, which when it came was doled out from the caddy with a sparing hand and brewed with water that was hardly boiling. Mrs Petworth drank with the tiny handle of the teacup held between forefinger

23

and thumb, the little finger extended elegantly into the air, as she had heard was fashionable. Her eyes, roving over her niece, settled waist-high.

'Not breeding yet, are you?' she asked abruptly. 'It's a wonder, as I was saying to your uncle only this morning, two lusty young sprigs as you are. I hope you mean to do your duty by your husband, ma'am, and not tight-lace your brats out of existence before they're born. Ah, when you get to my age you'll rue it sadly if you've no young ones about you, mark my words.' She sighed theatrically.

'It's early days yet, Aunt.' And so it was, Dorothy thought, sipping the cold tea. Before her marriage she had not dwelt as fondly on the so-called nuptial joys as might a girl with sisters or with many friends, and her wedding night had been not without apprehension. But no bridegroom could have been more kind than Lyndon. She had certainly expected rather more sentiment, something more romantical about the occasion. But Lyndon, as he himself pointed out, was not one for calling girls Celia, Delia or Cloelia, when their proper names were Betsy or Nan or Poll, and she need not expect him to act the amorous shepherd, always prating of hearts and darts and fires and lyres. Dorothy agreed that such posturing was exceedingly silly; if she wanted romances, she could read them for herself. When her husband took her on his knee, and kissed her, and called her his pretty pink, she who had never had a beau was as proud and happy as any bride in the kingdom.

Thinking of which, she strove to be pleasant to her aunt.

'You know, Aunt, we have good nurseries at Dove House, looking over the gardens. Lyndon would not wish his children to be reared in London, with so much smoke and fog. He says he looks to the day when he can teach our sons to play cricket on the Green, and when the times are mended, and the K—' she stopped abruptly. Aunt Petworth threw her a sharp glance.

'The what?'

She had been going to say 'the King enjoys his own again.' Laughing, she parried the question. 'There, I quite forget. My mind is so charged these days.' She rose quickly and went to the window.

'Mercy, what's that in the garden?'

Huddled on the door-sill of a lattice summerhouse was a small, grotesque figure. In the shadow there was only a general appearance of darkness, but it seemed to have its hands up to its face, and to be rocking to and fro rhythmically.

'What *is* it?' enquired Aunt Petworth fretfully, disinclined for an arthritic struggle to her feet. 'Not that dratted dog again, I hope?'

'No, I think it's a child. Or a dwarf . . .'

'I'll have neither sneaking children nor sneaking dwarves in my garden.' She heaved herself up and joined Dorothy at the window, where she gave a bark of annoyance.

'Well, if she hasn't had the brazenness to intrude herself into the summerhouse! Of all the outrageous impertinence – and after I distinctly told Mrs Paine to get shut of her.' She went to the fireplace and tugged the bell-rope. 'Get her out, I said, with her sulks and her fleas and worse, I dare say. Where *is* that woman?'

'But who is she?' Dorothy asked.

'A slave-girl that Captain Finch brought from Bristol. I said to Mr Petworth I wanted nothing of her, but he would have it that a nigra lends a good tone to a household, properly trained and dressed. A lot of use trying to train her! Ah, Paine,' as the door opened to admit a middle-aged woman in high cap and starched apron. 'You took your time coming upstairs.'

'I was tending the dough, ma'am,' resentfully said the cook, or housekeeper, whichever she might be. 'I had my hands to wash.'

'Yes, well, now you are here, perhaps you'll tell me how that slave comes to be back on the premises. Look for yourself.'

'I see her, ma'am. I don't know, I'm sure, how she comes there. I gave her to the beadle, as you asked, to be taken to Rump Hall.' (This Dorothy knew, was the workhouse.) 'Must have run back.'

'Then run her out again. Tell the gardener to give her a good beating and put her in the street.'

'Yes, ma'am.'

'Wait,' Dorothy said. 'I would like to see her. She seems to be in some distress. May I, by your leave, Aunt—' and before Mrs Petworth could speak she was in the hall and out through the door leading to the gardens. She sped to the summerhouse, where she found the girl lying prone on the floor, her body heaving with silent, painful sobs. As Dorothy knelt by the girl and touched her there was a convulsive movement away from her, one arm going up to protect the head. The ragged upper garment fell away, revealing a dark, naked shoulder with a raised weal across it, and the beginning of another weal lower down. There was a wordless cry of protest as she touched the shoulder.

'Hush,' Dorothy said gently, 'I won't hurt you. I won't even touch you if you don't wish it. Please sit up, and tell me what ails you.'

Slowly, painfully, the figure crawled to a sitting position, eyeing her from beneath dark brows with a look she had seen in the eyes of a frightened horse. Dirt, and the ravages of weeping, made the features hard to distinguish, but the skin was a dark brown, the eyes large and red-veined with tears. Dorothy could see that she was quite young, and judged her to be about twelve years old from her size. She put out a hand to her encouragingly. 'Won't you tell me, now?'

The gasping sobs lessened, as the slave-girl took in the apparition of the most beautiful lady she had ever seen. Timidly, shivering, she put out her hand, and Dorothy, trying not to notice the dirt, took it and held it in both of hers.

'There, now we are friends, I am going to take you away from here.'

The hand was pulled away as the girl cowered back. Dorothy heard 'No' from her. She recaptured the hand. 'They won't let you stay, my dear, so you'll do well to come with me.' This time there was no resistance, only a head bowed in resignation. The slave followed in Dorothy's footsteps back to the house.

In the hall Dorothy almost collided with her Uncle Petworth, whose large face turned very nearly the colour of his plum coat at seeing her companion.

'Good day, Uncle,' she said briskly. 'Aunt tells me you wish to be rid of this young person, and have nowhere to place her, so with your leave I'll take her to my housekeeper, who may find her of use. Will you pay my respects to Aunt and say that I'm in haste?' With

26

a sketch of a curtsey she turned and ushered the slave out of the door, followed by Mr Petworth's pop-eyed stare. He charged into the parlour.

'What the firing devils,' he asked his wife, 'is our niece doing along of that slave-wench, running off hugger-mugger without a civil word? Is she gone quite mad? By Gemini, Mrs Petworth, there's rum blood in your family.'

His lady's high cap wagged to and fro in bewilderment, like an agitated butterfly.

Those inhabitants of Richmond who happened to be shopping or at their windows on that afternoon echoed his surprise at seeing the young lady of Dove House walking familiarly (walking, not riding, mark you, and she with her own carriage in stables) with a figure that might have been either a chimney-sweep's child or an imp from Hell. The Honourable Mr Beaumont, they opined, had caught a Tartar when he took Miss from London to wife.

It was a relief to arrive at Dove House, for the slave-child's bare feet stumbled along pavements and cobbles, and she was exhausted. Lyndon, just mounted on his horse by the gate, stared open-mouthed at them, but Dorothy called up to him that she would explain later. In the house she turned her charge over to the plump, comfortable and well-spoken woman who smoothly controlled their household, and who was not inaptly called Mrs Mercy (though, as Lyndon said, she tempered justice with it).

'I found this child with my relatives, Mrs Mercy. She has had bad treatment, it seems, and they have no place for her.' Mrs M. might think what she pleased about the bestowers of the bad treatment; if the cap fitted her aunt and uncle, let them wear it. Dorothy was filled with anger against them and whoever else had abused the child, and with contradictory anger against herself for having rushed into a situation which might prove an embarrassment to all concerned. One might rescue a kitten from torment by boys, or protest to a horse-beating drayman, but to saddle one's household with an unknown quantity of a human being was quite another matter. Lyndon would certainly think so when he returned.

Mrs Mercy, charged to clean the newcomer up and do whatever

was necessary for her, departed downstairs calmly, a stately ship of the line with a dirty little collier following in her wake. An hour later she appeared in Dorothy's small Blue Parlour.

'I think she'll do now, madam. At least she looks like a Christian, which was not the case before. Lettice and I have bathed and combed her – there were only a few live things, which are gone now.' She lowered her voice. 'There are some nasty wounds, madam, but not turned ugly – I suppose because she's young enough to heal quickly. I've put salve on them. And the rags are burnt; little Dorcas's frock just about fits her, though if you mean to keep her more will have to be got, for Dorcas is crying in the wash-house for her gown.'

'Yes, of course, Mrs Mercy. I will see to all that. Where is she?'

Mrs Mercy moved her ample form to reveal, on the landing outside, a figure that approached nervously as Dorothy beckoned.

'Don't be afraid, child, let me look at you.'

But this was not a child. Of a child's height and slenderness, reaching barely to Dorothy's shoulder, but the figure outlined by Dorcas's red gown was the budding figure of a very young woman. The newly scrubbed skin was a rosy-brown, not black, and instead of the spreading African nose and thick lips Dorothy had expected there was a neat, high-bridged little beak and a full but shapely pink mouth. The hair, still damp, had been neatly coiled on the neck with some of Mrs Mercy's own prized tortoiseshell pins, and proved to be densely wavy, but not frizzy like that of the slaves who were landed at London Docks. The remains of a livid black eye and some scratches on the cheeks could not conceal an exotic, pathetic prettiness so far in excess of what Dorothy had expected that her spirits rose sharply.

'Why, you're quite handsome, child. Won't you come and speak to me?'

For answer the girl came forward on brown bare feet, and suddenly knelt before Dorothy, bowing her head.

'No, no! You mustn't kneel to me. That is not our way in England. Come, get up, and Lettice shall teach you how to curtsey. Do you understand me?'

A shy nod.

28

'Good, then you speak English. Have you a name?'

'Not . . . for long. On ship . . . no names, only nigra.'

'And before that, in your own country?'

The slave shook her head. Dorothy guessed that ill-treatment had come between her and memory.

'Well, never mind, we'll find a nice one for you. Are you from Africa?'

A headshake. 'James . . . Jamestown.'

Dorothy's geography was not strong. 'I must look at the map,' she said. 'Now, Mrs Mercy, take her downstairs again. I'm sure there's some task you can set her to in the kitchen.'

'More than plenty, madam, with company coming,' She ushered out the new member of Dove House's staff.

The American girl sat at the kitchen table, shelling young peas from the kitchen garden, which lay green-golden in the late sunshine, directly outside the window. She had never seen peas before, and marvelled at their tenderness and perfection. It would not have occurred to her to taste one, though there was no sign of a whip among the objects which festooned the great open fireplace: jacks and gridirons, spoons and ladles. Nor had a hand yet been raised to her by the large woman whose name brought back echoes of long-silent Bible classes, held by Massa's pious wife, or by the quiet man called Fowler who seemed to be in prayer over a number or bottles (and who was the Beaumonts' butler), or by the girl Lettice. Even the younger girl, Dorcas, who she knew was angry with her because her frock had been taken away, had only put her head round the door and made a face. It was very strange. Things had been different at the last English house, where there had been screamings and shoutings, a bed in a coal-cellar, and a final beating which had made her want to be dead, before they had kicked her towards a huge man who had dragged her out of the house with rough words. But she had torn herself away from him with the strength of desperation, and run back to the house because it was a place she knew, and she thought he was taking her to hell.

Already, and she marvelled at it, earlier memories were fading. She had been a child on a tobacco plantation in Virginia, working all day, living in the family hut by night, treated no better and no worse than the other slaves. Her parents had been very young, her brothers and sisters mere babies. The Bible classes had been nice, and the singing at night, and the occasional celebration of some happy event in Massa's family.

When she was turned eleven and growing shapely, one of Massa's elder sons had taken her, as casually and brutally as he would have slashed the head off a thistle with his cane. It was painful, but only to be expected, and she did not become a child-mother as so many others did. She could not remember the next bad thing that had happened. Massa's fortunes had been declining after a bad crop, and he had agreed to sell some of his slaves to an English trader who had put into Jamestown. The stranger had come round to make his choice, pointing his whip at her because she was young and healthy, lighter in colour and more delicate in feature than many of the slaves, for her grandfather had been white and her mother was of Indian blood. He had had to pay an extortionate price, and so took a cut at her with the whip whenever she caught his eye.

But that was not often, because on the journey which took her to England, crammed into the stinking hold with others who grew sick and died, gave birth or went mad, the slaves had no individuality. For their white masters they existed only as a cargo, at best as a species of animal with only the remotest resemblance to humanity. The salty clean air of the port of Bristol was wonderful when the remnant of the slaves were disembarked there, blinking in the light and groaning, half-crippled with confinement. She had hardly minded when she and some others who were not too disfigured were put up for auction in the slave-market, standing like cattle to be appraised, in chains and neck-halters which wore bloody sores in the flesh. A sea-captain had bought her. The woman at his lodgings would not have her, so she had been locked in an outhouse, where the captain visited and assaulted her fumblingly and incapably, being roaring drunk at the time. Because he could not succeed with her he beat her soundly, and the next morning she was made to climb to

30

the top of a coach which rolled and jolted its way to London, the captain beside her drinking from a stone bottle.

Nobody seemed to want her; neither he nor the big red-faced man who bought her from him in a tavern and took her in an old coach to his house at Richmond, where at first she thought her lot would be bettered, for it was a fine great house.

But not so fine as this. Here even the servants' quarters were full of mysterious, beautiful things. The air was scented with delicious food-smells, herbs and flowers. She could hardly hear what the people said, so quietly they spoke. 'Good wench,' they said, and 'Please' and 'Thank you', which had never been said to her before. She could hardly believe in the state of her own body, clean and smooth under the lovely red dress. Confused memories began to creep back of stories about heaven. Perhaps she had died and was there, and the beautiful young lady upstairs was – she was proud of herself for remembering – Mrs Virgin Mary.

These thoughts came one by one, and more and more lucidly, into her brain, which had been reduced almost to the brain of an animal. There was still fear in her, and apprehension; but the light was coming back. She bent her head over the last few of the pea-pods, popping them satisfyingly into the basin.

Mrs Mercy, by the roasting-spit, nudged Mr Fowler as he passed.

'Did you ever see such a change? I thought at first it was madness in the mistress, bringing her here, did not you?'

Mr Fowler nodded absently. He was on his way to decant the port.

The bustle of preparation was over, the dishes sent upstairs, and relief reigned in the kitchen; while above, in the dining-room, the clatter of cutlery on plates told that the dinner was proceeding as planned. Indeed, with one member of the party it was proceeding much faster than planned; Dorothy stole glances of amazement at the amount of food Mr Samuel Johnson was able to get into his mouth at a time, even allowing for the quantity which escaped on to his waistcoat, the tablecloth or the floor. To her shame, he noticed her glance and, turning to her with twisted smile, said, '*Impransus.*'

'I – I beg your pardon, sir?'

'And I yours, ma'am. That is, translated, I had not eaten of late. It was very ungenteel of me to address a lady in Latin at table, but the habit is strong and, I believe, in essentials a good one. Latin, to my mind and that of all sound-thinking men . . .'

'Sam,' said Mrs Johnson warningly. Swiftly he laid an enormous hand over her plump one.

'My charmer. You do well to correct my excessive verbosity. I did but mean to convey, ma'am, that I have not eaten so well, or indeed eaten at all in the sense of doing more than appease the worse pangs of appetite . . .'

'I suppose,' said Mrs Johnson with a tremble of tears, 'you mean the company to believe your wife don't feed you properly, sir.' She put her napkin to her eyes, and the ceruse on her cheek promptly came off, leaving a patch of white. Dorothy swiftly began chatting away to Lady Primrose to cover the embarrassing marital interlude that followed. It was too bad of Lyndon, she thought, to have brought this odd, ungainly man home – a huge, raw-boned grotesque with a nervous tic in the face, painfully short sight (he was at that moment peering into his plate for any morsel that might remain on it), an ugly, scrofulous skin, and a pulpit manner. And yet she felt some good in the man.

As for Mrs Johnson, looking many years older than her husband, she was the image of what one of Charles II's ladies might have grown into, once her charms were past. A tiny, over-dressed, over-painted Nell Gwynne, showing far too much bosom, her hair was fair rather than grey by courtesy of the camomile bottle. She flirted and twittered, put on pretty sulks and pouts, until Dorothy wished earnestly that it was time for the visitors to go. And with her husband she was so dreadfully direct: could she know what she was saying, or was it the effect of the wine she took so liberally? Mr Johnson, his hostess noticed, took none, only water, for reasons which she was sure he would be only too ready to give, if asked.

'A fine handsome place,' Mrs Johnson was saying, suddenly re-covered and staring round her. 'But rather showy for the country, an't it, Sam? Now if I was to have it, I should furnish it different. But what can you expect from a raw young girl, is what I always say.'

Dorothy could not help seeing Lyndon's half-amused, half-shocked stare, or being aware that Lady Primrose's gauze-draped shoulders were heaving with suppressed giggles. As for Mr Johnson, he was shaking his head in gentle reproof.

'Manners, Tetty, manners. Nay, don't look so, my love; it is fair enough for us to correct one another, if either be at fault.'

Mrs Johnson stared at him vacantly, as if quite unaware of what he or she had said. Lyndon mischievously made to refill her glass, but a headshake from Dorothy stopped him.

'As I was saying,' continued Mrs Johnson in quite a different tone, "tis so congenial to come into a good comfortable house after the places Sam and I have lodged in these past years. Lord, how times change! You know, my dear,' – turning to Dorothy – 'when I was married to Mr Porter and we lived in Lichfield I was very well off indeed, wasn't I, Sam? Used to everything fine about me. I *feel* it sometimes, indeed I do.'

'I'm sure you must,' Dorothy said gently. 'But life with such a learned gentleman as Mr Johnson must have many pleasures and compensations.'

'Oh, never think it hasn't!' cried Mrs Johnson emotionally. 'What it is to know such intellect, I can't tell you, Mrs . . . I quite forget your name. And Sam has worked so hard, for little enough reward. Scribble-scrabble, all day and all night, pamphlets and essays, even a theatre tragedy, and is still a poor man. Why, the other day I had to sell . . .' she began to sob '. . . sell the little silver mug his mama bought him in London when she brought him to be touched for the Queen's Evil.'

Sam Johnson put his arm round his wife with such a tender look that Dorothy saw him in a quite different light, and Lady Primrose appeared moved. He was whispering something to his wife.

'Yes,' she said. 'Yes, I have indeed a touch of the megrims. I would like to lie down, if you please.'

'If you would be so gracious, ma'am . . .' he besought Dorothy, who had already leapt to her feet, unused yet to bells and servants, to conduct the suffering lady outside to a day-bed in another room, and tuck her up under a shawl with a vinaigrette to sniff. Full of pity for the quaint couple, yet vastly relieved, she hurried back to the company, who had finished eating and were eagerly talking. As she entered, Lyndon said: 'My dear life, would it be agreeable to you, in view of the particular circumstances, to waive the custom of allowing the ladies to retire and the gentlemen to smoke and tipple?'

'I should like nothing better,' she said.

'And I,' put in Lady Primrose. 'I don't see why we should be banished just as the evening is growing interesting, and I *love* to tipple.'

'Alas, madam,' said Mr Johnson with a giant's sigh, 'you are fortunate. Finding myself unable to practise moderation in drinking, I must confine myself to abstinence. But since the ingestion of wine is but, at least in the intention, an aid to the pleasant interchange of discourse among beloved friends, why should not that discourse itself provide the stimulation, without the dubious action of the grape?'

'Yes, indeed,' said Lyndon, looking baffled. He refilled the guest's glass with water.

'*I* will take a glass of port,' Lady Primrose pronounced graciously. 'I fancy we may need a brimmer or two, since we've a certain toast to drink.' She looked round the table, bright-eyed, as Lyndon filled the glasses.

'Now,' she said, 'let's come to the business of the evening. Since, as you know, it's dangerous to congregate in numbers as matters are at present, we of the Brotherhood are meeting thus, in small gatherings, all over England to exchange the newest tidings.'

'Which are . . .?' Lyndon prompted.

'John Blaw of Castlehill has been in Paris these five or six weeks. He talked with the Young Gentleman and with the French minister, D'Argenson, who asked him how many troops would be needed to ensure a successful rising. Blaw told him some ten thousand, at which D'Argenson went into another room where King Louis was. Coming back, he gave Blaw His Majesty's word that the Young Gentleman should have that number by October. And for the army's use a great many broadsword blades have been bought in Paris.'

Lyndon laughed triumphantly. 'That's tremendous news!'

'There's some less tremendous. Poor Blaw was caught in Edinburgh after his return, and lies in the Canongate prison. They got Sir Hector MacLean as well, so there's an end to any hope of the Clan MacLean joining in the rising, with their chief in Government hands. Heigh-ho. Still and all, there's news from the Highlands that many chiefs are hot for the Cause and will rally their clans as soon as the Young Gentleman sets foot in Scotland.'

'So he *is* coming?' Dorothy asked.

'If he has to sail without another man to support him, so he has said. There's a ship provided, the frigate *Doutelle*, and I've no doubt King Louis will send an armed escort-vessel as well. But if he doesn't, no matter. The Young Gentleman has borrowed money from Waters the banker, and has written to the Blackbird to pawn all his jewels, for that would be a better use for them than wearing.'

'And he's well?' asked Lyndon. 'Well and in good heart?'

'Never better. All the winter and spring he's kept in training, walking for miles barefoot in all weathers. They say he has the spirit and strength of a lion. And yet,' Lady Primrose sighed romantically, 'he has the bonniest looks that ever prince wore.'

Dorothy was gazing at the portrait engraved on the wine glass she was holding. It showed, rather indistinctly, a longish face, long hair flowing girlishly over shoulders clad in ornamental armour. She supposed it failed to do the original justice; at least one would hope so. He was such a legend in himself. Lyndon talked of him incessantly, of reports from his father who had seen Prince Charles Edward grow from a sturdy boy to a handsome lad, brave, merry and alight with the Stuart charm. Lyndon's absorption in the Jacobite cause disturbed her a little at times. If it should fail, what would he do? All his abounding energy was poured into this planning and plotting. It was unsafe, too, to be a known Jacobite, even here in Surrey, and with loyal friends, if any friend could be relied on for loyalty. Every Sunday she was filled with trepidation as she knelt beside Lyndon in Church, and heard him change, in a whisper,

the names in the Prayers for the King's Majesty and the Royal
Family: 'Our Sovereign Lord, King James . . . we humbly beseech
thee to bless Charles Edward, Prince of Wales, Henry, Duke of
York . . .'

He and Lady Primrose and the now animated Mr Johnson were
talking excitedly of plans and dates and what might best be done.
Mr Johnson seemed to have the most violent views about the Elector,
and Lyndon was not far behind him. There was talk of funds, and
communications, and the port decanter was growing steadily
emptier.

'Confusion to the House of Hanover!' Sam Johnson cried, waving
his glass of water.

Dorothy, unused to wine, felt herself falling asleep. She was aware
of Mrs Johnson tottering back into the room, apparently quite in
spirits again, and of Lady Primrose sitting down at the spinet and
beginning to sing in a clear voice.

> 'There is a flower in yon garden
> Smiles sweeter than the thyme,
> It is a blithe and lovely flower,
> And I wish that flower were mine,
>   O, were mine,
> And I wish that flower were mine.
>
> 'The garden that this flower grows in
> With weeds is all o'ergrown,
> And if I were the gardener there
> I'd make that flower my own,
>   O, my own,
> I'd make that flower my own.
>
> 'It is a Rose, a royal Rose,
> With a dark and rolling eye,
> And is my choice above all those
> That would love me till I die,
>   Till I die,
> That would love me till I die.'

36

3

Life below stairs at Dove House was slightly disturbed by the addition of the slave-girl to the domestic staff. The doves were, so to speak, a little fluttered at first because they had for so long had their nest uninvaded, what with Mr Lyndon spending half his time in London until his marriage and with their being in consequence almost like the house's only residents. Mr Fowler was a quiet man, given in his spare time to studying the newspapers and walking by the river, head down, sunk in thought. Lettice the parlour-maid, who also acted as maid to Dorothy, was engaged to a tradesman of the town whom she intended to marry if and when he could wish his cranky old father upon some other relative, for, she said, she would never share her home with such a fellow. Sarah the between-maid spent much time chattering and gaming with friends in other households on the Green, while Cook, elderly and asthmatic, hardly spoke to anyone except on the subject of food; and the widowed Mrs Alice, laundress, devoted herself to the bringing up of her daughter Dorcas.

It was left to Mrs Mercy to civilise the foreign girl. There were tantrums and some tears from the intruder; some hard-learned lessons on the use of the privy and the advisability of washing the face, hands and hair, the care of clothes and the use of ordinary domestic objects which were quite unfamiliar to her. But for Mrs Mercy's great patience, and the girl's natural teachability, there might have been ugly scenes; as it was, the housekeeper's hand was never once raised in menace, and her slow, calm voice continued to reiterate commands and instructions until, as with the teaching of a child, they made their effect.

'At least the creature is not a Hottentot,' said Mrs Mercy to Cook, 'nor even a born slut, I believe. I think she may be fit to show upstairs before long.'

'Ah, very likely,' replied Cook. 'All I say is, let her keep her dirty fingers out of my pots and pans.'

The American girl's fingers were, in fact, brown and small, as she was herself, a mouselike form in a made-over old stuff gown of Lettice's (for Dorcas's complaints had been so loud that the red one had been restored to her). She sat where she liked to sit, in a shadowy corner, listening to the voices saying things which she understood better every day, watching the fair-skinned people who treated her as they treated the cats which sat on the hearth-rug with their paws tucked beneath them, or looked down with inscrutable green eyes from a warm shelf beside the fire. They were the objects of mild, patronising affection, being quiet and clean. It was, she had learnt, important to be both.

The day came when Mrs Mercy beckoned her from the corner.

'Come. Madam has asked for you. Wash your hands and put a comb through your hair.'

Madam and the master of the house were in an oak-panelled room which served Lyndon as study and smoking-room (not that he had much use for either) and as a place where accounts were kept. He had said that they should see the girl there in case she were not fit for the delicate furniture of drawing-room or parlour. 'God knows what got into you, Doll, to bring such a strange wild wench here. Haven't we enough mouths to feed? I have enough on my mind as it is.' He was, indeed, surrounded by papers and lists, and unusually irritable.

'At least let us see what Mrs Mercy has made of the girl,' said Dorothy. 'And you know, Lyndon, I could not have left her where she was, any more than I could have left a dog in such a situation.'

Mrs Mercy entered with her discreet tap. 'The girl, madam.' As discreetly, she withdrew, leaving her charge standing meekly by the door.

'Night and Silence! who is here?'

Dorothy had read old ballad-books on her father's shelves, tales of Elfland, of enchanted mortals and small fairy women, surely sisters to this one, with her tiny, perfect frame, dusky hair and skin, so rare in England of the day. Dorothy glanced at Lyndon for his reactions, and caught on his face a look which struck a sudden pang to her heart, though she could not have told why.

'Well!' he said, after a prolonged stare that brought a tinge of colour into the girl's cheeks. 'Quite a little *belle sauvage* you seem to have found, Doll. What's your name, wench?'

For the first time the long lashes lifted, and the black eyes met his.

'I don' remember . . . sir.' They had dinned it into her that Sir and Madam were the forms of address upstairs, not Massa and Missis.

'What do they call you, Mrs Mercy and the others?' asked Dorothy.

'Quashee . . . madam.'

'What a horrid name!'

'It's what they call all nigra women,' said Lyndon. 'Sambo for the men, Quashee for the women.'

'Well, she isn't nigra. I've seen many pictures of Indians, and I think she belongs to that race, not the African. In any case we must choose a pretty name for her. What would you like to be called, child?'

The girl very slightly shook her head. She was not used to being given choices. Lyndon laughed heartily.

'My oath! No need to rack your brains, Doll. An't there Kitty, or Sukey, or Moll, or Fanny or Peg? What does it matter?'

'The naming of a person is very important,' Dorothy told him severely, 'whether they are just born or beginning a new life. Now, I have had a very good idea. There was a Latin motto, my father told me, belonging to his school or college, I forget which, and it was "*Spero meliora*", meaning "I hope for better things". Now, don't you think that would be very nice and fitting – Meliora, I mean? Better things. She needs them, heaven knows.'

'By God, I knew I'd married a bluestocking.'

Dorothy beckoned the girl. 'Would you like to be called Meliora?'

The first smile anybody in England had ever seen on the girl's face widened her full lips – which were the soft pink of spindleberries – and showed brilliantly white teeth. It transformed her face. Very gracefully and correctly, just as she had been taught downstairs, she sank in a curtsey.

'I like very much, madam.'

Lyndon bent forward and chucked her under the chin before she rose to her feet. 'A pretty name for a pretty creature,' he said. 'We'll have a christening party and wet the babe's head with a few bottles of my father's '25 clary; make a Christian out of her if the parson don't object.'

Dorothy shook her head at him reprovingly, and Meliora said with gentle dignity, 'I Christian already, sir. All Christian on my massa's plantation.'

'That's excellent,' Dorothy put in quickly, before Lyndon could say any more, but he seemed unable to let the girl go, so pleased he was with her.

'And you serve our true and rightful Christian king, eh, Meliora – His Majesty King James?' Seeing her puzzled look, he added, 'You come from Jamestown, Virginia, they tell me, which was called after another King James?'

'I don' know, sir,' said Meliora. 'They don' tell me nothing like that.'

Seeing a political gleam in Lyndon's eye, Dorothy gently dismissed Meliora, who dipped another curtsey at the door before she went. Lyndon's gaze followed the small figure that moved so differently from the usual shuffle-and-slouch of the untrained servant; the back straight as a wand, the head high, the foot light.

'What an extraordinary young female! Quadroon, of course, with that colouring – a white grandfather most probably. My mother had a quadroon girl, I remember, some sort of maid. Not a patch on this little creature, though. I expect you're right and there's Indian blood there as well.'

Dorothy was so pleased by the transformation of the girl, so glad that her own elevation to place and riches had given her the chance to do some good in the world; and yet, if only Lyndon had not looked at Meliora so, and made so much of her.

Fiddlesticks, she told herself; he was always civil and friendly to servants, a good, fair-minded master, and after all it was a novel thing to acquire a coloured servant of such comeliness. She went briskly to the still-room and forgot her foolishness in the preparation of rosewater, which served so many purposes, from cookery to sweetening the air, scenting gloves and beautifying the complexion.

There was a luxurious pleasure about handling the heaped blooms of every colour, the red most strongly scented, burying one's hands in them almost to the elbows, drowning them in a blend of white vinegar and sugar that would preserve them for seasons to come; and then there would come the making of a perfume-powder from damask petals, dried sweet marjoram, shavings of juniper. Round about, on neatly stocked shelves, stood jars of candied violets, vinegar of elderflower and cowslips, syrups of marigold and gilly flower. Soaps for the kitchen and for the portable copper bath which Lyndon had installed, to the faint shock of his staff, for cleansing after cricket or riding. The soaps, too, boiled up from last winter's fats, were flower-perfumed.

That night Lyndon's love-making was more passionate than it had ever been. She lay awake in their wide, luxurious bed, wondering if the nurseries upstairs might next year no longer be empty.

There was an unquiet spirit abroad in England that summer. Little enough was doing in Richmond except for the Assemblies at the Great Room on the Green, a pleasure-place a few doors from Dove House; but Lyndon had in any case no time for local amusements. Every few days he was off to London, returning sometimes thoughtful, more often in high spirits. Sometimes he took Dorothy with him, Lettice going with them to maid her, and then she was expected to shop or visit old friends in Bloomsbury while he vanished to unnamed destinations. She knew better than to ask him what they were; the only time, since the dinner-party, that she had shown curiosity, he had laid a finger across her mouth and said with a smile, 'All in good time.'

One night they went to the play at Drury Lane, a silly enough piece, without even the rising star David Garrick in it. The evening's excitement was provided by the occupant of the Royal Box, whose entrance provoked a storm of cheers, whistles, screams and shouts from the pit and gallery. He was an immensely fat man, young to judge by the absence of lines on his porcine face, which was almost as red as his scarlet uniform, decked all over with ribbons and orders.

His small pigtailed head sloped, apparently neckless, into his shoulders, a bullfrog throat resting on his cravat, giving him the appearance of an inedible dressed-up pineapple. To the applause of the audience he returned a short stiff bow, his thick wet mouth unsmiling.

'Gracious Heavens!' said Dorothy. 'What a hideous person. Why are they cheering him?'

Before Lyndon could answer the band struck up the tune which had recently come to be called the National Anthem. Everybody stood as an actress came forward to the floats and sang it, loudly and clearly.

> 'George is magnanimous,
> Subjects unanimous,
>   Peace to us bring,
> His fame is glorious,
> Reign meritorious,
> Let him rule over us,
>   God save the King.

> From France and *Pre*tender,
> Great Britain *de*fend her,
>   Foes let them fall;
> From foreign slavery,
> Priests and their knavery,
> And Popish reverie,
>   God save us all.'

'Atrocious set of words,' observed Lyndon's friend Mr Percival Dod, who with his lady was sharing their box.

'Atrocious set of sentiments,' said Lyndon.

'But who is he?' Dorothy asked. 'Not the K – not the Elector, for I've seen him.'

'His third son,' Lyndon told her. 'William Augustus, called Duke of Cumberland, Captain General of British forces in the war in Flanders, where he recently lost the Battle of Fontenoy.'

'Oh. Then why are they cheering him?'

'I haven't a notion.' Lyndon yawned.

'Unless it's because he didn't run away,' suggested little Mrs Dod. Her husband added, 'They'll cheer for anybody these days, even Poor Fred that goes by the title of Prince of Wales, thick-skulled cowards that they are. We'll show 'em, one day.' He surveyed with contempt the seething crowds below them, who were now dividing their attentions between the oranges, shrimps and beer they had been buying, and the scraping of fiddles which heralded the overture to the play. Under cover of it Dorothy asked, 'What does "Popish reverie" mean?'

'Twaddle,' Lyndon replied. They settled down to watch the play, which contained many dragged-in references to invasion, peace, freedom, foreign foes and bold resistance, all heartily cheered. The spoken Epilogue, declaimed hand on heart by the leading actor, with his eyes riveted on the royal box, ended with a flourish:

'Now William's home, our faith's defender,
We fear nor Old nor Young Pretender;
This hope of the presumptuous foe
Could from his absence only grow :
He fills our hearts when safe at home,
And leaves no place for France or Rome.'

The subject of these lines appeared unmoved by them; possibly because he had slept through a great part of the final act and was barely awake yet. When he turned to leave the box, Lyndon and his party stood with the rest of the house, neither clapping nor cheering. Dorothy noticed curious looks directed at them from the fashionables in other boxes.

'Come,' Lyndon said. 'Let's go and take supper, if we've any appetite left after an evening's contemplation of the Fat Boy.'

They supped at the Dods', in Berkeley Street, where a cold meal had been prepared by the servants. It was a quiet repast. Each of them had in some way been affected by the atmosphere of the evening. When they had finished eating they drank the Loyal Toast, passing their glasses over the water-decanter on the table.

43

'The King, God bless him; and he who shall be King.'

'It will be soon now, will it not?' Maria Dod asked her husband.

'Very soon.'

'Dorothy is pensive,' Lyndon said. 'What troubles you, sweetheart?'

She looked up from the napkin she had been plaiting into folds. 'Nothing. Only . . . are they – the Elector and his family – so bad that we must risk war to get rid of them?'

'You had a good view of one tonight. That should have told you enough.'

'Yes, I know. The Duke is ugly and coarse, and cruel too, I think. And Papa used to tell me how the Elector insulted his wife with ugly German mistresses, and spoke so roughly to her before the Court that she cried. She had to hide her books, too, though she loved reading, because the Elector flies into a rage at the sight of one – at least that was what Papa said, and it seemed a dreadful thing to him. And he, the Elector I mean, hates his son the Prince of Wales and calls him a monster and the greatest villain that ever was born.'

'His own son!' put in Maria Dod in shocked tones, thinking of her own little Harry asleep upstairs. 'Just as *his* father hated *him*. It seems to run in the family.'

'Then what are you saying, Dorothy?' Lyndon asked, and she knew he thought she was making a fool of herself.

'Only, my dear, that it is very reprehensible not to love books, and to be rude to one's wife, and call one's eldest son a monster; but – but most families have their unpleasantness. Even the Stuarts, perhaps. Might it not be that the next generation would be better, perhaps, and that we should leave things alone, rather than fly into a war? Oh, I know that King James is our rightful ruler, and . . .' Her voice died away, for she saw the censorious look on Percival Dod's face, and the anger on Lyndon's.

'I am glad to hear you know that,' he said. 'I had begun to think we were entertaining a cuckoo in our Blackbirds' nest. Your late father's instruction seems to have had little effect. I must apologise, Dod, for my wife's curious lapse of taste.'

Angrily he swallowed the wine left in his glass. Maria Dod, seeing

Dorothy's flushed shamed face, put a hand on her arm and beckoned her from the table.

'Come and see Harry and small Mary. She was so tiny last time you visited us, and now she's grown immense. The nurse is very competent, thank goodness...'

Left alone, the men exchanged glances. Percival Dod's eyes were sunken shadows in the flickering candlelight; a flush of anger remained on Lyndon's cheeks. He laughed, a little shamefaced.

'I must apologise for myself, too. It was nothing. Women have these fancies, though why the nauseating sight of Cumberland should have set her off . . . well, away with it. Have you anything from Lady Primrose?'

'Yes, and the best of news. The Duke of Beaufort is firmly with us, and the Earl of Orrery, Sir John Cotton and Colonel Cecil, and the warmest is Sir Watkin Williams Wynne.'

'Any promise of money?'

'Well, no. Not on paper, and no sums named. But it will come, no doubt of that. Then there's Tom Carte, and Dr Barry, and God knows how many squires and country gentlemen who wish the Elector at the Devil and will send every farmhand and stable-boy they can muster, and guineas galore.'

Lyndon lit his pipe, blowing smoke up towards the cupid-painted ceiling. 'My young lady keeps harping on war. Do you think it will come to that, Dod?'

'Never in this world – give or take a skirmish or two, a few bloody noses. As soon as he lands on British soil the nation will be at his feet, mark my words. None of us doubts that. They say he could charm the wildest bird from its tree. Or rather Lady P. says so. Her brother-in-law of Dunipace won't dare set foot over her threshold if he don't turn out for the Cause.'

'And the King of France? Any news of that backing?'

Dod shrugged. 'I wouldn't bet much on it. It's said that He has been trying every way to get an audience, and been fobbed off at all turns. Somebody in Rome saw a letter He had written to the King, in a sort of desperation, saying He was in honour bound to invade now. I had it copied as he remembered it.' He fished a scrap of paper, tightly folded, from a pocket. ' "Let what will happen, the stroke is struck, and I have taken a firm resolution to conquer or to die, and stand my ground as long as I shall have a man remaining with me." '

Lyndon nodded. 'That's the spirit that will bring us victory. Damn Louis – we can do without him. And you, Dod – you've sent word?'

'Discreetly, yes. I've sold the Gloucestershire farm. I'd no time to work it, and it brought me two thousand.' He chinked guineas together. 'It shall all go to Him, and no robbery of my wife and family, for I've plenty from the Islington land to support them. I imagine it's the same with you.'

Lyndon shook his head. 'I wish to God I could sell the Grosvenor Square House, but it's entailed and neither my father nor I have the power to break the entail. There are those who think I'm rich – I believe even my wife does – but . . .' He sighed. 'Well, I've *some* assets. I shall do what I can.'

The tall clock in the corner began its mellow boom of twelve. Lyndon started. 'Jupiter, is that the time? The coachman will be drunk by now. Call my wife down, there's a good fellow, and I thank you for a very pleasant supper.'

Jogging through the summer dark, the coach rocking and creaking over the ruts and cobbles, Dorothy sleepily put her head on her husband's shoulder and took his hand.

'I'm sorry I disgraced you. I must have taken too much wine.'

He pinched her cheek. 'Slut.'

'No, I'm in earnest. You know I'm heart and soul for the Cause, Lyndon. Indeed I wish you'd tell me more of what's going on, but after tonight I suppose you won't trust me again, talking what must have sounded like treason in front of our friends. But it wasn't meant so, truly.'

She looked out at the black silhouettes of trees against a sky of dark sapphire pointed with stars. Somewhere an owl flew down towards its victim with a cry of 'Kee-wick'. It would have been nice to sleep until they reached Richmond, but she had been troubled by the look on Lyndon's face at supper and she needed words to explain. 'I think it was the theatre – all the shouting for that horrible Duke, and the talk of invasion and enemies, and something . . . I think it was fear among the people. I suddenly knew how it would be, the feeling of war . . . bloodshed and dying, things I've only read about, things that might happen in England.'

She felt him shaking with amusement, and was disappointed. 'Don't you understand?'

He turned her face up to his, pushing back her hood and tweaking forward the unruly tendrils of hair to lie on her forehead, and tilting up the tip of her nose. 'I know that you're a very sweet, simple young person – which is the very reason why I married you – and that you'll find out one day that life is very different from your story-books. But Doll, I hope and trust it won't be bloodshed and dying, this enterprise of ours, but glory and victory and the end of foreign rule.'

'The New Jerusalem,' she said drowsily. 'Jerusalem the golden, with milk and honey blest . . .' She slept, not hearing the shriek of the small creature in the hedgerow as the owl pounced down upon it.

4

'We've as good as decided on August, madam.' Lettice folded her hands in a matronly manner in front of her apron. 'Thomas having got a promise from his brother Fred to take his Dad – that's the brother who lives at Taplow, you remember – well, there's no reason why we shouldn't marry as soon as the banns can be called. Not but what I hope,' she added primly, 'that people won't say there's improper haste in the matter.'

'I'm sure they won't, Lettice,' said Dorothy, thinking that Lettice's well-starched manner and distinctly plain face hardly suggested unbridled passions. 'I hope you and Mr Peasmarsh will be very happy. I shall miss your services greatly, of course.' This was more polite than truthful. There was an impersonal quality about Lettice, a suggestion in her demeanour as lady's maid that the lady in question was too young and of too lowly an origin to be worth troubling about; or perhaps it was that she simply had no interest in the fripperies of the toilette or the arrangements of hair. Dorothy had only seen Mr Peasmarsh in an environment of hams and cheeses, a solid, harassed-looking man who would never see forty again; she hoped he was not expecting sparkling vivacity in his wife.

However that might be, Lettice's departure would mean taking on another parlourmaid sufficiently accomplished to act as abigail as well. It was not an agreeable prospect, for to a young woman who had always dressed herself and done her own hair the ministrations of other hands were irritating. Lettice might be spoon-faced, but at least she was quick and efficient. Perhaps she could dispense with a maid altogether? But Lyndon would think it undignified; he would expect to find himself being asked to lace her stays.

The idea which followed this one into her head was probably just as ridiculous, but worth investigating. She rang the bell for Mrs Mercy.

'How is Meliora getting on downstairs, Mrs Mercy?'

'Oh, well enough, madam, I daresay. She seems a very well-conducted young person.'

'What are her duties?'

Mrs Mercy's calm features showed a gleam of surprise. 'Why, having no precise instructions, madam, I have set her to helping Cook.'

'As kitchen-maid?'

'Yes, madam. She is clean enough now to handle the food and the crockery.'

'Does she learn quickly?'

'I haven't taken much regard, madam, having once trained her to be decent.' She mused. 'I believe she does speak a good deal better than at first. These people are like parrots, I expect, quick to pick up words. I had an aunt whose parrot could repeat the Lord's Prayer; though it also swore shockingly.'

'I hope Meliora won't do that. Do you think, Mrs Mercy, that she could be trained for better work – to take Lettice's place as parlour-maid, and to attend me?'

'Well, I'm sure I couldn't say, madam.' The housekeeper's tone indicated disapproval. 'I should have thought a local girl would have been more suitable. There's the question of honesty, for one thing.' Her eyes dwelt on the silver candle-branches, the delicate porcelain figurines, the miniatures painted on ivory, her mistress's fan and the rings on the hand that held it. 'One never knows what bad acquaintance such people may have picked up, though I'm not saying it's the case. I'd not make up my mind too quickly, if I was you, madam.'

'I shall not. But I would like to speak to the girl, if you'd send her up, please.'

'Very well, madam.' Mrs Mercy rustled out, and within a few moments a timid knock announced Meliora. She had changed since the last time she had appeared upstairs. Somebody had found her a cap and apron, which gave her an altogether more conventional appearance, and she had lost what Dorothy thought of as her sleep-walking look. Now she was awake and knew her place in the world. Her answer to Dorothy's questions were made in astonishingly

49

improved English, with a very slight tinge of Surrey in it. Yes, she said, everybody downstairs was kind to her; she was quite content. There was a gentle, composed air about her which came from the habit of resignation to her circumstances, but was curiously peaceful in its effect. The small slender fingers with their dark nails were quiet, not restless as so many fingers were. Dorothy could envisage them handling delicate things, tidying and tending as if they cared for the objects they touched.

'I shall ask Mrs Mercy to give you a trial as parlourmaid, Meliora,' she said. The great dark eyes widened, unbelieving.

'Me, madam?'

'Yes. Lettice is leaving us to be married, and I think you might be suitable to take her place. If you are not equal to the work you will have to go back to the kitchen, of course. You must listen very carefully to everything you are told, and try to do very well, so that you can rise in the world. I trust you, remember, Meliora.'

Meliora stood very still, then suddenly dropped on one knee and carried Dorothy's hand to her lips in a swift ritual gesture.

'I serve you always, madam,' she said. 'Till my life end.'

She knew that in the kitchen they thought her mistress was mad to promote her, and Lettice's sniffs and snapped instructions left her in no doubt of that young woman's feelings. Orders were thrown at her too fast to take in, every mistake she made was scolded or derided. It seemed that she had not after all left enmity behind when she entered Dove House.

'Tck, tck, tck, fingerprints on the furniture and that silver bowl left half polished. I don't know what this house will come to when I go, I'm sure, but I think 'twill be rack and ruination. Putting a heathen black person in charge of a residence that nobility and gentry and the highest in the land might visit and never see anything worse than they see at home, it's a crying scandal.'

'I am not heathen black,' said Meliora gently. 'The Vicar gentleman he christen me Meliora Anna, for Madam's dear mamma. He say I not baptised properly in Jamestown.'

Lettice tossed her head. 'Well, behave like a Christian, then. Look at the dust on that table. And if I find you pocketing the candle-ends I'll tell of you to Madam.'

'That will do, Lettice,' said Mrs Mercy, looming behind her. 'Praise blesses, blame bans, remember. The girl is doing quite well, and will improve.'

After the departure of Lettice to make Mr Peasmarsh a happy man, it was wonderful to Meliora to be in sole charge of the beautiful objects in rooms the lower servants would never see. She found a sensuous pleasure in touching the sheen of satin, the rough richness of brocade; in polishing with beeswax the surfaces of furniture made from the fashionable new wood, mahogany, that came from the West Indies, and could be polished until it had the appearance of a great chestnut. Walnut, dappled like a horse, had a different feeling altogether. The spinet was of walnut. When she was sure nobody was about, she would touch, very lightly, its ivory keys, and hear its silver whisper of sound, like the voice of one of the tiny painted nymphs who sported among flowers on its lid. The silver tea-kettle had a crusted feel to its embossed handle, but the dining silver was quite different, the forks and spoons cool and smooth like the bodies of fish. She particularly loved to touch the two-handled bowl which Lettice had accused her of polishing imperfectly. The two long-haired, long-robed figures engraved on it were, she knew, angels, and her mistress had told her the meaning of the words beneath the shield – *Un je serverai*: I serve one alone. That, Meliora thought, meant herself, dedicated to the service of the heavenly young lady who had taken her out of a nightmare and brought her to this place where, as the hymn said, all wounds at once are healed and tears for ever dry.

She served the Master as well, of course: that strong, laughing, handsome young man who chucked her under the chin or shouted a compliment at her when they met in room or corridor. He seemed to care for nothing but his horse and cricket, but Meliora, because she had a secret spring of knowledge from her Powhatan ancestors, could tell that some great business occupied his mind, kept him from sleeping, and lay over the thoughts of Madam as well. It was in any case impossible not to notice the frequent visits paid to him by gentlemen who arrived in coaches boasting no coat of arms, and stayed behind closed doors talking, sometimes until late in the night.

No word of these meetings was said in the servants' hall. Mrs Mercy, who had been in the service of Mr Beaumont's mother as a girl, knew what they meant and held her peace. Mr Fowler knew, but kept his own counsel. The others had no curiosity about gentlefolk's business. Only Meliora saw the shadow of conspiracy come in behind the gentlemen, and go out behind the Master when he drove up to London, and she knew that there was great danger in the shadow. The sound of war-drums was in her ears when she saw it, and the colour of blood before her eyes. But she could say nothing, even in the quiet moments when she pinned up Madam's hair or fastened jewels at her neck. The first time she heard mention of it was one day in late July when a heavy hammering came at the front door, and Mr Fowler, who was busy with his pantry-book, sent her to answer it.

A wave of shock went through her when she saw who stood there. Rouged, bepowdered and wigged, Mrs Petworth held stiffly to the arm of her large old husband, and at the sight of them nightmare recaptured Meliora.

'So, it's true!' Mrs Petworth said, triumphantly thumping her cane on the ground. 'Ye see, Mr Petworth, the wench is here, just as was told us. Lud, what a fine lady, prink-pranking like any Christian! Whatever is the world coming to?'

Ozias Petworth's faded eyes, prominent like a snail's, raked the maid's figure insolently before he pushed her aside, almost knocking her to the ground.

'Out of the way, and tell your mistress her kin are here.'

Dorothy, sewing at the window of the Blue Parlour, looked up annoyed at Meliora's trembling announcement.

'I knew they would come out of curiosity, sooner or later. Plague take it, I shall have to see them, and I won't do it alone.'

She called out of the window to Lyndon, who was playing on the lawn with his new mastiff bitch, Belle.

'Bring them upstairs, Meliora.' She saw the pallor behind the brown of the girl's cheeks, and added, 'There is nothing they can do to you, you know. Show them in, then bring tea.'

When, a few minutes later, Meliora entered with the tea accoutrements, she felt storm-waves of anger in the room. Dorothy, pink-faced, was tapping her fan rapidly against the palm of her other hand, and Lyndon stood by the fireplace with a face of fury and his hands in his pockets, inelegantly jammed, as though he feared he might commit some violence if he took them out. The Petworths wore the satisfied air of people who had said what they had come to say, and caused the utmost unpleasantness by doing so. Meliora knew she had been discussed. As she opened the door Lyndon was saying, 'Relative or not, any man who speaks so to my wife leaves my house, with my boot in his breeches. So take care.'

Dorothy said quietly, 'I think we had better talk of something else, my love. Have you visited Town lately, Aunt?'

'Neither money nor inclinations,' snapped Mrs Petworth. 'What's there to London but a pack of thieves and whores?'

'Besides,' added her husband with a malicious eye on Lyndon, 'ain't we got the pink of society here in Richmond, what with His Gracious Majesty riding down o' Sundays to dine at White Lodge?'

'You can see him shootin' turkeys if you've a ticket to get into the Park,' said Mrs Petworth. 'And now Princess Amelia's become Ranger she spends more time at the Lodge than at St James's.'

'And, I hear,' said Lyndon coldly, 'has closed the Park to all but a few, thereby robbing free citizens of the rights they've enjoyed since the time of King Charles the Martyr.'

'Come, come.' Mr Petworth was luring him on to an outburst. 'Let's have no harsh words about the monarchy. There's enough treason in the air nowadays, with all this talk of the Pretender's son bringing a herd of Papists over to massacre honest Britons and put an end to all civil liberty.'

Lyndon turned his head aside, saying. 'Twaddle.'

'Twaddle you may say, my lad, but you'll sing another tune when the dangblasted priests are burning men and women at Smithfield, and Protestants are being murdered in their beds, rot my eyes. Aye, that'll show up these fools that rant about the exiled Stuarts. Exiled be damned! We threw 'em out for the papistical tyrants they were, and out they shall stay.' He leaned forward, hands on knees, enjoying Lyndon's silent fury. 'Well do I remember the song we drummed 'em away with, for my dad used to dangle me and sing it, and may I be everlastingly fired if I didn't hear 'em singing it in the streets t'other day, when I went up to see my lawyer.' He broke into a hoarse and unmusical bellow which was hardly recognisable as the tune of 'Lilliburlero'.

'The Pope sends us over a bonny brisk lad,
 Twang 'em, we'll bang 'em, and hang 'em up all.
Who to court English favour, wears a Scotch plaid,
 Twang 'em, we'll bang 'em, and hand 'em up all.
 To arms, to arms,
 Brave boys, to arms!
A true English cause for your courage doth call,
 Court, country, and city,
 Against a banditti,
Twang 'em, we'll bang 'em, and hang 'em up all.'

Dorothy glanced nervously round the room, half expecting to see the family portraits crash to the ground in outrage. Hurriedly she said, 'Why a Scotch plaid?'

'Because, my dear, the Pretender's son's relying on Scotch help to raise an army, an army of bare-arsed gallowglasses that never saw a battlefield nor the right end of a cannon. French money and Scotch soldiers, that's his hope, and may he and the whole pack of sedition-mongers rot in hell.'

Without a word, Lyndon walked out of the room, closing the door with a quietness more eloquent than the loudest bang. Mr Petworth began to heave with laughter.

'Damme, if your good man don't seem hipped, niece! Have I said somewhat to offend him?'

Mrs Petworth contributed a faint giggle. 'His own father's an outlaw.'

Her husband pretended recollection. 'Now it comes back to me. The good man was out in the 'Fifteen, and has since found the air of Italy healthier than England's. Your pardon, niece Doll, I'd quite forgot. Well, well, an old man's memories are short.'

Dorothy's face was calm, though her hands shook. 'I think your memory is excellent, Uncle,' she said. 'Now, if you'll excuse me, I have matters to attend to. Meliora, show Mr and Mrs Petworth out.'

'Hoity-toity! we know when we're not wanted.' Mrs Petworth, nose in air, led the way. At the front door Ozias suddenly turned on Meliora and, leering, gave her bosom a painful pinch.

Dorothy ran down the stairs and out through the garden door. There was no sign of Lyndon, only the bitch Belle lying in a patch of sunshine. Picking up her skirts and cursing her wide hoop, she tore across the lawns, through the orchard, towards the stable-yard. He was there, saddling the young roan with a furious, intent face. As he fastened the last buckle and led the horse to a mounting-block she caught up with him, panting.

'Lyndon, wait!'

He leapt into the saddle and impatiently jerked the reins away from her hands.

'Wait! I'm sorry you're vexed. But what could I say, what could I do?'

'Anything but sit there like a milksop!' he retorted savagely. 'Why did you let the old boor in at all? If you must talk treason with your Whig relatives, do it somewhere else in future. I'd have killed him if I'd stayed, I tell you that – killed him! Damn you, let go my bridle.'

She shrank back, thinking he was going to strike her with his crop, but he used it to give the horse a cut across the neck that startled it into movement. A frightened stable-lad ran out to open the gate, and Lyndon was gone, at a rapid trot that she heard breaking into a gallop in the lane, growing fainter until the hoofbeats died away. She stood, unable to stop the tears that welled into her eyes and ran down her cheeks. The boy was looking at her curiously; she turned and walked slowly back towards the house.

She was in bed when he came back. His clothes were dusty, and he smelt of wine, but his look, thank God, was cheerful, and he was humming tunelessly as he went into his dressing-room. Returning, he looked down at the flushed face and swollen eyes of his wife, smiled and stroked her cheek.

'What's amiss, poppet? Not still fretting about my little burst of ill-humour?'

She nodded, half crying again. 'I didn't know you could be so a-angry.'

Yawning, he unbuttoned his waistcoat and dragged the ribbon from his hair, shaking the dust from it. 'Think nothing of it. I was in a pretty rage, I know, hearing my Prince and my father spoken of like that. But I should not have raved at Dolly. There, child. Lord, your handkerchief's soaked! Take mine – not that it's very clean.'

She mopped her eyes and sat up among the pillows. 'Where did you go? I was afraid you'd ride recklessly and break your neck.'

'I? You know me, a positive centaur, half a horse. Oh, I galloped my temper off through Petersham and Ham, then back by the boundaries of the Park, even within it at one point, without the permission of Her Most Gracious Highness the Princess Amelia. Did you know the Elector's in Hanover? One of the gatekeepers told me, and I gave him a sixpence for the good news. On the way home I saw Colonel Duncombe walking in his garden, and went in for a pipe and a cup or two. Young Paul was there, for it's the law vacation. For once he was near to being merry.'

And I lying here, she thought, imagining Lyndon brought home on a door and me a widow. She turned to him.

'Will it be long to wait now?'

'What?'

'You know. Uncle Petworth said . . . the landing.'

'No. Very soon now. Good night, my sweet life.'

'Who the Pretender's son?' Meliora asked Mrs Mercy.

'Who *is* the . . .' the housekeeper began mechanically to correct, before snapping, 'Mind your own business, girl. Where have you been hearing such talk?'

'I wait at the tea-table, ma'am, and I hear it there.'

'Don't you know the first rule a servant must learn is not to listen to what the quality say? When you're in waiting you're deaf, to all intents and purposes, even as the deaf adder which stoppeth her ears. Well, I suppose you haven't had time to learn everything yet. But mark me. Now take your brush and dusters up to the attics, for the flies swarm there this time of year, and we don't want 'em breeding for the winter.'

Meliora trudged up the back staircase and the one beyond that, to the long top floor of small rooms with dormer windows and sloping roofs. In the bigger ones the lower servants slept, only Mrs Mercy and Mr Fowler having rooms in the basement. She shared one herself with flighty Sarah, who came home sometimes at an hour of night Mrs Mercy would not at all have approved; but she had never entered the smaller ones at the end of the passage, used as lumber-rooms. It was true, as Mrs Mercy had said: they faced west, and their small seldom-cleaned windows were dancing-floors for black, buzzing crowds of flies. Meliora, who had seen flies in Virginia to which these were mere gnats, fearlessly unscrewed the window-catches and ejected the dancers, then slammed down the sashes and thoroughly washed panes and frames with a good strong solution of lye, made from wood-ash and highly efficacious against pests.

She was finishing the second window in the far attic when she became conscious of a sudden shiver of cold down her spine. It was odd, for the room was close, having been so long shut up, and she was warm with working. She looked round for some source of draught, but there was none. The shabby little room was bare but for a few pieces of broken-legged furniture and some travelling-bags, ancient things with the Earl's crest on them.

She grew colder, and realised that her teeth were beginning to chatter. Very deliberately she wrung out the cloths, putting all her concentration into the simple act to drive back the knowledge that the coldness came from fear; an awful, gripping fear that made breathing an effort and raised the tiny hairs on her bare forearms. Fear of what, of whom? Had she not left fear behind in the Nightmare? Yet here it was, black and blinding, shutting out the English summer day and taking her back beyond knowledge into the superstitions of her Indian and negro forefathers. Somehow she reached the door, shut it on the horror inside, and ran.

When she pelted into the kitchen, the bucket she still carried clanking and slopping its contents on the floor, Cook was stirring the stock-pot on the hob. She dropped her ladle, and the grey cat at her feet leapt in alarm on to a shelf.

'Lor, what's the matter, Mel? Thieves or fire?'

Meliora shook her head, then broke into an incoherent and ungrammatical account of her experience, later translated by Cook to Mrs Mercy and Mr Fowler as 'She said as there was a spirit in the attic and it frit the life out of her'. Reprimanded for giving way to hysterical nonsense, she learnt her first lesson in the advisability of maintaining decorum if one wished to be accepted by the English.

That night, over their supper-beer, Mrs Mercy discussed the occurrence with Mr Fowler.

'I wouldn't have thought twice about it, Mr F., for goodness knows what fancies these people get into their heads. But it was the very room where that terrible thing happened.'

Mr Fowler drained his glass, relit his pipe, and enquired what terrible thing.

'Well, it was back in his lordship's mother's time – the Dowager Viscountess she was, of course. There was a lot of Beaumont relations then, and in the summer there'd always be a houseful getting away from the stink and dust in London. One year her ladyship's sister came to stay, with her family, some quite small, for she was a good deal younger and not all that long married. It was a wet summer, as things turned out, so the children played about the house and stables most of the time. They were none the worse for it, and they went back to London with good Surrey roses in their cheeks . . . *all but one.*' Her voice sank to a whisper, and she glanced round her sitting-room to make sure that no unlicensed ears were listening. 'It was the youngest of her ladyship's boys, an out-and-out little terror, always in mischief, and the nurse's despair. The day came when the children had been all over the place, running and shouting and tiring of themselves out. But at bedtime . . .'

Mr Fowler took his pipe out of his mouth.

'But at bedtime the youngest boy was not to be found. High and low they searched, but not a trace of him could they come by, either then or after his poor mamma had had to take the others back to London, thinking him fallen into the river. Until . . .' She paused and fixed the butler with an awesome look. 'Until the housekeeper as was then went up to the attics. They was little used for sleeping, Mr Fowler, for in those days servants were more often than not made to sleep down here, higgledy-piggledy, or in the outhouses, not in comfort like us. And there, in the small attic at the end, they found the poor infant; or what was left of him. In a box-trunk that he'd climbed into and pulled the lid down on himself, and smothered to death.'

'Dear, dear,' said Mr Fowler. 'What a truly awful fate.' He shuddered slightly. 'I rather wish you'd kept me in ignorance, Mrs M.'

'I told you,' she said, 'because I believe, true as gospel, that young Meliora met with that unfortunate child's spirit, or fetch, or bogy, or what you like to call it.'

'But,' Mr Fowler pointed out mildly, 'other servants have been up there, surely, and they've reported nothing untoward, at least in my time.'

'Nor in mine. And my opinion is that only certain folk feel or see such things, and she is one. I shall not beat her for being fanciful, Mr Fowler, for I know better.'

'And she could not have heard this story from anyone?'

An emphatic headshake. 'I've told it to nobody, being all too well acquainted with the foolish fears of maids. If that pot is empty I will send Sam to the brewhouse for more. My sensibilities are quite shaken, I declare.'

Meliora was fond of going to church. She liked the singing and the playing of the band in the gallery, the prayers and the ritual, though the sermon was always very long and to her largely incomprehensible. Most of all she liked the glass pictures in the windows, of God and His Son and His Son's Mother and the beautiful saints and angels, and was moved to tears by contemplation of the anguished form nailed to the cross. If she could have such an image, a very small one, to have always with her, she was sure that it would keep away any menacing evil. There was no such thing to be bought in Protestant England, of course, even if she had had any money. She wanted one so much that she felt she might even steal one if she could find it, though she knew that was very wrong.

An honester solution was presented. Sarah, coming home with her through the gardens, had pointed out a tree with reddish leaves and clusters of small berries of deep orange-pink.

'Rowan's turning early,' Sarah said. 'That mean a hard winter, that do. He's a fairy tree, is rowan, which I don't expect you ever heard, Mel, not having English trees where you comed from.' Meliora looked blank. 'Fairies, *you* know, little atomies what creeps out of a night and sweeps the kitchen if you puts a saucer of cream down for 'em.'

'They are cats?'

Sarah burst out laughing. 'Cats? Jiminy, what a green goose you are, Mel.' She explained as well as she could about the properties of fairies, their shyness, their attachment to certain wells, glades, flowers and trees, and the protection they extended to favoured humans. Meliora gazed speculatively at the tree, and, when they were near the house, went back on the excuse of having dropped a new halfpenny Madam had given her. Once again at the tree, she carefully broke off two twigs, one longer than the other, murmuring apologetically to the fairy tree as she did so.

In a quiet corner of the scullery she bound them together with a piece of wire, and held the result at arm's length to admire it. Yes, it was a real cross; even if the Saviour Jesus was not upon it, she could imagine him there. Her small fingers secured the cross to a piece of string which she hung round her neck, arranging this, her one ornament, neatly in the valley between her breasts.

Which was where Lyndon saw it, when she opened the door to

him. His gaze, for once, was not admiring. Mrs Mercy was surprised to be summoned to the library, where her master ordered her sharply to make the coloured girl take off her home-made crucifix. 'And never let me see her wearing it again. It – isn't safe these days, Mercy.'

Master and servant exchanged an understanding look.

Obediently Meliora removed her cross, but it went into the pocket she kept permanently tied round her waist under her looped petticoat.

On the last night of July, Mr Fowler, who had been in a refreshing sleep for some three hours, was startled awake by a thunderous knocking at the front door, just above the room in which he slept. Muttering words that were foreign to his mild nature, he fumbled about for a candle and a flint and tinderbox with which to light it, dragged a cloak round his shoulders, seized a kitchen poker in passing and went to confront the knocker. Thieves, or the Watch? He unbarred the door but kept its massive chain fastened, peering out through the crack.

' "Wake Duncan with thy knocking? I would thou couldst!" Good evening, friend,' said a thick, amiable voice from the summer darkness. Mr Fowler's candle illuminated a hulking form in a riding-cloak, short-sighted eyes peering forward into his.

'Good God, sir!' he said. 'Pray come in.'

'Thankee,' replied Mr Samuel Johnson.

5

Raising his huge head occasionally from the plate of cold meats hastily collected from the larder, and the mug of steaming toddy of which his principles for once allowed him to partake, Mr Johnson beamed upon the company. Lyndon wore a handsome Turkish-patterned dressing-gown and Dorothy's hair streamed about her shoulders, but their faces were as bright with expectancy as though the sun had just begun to touch the earth.

'I beg your pardon,' he said, munching, 'for this unheralded visit. You may call me a rascal, sir, for intruding upon your household at such an hour. I beg you to believe I had the best, the most cogent of reasons.'

'Yes, yes,' said Lyndon impatiently. 'Pray come to it.'

Mr Johnson, after lovingly contemplating a sausage, laid it aside and drew from his pocket a letter, heavily sealed. He laid it on the table.

'I dined last night at Lady Primrose's, where our repast was interrupted by the arrival of – of a gentleman. After our company had heard the news he brought—'

'The company being the Brotherhood?'

'Members of it, sir. To resume, after we had heard these tidings, all thought of food was put by. I have never . . .' He shook his head wonderingly. 'I never thought to see a company so completely overset. I begged – and I hope it may not be deemed presumptuous – to be the bearer myself of the tidings which Lady Primrose desired to reach you as soon as possible.'

Lyndon reached out and took the document. 'By your leave.' As he tore the seals and read it, Dorothy saw his face freeze for a second in disbelief, then become transformed. He read the paper again and laid it down; his hands were shaking.

'He has landed,' he said. 'Six days ago Prince Charles Edward landed on the Island of Eriska, to the west side of Scotland.'

'I know it,' said Sam Johnson. 'And I praise God for it.'

'Amen.'

The tall clock in the corner gave its ponderous tick-tock, but Dorothy did not hear it. It seemed to her that time had stopped, for something had happened beyond its reckoning. Something had happened which was going to change their world, for ever. She felt cold and strange; her teeth were chattering.

'Your lady is pale, sir,' said Sam Johnson. Very gently he placed the toddy-mug in her hands, the side from which he had not drunk towards her, and gratefully she sipped at it. Lyndon was still staring at the paper.

'Only a few were with him,' he said. 'The Duke of Atholl, Sir Thomas Sheridan, one or two others. As the ship sailed towards the island, the Duke perceived a great eagle circle above it, which would not leave them, and observed to the Prince that the king of birds was come to welcome him to Scotland.'

'But the French forces?' Dorothy asked.

Lyndon shook his head. 'The King of France failed him at the last moment. Think nothing of that. When he raises his Standard the Scottish chiefs will flock to him, and England will send every loyal man she has.'

'I am not a man of war, sir,' pronounced Johnson. 'For that matter, I make no claim to be a politician, and I had as lief endure one sort of government as another. But I cannot see without wrath the usurpation of the old ways and the old rulers by those who have neither rights nor virtues. Have you ever visited Scotland, sir?'

'No. No.' Lyndon was hardly listening to him.

'It is, I believe, a wild mountainous region, where, however, the natives retain a kind of simplicity of life which may indeed approximate to that of the ancient state of Britain. My father, as you may know, was a bookseller, and I well recall in my childhood poring over a certain book, a *Description of the Western Islands of Scotland*, in which I am sure there was mention of this Isle of Eriska. It is curious, madam,' – turning to Dorothy – 'to reflect how small a place may contain so great a destiny.'

In the strangeness of the moment she saw what she had not seen in him before: a quality of immensity which had nothing to do with his size. The peering eyes met hers over the rim of the mug, and for the first time she saw them as the eyes of a visionary.

'Very curious, Mr Johnson,' she answered. 'I hope His Highness was not met by Scottish witches.'

He threw up ham-like hands in astonishment. 'Mrs Beaumont, I believe you are yourself a witch! I was at that moment dwelling on the prophecy, "All hail, Macbeth! that shall be king hereafter". It is not astonishing that such words should come into *my* head, for I'm at present employed on *Some Observations on the Tragedy of Macbeth* – but that they should come into *yours* . . . To my mind, madam, the most irresistible charms in a female are intelligence combined with beauty, and in you I behold both.' He bowed – as well as anyone could who was seated at a table with a napkin tucked into his cravat.

Dorothy smiled, 'I'm honoured, Mr Johnson. Now we shall leave you to finish your supper, and retire.' She touched Lyndon's arm. 'My dear.'

He looked up, blinking. 'Yes? Yes, it's late. Tomorrow we can talk, and plan . . . The butler will show you up, sir.'

As the door closed behind them, Johnson sighed heavily. He possessed a large and susceptible heart, and it was a sorrow to him that his beloved Tetty had become so extremely unromantical after their marriage, and was, even to his chivalrous eye, incomparably less attractive than the charming Mrs Beaumont, who could also quote Shakespeare, was obviously a good Jacobite, and whom he guessed to be a very romantical young lady indeed. The man who would one day be known as Doctor Johnson, the Lexicographer, the Sage of Fleet Street, the Great Cham of Literature, sighed again and resumed his supper.

In the weeks that followed, the rule of silence which Mrs Mercy had imposed on herself and her staff was broken. Not only Meliora but the entire household became aware that their master's sympathies lay with the young man who had boldly come to win back the throne for King James. The papers called him the Pretender's Son, the Young Chevalier de Quixote, the Foreign Invader, the Boy, and even ruder things. Richmond, so near to London, heard news post-haste, and gossiped exicitedly in the streets, the Castle Inn, the Star and Garter, wherever people gathered together. Six men-o'-war had been ordered to sail immediately for the coast of Scotland. General John Cope was mustering military forces. The Prince had raised his Standard at Glenfinnan, and the Highland chiefs were rallying to him. Descriptions of him varied wildly. He was 'a tall youth of a most agreeable aspect', a foreign-looking personage disguised (omin-ously) as a priest, an ogrish creature in full Highland costume. There were ten thousand, or was it a hundred thousand, French troops coming over to back him, and a legion of Romish priests sworn to bring back the Inquisition, the rack and the flames, and a proclama-tion had been issued accordingly that all Papists and reputed Papists should depart from the Cities of London and Westminster, and within ten miles of the same. The King, thank God, was back from his German dominions, and would set everything right.

Lyndon threw down the *Monthly Chronologer*.

'Idiots! Jackasses! what do they know of him, or the Cause? I have it on the best authority that far from being a bigoted Papist he leans too far the other way for the King's satisfaction. Do they think we live in the times of old Harry or Bloody Mary?'

'Very probably,' said Dorothy. She had spoken sharply to Meliora that morning for coming weeping to her with a tale that the Pretender's son was going to introduce slavery into Britain, with its attendant whips and chains. 'Nonsense, child. Do you think your master would support such a ruler? Go and wash your face, and next time you hear such a tale, give the teller a back-answer.'

To Lyndon she said, 'People will only learn truth by experience. When he comes among them, they must see that these are only silly stories. You – you have no doubt that he *will* succeed?'

'I'd as soon doubt that the sun will rise tomorrow. He's marching towards Edinburgh, carrying all before him. Lochiel has captured Perth, and King James is proclaimed there. Lord George Murray has joined the Prince, and Ogilvy, and Oliphant. Soon he will be at Scone, where his ancestors were crowned.'

' "Whom we invite to see us crown'd at Scone",' murmured Dorothy. Why did the play of *Macbeth* come so often into her mind these days? She had heard her father say at some time that it was considered unlucky in the playhouse. But then it was the story of a wicked Scottish king, and present events, God willing, would earn Scotland a good one. She pondered on a miniature which had been taken from its hiding-place and now hung in a place of honour. It had been smuggled from Rome in a package from Lord Gainsford, and was said to be a good likeness of His Royal Highness. If so, the artist might have done more for Jacobite propaganda by a little flattery, for it was no more prepossessing than the engraved portrait on the drinking-glass. The face was abnormally long, the features slightly effeminate, the expression simpering, the complexion pink and white and the eyes a watery blue. How different from Lyndon's manly looks! It was odd that such a delicate-seeming creature should march at the head of an army of wild Highlanders, should even have a personal camp-follower, his mistress Miss Jenny Cameron, a lady whose reputation provided the gossip-scribblers of Grub Street with endless fun.

It was Sunday, 22 September. Even the servants, normally inclined to slump in their pews and whisper when unobserved, were alert for any reflection of the Scotch Affair in the service. Only the figures in the wall monuments, and the three sculptured heads above the North Transept door, of people who had lived under an earlier Stuart, were indifferent as the clerk read with unusual animation the First Lesson, that lascivious-sounding chapter denouncing the prophet's wanton wife, or possibly the idolatry of the people – it depended on what one made of it.

'Therefore, behold, I will allure her, and bring her into the wilderness, and speak comfortably unto her.

And I will give her vineyards from thence, and the valleys of Achor for a door of hope; and she shall sing there, as in the days of her youth, and as in the day when she came out of the land of Egypt . . . and I will say to them which were not my people, Thou art my people; and they shall say, Thou art my God.'

'For God, read King,' muttered Lyndon to Dorothy.
'Hush.'
The Vicar had been commanded to read out to his congregation a copy of a letter from the Archbishop of Canterbury to the clergy of his diocese.

'A considerable number of rebellious persons having appeared in arms in Scotland, and now advancing southward, and these nations being also threatened with a powerful invasion from abroad, in order to advance to the Royal Throne of these Kingdoms, a Popish long-abjur'd Pretender, to the manifest hazard as well of our holy establish'd religion and civil liberties, as of the sacred person and government of our most Gracious Sovereign King George, you are hereby desir'd and admonish'd, agreeably to your own duty, by your Example, by your Exhortations, as well private as public, and by all other means in your power, to excite the people under your care to exert, on this most important occasion, the preservation of our most happy constitution in Church and State.'

Lyndon wrote on the margin of his prayer-book, 'Don't he wish he may get it!' causing Dorothy to stifle a giggle in her handkerchief. The staff were gaping and grinning; the clerk had his eye on them.
It was by the strangest fortune that, emerging into the main street from the pathway that led to the church, they should meet head on with a small cavalcade in whose centre rode, in a shabby coach, none other than their gracious sovereign King George. He had not changed since Dorothy's father had shown him to her long ago, except that his red face was more lined and puffy, and angrier even than she remembered. An ugly woman in a feather-dotted wig rode beside him. As he drew level with them, the people coming from church paused and doffed hats, some loyalists bowing low. Lyndon,

at the edge of the pavement, only two yards or so from the carriage, stood his ground, hatted, an insolent smile on his face. As Dorothy instinctively made to curtsey he gripped her arm and pulled her upright.

For a second or two the eyes of King and rebellious subject met. The King's face grew red as a turkey-cock's wattles; he seemed about to spit. Then the coach moved past them, and they were the object of stares and a few jeers from those around.

'Oh, God!' said Dorothy. 'He'll never forget you.'

'It makes no difference whether he does or not. When I call at St James's he will not be there. Come, my dear.'

Their neighbour Colonel Duncombe caught up with them. 'That was a plaguy risky thing you did there, Beaumont,' he said, only half jokingly. 'We all know your sympathies by now, but do you want to find yourself in the Tower?' With a flourish of his cane, he passed on, not anxious to be associated at that moment with a known renegade.

After dinner Lyndon asked Dorothy if she would like to ride with him. It was a cool, sunless afternoon, the Hill almost empty of people, a breeze blowing up from the river. At the top, where the great tapestry of Surrey stretched below them, and a gently declining road led to the village of Petersham, they drew rein, as everyone did at that spot, to breathe their horses and admire the prospect. Lyndon had been very silent since church. Dorothy knew that he was preparing something in his mind that he must tell her; something that she did not want to hear, yet must. She turned to him, looking a question, and there was relief in his answering look.

'I'm going away, Doll. Tomorrow.'

She gasped. 'So soon!'

'I must reach him as soon as I can, now that he's close to Edinburgh. It would have been madness to go before, into those wild Highland regions with no guide. At least Edinburgh's within civilisation.'

'But . . . you have no men, no forces. What will you take to him?'

'Myself. And what I can spare besides.'

A gust of wind from the valley brought a spatter of rain with it.

She was glad, for it gave her an excuse to draw her hand across her eyes, suddenly filling with tears she must not shed. Fool, she said to herself, fool, fool, and brought her ungloved right hand sharply up against her saddle, with an impact which hurt enough to stop the threatened tears.

'And what shall I be doing?' she asked, calmly enough.

'Why . . . keeping house, I suppose. Keeping all safe for my return.'

'White-armed Andromache waiting at home for Hector?'

'Who?'

'Oh, never mind. Lyndon, I couldn't bear it, I should go mad with the waiting and not knowing. Let me come with you!'

He stared at her, then laughed. 'As what, pray – part of my retinue? You don't propose, I hope, to disguise yourself as a page, like one of the ladies in your romance books? You've too damn' good a figure, for one thing.'

'Don't laugh at me. I want to come as your companion. As your wife, Lyndon. Is there anything odd in that?'

He stroked his chin. 'Why . . . I hadn't thought of it. There's the danger—'

'I'd rather be in danger than out of my mind with worry.'

'Besides, who'd look after Dove House?'

'Mrs Mercy, of course. She has, after all, been doing it for twenty years or so. It will put her neither up nor down if I'm away, and she can inform us of anything we need to know. She writes a good hand. Oh, pray don't make objections and try to put me off, for I'm quite, quite resolved to come with you.'

'I believe you are – you funny little puss.' He was suddenly serious. 'Doll, you're not breeding? This isn't some woman's whim you've got? For if you were, I'd not risk taking you into God knows what perils.'

She shook her head. It had been a grief to her that in these nine months of marriage there had been no sign of a child, but now she was glad. 'I'm not breeding. I can ride as far and as well as a man.'

He was biting his lip, silent and brooding. Two young men passed them, and one suddenly turned and pointed back at Lyndon, re-cognising with shocked glee the man who had out-stared King George. Ignoring him, Lyndon drew his horse closer to Dorothy's, and tilted her face up towards his.

'Look at me, Doll. I want you to swear something to me. Are you heart and soul for the Cause and the Prince?'

Calmly and steadily she answered, her eyes on his, 'I am. I swear it.'

Only a man, of course, would have counted on leaving home for an unknown country at a day's notice. There was so much to be done, linen to be washed and pressed, clothes and belongings to be chosen and packed. From a place of quiet and order, Dove House became a maelstrom. Yet Mrs Mercy controlled the household panic as though it were the most ordinary thing in the world for her master and mistress to be going off to the wars.

'Mr Lyndon will be taking Leach to drive the coach and Nicholas to valet him, I suppose, madam?'

'Yes.' Dorothy disliked the young footman Nicholas, who was inclined to impertinence and whose honesty she had reason to suspect, but Lyndon found him congenial because he was always ready to abandon his duties for a game of cricket (which in fact he played very well).

'And Madam will need a maid.'

'I shall take Meliora.' Mrs Mercy was looking dubious. 'Unless you think she would be unsuitable in any way? Take fright in a strange place, perhaps?'

Mrs Mercy smoothed her apron. 'As to that, I can't say, madam. I hear the Highland people are very wild and savage, but I should be surprised if they are any worse than what she has seen in her time. No, I have no anxiety for *her*.'

As Mrs Mercy said no more on the subject, Dorothy was not to know that she felt a motherly anxiety for her mistress. Mr Lyndon was a good husband, she had no doubt, and probably knew what he was doing in embarking on this adventure, but Mrs Mercy suspected

70

that he had not the slightest notion of how to look after a young creature brought up in peace and quiet by a fond parent, and never further away from home than a matter of a few miles; not to mention being so content in her new house with fine clothes and servants. For a wild moment, which she could hardly credit in herself, Mrs Mercy wished that she might go instead of Meliora.

But Meliora was sparkling with delight. Her deft hands folded and packed as she chattered away of the excitement they would have, the strange places and people, the young Prince whom she frequently confused with Jesus in the church window, her own gratitude at the honour of being chosen to maid Mrs Beaumont. Besides, it was fun rousing the envy of the other domestics. Cook and Mrs Alice the laundress obviously would not have expected to be chosen for the honour, but Sarah, formerly friendly to Meliora, took it into her flighty head to become violently jealous and to twit the coloured girl at every opportunity.

'Likely you'll find a sweetheart among them Scotchmen, Mel. I'm told they're heathens, the lot of 'em. Anyway, if there's a war you'll be ravaged, that's for sure. Oh Lor, I'm glad it's not *me* goin'. East west, home's best, I always say.'

Lettice Peasmarsh, dropping in to show off her new high style as a matron, in an extraordinarily elaborate fontange cap and a stately black gown, was likewise put out at the thought that she might have been the one chosen to travel and see Life, had she not left to marry. Sipping tea in the kitchen, she radiated gloom.

'Going into the jaws of danger, in my opinion. Look at his lordship, not set foot in his own country these many years, all for flying in the face of the lawful Government. Wouldn't surprise me if Mr Lyndon never come back at all. And what there is to cry for, young Dorcas, I don't know, for them that sow the wind shall reap the whirlwind: *Hosea*, Chapter Eight. As to King George, God bless him, I say. Mr Peasmarsh has high hopes he may get the patronage yet, for old Mr Ekins is past supplying royalty, in my opinion. We shall see a lion and unicorn on our shop-board, mark me.'

'I wouldn't talk too much about Mr Lyndon's affairs outside these doors, if I was you,' said Mrs Mercy. 'Nobody knows yet which way the cat will jump. You don't want to get the household into trouble, do you? A still tongue makes a quiet mind.'

Nicholas was far from displeased that Meliora was to go with them. He had had his eye on her ever since she had been cleaned up and made presentable. An experienced fumbler of maids behind doors and in haystacks, he swiftly summed her up as a pretty piece, in her outlandish way. She could provide him with quite a novel variety of wenching, and he felt sure she would give no trouble, having been brought up among savage Indians. Neatly transferring a quantity of excellent snuff from his master's box to his own, he thought of the delightful prospect, which would undoubtedly enliven the long journey to Scotland. He had heard a lot about wayside inns, their rambling passages and dark stairways.

On the morning of their departure, Meliora stood in the drawing-room. Silently, her eyes caressing the room, she took farewell of the dark shining furniture that had known her hands so well, the French clock on the mantel, a gilt Venus smothered in gilt cupids, the rose-cheeked porcelain people on either side of it, smiling Phyllidas nursing woolly lambs, ogling Corins with sheep-crooks beneath bright green trees. Where they were going there could be no such rooms, of course; perhaps there would be shacks such as she remembered in Virginia.

The door opened and Dorothy, already cloaked, appeared.

'There you are, Meliora. We're almost ready to leave. Make haste.'

Something unfamiliar about the room struck her, something missing.

'Gracious! What's become of the silver?'

'Mr Fowler and Nicholas take – took it, madam, last night.'

'Oh – to the bank vaults, I suppose. Yes, it will be safer there. I hadn't thought of that.' She paused and smiled. 'I had such a beautiful dream last night, Meliora. I can't for my life remember what it was, but I woke feeling so very happy, quite transported. Now isn't that odd, considering what a haste and a muddle we've been in?'

'The spirits send it you to say all shall be well, madam.' Meliora touched the rough crucifix in her pocket.

'Did they? Most obliging of them. Oh, I'm sure it will – of course it must!'

Lyndon's shout summoned her from the hall and she ran out, light-footed, her cloak flying. Meliora followed. Turning at the door before closing it behind her, she blinked in surprise. The great room was completely empty. Uncurtained windows flooded light on to bare boards and walls on which only the marks remained where pictures had hung and candle-sconces had been nailed. In the empty grate a heap of soot had collected; there was thick grey dust on the mantel.

It was an illusion, a trick of the light, caused by the sudden giddy buzzing in her head. She shut her eyes; when she opened them all was as before. Quickly she closed the door and went out to the waiting carriage.

6

However warlike was the spirit attributed to the English people by
the newspapers, the landscape through which the Beaumonts
travelled showed no evidence of it. The harvest was safely in, the
fields lay shorn and calm; the Thames, beside them, was more blue
than grey under a sky in which the only clouds were the colour of
clotted cream. Here and there they would see in a meadow the stiff
corpse of a cow, dead of the murrain which was infecting herds all
over Europe.

'Thank God we have no home farm,' Lyndon said. 'There's a
new remedy for the disease, I hear, tried out in Sweden, a fangle
of snakeweed, valerian and camphire, laurel and elecampane and
Lord knows what beside, but it's tedious to administer and seems to
do little good.'

Dorothy knew that his mind was not on the unfortunate cattle, or
on anything else seen on the familiar journey to London. It was not
until they had crossed London Bridge, that strange street above
water with its ancient houses and shops, and had taken the intricate
way westward to Essex Street and Lady Primrose's house, that he
came to life, and talked animatedly to my lady of rumours and
counter-rumours, as they sat over a cold repast in her dining-room.
She was, thought Dorothy, looking a good ten years younger than
her age, with a white cockade of muslin tucked in her curls. Yet
even she had a word of doubt.

'Nothing yet from Watkin Williams Wynn or Lord Barrymore.
Chicken-hearted, I suppose. I have sent round a letter for them to
sign, if only to send the King as a pledge of good faith. But then,'
shrugging, 'it seems the Prince is managing very well with only his
Scotsmen. The Elector thought himself cock of the walk, and is in
a panic about it all. O Lord! I'd give a thousand pounds to be
coming with you, and I would indeed, indeed, if I didn't think
there was more use for me here. I suppose you will be presented to

74

the Prince, Mrs Dorothy, and dance with him, even. Be sure you get a good likeness of him and send it me, for I can't wait till he gets to St James's. I hear there's to be a battle. Do you suppose you'll be in time for it? How long is it to Edinburgh?'

How long is it to Edinburgh? Long enough, Dorothy thought, during the days of jogging over the ruts of the Great North Road, thankful for the fresh September weather that was neither too hot nor too cold. The countryside was a glory of autumnal colour; russet, gold and crimson blazing in forest and coppice, rosy creeper veiling house and barn, beech hedges turning to dry brownness. The carriage windows were kept open by day for freshness, the stuffy smell of leather overpowered by the heady scent of woodsmoke from pyres of garden refuse. Dorothy, the townswoman, was charmed by all they passed: the villagers who leant on fences or over farm-gates, staring at the carriage as though it were Elijah's fiery chariot, the red squirrels rushing up trees at their approach to chatter at them from the boughs overhead, the pigs and fowls that wandered unconcernedly in the road, miraculously avoiding disaster by a neat side-step or a timely flutter and squawk.

Lyndon, the seasoned traveller, watched his wife with amusement as she leaned out to marvel at some perfectly ordinary sight. On the opposite side of the carriage Meliora was even more wonderstruck. Her previous experience of travelling had been part of the Nightmare. Now the ugliest things to be seen were those that hung from wayside gallows-trees, and even they were no more than dangling bundles of blackened rags festooned with scavenging birds. She had seen slaves hung for insubordination; her eyes rested only briefly on the nasty gallows-fruit. Nicholas rode outside with Leach the coachman, so she was free to listen to the talk of her master and mistress and print on her impressionable mind how they spoke. By the end of the long journey the thickness would have gone from her speech and her imitation of Lyndon's slightly drawled vowel sounds would cause other servants to stare at the Indian foreigner who talked ladylike.

They stayed at the great coaching-inns where, Lyndon said, they would be better lodged and fed than in the bug-infested smaller houses where one might equally well have one's pocket picked or one's throat cut. There were fleas, true, at such noble inns as the George at Stamford and its relations along the Great North Road; but then there were fleas everywhere. It was Meliora's duty to scatter the sheets with a powder of sulphur, made from Mrs Mercy's own receipt, which at least discouraged the horrid creatures.

But the inns were places of danger more subtle than the roads, where highwaymen might lurk. As they supped at St Neots, in the inn's dining-room, other travellers exchanged news and views on the weather, the Princess of Wales's coming child, the cattle pest and the Young Pretender. Only in England, perhaps, could their talk have been so mild and unperturbed. Where, Dorothy wondered, were the anticipatory shudders at the return of the thumb-screw and the rack, the terror of half-naked savages coming among them?

Lyndon shrugged contemptuously. 'All scribblers' lies. The common people care nothing for who rules them. When the Prince rides into London they'll crowd the windows to cheer him. As for the women, I don't doubt they look forward to a hearty Highland rape, with husbands like these.' He gestured towards a well-fed, slow-spoken group of John Bulls at the next table. One of them, less bucolic than the rest, looked up and turned his large head towards Lyndon.

'I'd watch your tongue, friend, if I was you.'

Lyndon's brows rose. 'I? What have I said?'

'Enough to stand for treason.'

Lyndon was half on his feet, but Dorothy pulled at his sleeve urgently. 'Lyndon, no! Sit down. Make nothing of it.'

He looked rebellious, but saw the wisdom of her warning and sat down, saying with a pleasant smile, 'I fear you mistook me, sir. Only a jest.'

The other scowled. 'A poor one, then.' But he turned back to his table-mates, and was lost again in a plateful of roast beef. Dorothy hurried through the pudding, and as soon as was decent yawned her way to bed. Lyndon followed, still with the look of a cross, chidden child. In their bedroom, the door locked, she turned on him.

'For God's sake, be careful. Do you want to reach Scotland, or to be taken up and dragged back to face a court in London? They may be yokels or merchants or I don't know what, but they're not indifferent. Can't you keep your opinions to yourself, for all our sakes, till we get there and you can speak out in the right company? Be reasonable, I do beg and pray you.'

He shook off the hands that held him. 'They make me mad. I thought any man could speak his mind, even under the Elector.'

'You know better than that. Why have we been careful so far? Would even Lady Primrose speak out in public?'

With one of his sudden transitions of mood, he smiled, and bent to kiss her flushed cheek. 'You're very right, my dear. Well, as Mrs Mercy would say, Patience is a flower that grows not in everyone's garden, but such as I am I'll try to cultivate it. You shame me, Doll, indeed.'

'I don't mean to shame you. I know how you feel. Only be content to say it to me, in private, as much as you like. Who should listen better than I, with so much to learn? I like to hear you talk – only I'm afraid for you if others hear.'

'My clever Doll. Come to bed.'

The George at Stamford, reached late in the evening after another long day's drive, was a huge, rambling house built round an inn-yard pretty with pot-flowers and wreathing vines. They were given a room that looked to the river, away from the clatter of the street and the cry of the watchman. But Meliora, who had so far either slept in a dressing-room next to her mistress's, or shared a bed with another maid, was put in a tiny room at the top of the house, vacated for the night by one of the inn-servants because of the unusual press of travellers. She was pleased at her unusual freedom, and at the pretty view from the small window, the moon behind trees, a square church tower black against a sky whose stars were bright with early frost.

Her bodice unlaced and her small hoop laid aside, she stretched in comfort, yawning like a sleepy cat. She had grown since she came to Richmond; her clothes were tight and her whalebone bodice in particular hurt her, but she would say nothing to her beloved Mrs Dorothy. Cool, in her shift, she turned back the coarse sheet of the pallet-bed. There were no fleas, she thanked the assorted heavenly company to whom she prayed every night. She was half in bed when the wooden latch clicked and the door opened.

Nicholas stood there, grinning in the moonlight, coatless, his breeches half-unbuttoned. She pulled up the sheet round her neck.

'What you want? Get out!'

He ambled forward. 'Well now, there's a nice thing to say to a chap that's waited since I don't know when. A room to yourself, no less. I thought you'd be frightened to be alone, so I come to keep you company, Mel. Why let the masters have all the fun, eh? Come, you ain't playing coy, surely? 'Cording to what I heard, you nigra wenches is as hot as mustard. Kiss different to English ones, I'm told. Well – what you waiting for?'

She had retreated almost to the wall, the white of her eyes brilliant. 'Out!' she spat at him. 'Or I scream for someone!'

He laughed. 'Likely they'd come, ain't it? Now give over, Mel, do.' He snatched at the sheet, which dropped from the dark tantalising shoulders, and wrenched at the neck of her shift. With the sureness of a tigress she struck out at him, her long hard nails raking his cheek open. As he leapt back with a yell she snatched from her hair the steel bodkin that held the mass of it under her cap by day, and menaced him with it.

'You come nearer, you go out no man, I promise you.'

Now she was advancing and he retreating, uttering cries and curses as the small hand and its improvised dagger came nearer to what Nicholas prized most. At the door he fumbled for the latch, one hand behind him, the other clutching his breeches.

'Hellcat! Bitch! Filthy black doxy!' He was out and away, his boots clattering along the corridor. Meliora got out of bed, bolted the door, placed the bodkin on a chair and knelt composedly at the bedside.

'Thank you, Father God, thank you, Saviour Jesus, thank you, Mother Mary and Prince Charles Edward, not to deliver me into the power of the dog. Make me always good and preserve my mistress and master. I wish you all a very good night.'

They were through the flat Midlands, up among the Dales, the immensity of Yorkshire spreading on each side of them, the road increasingly rougher. Dorothy had never seen a wonder like York's massive Minster and city walls, or, when they had passed York, grandeur like the hills of the North Riding, though Lyndon said they were as nothing to the heights she would see in Scotland. They were going by the less frequented road, towards Newcastle, not Carlisle where the Elector's forces were gathering. From the east came the salt breath of the German Ocean; to the west lay a prospect of towering fells that he said hid the lakes, Grasmere, Ullswater, Derwentwater, and even higher mountains above them. Eighteenth-century taste did not admire such scenery, regarding it as awe-ful, rude, fierce and beetling. But Dorothy could not look at it enough, staring until the sun sank behind the mountains and night came on.

The people spoke differently in these villages, and were unwelcoming. They looked at Meliora with deep suspicion, not with the frank curiosity of the South: as though her colour made her an enemy stranger. Dorothy remembered from her history books how often they had faced invaders, Rome, Saxon and Dane. If invasion were coming again they would not meet it with a smile or with indifference. Not far from Newcastle the travellers lodged for the night at Blanchland, a secret, lovely village of stone among wild fells, at a small inn among the ruins of an abbey.

'Your namesake lived here, Doll,' Lyndon told her. 'Dorothy Forster, who helped her brother to escape from Newgate after the 'Fifteen. But Derwentwater wasn't so lucky.'

'Who was he, love?' She was glad to encourage him to talk, so silent and withdrawn he had been on the journey.

'Young Jamie Radclyffe, the third Earl. He grew up with King James at St Germain, and fought gallantly for him, but they took him at Preston. His young wife went to London and threw herself

79

at the Elector's feet to plead for him, and even the House of Lords petitioned for a pardon. But it was all no use. German George had his head chopped off on Tower Hill. It was said that strange lights glowed in the sky that night, and every year since on the anniversary. They brought him home secretly and buried him at Dilston, here in Hexham Vale, and his people made songs on him: 'O Derwentwater's a bonnie lord . . .'

Dorothy shivered. 'A wonder the Queen – the Elector's wife – couldn't have saved him.'

'The Queen? Left behind in Hanover, locked up for life, all for taking a lover, when Geordie flaunted his ugly whores wherever he went. Much pleading *she* could do, even for herself. Well, at least Jamie Radclyffe got the easier death.'

'Easier than what?'

'Why, the full sentence for a traitor – to be hanged, drawn and quartered. The Elector was all for it, but Jamie's rank saved him.'

The little panelled room seemed to be closing in on them. 'Don't let's talk of such things,' Dorothy said. 'All that is past now.'

Lyndon went to the window, which shook with the violence of the rain sweeping down from the fells. 'I shall go out and walk. I must have air and exercise, after being cooped up like a fowl at market.'

'I'll come with you – I don't mind rain.'

But he was at the door. 'No, I'll walk further alone.' A few moments later she saw him from the window, in his riding-cloak but bare-headed, striding through the abbey archway that led to the road to the Devil's Water, and a battlefield of long ago, and the hidden grave at Dilston. How changed he was from the cheerful young Surrey squire she had married. And yet . . . her father's words came back to her: 'He will take you on hard roads, on stony ways; he has a Holy Grail before him, and such knights have never made easy company.'

It was true, and she must accept it.

All that day he was away, and all that day the rain came down unrelentingly. When he returned they decided, to the relief of Leach, that they should stay at Blanchland until the weather lightened, to rest the horses and themselves from the strain of travelling in those hilly regions. Lyndon, feverishly impatient, took himself off every morning, and Dorothy passed her time in teaching Meliora to read. It was surprisingly easy once they had got over the hurdle of the Cat which sat upon the Mat and ate a Rat. Dorothy had sent to a London bookseller, John Newbury, for one of the new children's books he had published; before his day they had had to make do with gloomy religious tracts. It was *A Little Pretty Pocket-Book, intended for the Instruction and Amusement of Little Master Tommy and Pretty Miss Polly*, and Meliora loved it, following the words with her finger and most contrite at her mistakes. When she had done particularly well her reward was that Dorothy should read to her from what they called the *Beast Book*, a battered old volume of travellers' tales. Crouched by the hearth, her knees up to her chin and her eyes huge, Meliora listened raptly again and again to the same passage concerning Extraordinary Phenomena.

'The wonderful Possum, the squealing Raccoon; the silver-breasted Mock Bird, the Turtle's melancholy wailing, the nimble Catfish, the dreadful Alligator, the heavy Porpoise, rolling in sluggish wantonness.'

What warm climes, strange creatures and brilliant flowers and trees did it conjure up, from her own or her ancestor's childhood? Dorothy had seen her look at the driving rain that blotted out everything, and watched her glowing colour turn grey in the cold – as bright fish, the *Beast Book* said, turned when they were caught. Nicholas teased and taunted her at every opportunity; Leach looked down at her as though she were a horsefly on his many-caped greatcoat. The inn-people avoided her. It had been cruel to bring an exotic creature here on this strange quest for a king.

But on the third day the rain stopped, leaving only a shine of wet on the grey stones, and a heavy fall of leaves. Two more days brought them to a steep ascent which taxed to the limit the already fatigued horses they had brought from the last posting-stage. A north-easter was blowing, making the carriage rock dangerously, the luggage in the boot crashing from side to side. Slower and slower went the horses, till the summit was reached and they paused for breath. Lyndon put his head out of the window, calling 'Stop!' and, pulling Dorothy to her feet, opened the door and helped her out. She drew her breath in a sharp gasp of delighted wonder. On the other side of the slope the sun was shining, and before them lay a panorama of green marshland and brown moor, backed by a great range of mountains, the Cheviots stretching away in the distance: Carter Fell, the Carlin's Tooth, Peel Fell, Hartshorn Pyke, in the east, to the distant heights of Ettrick and the Peebleshire Laws to the north-west; in the foreground grey peel towers and stones that were the fallen walls of Roman camps. And over the mountains spread, like a rich carpet, the purple and rose-bloom of heather. It was a scene that brought tears to Dorothy's eyes.

It was very quiet; only the sound of the wind, the steamy breathing of the horses, the haunting cry of peewits. Lyndon put his arm round his wife.

'We stand on the Border,' he said. 'There lies Scotland.'

Long before they reached Edinburgh they heard, over and over, in every place of halt, that the town had been triumphantly taken by the Prince and his Highlanders. The Castle still held out for the Elector, but there had been a battle at Prestonpans, by the shores of the Forth, in which the English forces under Sir John Cope had been utterly routed. As the Prince, whose generalship was better than his spelling, wrote to his father, 'they ran like rabets'. Now he held court at Holyrood Palace, a Stuart come into his own again in the home of his ancestors. In Edinburgh the guns were quiet, the swords sheathed until the next battle, the populace on the whole reassured by the behaviour of the kilted men from the North.

Yet an air of expectancy lay over Edinburgh, lurked in the narrow cobbled streets beneath the Castle, peered out of closes and wynds, hid behind the shuttered windows of the tall houses which teemed with inhabitants, whispered in the gusts of wind that swooped down between them. The cold air was thick with mist, forced down by the pall of smoke from thousands of chimneys, and the entrances to the closes were befouled and odorous, and barely wide enough to admit a lady's hoop; though many a titled lady lived in the warrens that were called Lands, cheek by jowl with every kind of person from decent merchant and pious minister to prostitute. A secret city, an ancient, conspiratorial city, and a dirty one, Auld Reekie yet held the charm a once-beautiful woman may keep in her ravaged old age.

They found it difficult to get lodgings. The inns were overflowing with Jacobite visitors as well as with the Prince's followers. Nicholas's cockney accent was greeted with surprise and derision, and at one tavern he almost got into a fight. Angrily, Lyndon ordered him back to the coach.

'I'll ask myself, since you can't make yourself understood.' And ask he did, but with no success at the first places he tried. Dorothy began to feel increasingly weary. It was anticlimax to be in Edinburgh at last, and she felt the oncoming of a cold. The muggy air that filled the coach every time the door was opened got into her lungs, making her cough and choke. By the time they had tried fifteen or sixteen taverns she was near weeping, a condition which irritated Lyndon's already exacerbated temper. He thrust his brandy-flask at her.

'For God's sake don't let's have tears to add to the rest of it. Curse and confound this blasted, uncivilised town! Are we never to get a bed for the night? Damme if I won't drive to Holyrood and bang on the door . . .'

He looked capable of that or any folly, and Dorothy, strengthened by the brandy, said, 'If you do you will probably be shot. Why not knock at one of the houses and ask if they let lodgings? We might do better there.'

Lyndon grumbled, but obeyed, performing a furious tattoo on the door of a tall house in the Canongate which looked reasonably respectable. A woman answered and, after careful inspection of the crest-bearing coach and Lyndon's gentlemanly attire, said, to his vast relief, 'Aye, ye may lodge here the nicht if ye'll pay noo. A lone widdy canna take risks, wi' bairns to feed.'

Money was handed over, enough baggage for the night unloaded, and Dorothy, shivering and stiff, was escorted into the house, which smelt little more fragrant than the streets outside, while Leach drove off to house the coach at the stable indicated by the landlady, where the postboy could also sleep before taking the horses back to the inn next day.

'This way, mem.' Dorothy followed Mrs McMurdo, as she proved to be called, up seemingly endless flights of dark narrow stairs, to a room containing little more than a bed, table and chairs. 'The black'll come wi' ye?' the landlady had asked, and Dorothy was thankful that she made no more ado about Meliora's presence. Ladies in Edinburgh were much given to native servants.

At Dorothy's request and the passing of more money, a fire was lighted in the small grate and more candles fetched. Mrs McMurdo, who indeed had bairns to feed and was by no means an unfeeling soul, surveyed the English girl's flushed face and listened to her cough. 'Aye, ye've a sair hoast there. I'll fetch ye up a treacle posset, and mebbe ye guidman'll be glad o' a dram for ye both.' With Meliora's help, a warming-pan was found and applied to the sheets, and Dorothy got thankfully between them. By now she was feverish, hardly noticing the arrival and departure of Lyndon, who had been invited to sup downstairs with some other lodgers.

They were all, fortunately, Jacobites, joyful and triumphant, and they introduced him to Scotland's great drink, usquebaugh or whiskey. Very faintly, two pairs of stairs up, Dorothy heard their shouts and laughter, while outside, in the Canongate, someone went by drunkenly singing.

'O Logie o' Buchan, O Logie the laird,
They hae ta'en awa' Jamie, wha delved in the yaird,
Wha played on the flute and the viol sae sma',
They hae ta'en awa' Jamie, the flower o' them a'. . .'

This lugubrious ballad was followed by the sound of someone being violently sick in the gutter. Dorothy buried her head in the slowly warming sheets and sniffled miserably.

Meliora had been put in a room next to her mistress. It was little more than a section of landing with a wall-bed in it, a narrow recessed plank let into the panelling. Meliora was as cold and tired as her mistress, but more used to enduring, and she was asleep almost as soon as she had climbed into the coffin-like bed.

Lyndon, coming unsteadily upstairs some two hours later, saw by the light of the candle-stump wavering in his hand a recumbent form under a coverlet. Curiously he turned back the top of it, revealing a dark curly head.

'Oho!' he said, and ruffled the curls, settling himself on the sharp bedside.

Meliora woke with a start to find the shift pulled off her shoulders and her master's hands and lips caressing her. It was almost a repetition of the night at Stamford, except that the invader there had been a fellow-servant of no account. Now it was different. Generations of slave-blood told her to lie quiet, obedient to her master whatever his will. The dark gods would have her lie there quiescent, as she had lain in a field so many years ago to be ravished. Then good sense and civilised influences prevailed. She struggled just as arduously as any Pamela for her honour against the whiskey-breathing man who was trying, very incompetently, to get into her bed.

It was thus that Dorothy, wakened by the noise, found them. Stupefied as she was by her cold and the influence of Mrs McMurdo's draughts, she took in the situation at a glance; Meliora's wild eyes and Lyndon's fumbling hands. At her appearance they froze into a statuary group, a nymph and satyr.

'Meliora,' she said calmly, 'I'm sorry to trouble you, but I cannot find the box of handkerchieves. I know it must be somewhere in the brown trunk. Would you be so kind as to look for it?'

'Yes, madam.' Meliora was out bed and had vanished into the room, and Lyndon, uttering something under his breath, was on his feet, staggering. He caught at the sleeve of Dorothy's robe as she turned to follow Meliora.

'Nothing, nothing, Doll. Jus'. . . a little drunk. Good fellows downstairs, good loyal men. Thought it was you . . . in the bed, found little wench instead.'

'Yes, I see. I think you had better go to bed now, or you'll rouse the people of the house.' Obediently he went into the bedroom, and after the token removal of coat and breeches was asleep, snoring. Dorothy climbed in beside him, carefully settling herself at the extreme opposite edge.

I shall never blame Meliora, she told herself. I must never blame anybody, unless those sots downstairs. Wretchedly she drifted off to sleep, as Edinburgh began to come to life.

Next morning Lyndon appeared to have forgotten all about the episode on the landing. He was in haste to go to Holyrood, and Dorothy observed with wry amusement how quickly he spruced himself up with the aid of Nicholas into a well-dressed English gentleman fit to appear before Royalty. Dorothy, feeling too unwell even to get up, bespoke the rooms for the next few days. After all, they were unlikely to get better ones. Lyndon came back that evening in a state of high excitement.

'I had to wait three hours for an audience, there were so many to see him. Gordon of Glenbucket has just come to the Standard with four hundred men, and Lord Ogilvy with six hundred. Then at last I was shown in. Oh, Doll, if I could tell you how gracious he is! He seemed to know as much of me as if I had been his brother. He told me that my father had been to see the King and offered what help he could, and said how much he prized the loyalty of such English gentlemen as had rallied to him, for they were few enough and risked all. King Louis has sent him arms and men at last – what do you think of *that*? And he has every confidence that he can invade England successfully, and soon.'

Dorothy blew her nose and tried to concentrate, against the buzzing in her head, on what Lyndon was saying. 'What is he like?' she asked.

'Like? What a woman's question! How should I say what he's like? Like his pictures, I suppose, and any princely person you may imagine. He has no tartan about him, I remember that. Quietly dressed, I think, like an ordinary gentleman. After the audience I talked with one of the chieftains in the ante-room and, Doll, it's just as I used to tell you – though a Papist he is all for the people keeping their own faith, and has directed that Presbyterian services shall be held as usual in the churches, and the Elector prayed for if the ministers wish it. And as for his mercy to his enemies, this gentleman couldn't say enough for it. After Prestonpans he refused to rejoice over the English killed, saying they were his father's subjects, and the prisoners were treated like lords. Who would not follow such a prince? Oh, if you could but see him, Doll!'

'I hope I shall,' she replied, a trifle sharply. 'It would be a pity to have come all this way for nothing. This pesky cold should clear within a day or two, and then I hope I may be presented.'

She noticed a look of faint surprise cross Lyndon's face. Had he not, she wondered, intended to present her to the Prince? And if not, what was she doing in Edinburgh at all? Her head was too thick for conjecture. She laid it among the hot pillows again, and sniffed the camphor mixture Meliora had brought for her.

Next day she was astonishingly better, able to go out for the first time. The clear cold air blowing from the Nor' Loch in the valley below the town was exhilarating, lifting the heaviness that had been on her. She was beginning to recognise the kinship between herself and Scotland through her Nairne mother. In this rugged place, that crouched between the hill called Arthur's Seat and the Castle Rock, she looked back on her life in London and Richmond as dull and sluggish. There was danger here, but exhilaration too. She felt light and happy, excited, indulgent towards Lyndon's boyish exuberance and pleased at the thought of some cheerful company again after so many long days of travelling; for Lyndon, somewhat sheepishly, had brought her a letter of invitation from Mr Secretary Murray of Broughton, inviting her to attend a levee at Holyroodhouse that same evening.

The dresses in the baggage had been so long in the boot of the coach that they looked far from spruce, but Meliora's attentions with the smoothing-iron would soon remedy that. Dorothy ranged the best of them out on the bed.

'Which shall I wear, now? The sprigged muslin is pretty, but a little rustic, I think. The carnelian's too dowdy and the blue will make me look pale.' She held it up against her, glancing in the fly-spotted mirror.

'Ugh! What a fright I look, quite red-nosed. Perhaps this would do.'

She picked up a brocade gown of white, with a thread of silver in the raised flowers that covered it.

'Women and white look best at night, they say. It's very plain, of course, but why should that matter? I don't suppose anyone will heed me, with so many fine ladies in the town.'

But she was worth the looking at as she stepped into the sedan-chair that was to take her to Holyrood. Meliora had dressed her hair high, with ringlets at the back, and for ornament only a small pearl crescent. A neck-band of black velvet made her exposed bosom look even whiter, and excitement had brought to her cheeks a brighter colour than rouge could lend. As she was dressing, Lyndon had come in and given her a silk scarf of Royal Stuart tartan, saying, 'I am told all the ladies are wearing these at Court; I thought it might look well on you.'

It did, indeed, a scarlet splash of colour against the white bodice, lightly draped over one shoulder and tied at the waist.

'We shall make a handsome pair,' she told him, for he was splendid in buff satin coat and white breeches, with Mechlin lace at throat and wrists.

The Palace of Holyrood blazed with lights, its courtyard thronged with coaches and chairs. Even when, at last, they were deposited at the door of the inner courtyard, the Abbey Close, by which guests were admitted, they found themselves in such a crush of people that they became separated. With Lyndon out of sight among the satins and tartans, Dorothy could only move with the crowd, at a snail's pace, up the staircase and along a corridor through the wall of which came the sound of conversation and music. Finding herself on the edge of the crowd she took the chance of leaving it, and opened a door which should lead into the Assembly Room.

So, indeed, it did. But it admitted her to the opposite end to the one from which the crowd she had just left was approaching, in stately ranks. The startled Highland guard whom she almost knocked over was too late to stop her precipitate and conspicuous entry, and she found herself, the target for many pairs of scandalised eyes, almost falling at the feet of a young man with a star on his breast and a garter about his knee.

And, at the same instant, falling for the first time deeply, irretrievably, utterly in love.

7

He was not in the least like his portraits. How on earth could Lyndon have said so?

Tall and broad-shouldered, the height and breadth emphasised by the blue dress coat and tartan trews he wore, an air of natural command radiated from him which those feeble likenesses did not even suggest. The long Stuart face was not pale, but sunburnt and freckled, a soldier's complexion; the brilliant, compelling eyes not blue, but a deep velvet-brown; and the mouth which miniaturists had rendered as small and effeminate was manly, with a humorous curve to it. It was a face not merely superbly handsome, but full of good nature and good temper. He wore a fair, unfussy tie-wig, with his own sun-bleached hair combed over it at the front, and he carried his head with a pride which had no arrogance in it, but simple majesty. Seeing him, there was no need to ask why Highland chieftains had put the lives of their clansmen in his hands, or why even the most confirmed Whiggish ladies of Edinburgh gazed enraptured at him from their windows. This was he the Highlanders called Tearlach, the Gaelic for Charles, and others, in affectionate familiarity, Bonnie Prince Charlie.

The strong arm of the sentry saved Dorothy from the ultimate embarrassment of falling at the Prince's feet. Deftly he pushed her behind him, and, when the Prince's attention was engaged by a couple being presented to him, ushered her tactfully through the door, with a whispered injunction to rejoin the crowd at the main door. There she found Lyndon waiting for her with a face of thunder.

'What the devil were you doing, bursting in like that? The whole room was staring at you. Do you want to make us a laughing-stock?'

At any other time she would have been contrite, apologetic; but in her present state of euphoria she laughed, fanning her heated cheeks from which the blush had not yet faded.

'Yes, it was very clumsy of me. We will go in separately, if you like, so that people will not know I am with you.'

He jerked her arm into his, 'Of course we will not go in separately! Dorothy, sometimes I take you for a perfect fool.'

So she was Dorothy tonight, not Doll; out of favour, and she cared not in the least. As they moved slowly up the long room, with its hideous oil-paintings of dead and gone Scottish kings, her father's words came back to her. 'Would you bear logs for him, Miranda?' he had asked her, when Lyndon came courting; and she had said lightly that she was very strong. But her inexperienced heart had not known what he meant. Now she had seen the person for whom she would bear logs. 'The very moment that I saw you did my heart fly to your service.'

The heart was beating tumultuously as they approached the top of the line of guests. She half dreaded the moment when they would arrive there. Suddenly it had come, and she was curtseying low, hearing Lyndon introduce her, giving her hand into the long-fingered brown hand extended to raise her. And at last she was looking into the beautiful eyes inherited from his Polish mother, and receiving the famous smile.

Prince Charles Edward was only too used to the adoring gaze of ladies, though his smile was never the less warm for that. His right hand ached from being grasped and kissed by more people than he could count, in that one evening alone. He was as strong as a cart-horse when it came to fighting and marching, but these social occasions exhausted him more than a prolonged battle would have done. A superb diplomat, he had the talent for making anyone presented to him feel important, and the ability to remember names and titles. It was refreshing to greet an English lady for a change, so disappointing had been the response of the nobility across the Border, and he at once remembered what he knew about the Beaumonts.

'Mrs Beaumont. One of the ladies who has been so kind as to supply my tables. We have been well off for arms, thank God, but poorly set up in matters domestic. Holyrood, as you see, is a bare enough place.'

Dorothy listened in enchantment to his voice, light, pleasant and confident in tone, slightly strange in accent, with overtones of his French and Italian background and a tinge of the Highland speech his quick ear had picked up since his landing. It was charming, but she had not the slightest idea what he meant. Her 'Your Royal Highness?' must have carried a question, for he smiled and showed her the silver wine-goblet he held. It bore Lyndon's coat of arms.

Enough self-possession was granted to her to say, 'Your Highness is more than welcome to anything we can give.'

She caught Lyndon's sidelong glance and knew she had said the right thing. It was obviously enough to say, for the next guests were moving up behind them. She curtseyed again, Lyndon bowed, and they moved on. Out of earshot of the Prince, she turned sharply on Lyndon.

'Why did you not *say* about the silver? I saw it had gone, but I thought . . . Did you think I would forbid it?'

'It was not for you to forbid or agree. The silver's mine, or my father's. I said nothing because women are not always reasonable about these things.'

'I am always perfectly reasonable! You know I would do anything for . . . for His Highness.'

Lyndon's tone was cool. 'No, I can't say I ever thought you mighty keen on this enterprise. I'm happy to know you've had a change of heart.'

This was painfully true, but Dorothy was not prepared to admit it. Instead she asked: 'How much did you bring?'

'All of it. Would you expect me to have gone through the knives and forks, picking this and rejecting that?'

'Of course not. How ridiculous you are. Oh, Lyndon, I know you're vexed with me for coming in through the wrong door, but it was only a silly mistake and I'm sure very few noticed it. Must we quarrel all evening? I'm truly pleased about the silver. Now do let us enjoy ourselves, pray.'

But he had turned his back on her and was leading out a young lady in yellow in the minuet which the musicians had just started to play. She sat down at one of the small occasional tables at the side of the room, and looked round her. Lyndon's peevishness was unimportant besides these glories. The figure at the end of the room was invisible now behind the swirl of dancers, a great moving patchwork of silks, satins, tartans and velvets, twinkling with jewels seldom displayed, some, perhaps, got out of pawn. She was quite content to look on, hoping for a glimpse of the prince.

A voice startled her. 'Would you allow me to lead you out, ma'am, if you're not engaged already?'

The voice belonged to a slender, quietly dressed man. His grey wig gave him the appearance of being older than his age, which was perhaps thirty. His dark, aquiline-featured face had a thoughtful look to it, a little like her father's. She took to him at once.

'Thank you, sir.' They took the floor together, their steps matching well. He danced with a grave precision, neither turning his ankle affectedly nor flirting with his eyes, as she noticed so many gentlemen did. The dance finished, he led her back to the table, bowed and introduced himself.

'Allan Carr, at your service, ma'am.'

She inclined her head. 'Mr Carr.'

'May I bring you a glass of wine, or a cordial?'

'Some wine would be refreshing.'

She drank gratefully when it came, for it was cool and sparkling, and the candle-heat from sconces and hanging candelabra was becoming almost unbearable. Mr Carr, she noticed, only sipped his. Impulsively, perhaps because his quietude was of the kind which invites confidences, she told him of herself and Lyndon, and the Beaumont family's Stuart allegiance. He nodded.

'I have met Lord Gainsford at the King's court in Rome.'

'You are one of His Highness's gentlemen, sir – a chieftain, perhaps?'

The Scots lilt was strong in his voice. 'Alas, nothing so noble. As to gentleman . . . perhaps a physician may call himself so, though there are those who have other names for him.'

Her eyes brightened. 'You're His Highness's personal physician, sir?'

93

'No, ma'am. Nothing so exalted. Sir Stuart Thriepland holds that office, though there was never a prince less in need of him, thank God. I and other surgeons attend the army in times of battle.'

'That must be terrible work.'

'At Prestonpans it was wonderfully light work. There were only a hundred killed and wounded on our side, but so many of Cope's forces that the Prince sent into Edinburgh for extra surgeons.'

'For the *enemy*? Was that not carrying mercy to an extreme?'

'I believe His Highness to be the most merciful general who ever led an army. After the battle he refused to leave the scene until all the wounded had been attended and carried away on litters. He would not even touch food himself, until I insisted that some sort of meal should be brought to him on the field.'

Dorothy sighed in admiration. 'Do you think the next encounter will go as well, sir?'

'Who can say? Much depends on the English command. They'll never send Cope against us again, after the drubbing he got, but it seems there's another candidate. Since we have a hero, they must have one for themselves. The Elector has recalled his son William of Cumberland from Flanders, presumably because he distinguished himself at Fontenoy, even though it was a lost battle.'

'I saw him once at the play. Is he as odious as he looks?'

With some relish, Allan Carr launched himself into a lively account of the man whose brutality in war had left a nasty taste in the mouths even of hardened soldiers. He was twenty-four, a year younger than Prince Charles, but looked many years older because of his monstrous fatness. Food, drink and women were his principal preoccupations when not directing slaughter; Allan softened the rumours that had reached Scotland and even Rome of the Duke's popularity among prostitutes, from whom, it was said, he had caught the pox so badly that no progeny could be expected from him. Among these ladies he was known as the Fat Boy or Sweet William, a facetious title owing more to sweatiness than sweetness, and his personal circle included the most raffish members of a raffish Court.

'Such,' said Allan, 'is the man the Whig journalists have drummed

94

up into a popular idol. I only hope our Highland broadswords will put the fear of God into him as they did into poor Johnnie Cope. Let us not talk about him in such a noble company as this.'

He pointed out to her some of the people present: Lochiel 'the Gentle', head of Clan Cameron; arrogant young Lord Elcho; Lord George Murray, stern-featured, the Prince's most loyal adherent, who yet had an unfortunate knack of getting on the wrong side of him; old Sir Thomas Sheridan, the Prince's one-time tutor, nodding off over the bottle of whiskey with which he had thoughtfully come provided; Secretary Murray of Broughton, dashing anxiously about to make sure that all was going well, and his beautiful dark wife Margaret, one of the loveliest ladies in the assembly. Dorothy was bold enough to ask a question which had been in her mind.

'Which lady is Miss Jenny Cameron?'

Allan Carr looked astonished. 'Jenny Cameron?'

'The lady who . . .' Dorothy blushed. 'The journals said she is a very close companion to His Highness.'

'Oh!' He laughed with real amusement. 'I tell you, ma'am, these Grub Street gentlemen are only a little lower than God himself. They can change a bad man into a good one, as they have done with Cumberland, and create a woman who never before existed. The truth of the story is that a lady who had been Miss Jeannie Cameron of Glendessary, but was then Mrs O'Neil, came with her brother Archibald Cameron to the raising of the Standard at Glenfinnan, and afterwards went home, sending His Highness a present of cattle. She was a handsome female of at least fifty, I would say, and to my knowledge she was never presented to His Highness. This tale was sent back, twisted, to London, and thus it came to you.'

'I see. How ridiculous!'

Dorothy was unreasonably relieved, a fact which Allan Carr was not slow to note. In Mrs Beaumont's charming face he had already discerned the familiar symptoms of infatuation with his royal master. While he had been talking, her eyes had continually wandered away from him towards the end of the room, and it had been obvious that the impressive figures of the Highland chieftains had interested her but little. Ruefully he reflected that when, for once, his bachelor existence was offered the chance of attractive female company apparently unattended (what was that unaccountable husband of hers doing to desert her for the evening?) she should prove an Ariadne pining for the Royal Theseus who would certainly disappoint her; for, in spite of his enormous attraction for women, the Prince had very little time for them, preoccupied as he was, body and soul, with his great enterprise.

'Does His Highness not dance?' Dorothy enquired, looking in vain for him among the couples who were now moving into the foot-tapping rhythm of the Highland reel, played by the Prince's own piper. The noise was outlandish and hideous to English ears, though she would have listened to it all night if she could but have watched the graceful figure in blue and scarlet.

'I have seen him dance many times, in Italy, and very well too. But here he thinks his time and energy better given to conference. Besides, the selection of one lady rather than another would cause jealousy and faction, the last things he would wish.'

At that moment Lyndon appeared out of the crowd to claim his wife's hand in the dance, a decorous gavotte which had replaced the delirious reel. Dorothy introduced the two men, who chatted politely before Lyndon led Dorothy out on the floor. Allan Carr looked after them. He had been charmed by the pretty English girl with the frank manner and transparent enthusiasm for the Prince. He hoped her husband's apparent neglect of her was only due to his anxiety to mingle with the Jacobite society of Edinburgh.

The Prince had disappeared. It was his habit to retire as soon as he decently could from such assemblies; he would be up early next morning to hold council with his officers. On some nights he supped in public to give his guests full value, but this was not one of them. He was becoming anxious about the waste of his funds on entertaining. He had a much more urgent use for them.

As Dorothy had little appetite for the supper laid out in the next room, she begged Lyndon to leave early so that they might be sure of getting chairs. The Royal Mile was not the most savoury place to walk in by night, at the best of times, with its dark lurking-places and the local habit of disposing of sewage by way of the window, and these nights brought the chance of a random shot or two fired from the besieged Castle. The slender gilt sedans borne by Highlanders who swore at each other in Gaelic and overcharged English passengers afforded some degree of shelter.

As Meliora helped her to undress, Dorothy gave yawn after yawn. She was not tired so much as drained, exhausted – and she wondered why. Exhausted by dancing a little, drinking a cup or two of wine, staring like any greensick girl at a handsome prince? Was it the effect of the wine, perhaps, or the heat of the room?

Meliora had not pestered her with questions, but, plaiting her hair ready for bed, she said, 'Madam has seen a star.'

'A star, Meliora? I don't even recall looking heavenwards tonight.'

'No, no. The Bible star.'

Dorothy had been to church every Sunday of her conscious life, and took Meliora's meaning. St Matthew's Gospel was as familiar to her as her own name.

' "We have seen his star in the east, and are come to worship him." Is that what you mean? The star above the stable?'

'Yes, madam.' Meliora was shaking out the folds of the white dress.

'But . . . His Royal Highness is not a divine personage, child. He wears the star of the Order of the Garter; are you thinking of that? It's but an ornament, you know.'

Vigorously Meliora shook her head. 'No, madam. The star you will follow, always follow.'

Her eyes were very large and had a far-seeing look to them, the black irises almost encircled by the whites. Dorothy bade her good night, and when she had gone went to the unshuttered window. The usual smoke-pall hovered over Edinburgh, but above it the sky glittered frostily with a multitude of stars, and one of particular size and brilliance seemed to hang directly over Holyroodhouse. Into Dorothy's mind came the story of a new star that had appeared in the skies on the night of the Prince's birth. Perhaps it watched over him still.

When Lyndon came to bed, well flown with wine and in high good humour, he at once began to make love to her. Suddenly irritated, she turned her face away from him and edged towards the side of the lumpy bed. He sat up, staring at her.

'Why, what's the matter, Doll? An't you well? Have you the . . . no, that's past, I remember. What then? Is it that I was sharp with you tonight? It was only that I want us to make a good showing in front of . . .'

'Yes, I know. I know. I've forgotten it already.'

He shook his head in puzzlement. 'You've never been cold to me before. It's not because of the little wench, that night? I told you, I was drunk. I've never been unfaithful to you, Doll.'

Wearily she rolled over to face him. 'I don't doubt that. Please don't ask me tonight. There's no reason, just . . . foolishness.'

'There must be a reason.'

With instinctive guile she said, 'I want to stay with you – with the Prince's army. It would never do to be breeding at this time.'

Lyndon gave a sharp laugh. 'Well, upon my soul! If all Jacobite wives are of the same mind, there'll be some disappointed husbands tonight.'

He reached out and extinguished the candle. She was ashamed of herself for her rejection of Lyndon, puzzled by her own feelings. The star in the eastern sky still shone brightly, distorted from where she lay by the thick irregular glass of the window-pane. She smiled to herself.

'Meliora was right. I must be starstruck.'

On the morning of 30 October a heated argument was going on in the council-chamber of Holyroodhouse. The vexed question, to invade or not to invade, had at last to be decided. Around the long refectory table sat the chieftains: Clanranald, Glencoe, Ardshiel, Lockgarry, gouty old Atholl, Keppoch. Young Lord Lewis Gordon, who slightly resembled the Prince and had lent him his name in the past as an alias, sat next to fiery-haired Lord Ogilvy; beyond him tall, amiable Lord Kilmarnock and the two Irishmen, Sheridan and O'Sullivan, together as always, presenting a united front against the Scots. On the right hand of the Prince sat Lord George Murray, looking dour, and on the left Murray of Broughton was scribbling busily with a furrowed brow. The Prince's mouth was set in a mutinous line, and he was tapping impatiently on the table. Lyndon, who had been graciously allowed to sit in on the council, guessed from his face that the matter they had met to debate was a foregone conclusion.

'Gentlemen,' said Charles, 'I think we are all agreed that a decision can no longer be delayed. Winter is coming on – if we are to march south, it must be soon. Nothing can be settled until London is taken.'

'But,' said Lord George heavily, 'as I have before pointed out to Your Highness, there would be more advantage in . . .'

'In remaining here and consolidating my father's kingship in Scotland. I would remind you, Lord George, that we are daily losing men by desertion.'

He looked pointedly at the chieftains, whose clansmen were indeed returning to their glens in large numbers, with their booty, as had always been their custom after a raid.

'While our forces are dwindling the Elector's are increasing. We must have more recruits, and we shall not get them by staying here. If we march on Newcastle we can tackle Wade's troops easily – he has only a handful more men than we.'

'With Your Highness's leave,' interrupted Lord George, 'would it not be better to march – if we *must* march – to Carlisle, where our English friends could more readily join the Standard? We shall then be close to Lancashire, which we know to be well affected towards you.'

There was a murmur of agreement from several of the council, none of whom had more than a sketchy acquaintance with the geography of England. Lyndon opened his mouth to point out that in Cumberland they might well find themselves up against Henry, Viscount Lonsdale, who was Lord of the Bedchamber to the Elector and had in his time been Constable of the Tower and Lord Privy Seal. But the moment passed before he could be heard. The arguments were flying to and fro, the Prince pressing for the Newcastle direction and the majority of the council voting for Carlisle. Suddenly Charles leapt to his feet, scarlet with anger.

'The Council is adjourned,' he said, and swept out of the room.

Next morning, when they met again, his face was calm. Briskly he rapped the table for attention.

'Gentlemen, I have seriously considered your arguments over-night. Now, on reflection, I'm inclined to think you are in the right.' A sigh of relief went up from Lord George. 'Therefore I am ready to follow your advice. I suggest that we devote ourselves to discussing the route and the necessary marching orders. Now, my own proposal is that the army be divided into two columns. One I shall, naturally, lead myself, with yourself as second in command, my lord.' Lord George Murray bent his head in acquiescence. The Prince spread out a map. 'We march as far as *here*.' His finger rested on the town of Kelso. 'Then we turn south-east by way of Jedburgh, en route for Carlisle. As to the other column, under my lords Atholl and Perth, that will proceed directly south . . .'

As he outlined the plans, Lord George exchanged a look with his brother, the Duke of Atholl, a man attainted in '15 and officially robbed of his title, but unswervingly loyal to the Stuarts. It seemed that after long strife in the council-chamber the two Murrays were to be recognised as wise leaders and guides to their headstrong young master. Their glance said to each other that what he did wrong they would put right. It was inconceivable that one as inexperienced in warfare as he should know what to do for the best. It was Lord George's private opinion that the victory of Prestonpans had been a fluke. Nobody bothered to remember that Charles had been initiated into war at fourteen years old, fighting for the Spaniards against the Austrians under heavy fire, to the extreme horror of his father, or that he had studied strategy ever since.

And so it was settled; they were to begin the march to England on 1 November, in just two days' time. Old Sir Thomas Sheridan turned to O'Sullivan as they left the council-chamber.

'It is not a lucky day, not lucky, the Eve of All Souls'. We should be fasting and praying for them in Purgatory, I'm thinking, not going to war.'

O'Sullivan laughed and clapped him on the shoulder. 'My dear good Sir Thomas, you forget I was a priest before I turned soldier. November the first is All Saints', when the Blessed Ones themselves will be praying for *us*. Sure, that's why His Highness chose it.'

Sir Thomas greatly doubted this. His former pupil had shown a very distressing tendency in the past to display irreverence to the Old Religion, had even shocked his poor devout mama by declaring, 'I snap my fingers at the priests, the monks are great rogues, and the Mass cost my grandfather three kingdoms.' Silently Sir Thomas implored his patron saint to have a special care over the prince whom he still thought of as his beloved Carlucchio, of their Roman days, before they ever came to this bleak heretical country.

'Carriages? *Mon Dieu*, what carriages? I ordered none.'

Charles banged his fist on the table, making the scattered papers dance and the inkwell lid fly open. Mr Secretary Murray had just brought him the final details of the march arrangements for men and transports.

Murray looked miserable. 'For the ladies, Your Highness.'

'I was not aware that any ladies had been recruited.'

'No, sir. Of course not. But there is Lord Ogilvy . . . he is new-married and . . . sir, Lady Ogilvy is uncommonly beautiful, and they are most devoted. He asks your leave to take her.'

Charles sighed with exasperation. 'Very well. As he brought me six hundred men I suppose I can't refuse. But I'll thank him not to waste his time in dalliance. Damn it, why do men marry when there's work to be done? Well? What other ladies are we to have the pleasure of escorting?'

'There is my wife, sir. We – she has been a good worker for the Cause.'

Charles nodded. 'Mrs Murray has been of the greatest help in re-cruiting, here in Edinburgh. Many a white cockade has left her hands for a good fellow's bonnet. I look on her as almost one of my soldiers. Anyone else?'

'Lady Kilmarnock, sir. You remember she persuaded the Earl to break with the Government and join your Standard. She was Anne Livingstone, a most zealous Jacobite. And then there is Mrs Beaumont.'

'Mrs Beaumont? Oh, Lord Gainsford's family. The silver, yes.' He picked up a list and studied it. 'I'm not precisely clear what Mr Beaumont proposes to do further in the campaign. He is not a trained soldier, I see. What use can he be to us?'

'He is very active in sports, sir, and a good swordsman I believe. I think he would prove both brave and tireless. And his lady is very ardent for the Cause. Dr Carr, who has become a friend to both of them, says she would be willing to act as field-nurse under his instructions, or do anything else that would be helpful. She is not a noblewoman born, I understand, but her mother was a Nairne, some kin to Lord Nairne and the Murrays, I find.'

'Very well.' Charles scribbled his signature at the foot of the list, then paused. 'That makes only three carriages. For whom is the fourth?'

'For yourself, sir, if you wish to use it at any time.'

Charles said something very strong in Italian. 'Do you think I am a milksop, a *choineachain*, a *caillich*? – that's a babe and an old woman in the Gaelic, Murray, of which I dare say you know less than I do, for all the short time I've spent in the Highlands!' His laugh was like the sun coming out, and Murray, not for the first time, thanked the good fortune which had given him a leader whose bad humours were never more than summer storms.

'Indeed, sir, I'm only a Lowlander myself and not learned at all in the Gaelic. But it's not surprising that Your Highness learns so quickly, when you already have the French, Italian and Spanish. I had no thought to insult you by proposing a carriage – it was Lord George's idea.'

'Then you may tell Lord George I shall march with my men as always – barefoot if need be. It would be no novelty to me, or hardship either. Now, let's settle this business of Elcho's cavalry. At least they have some uniforms . . .'

* * * * *

Dorothy flung her arms round Allan Carr, as though, he thought wryly, he were her grandfather or at best an aged uncle.

'So he agrees! He'll be happy for me to go with the army! Oh, I'm so transported, Dr Allan. How can I thank you, how?'

Gently he disengaged her, for her embrace was disturbing.

'It was nothing to do with me. I merely spoke to Murray, and His Highness seems to have agreed. I doubt if he expressed any opinion. I should take it as the fortune of war, if I were you. Of course he's pleased to have any help that may be forthcoming, though he would not have a lady at risk in whatever may lie ahead of us. And I think you should learn as much as you can from my books.'

They were in a pile on the table in the mean sitting-room of the Beaumonts' lodgings, surrounded by a heap of belongings and trunks. Allan, with time hanging heavy on his hands now that all the wounded men had been accommodated for the journey, and the more seriously ill left behind in safety, had instructed Dorothy in the first principles of help for men who might be suffering from a variety of ailments between chills and fearful wounds. He was agreeably surprised to find how far from squeamish she was in discussing such details as amputation and gangrene. His admiration for her grew with acquaintance, and he feared greatly that it was more than admiration.

'Here, you see,' he picked up one of the text-books, 'there is a chapter on cauterisation. You may well find, in the case of an injury too serious—'

The door burst open. Lyndon stood before them, patently in a rage.

'My dear, what is it?' Dorothy ran to his side. 'What's the matter?'

'I've been robbed, that's the matter! My dress sword, my gold snuffbox, my diamond stock-pin and two pairs of brocade weskits, all gone with that villain Nicholas.'

'But – he was here this morning . . .'

'Well, he's gone now, and my goods with him, and more than a trifle of money if it were counted, I dare say. You'd better see to your jewellery. Even that poor child Mel's trumpery brooch that you gave her has gone. All because he's too chicken-livered to face the march,

I suppose. Well, good riddance to bad rubbish, and may he meet the hangman before he meets his Maker.'

It was true; Nicholas had vanished, and with a good haul of their possessions. They could only make the best of it; footmen were not going to be greatly needed on this expedition.

'For myself, I have never had one,' said Allan, 'and never lacked one either. It seems you're well rid of Master Nicholas, and you still have your faithful servant girl.'

'Oh yes!' Nothing could dim Dorothy's radiance now. 'Meliora would follow us into hell, I dare say, if we were going there.' A sudden doubt seized her. 'We shall be in *his* column, shan't we – not with the other?'

Allan smiled. 'Yes, indeed. I have seen to that.' And to my own unease, he thought. There was a frivolous English theatre-piece, *The Beggars' Opera*, he had seen once in London, with a deceptively named hero, Captain Macheath, who had sung a song he now recalled all too well: 'The fly that sips honey is lost in the sweets, And he who tastes Woman, Woman, Woman, ruin meets.'

Mrs McMurdo stood at her house-door, her arms folded beneath her apron, two of the bairns at her side. Those of her neighbours who were not crowded into their own doors hung from the windows to see the last of the Jacobite army as it marched away, southwards, colours flying and pipes playing, ragged tartans and bright blue uniforms, little Highland horses and heavy baggage-wagons grinding over the chuckie-stanes of the ancient street. From the Castle above came a derisive salute of cannon, Mons Meg roaring her farewell to the Prince who had left her unconquered. From one of the steep wynds that led up to the Castle came three red-coated Government soldiers, dragging something between them that cried and groaned as its bloody head bumped on the ground. The bailies of Edinburgh had given Charles their solemn assurance that the seriously wounded who had been left behind would be well treated. He had taken one of them, Bailie Wilson, hostage as security, but with his usual good nature had released him. Now they had dragged one of the most injured Highlanders from his bed, and were pulling him through the streets like a sack of coals, jeering and cursing the wounded rebel.

But he no longer heard them, or anything else, and he would never see his home by Loch Morar again.

8

If Dorothy had thought that to travel with the army would afford delightful opportunities for meetings with the Prince, she was to be disappointed. She shared an oldish carriage with Mrs Murray of Broughton and their respective maids, at the rear of the detachment, with hundreds of soldiers between them and the front ranks in which the Prince marched. Their closest companions were the ragged, barefoot women, many with children in arms, who followed their men to war, as the custom was. Dorothy regarded them with pity, but Margaret Murray laughed.

'What would they be doing left behind? The old women and nursing mothers stay at home to do the herding and spinning. These are the strong ones, like Highland cattle.'

But it was distressing, as the column left Scotland behind, to see the poor creatures floundering and shrieking in the high-running waters of the Tweed, in the wake of their menfolk. Dorothy began to recognise features of the Border country she had travelled through with Lyndon; could it only have been a few weeks ago? He was nowhere to be seen now, for he was riding with Elcho's lifeguards, the smartest and most martial section of the army. It suited him well – as well as his blue uniform. He was strong, fit, used to the exertion of sport, a good shot, and with a skill in swordsmanship learned from an excellent *maître-d'armes*. He got on well with his commanding officer David, Lord Elcho, a little younger than himself, educated at Winchester and very much more an Englishman than a Scot; the only thing that marred their relationship was Elcho's habit of referring disparagingly to the Prince who – to Lyndon – was beyond reproach. They had known each other since both had been boys in Rome, when the seeds of jealousy had been sown in Elcho's mind which were to produce bitter weeds in future years.

The weather grew worse as they approached Carlisle. October in

106

Edinburgh had been like late summer, but now the icy winds were blowing and flurries of snow eddying in the chill air. The two women, shivering in their warmest wraps, heard the guns of Carlisle Castle speak in the distance as their carriages and the baggage-waggons waited in the rear while the united forces, the Prince's and Atholl's, went into the attack.

'Do you think they can succeed?' asked Dorothy.

Margaret shrugged. 'If His Highness's plan don't cross Lord George's too much. They are oil and vinegar to each other. Lord George will sit up all night playing toy soldiers to work out his method of attack, while the Prince trusts to Providence and marches in without a hand raised against him.' Her eyes glowed. 'Oh, if I were but a man and could march at his side! Colonel Anne and I, we'd make better lieutenants than a dozen of your paper-planners.' The lady affectionately known as Colonel Anne was the wife of Angus Mackintosh of Mackintosh, a gentleman who, having slid over to the Hanoverian side and regretted it, failed to find the courage to rejoin his Prince. It was left to his wife to raise the banner of the clan and go recruiting, in a tartan riding-habit with pistols at her saddle-bow, winning Clan Chattan to the Standard. Margaret had done her share of recruiting, too, in Edinburgh, drawing as many men by her sparkling beauty as by her promises of glory. The sparkle was dimmed now, as they sat in the coach waiting. Her husband was with the Prince, and she was restless and out of touch with events.

A heavy November fog was coming down. In the carriage they could hear movements and voices, hoofbeats, occasional shots. They had slept badly, at a cold village house, crowded into one small noisome room, and their nerves were frayed. It was a relief to hear something definite, a burst of shouting and the characteristic Highland battle-yells. The two maids huddled together, and Dorothy turned to Margaret.

'What is it? Are they going to fight?'

'Surely not. We would have heard . . .' But what they did hear was a frantic rapping at the carriage window, at which there appeared, through the freezing fog, the face of Murray of Broughton.

Fumblingly, Margaret's cold fingers opened it. Excited, triumphant, he leaned in and kissed her.

'The Castle's surrendered, they say, without a drop of blood shed! I'm sent post-haste to find out whether 'tis true, and arrange the terms of surrender.' Then he was gone into the fog, leaving them staring at each other in wonderment.

It was true. A garrison of old men, under a protesting officer, had yielded Castle and town, and King James was to be proclaimed at the Market Cross.

Margaret Murray, to whom female company was unrewarding, left Dorothy with barely a word as soon as they were within the crumbling walls of the old town, to seek out her husband at the heart of affairs. Dorothy bewildered, left the carriage in the hope of seeing someone she knew who would tell her what to do. But she was back in an England completely unfamiliar to her, and the fog added a nightmare tinge to everything. She went back to the carriage, where Meliora waited with a native resignation which her mistress envied. They had lit a lantern to give them some light and cheerfulness, and Meliora was patiently copying, in very large black letters, her favourite passage from the *Beast Book*: 'T-h-e dread-ful Alli-gat-or, t-h-e heav-y Por-poise, roll-ing in slug-gish wan-ton-ness.'

Dorothy looked over her shoulder. 'I wish *we* were rolling in sluggish wantonness, I must say. It would make a most agreeable change. If nobody comes to fetch us I suppose we must sleep here.' Both sighed. The Beaumont coach had seemed palatial compared with this vehicle.

But, mercifully, a harassed billeting officer arrived in due course and led them through a warren of streets to a house in a narrow wynd off the Shaddongate. Banging forcefully at the door and getting no reply, he at length opened it and ushered them in. The small room, a sort of kitchen-parlour, showed signs of someone's hasty departure. On the hob a pan had boiled over, the contents dripping into the hearth, a pastry-board on the table bore a half-rolled piece of dough, and a child's rag doll sprawled on the floor. The only sign of life was a black cat, leisurely washing itself in front of the fire.

'Bide here,' the officer told them, and went off in noisy search.

After a few moments they were startled by a shriek from above, followed by the reappearance of their friend dragging a terrified, gasping woman behind him. Her hair had come down and her dress was disordered, as though she had been hiding in a cupboard. There was dust on her hands from the floor where she had lain crouched.

'Noo, noo,' her captor was saying soothingly as she cowered away from him, 'there's nae call for sic a carry-on. We'll no' hurt ye, wife. 'Tis juist a bit room we need, for these twa leddies.'

The woman took a look at Meliora and gave a scream loud enough to bring down the cooking-pot from its hook above the fire. 'The de'il! The de'il!' she moaned, throwing her apron over her head and shrinking back against a wall. The cat gave her a disparaging look, and continued to wash.

'Havers, wumman,' said the officer. 'There's nae de'il here. Sit ye doon and ha'e a wheen o' sense, will ye.'

He coaxed her apron down and propelled her into a chair by the table, where she sat rocking, her hands between her knees, staring wildly at her three visitors. Fortunately, apart from Meliora's alarming complexion, they were respectable enough in appearance, the man dressed like any Christian and not, as she had heard of these invaders, a bearded savage half naked and brandishing a bloody knife with a baby spitted on the end of it. Neither he nor the women had tails, so far as she could see. The officer, a patient man and a Lowlander whose speech she could comprehend, managed to get into her head that all he wanted was a room for the lady and her maid for as long as the Scottish army remained in Carlisle.

The room was the usual bare apartment with a box-bed in the wall, scarcely more appetising than the pallet of discoloured blankets provided on the floor for Meliora. The billeting officer handed over a guinea to the woman, who stared at the untold wealth unbelievingly.

'His Royal Highness aye pays for billets,' he said. 'He'll no' let private citizens go poorer for leein' in their hooses.' And, saluting the ladies, he hastened away to deal with other matters.

Dorothy looked about her. They had spent several nights in cottage homes during their journey, but none had been as sordid as this, with its dirty window almost touching the opposite wall of the wynd. The weather, too, had never been so cold.

'Well,' she said to Meliora, 'no use repining. I dare say many of our people lie worse than we do – especially since the tents from Edinburgh were left behind. Poor girl, you must feel the cold even more than I.'

'I go out and buy food,' Meliora replied cheerfully. 'There soup in the pot downstairs – I smell it – and if I bring meat the lady will think we angels, not devils any more.'

This proved to be a true prophecy. Mrs Haughie was delighted to cook a piece of beef, and to add other items to the broth already simmering over the fire. An invitation to join her guests was readily accepted, and another member of the feast was provided, her son Jackie, a red-haired silent child of seven or eight whom she had kept hidden until then, under the impression that he, if anything, would be on the Scottish bill of fare: Hielanders were well known to be cannibals with a particular taste for children's flesh. She could not altogether rid herself of a conviction that Meliora's origins were infernal, but two females, especially generous ones, were far better billetees than she had expected.

'She have a son, but no husband,' meditated Meliora when they retired to their room. 'Dead perhaps.'

'More likely hiding outside the town. Captain Jameson said that as the troops were marching in they were nearly knocked down by townsfolk fleeing out. Perhaps he'll come back and join the Standard.' The Prince's headquarters were at Brampton, a village seven miles out of Carlisle. Surely, now that the town had surrendered its keys, he would come in? Any amount of discomfort was bearable if she could look forward to seeing him again.

Two days later her wish was fulfilled. On Sunday he entered Carlisle at the head of his clans, a body of pipers marching before, playing triumphantly the tune of 'The King shall enjoy his own again' – the Hundred Pipers who would go down the years in song. For once he was not on foot, but riding the great white war-horse that had been sent to him by an old Jacobite too frail to join him. If he had looked handsome in Edinburgh, he was magnificent now, a towering figure in full Highland dress, gold lace on his coat, a silken white cockade in his blue bonnet of velvet. His wig today was a light grey, making the young face appear even younger, radiant in its pride.

All Carlisle, it seemed, stood about the Market Cross to stare at him. They were not cheering, though one hardly noticed that for the noise his own men were making. Dorothy saw one grizzled, half-ragged Highlander weeping, and Lochiel's happy face. Snow lay thick on the ground, the snow which had shut up Marshal Wade and his men in Newcastle, making it impossible for them to come to the rescue of Carlisle.

Dorothy impulsively pushed her way to the front rank of the crowd, without much resistance, so apathetic they were. The Prince was speaking, greeting his new townsmen, promising them release from the yoke of Hanover and freedom of thought and religion. From their blank faces, it was doubtful that many of them understood a word that clear voice was saying. As he ended, raising his bonnet and flourishing it to the crowds, Dorothy took from the shelter of her cloak a white rose, small and perfect, which she had found incongruously growing on a bush in the yard at the back of Mrs Haughie's dwelling, and had picked and kept fresh in water. She was standing at the Prince's stirrup, the white horse not stirring at her closeness but bending its gentle head to the light touch on its reins. She stood on tiptoe and held up the rose to its rider.

A gauntleted hand took it, and placed it in the breast of his coat, tucked behind the blue Garter ribbon. 'Thank you, mistress,' he said, with the smile that had changed many a Whig lady's politics. She had hoped, perhaps, for recognition, but it had been too much to expect, since he had only seen her once before, in her finery at Holyrood. The horse was moving, a path was being cleared for it through the people, and still she stood by the Market Cross, her heart beating violently, her cheeks blazing in spite of the cold.

'I am enchanted,' she said to herself. 'I lie under a spell, and how can it be a good one, since I am a married wife? Yet what can be bad that comes from him?' There sounded in her memory, through the retreating murmur of the crowd and the renewed rejoicing of the pipes, a woman's voice singing in a drawing-room, to a spinet, one summer night.

'It is a Rose, a royal Rose,
With a dark and rolling eye,
And is my choice above all those
That would love me till I die.'

'May I walk with you a little, Mrs Dorothy?'

She turned with a start to see Allan Carr beside her. Gallantly he offered her his arm.

'The snow is slippery where so many feet have trod. And how have you been in this triumphal progress, ma'am?'

Glad to be no longer alone with her thoughts, she launched into a humorously exaggerated description of the journey from Edinburgh. 'Yet I've little enough reason to complain, when so many soldiers have been far worse lodged.'

'Aye, indeed. Or not lodged at all, poor fellows. Last night many slept under hedges. At least it has been a peaceful time for me – only two casualties in the siege, and no sign of a battle yet.'

'Is there to be one soon?'

He shrugged 'Who knows? Cumberland has mustered, it's said, but where we meet him depends on much, especially on the weather and the forces we have ourselves. I wish we could see more recruits. His Highness hoped that once over the Border the English loyalists would rush to him, but there's no sign of that yet, or even of men of this region joining the Standard. Oh, Carlisle is grateful enough not to have had its houses plundered and its citizens murdered, but not one will volunteer.'

In unspoken agreement they were following the crowd, some way behind it. 'Mr Beaumont seems to have taken unco' well to the soldiering life,' said Allan, catching a glimpse of the bright Elcho cavalry uniform high above the heads of those on foot.

'Yes, he has. That is, I think so, for we have hardly seen each other since we left Edinburgh.'

So he was still leaving a lovely wife to her own devices, though now with rather more excuse. Not that she sounded greatly grieved over it. His diagnosis of Dorothy's condition at Edinburgh was still true : a case of severe inflammation of the heart. He hoped and trusted, for everyone's sake, that it could be painlessly cured, and wished fervently that the beautiful eyes of his Prince were employed in recruiting men rather than in bedazzling women. But that, of course, was hardly His Highness's fault.

He was visible again now, before a handsome double-fronted house in English Street, waving his bonnet once more to the crowds before disappearing through the entrance to the courtyard. Allan felt Dorothy's grasp of his arm slacken as tension ebbed from her, then tighten again as her foot slipped on the treacherous cobbles.

'Take care,' he said gravely, and in his mind added 'my dear'.

She smiled up at him, glad of his strong arm to hold.

The snow which had crept over from the east grew thicker as the army left Carlisle to march south. Bitter winds froze it as it fell, making an icy purgatory of the journey for men and horses. Even the occupants of the carriages were little better off, thrown from side to side on the rocky snow-piled roads. Dorothy and Meliora were bruised from their constant falls, aching and stiff with cold. It was almost a relief when the order came to leave the carriage and walk up the steep fell-slopes which the horses could not negotiate with passengers behind them. Then, at least, to be inside again seemed comparative luxury. Dorothy gave thanks for her own stamina. She had never suffered from anything worse than a cold or a childish fever; she was well fed and strong of heart. There was even, to a girl brought up in London, a stimulation about the wild country and the wilder weather.

9

A freezing fog lay over Lancaster as the Prince's column reached it late in the afternoon of 25 November. Dorothy thought that, seen at its best, it would be a highly romantic town, grey and ancient and rough-stoned, nestling beneath John o' Gaunt's battlemented Castle and the noble Priory Church beside it on its eminence. To the west lay the sea, and the river Lune curled away between meadows and tree-lined banks.

But today Lancaster was by no means looking its best, and those of its citizens who came out to watch the Jacobite approach appeared too paralysed by the cold to show the enthusiasm expected of them. The march from Carlisle had been gruelling: a bitter wind in the army's face, snow, ice, and the terrible Shap Fell to be braved before the welcome halt at Kendal. The Prince had trudged all the way on foot with his men, refusing any advantage they did not have; half asleep with weariness at times, holding on to the shoulder-belt of an Ogilvy so that he should not fall, he showed himself to be a leader in a million. If Lancaster had expected a shining figure of chivalry at the head of the Scottish army, it was disappointed; but the young man in bedraggled Highland dress smiled on them as he had done on the folk of Carlisle and Kendal, and there was no mistaking his identity.

As for billets, it was as usual first come first served. Dorothy, in the last line of carriages and waggons, found herself assigned to a cheerless primitive house in China Lane, once again in company with Mrs Murray of Broughton. That lady was in a high temper and had no hesitation in making it known.

'I vow I am quite beside myself, Mrs Beaumont. I think I have done the Prince enough service to deserve at least to be lodged as well as my husband. *This* place . . .' She looked round scornfully at their dreary surroundings. 'They might as well lay us in a byre. Or in the Castle dungeons – aye, that would be just suitable. Well, John shall know of this. Morag!'

Her little Highland maid eventually appeared from somewhere below stairs, and was charged with a message to Mr Murray of Broughton, couched in no mild terms.

'Where will I be finding Mr Murray, mem?'

'How should *I* know? Go out and put your tongue to its proper use.'

The battle was without question to the strong, Dorothy thought, when an hour or so later the maid returned with a note from Mr Murray.

I am most sorry my Deare not to have placed you better, but am bid by His Royal Highness to invite you and Mrs Beaumont to sup at his lodgings this night at 7. We will then talk of what may be done.

'There, did I not tell you so?' said Mrs Murray triumphantly. 'The Prince will sort all out and we shall lie well tonight.'

Dorothy was less concerned with their comfort than with the appearance she would make at the meal. She had not had a bath for a fortnight. The steaming hot water and fragrant orris-scented soap manufactured by Mrs Mercy seemed to belong to another life. The only mirror available was a tiny gold-framed one which travelled in Mrs Murray's luggage, but even from that Dorothy thought it a good thing that elaborate hair-fashions were not stylish at the moment. There was little she could do beyond brushing her hair backwards and confining it under the pretty lace cap she had been keeping for best. Her white and silver dress, unworn since Edinburgh, was crushed and limp, but it would have to do. From somewhere Meliora obtained a bowl of warm water, enough for the sketchiest wash, after which she anointed her mistress liberally with rose-water. On the whole, Dorothy was glad not to have the use of a pier-glass to view the result. She paid heavily for some fuel to make a fire in a rusty grate which seemed not to have been used in the last fifty years or so, and established Meliora beside it with a kettle of hot water and the flask of eau-de-vie which Lyndon made her carry.

Margaret Murray, equally unwashed and ungroomed, looked superbly beautiful in pale blue, with a jewelled ornament in her dark curls. At another time Dorothy might have been envious; now she merely admired, trying to stifle her own immoderate excitement.

The house was in Church Street, the old thoroughfare leading from the Church and Castle to the centre of the town. It was grave, grey, sturdy and foursquare, with a handsome pillared portico and iron railings. They arrived at its door by means of chairs, a conveyance they had not associated with Lancaster; but where Margaret Murray was, dignity and civilisation followed. The dream-like feeling followed Dorothy into the house. Somewhere in the link-flared gloom of the street a piper was playing 'Hielan' Laddie', and there was the sense of excitement she had learned to associate with their arrival in any town.

The dining-room was merchant-rich Lancaster at its grandest, fine panelling and a moulded plaster ceiling. From the candle-shine and warmth came Murray of Broughton.

'Meg, my dearie. You had my letter safe, then.'

Dorothy moved out of earshot of the lady's sharp retort. Lyndon was greeting her, introducing the bold-eyed Irishman John O'Sullivan, Sir John Macdonald, who seemed from his accent to be French, reuniting her with pretty young Lady Ogilvy, the gracious Lady Kinloch, Dr Archie Cameron, old Sir Thomas Sheridan, who had a dreadful cold. Dorothy chatted to this one and that about the journey, the English reception, the weather; always the weather. Sooner or later, she felt, someone must tell her to take her eyes from the door.

The Prince was ushered in by a harassed-looking man she later found to be Gib, Keeper of the Royal Household. He stood in the doorway surveying the guests. The room was bright already, but he seemed to bring more light in with him: he wore the blue silk coat of Edinburgh, a richly embroidered silvery waistcoat, and trews of the white Dress Stuart. It was not his practice to change out of his Highland gear during the march, but Morrison, his valet, had persuaded him that it must be dried, and fine clothes assumed just this once, 'tae compliment the leddies'. Confound the ladies, Charles had thought, wearily submitting to being cleaned up and dressed. He would like to have eaten supper quickly, with a map propped up in front of him on the table, then gone to bed to sleep off the fatigues of the day, and here he was having to make conversation and pretend not to have a care in the world.

He was now moving through the little gathering of curtseying women and bowing men.

'I was most sorry, Mrs Murray, to hear of your uncomfortable lodging – and yours, Mrs – er – Beaumont. Perhaps a good supper will drive the chill from your bones. Lady Ogilvy, you're in high looks tonight. Sir Thomas, my dear, pray don't stand on ceremony but come to the table. O'Sullivan, as you're the nearest thing to a priest among us, perhaps you'll say grace.'

'I doubt it'll be acceptable, sir, coming from a soldier's lips.'

There was a general laugh. O'Sullivan's colourful language was well known. But he pronounced the Latin grace patly enough, and they fell to the supper. It was simple enough, fish fresh from Poulton Bay, a dish of pork tenderer than Scots palates were used to, and boiled fowls in a sauce. Conversation flowed, for it was impossible to maintain formal constraint in Charles's company. At the head of the oval table, with Mrs Murray on his right hand and Sir Thomas on his left, he distributed his attention with perfect fairness between the whole company, affable, courteous, and quick-witted. To Lyndon he talked of cricket – 'which may seem a surprising pastime for one brought up in Rome, but my brother and I used to play at all the English sports – I think it was a servant taught us that one. I will admit to you that I preferred golf, but that was maybe because I could play it and walk long distances at the same time.'

'Your Highness has not changed your tastes greatly, then,' said Lyndon.

'Nor have I. But now there's more than sport afoot. Did you not tell me your country house was at Richmond in Surrey? Then I'll tell you that I owe that place my life, in a manner of speaking. My father the King was so delicate at birth that very soon afterwards they took him from St James's to Richmond Palace, for the better air by the river. But when he grew no better they sent for doctors who poured the most fearful stuffs into the poor infant, including Canary Wine and Dr Goddard's Drops.'

'*Dhé*!' exclaimed Dr Cameron. 'The Drops are distilled hell-fire, sir. One falling on a piece of cloth will burn a hole through it in half an hour.'

'Aye, that was what my grandfather said when he heard of it, and at once he and the Queen went down to Richmond and ordered that the child be put on the breast, which was done by a tilemaker's wife, and my dearest Papa at once recovered. So you see that I have to thank Richmond.'

'So have we all, sir, devoutly,' said Lyndon.

'You spoke just now of your brother, sir,' said Lady Kinloch. 'Is he very like you? We have not seen his portraits as we have yours.'

His Highness laughed. 'Oh, Henry is a much prettier young man than I am. Much cleverer at his books, too, and very pious – something they'll never say of me, eh, Sherry?'

His old tutor shook his head reprovingly. 'Years will bring wisdom.'

'Aye, mebbe.' Dorothy noticed with amusement that he was rapidly picking up Scots words and expressions, even the occasional Gaelic '*Dhé*!' instead of '*Mon Dieu*'. England was going to have the first Scots-spoken king since James I, when Charles III came into his own.

She was relieved to find that Sir Thomas, in addition to suffering from a cold, was extremely deaf and only too glad not to be engaged in chatter, while Dr Archie, on her other side, was a man of few words. She had leisure to study the face she seemed to have known all her life : the quick bright looks from one person to another, the mouth that was almost haughty in repose, the next moment merry as a schoolboy's, the foreign hand-gestures that made the rest of the company appear stiff and inexpressive. She was touched by the very human scars at the side of the chin, left by boyish acne or perhaps by a light attack of smallpox. Her gaze crossed the sardonic one of Colonel O'Sullivan, who had mentally marked her down for a pleasant little flirtation after supper, when her boring English husband was out of the way on guard duty. Evidently it was not to be. Damn the jades, thought O'Sullivan, if they would only leave the Prince alone . . .

Charles and Dr Archie were discussing the intentions of Field-Marshal Wade, now encamped at Newcastle.

'I sent a spy over to find out his plans,' said the Prince. 'At any time now he should be here. It completely baffles me that a commander with some fourteen thousand men under him should be content to skulk in a hole like a rabbit with the ferret after it. Surely we are the rabbit, and he the ferret, if numbers count?'

Lyndon laughed. 'Poor old Grandpa Wade qualifies admirably for the status of rabbit, sir – if numbers count.'

'I don't follow you, Mr Beaumont.'

'The numbers of his illegitimate offspring, sir. That is why we call him Grandpa. He has never been married, but his sons and daughters are quite on a Biblical scale.'

The Prince, looking faintly shocked, said, 'Well, well. I'm told he's nearing seventy. It may be old age and not strategy that keeps him from attack. Pray, don't you think this Malaga excellent? It was given me in Kendal, of all cold cheerless places to find a good wine. Won't you take a little more, Mrs Murray?'

Several of the guests were happy to take a little more, but Charles drank hardly two glasses, Dorothy noticed. She saw him watching the clock, and was not surprised when he suddenly rose, and with a dazzling smile dismissed them all.

'We must be on the move early tomorrow. Gentlemen, ladies, good night to you.'

He was gone through the door at the end of the room, and they were in the hall, being cloaked and coated by the servants. Lyndon gave Dorothy a quick embrace.

'I'm on guard duty tonight, my dear. Sometime tomorrow I may catch sight of you. Take care.' Feeling a shade forlorn, she turned to Mrs Murray who was in animated conversation with O'Sullivan.

'Perhaps we may walk together, ma'am.'

Margaret Murray's eyebrows performed a graceful arch. 'Oh, did

I not tell you? John has found me a corner here. Now you and your woman will have more room and another blanket or so.' She turned away, leaving Dorothy to make her own way out. It was astonishing how quickly a company of people could melt away. She was alone, standing under the portico by the link-extinguishers. Outside there was no torch-bearer to lead her through the streets, no chair-man to convey her. Not far to go, certainly, but the streets were dark, and it was not pleasant to be a woman of the invading army in a strange town. Well, it was all part of the fortune of war. She stepped into the street and the cold mist just as the door opened behind her.

The Prince was there, wrapped in a heavy roquelaure. For a moment he failed to recognise her.

'Mrs Beaumont! I thought all the guests were gone. Are you waiting for someone – a chair?'

She curtseyed. 'I thought there would be one about, sir. But it seems there's not.' She explained briefly about Margaret Murray.

He frowned. 'A lady should not be left to find her own way back to her lodging. I'll find a servant . . .' But with his hand on the door-knob he turned back to her. 'No, I'll escort you myself.' As she began to protest, he said, 'I was about to take a walk, in any case. You have no idea how restless I am. I can't stay still unless I'm abed.'

'But after a day's march, sir . . .'

'It makes no odds. I need no more rest than my lads do.'

'But sir, it is not safe. If you were captured, how should I then feel?'

'I shall not be captured. Lancaster is a loyal town. Now, where are you lodged?'

'China Lane, sir. It is . . .'

'I know where it is. I never move into a place but I have a plan of its streets. So: China Lane is to our right. However, we will not go down China Lane. We will go through the garden, which my host kindly showed me this afternoon. The gate is across the street.'

For such a large-framed man he moved like quicksilver, back into the hall, where he took up a horn-lantern and lit it from a tinder-box which he produced from his pocket. Dorothy perceived that he was a person who would always have the necessary article in his pocket –

tinder-box, pen-knife, oatmeal bannock. Armed with the lantern, he rejoined her and steered her across Church Street with a hand under her elbow.

'This garden is unusual in being separated from the house by the public street. It is something to do with the lie of the land at the back.' The iron gate clicked and they were in the garden, under misty dripping trees, walking on wet squelching grass which could be doing no good to the Prince's fine buckled shoes, the faint gold light of the lantern tossing in front of them. It was, Dorothy thought, exactly like a dream, walking through an unseen landscape, on the arm of Scotland's Lord, the Young Chevalier, who was chatting amiably about the geographical configuration of Lancashire and his confident expectation of adding to the army at Preston.

'It was an unlucky place for my father, but I feel it will be lucky for me. This time there'll be no martyred Derwentwater. Ah, this must be Marton's Folly – or do they call it Marton's Tower?'

They had stopped before a small building, on the front of which the lantern picked out elaborate carvings, pillars and capitals. The Prince examined it with interest.

'Very Italian. One might almost be in Rome again . . . I was told the late owner followed the arts. This was his music pavilion, built for him by craftsmen from Italy.' The light showed her a mischievous face. 'Shall we go in, ma'am? A breath of the warm south would be no bad thing tonight.'

She was trembling so much that she could hardly speak, but managed to get out, 'If you wish, sir.'

He was aware of her shaking. 'Don't be afraid. I promise you there'll be no spies lurking inside. A ghost or two, perhaps the late Mr Marton . . .'

He pushed open the damp-swollen door and they were inside.

Dorothy drew in her breath with astonishment. Doves and cupids painted in rich colours looked down from the ceilings; cornices of fruit and flowers were clouded over with cobwebs. Carved fireplaces held empty grates, delicate furniture wore the bloom of damp, musical instruments stood draped and silent.

'The palace of *La Belle au Bois Dormant*,' said Charles. 'But where is *La Belle*, and where are her courtiers? Let's have some more light.'

He was going round the room, lighting candles, some of which had burned down in their sconces, while others had never been lit. A faint blue sputtering, and the whole room was bathed in golden light that brought back the colour to painted nymph and gilded chair. The Prince was on his knees at the fireplace, filling the grate from a pile of brushwood that lay on the hearth. In a moment it was alight, blazing and roaring up the chimney, lighting the room with comfort.

'Let's play at courts, ma'am,' he said, laughing. 'A little interlude in a hard campaign. Take off your cloak and you'll feel the warmth better.'

He had already thrown off his own, and she saw with surprise that he no longer wore a wig – as he had done at supper – and that his own hair was short and inclined to wave and curl, sweeping back from his brow and touching the back of his neckcloth. Amber lights played in it from the fire and the candles: he was indeed the yellow-haired laddie of the songs. She watched him wander from one instrument to another, rejecting a harp, touching a viola, and finally pulling back the cover of a harpsichord, a large two-manual which dominated the room. Suddenly he sat down at it and began to play. The long-silent thing awoke under his strong touch, sweet notes clashing into the damp air now tinged with the scent of wood-smoke. She sat on a little Louis chair, still as a mouse, watching and listening.

He drifted from the cheerful fireworks of Domenico Scarlatti to a gentle air from a sonata of Corelli, a tune for courts and lovers and warm Italian nights, for cypresses and fountains. His face, noble as a profile on a Roman coin, was rapt, absorbed in the music he had played easily and skilfully since he was a child, so easily that his father and his tutors were forever scolding him for it. All very well for a young prince to be accomplished in the arts, but what about the sciences, philosophy, Latin? It was no credit that he played so well, they said.

Gently the theme moved into variations, ever sadder and sweeter, repeated its first statement, seemed to sing its own melancholy words. The silence of the listener communicated itself to the player. He half turned his head, and caught on her face such a look of naked adoration that he brought the piece to a premature, quiet end. He knew, too well, what he could do to a susceptible young heart; in this romantic lonely place, with such music about them, it was not fair to go on.

As he stopped, she rose and went to him. 'Oh, I pray you, don't stop! I never heard anything so beautiful . . .'

He stood up and looked down into the pleading face. Charles had never been in love, except with the country he had come to win. Plenty of women had offered themselves to him, from predatory Italian ladies twice his age to their daughters no older than Juliet who saw in him a great matrimonial catch, and in consequence he had developed a terrible shyness with females which had drawn lewd comments from Whig observers. He was getting over it, among the cooler dames of Scotland and England. Here was a young lady quite dreadfully in love with him and not ashamed to show it. He knew that her plea had not been merely for the music. He was too kind to refuse anybody anything, within reason, and she was very pretty, and very close to him, the faint rose-scent she wore mingling with the blue wood-smoke. He bent down and kissed her.

Her arms came round him, clinging. They were locked in an embrace neither had intended, and to his own surprise he felt his arms tightening about her, his mouth on hers again. Impossible not to think of the loneliness of the little pavilion, of the misty night outside; or the broad sofa in the corner of the room.

Suddenly sense prevailed over growing passion. Gently he pushed her from him, and when she resisted he took her by the arm and led her to a chair. She looked up, reproaching.

'Why?' she asked.

'Because, my dear Mrs Dorothy, your husband is one of my serving officers. And because, in any case, I could not take advantage of a young lady in such a situation.'

'I should not mind. I am not a . . .' Virgin, she had been going to say.

'No. But you see, a Prince cannot do things an ordinary man might do. Would you wish yourself to be slandered as poor Mrs Jenny Cameron has been? Not to mention my reputation. Any moment now they will come looking for me when I'm missed from the house. Do you see?'

She nodded, unable to speak.

'Now,' he said, 'we will go.' He put her cloak round her shoulders and arranged its hood over her hair, in which damp mist still sparkled, before putting on his own roquelaure. Going round the room he blew out the candles and stamped out the dying fire. 'It would be ungrateful to burn my host's pavilion down.' At the door he paused and, putting down the lantern, kissed her again, this time on the brow, before leading her out into the garden. Silently they walked to the little gate which he knew was at the end of it, an exit into China Lane. When they reached it she took his hands and held them to her breast.

'Will you . . . how can I say it? Will you promise me something, sir?'

'What can I promise?'

'Only to . . . send for me. If I can ever help you . . . do anything, anything at all. You'll think me bold and shameless. But I would die for you, indeed.'

He smiled. 'I hope you will not have to. I hope few will have to.'

He bowed, opening the gate for her. From the distant house voices were shouting, lights bobbing in the gloom as anxious guards came out to search for him. She stood alone, in narrow, dismal China Lane. Wild happiness, unbelief, the consciousness that she could never be the same person again, fought with a kind of shame that she, a married woman, should have invited, confessed . . . what must he have thought of her? There was grief, too, for what could not and must not be.

In panic, she began to run, without direction, colliding with a cloaked figure which had just turned the corner of the street – and found herself in the arms of Allan Carr.

'Dear me!' said Allan. 'You're in a mighty hurry, ma'am.'

10

Allan was more than a little alarmed at his dear Mrs Dorothy's obvious agitation. His first thought was that she had been attacked, even raped. In the faint light from a cottage window he peered keenly at her face, but what he saw there was surely not outrage.

'What in heaven's name are you doing out alone?' he asked. 'This is no place for a young lady to be unattended, and no time, either.' In a nearby street a watchman was going his rounds, giving his monotonous cry. It was eleven o'clock, over-late for rambling.

She controlled herself enough to speak. 'I supped at – His Highness's lodging. I was going back to – to mine, only I fear I've forgotten where it is.'

'But why the Devil – why is Mr Beaumont not with you?'

She explained, stammering, about Lyndon's spell of duty and Mrs Murray's defection.

'But *somebody* should have accompanied you. A servant, or one of the Highlanders. Could they not have sent out for a chair? If I had not been called to a wild Maclean who'd got his head broken in a brawl, you might have wandered the streets of Lancaster all night. To be sent away alone, a lady in a strange town!'

'I was not alone,' she said in a voice he could hardly hear. 'His Highness was good enough to escort me through a private garden. He – he was taking a walk himself, and most kindly offered . . .'

'I see. Very civil of him, and rather dangerous, I should have thought, without an armed guard.' He knew now something of what had happened, though how far it had gone he would rather not know. So Charles the Chaste, as the Whigs mockingly called him, had his human moments, and must needs indulge in one at the expense of the girl whom Allan, rightly or wrongly, found that he loved. Silently he cursed, good Christian though he was. He cursed Lyndon Beaumont's neglect of his wife; he cursed, reluctantly, his Prince's irrestistible attraction for the female sex. Not least, he cursed his own susceptibility.

'Well,' he said aloud, 'do you think you could recognise the house where you lodge?'

'I think so. It had two gables and a stone over the door, carved with a date. If you could spare the time to go with me . . .'

'I have all the time in the world to go with you,' he replied truthfully. 'Perhaps you had better take my arm.'

She looked up at him, smiling. The tears had dried, and he wondered how, in circumstances that would make most women look like drowned rats, she seemed a flower turning its face to the sun. He supposed it was his own damned infatuation.

'I am *so* glad I met you,' she was saying. 'It was really most felicitous.'

As they began to walk, he tried to think of precisely the right things to say. Could he warn her, or was it too late? He was beginning to feel the snare of a hopeless infatuation lacerating his own heart, and he wanted so much to free her from hers.

'Extraordinarily gracious of His Highness to escort you, though I'm sure it was a pleasure to him,' he said, carefully choosing his words. 'The Stuart charm is a very real thing, is it not? They say it was a gift from a – from one of the Little People, to a Stuart in times past, and that she warned him it might prove a curse as well as a blessing, to those who came under its spell.'

The most recent victim of that spell was listening eagerly; he hoped he was making some impression on her. 'True enough of many of them, would you not say? There was King James IV who died at Flodden; ye'll have heard the lament for the Flowers of the Forest? Now *he* had it. And so had his granddaughter Queen Mary, in abundance. She died for it, and Rizzio, and Châtelard, the poor fool who hid under her bed for love of her. And her husbands, Darnley and Black Bothwell. They say *he* died mad in a cramped prison cell in Denmark. Her son missed the charm, and her grandson King Charles the Martyr had only a tithe of it – yet many died for him, and for his son, Charles II, the Black Boy, as ugly as sin, who could charm a bird from a tree or the heart from a lady's bosom.'

'But tell me about our own King,' Dorothy said. 'He must surely be one of the most charming of all' (with such a son, she added to herself).

Allan thought back to his youth at the court of the exiled King James III, the unpretentious Palazzo Muti in Rome; to the silent man with the long melancholy face, deteriorating into puffiness the last time he had seen it. He himself had never known the Queen, she who had been the fairytale Princess Clementina Sobieska of Poland. There was a portrait at the Palazzo of her radiant, triumphant after her romantic elopement to join her King, with jewels in her fair hair, and a sparkle to match them in her dark eyes. Nearby, in the Convent of Santa Cecilia, was another portrait. She had taken refuge there after the decay of her marriage; the picture showed her a gaunt, ecstatic nun, kneeling before an altar, the crown and sceptre laid aside at her feet.

'His Majesty is great and noble,' Allan said. 'I would not call him a spellbinder. Sometimes the charm leaps a generation.'

There was nothing more he could say that would not sound like a blatant warning, and he was afraid of giving away his own feelings. Fortunately at that moment Dorothy recognised her lodging. At the door she thanked him prettily. 'I really cannot think what the Beaumont family would do without its physician,' she said. 'Good night, Dr Allan.'

And that, thought Allan gloomily, walking away, is precisely what I appear to her – a grave old quack with an infinite fund of boring historical information. She will not heed a word I've said. Her dreams tonight will be of him, not of me.

Preston raised everyone's spirits. They were met with smiles and cheers and frantic waving of hats and hands. Women held up their children to see the Prince; the joyful church bells mingled with the skirling of the pipers who marched with the first column.

Whaur hae ye been a' the day,
Bonnie laddie, Hielan' laddie?

'You see, I was right,' Charles told his council. 'My father's army was quite wrongly disposed in '15. There was no bad luck about it, merely bad generalship. Perhaps now you will all stop heeding old wives' tales and listen to me instead. We are across the Ribble, and all we need now is a fine force of recruits. I told you Lancashire was loyal.'

'So far,' said Lord George Gordon, 'only three gentlemen have come to join us – Mr Francis Towneley, Mr David Morgan and Mr William Vaughan, the latter two Welsh – together with a few of the common people. It is hardly a gratifying number.'

'No matter, it's a beginning. It will be better at Manchester.'

Lord George said nothing, but exchanged a look with Lochiel.

It was better at Manchester, certainly. A bold young Scot named Dickson, captured from Cope's army at Prestonpans and an ardent convert to the Jacobite cause, had got leave to ride on ahead, with his wench and one drummer, armed with his master's blunderbuss, and at Manchester recruited singlehanded and by dubious means an army of a hundred and eighty men. The Mancunians seemed to include, besides the barefoot poor, a great many wealthy fashionables, who erupted from their fine houses and drove in from the country to see the takers of their town. There were a great many ladies among the crowd, a fact which did not escape the growing band of doubters among the Prince's council-members and officers. The warm-hearted women of Manchester, not over-blessed with charm in their own menfolk, fell in love unanimously with Charles. The night he stayed at Mr Dickenson's house in Market Stead Lane, one of them wrote, by her midnight candle, to a friend.

'If you but saw him once . . .
Do see him once! What harm is there in seeing?
If after that there be not an agreeing,
Then call me twenty rebel sluts if you,
When you have seen him, ben't a rebel too!'

Crowds of would-be feminine rebels waited outside Mr Dickenson's lighted windows, hoping for a glimpse of their hero. Others danced round the bonfire at the Market Cross, where King James had been proclaimed. In the evening Dorothy and Lyndon, with a young Macdonald from Elcho's cavalry, stood watching the dancers, English folk laughing and clapping the antics of the Highlanders who, fortified by spirits from the taverns, were performing wild flings and jigs to the accompaniment of their own shrill whoops. There seemed to be rough music everywhere, pipes, fiddles and singing. Aeneas Macdonald picked up one of the tunes and began to chant it. It was a catchy air, but the words seemed unfamiliar. Lyndon caught something about 'her name was bonnie Doll' and then '. . . the Prince's moll'. Then, in a comparative lull from the noise around them, he heard:

'Syne he cam' marching doon the street,
And tirléd at the pin,
And wha sae ready as hersel'
To let the laddie in?
O Charlie he's my darling, my darling, my darling,
Charlie he's my darling, the braw Chevalier.'

Lyndon tapped Aeneas on the shoulder. 'That song. I never heard those words before. Is it bawdry?'

Aeneas looked surprised. 'Not so bad as some. 'Tis a bit o' verse Elcho made up last night. It seems the Prince indulged in a wee escapade when we lay at Lancaster.'

'Indeed? That's not like him. Did Elcho say what it was?'

Dorothy felt a flood of scarlet surge over her face and neck. Even in the flickering light, she turned away so that Lyndon should not see it. She had not said a word to him, or even to Meliora, about her dream-like adventure; and now to hear it made a thing for common jest!

'Oh, some folly with a young madam. Elcho got it from a servant. Well, I for one grudge His Highness no pleasure. God knows he gets little enough.' He returned to whistling the tune.

Dorothy glanced at Lyndon. She knew him well enough to tell that any faint suspicion which may have crept into his mind had been examined and rejected. The company had all been together, all the time, in the house at Lancaster; he had said good night to Dorothy, probably imagined that he had seen her leave the house. Elcho's malicious squib had misfired – so far. But there was danger to Charles, not to her, if their names were to be even jokingly associated. She disliked what she had seen of David Elcho; otherwise it might have been possible to beg him not to spread his silly parody any further. As it was, she could only hope the Prince's popularity would prevent it catching on in the ranks. (And so indeed it proved. For they made new verses, and sang the refrain over and over, until it went through the head like a pulse-beat: Charlie is my darling, my darling, my darling, Charlie he's my darling, the Young Chevalier.)

At the Market Cross the merriment would go on all night. From the comfort of a tavern, through the steam of hot toddy, they could see by moonlight the whirling figures, the improvised banners at windows. A coarse straw effigy of the Elector was flung on the bonfire, to rousing cheers, making it flare up in a burst of sparks. Snow lay on the old crooked roofs, untouched in the moonlight.

'Tomorrow is the first of December,' Lyndon said. 'The English leaders will join us at any time, and the Welsh at Derby.' He squeezed Dorothy's waist. 'Mark me, we shall be home for Christmas.'

But at Derby, when the tired, cold army arrived there, no news awaited them of English or Welsh support, and the townspeople were wary and unwelcoming. The Prince went straight to the Earl of Exeter's house; he had urgent plans to make, for Cumberland was said to be no further away than Northampton. His men, on their best behaviour in street, shop and billet, talked excitedly of the coming battle. A spy from London brought news of the panic there caused by the presence of the Scots army as far south as Derby.

'The Elector's packing his bags, they say, and has a boat lying at Tower Bridge to take him to Hanover. The Bank of England's paying out in sixpences, the shops have shut, long faces everywhere. They think the end of the world's come. Cumberland's under-manned, the camp at Finchley's no more than a handful of raw recruits. Oh, and a letter was sent on from Lady Primrose to you, Mr Beaumont.'

Lyndon took it. 'My father's seal. This has travelled a long way.'

Dorothy watched him break the seal and read the letter. He looked up from it, half pleased, half puzzled. 'He's coming home. Father is coming home, Doll. What's the date?'

'December the fourth.'

'And this was written in mid-November. He should be at home by now.'

'Not in Berkeley Square?'

'No, at Dove House – I told him we'd closed up the other. He says – but read for yourself.' He passed over the letter. She read it aloud.

'Since the news is so favourable, and we may have every hope of an early Victory, I am minded to lay my bones in my own Country and die with my grandchildren about me. I feel my life will not be long, Dear Son, especially in this climate to which I was never inclined. I collect yr good Lady will be at home to receive me and give me some fond daughterly care, wh. I do not receive as I am now situate. His Majy. graciously bids me convey his love and thoughts to ye Prince, of whom he hears nothing but great and good reports. Ye P. Henry should by now be at Calais to enlist French help, and Ld. John Drummond is gone to Scotland with more than 800 Irish and Scots. (This for yr. eye and ye Prince's ear alone.) I look to see you, Dear Son, at ye happy conclusion of . . .'

Lyndon took the letter. 'And so forth, and so forth.' They stared at each other, the piece of paper between them, each perturbed.

'I can't go,' Dorothy said flatly. 'My place is with you.'

'He's an old man, and sick, Doll. Who else is there to look after him?'

'Why not Mrs Mercy?'

He shrugged. 'A good woman, but . . . suppose he should die before we return?'

'You said at Manchester we should be home for Christmas, only three weeks from now. If he was well enough to travel from Italy, surely he can last so long. Lyndon, how can you ask me to leave now, when we're so near to victory?'

He turned his back on her, looking out of the window. They were quartered in the house of Alderman Franceys, the apothecary, who seemed to have brought faint fragrances of camomile, rosewater and verbena home with him, for the room smelt sweetly of them. In the parlour upstairs Lady Ogilvy and Mrs Murray of Broughton were walking about noisily on high clacking heels, settling themselves in.

'If there *is* a battle, as seems likely,' Lyndon said, 'it will be no place for women. In any case,' he added bleakly, 'His Highness has never been in favour of ladies travelling with the army. I dare say he would be only too pleased to hear you were gone. You say your place is with me. I think it is with my father.'

'I'm sorry I shall not be able to present him with a grandchild – even the promise of one!' Dorothy threw back at him in a flash of temper.

'Is that my fault?' he snapped back. 'You've hardly been in the vein since we left Scotland. One would think you'd got yourself a swain on the journey.'

As the colour rose in her cheeks, he turned her sharply to the light. 'Is that it? Have you a sweetheart you keep dangling on a string – Dr Allan Carr, for instance? Whenever I see you he seems to be just round the corner. Is it true, Doll? Come, I *will* know!'

With a wrench she pulled herself away from him. 'Pray don't make yourself ridiculous! I won't talk to you. I'm sorry for your father, but if I choose to stay I shall stay.'

Between tears and temper, she ran out of the room and into the one Meliora shared with Margaret Murray's young maid. Meliora heard the story impassively, then she said, 'It will dispose itself, madam. The morning will tell what you must do.'

'The morning? Yes, there's a council of war early tomorrow. Perhaps when we know about the battle . . . yes, that must decide it. How wise you are, Meliora. Now make some tea, and then unlace me, and I shall compose myself with the novel Lady Ogilvy lent me. It's silly stuff but better than quarrelling.'

But after an attempt at reading she put the book aside. Heroines in stories seemed to have no such decisions to make. They were either about to be ravished, in which case they would certainly be rescued at the last moment by some gallant Sylvanus or Eglantine, or they were deliciously involved in a silken network of amorous intrigue. She was already sorry to have been sharp with Lyndon; when he came back she would make all well between them.

The next day passed without news. A grey wintry quiet had settled over Derby. The bellman went about the streets, calling upon those citizens who had not paid their taxes to deliver them at once to the Prince's treasury; the drummer of the Manchester Regiment beat up for recruits. And the city listened and waited. Dorothy walked to Full Street, to look through the gates at Exeter House. There was no movement to be seen. The day seemed endless. She was glad when dusk began to fall and candles could be lighted. Mrs Murray had gone out riding – recruiting, probably. Lady Ogilvy had made friends with Mrs Franceys, and they were chatting cosily in the parlour above. Meliora was mending a petticoat which had a large tear in it; whenever Dorothy looked at her the stitches seemed to have progressed no farther. Her little enamelled watch had said half-past five for hours, it seemed.

The outer door slammed. She jumped to her feet as Lyndon entered. Without greeting her, he pulled off his hat and threw it on a chair, his cloak following. His face was like death.

'We are going back,' he said.

'Back? Where?'

'To Scotland. The talks went on all morning. He argued and pleaded with them, but they were all against him, all but a few. I was one, and Perth, and Sir John Macdonald, but Murray and the others were too strong. We retreat tomorrow.'

'*Retreat!* It's impossible. The reports – London is in panic . . .'

'And Cumberland hesitating. We only had to press on and the game would have been ours. He said so, he begged them, one by one, not to betray him. He said he would rather be twenty feet underground than turn back. He wept, Doll. I never thought I should see him weep. When they had beaten all his arguments down, he said,

"In future I shall summon no more councils." We left him sitting by the window. I never shall forget it as long as I live.' Lyndon smashed his fist down on the table, again and again. 'God damn George Murray! Damn him to hell!' He leant against the mantelpiece, his hand over his eyes. 'I went back to speak to him – to the Prince – and he said something about a bad wicket. That he should remember, at such a time, a conversation . . .' He was unable to go on. Dorothy went and stood by him, an arm around his shoulders.

There was nothing for it now but to return to Richmond. A carriage and horses were hired, the baggage packed, a letter sent by messenger to warn Lord Gainsford of her arrival. Lyndon was to join his regiment by eight in the morning. There seemed little to say. Lyndon's spirits were as numb with shock as those of the other officers who knew of the retreat. It had been kept secret from the men.

'We may be in for a battle, or a siege. Or merely an endless march to skulk in the heather. I hope Murray and his council will be pleased with that. I'll get word to you somehow, wherever we are. Farewell, sweet. My best duties to my father.'

They kissed, and she watched him walk away, an incongruously bright figure in blue and scarlet. After a few minutes she dressed for outdoors and went to the Market Place, to stand in the crowd, shivering and expectant. As the clocks struck nine the gates of Exeter House were opened. Charles rode out, on the great horse. He was swathed in a dark riding-cloak. To the half-hearted cheers he returned no smile, and looked neither to right nor left. His grim face looked ten years older than last time Dorothy had seen it. Soon he was lost to sight on the road that led to Ashbourne, the way they had come two days ago.

Somewhere a piper was playing 'Bonnie laddie, Hielan' laddie'. The brave tune seemed to mean nothing now.

11

'Dear, oh dear me!' Mrs Mercy laid down the copy of the *Intelligencer*. 'Here's more news to be kept from his lordship.'

'What worse can there be?' Dorothy said wearily. It was 18 May 1746. She looked out at the gardens of Dove House, lovely with striped tulips, early roses, and in the distance the orchard trees, young apples and cherries budding among fading blossom on the boughs, in the sunshine. It seemed so long since the winter day when she had come home to find Lord Gainsford helpless from the stroke he had suffered on hearing of the retreat from Derby. They had nursed him all winter; she, Meliora and Mrs Mercy, watching with relief the use come back to his limbs, though the left side of his face was twisted in a downward droop, and his voice still thick and slow.

His mind, however, was unimpaired. He had insisted on being told any news that might reach them of the progress of the Scots army, and they had met his demands with heavily edited versions, telling him of the Prince's occupation of Stirling in January and the rout of Cumberland's army at the Battle of Falkirk, but suppressing the ominous, humiliating retreat of the Jacobite forces further and further north, until the terrible sixteenth of April, when on Culloden Moor near Inverness the flower of the Highland arms was cut down, shattered by Cumberland's cannon, trampled under the hooves of his cavalry, slashed to pieces by his swords. It was another Flodden. But even Flodden Field had not seen such bloody slaughter, or such savage reprisals as those taken by the soldiers of the man who would be known for all time as 'Butcher Cumberland'. The gross, blubber-lipped Duke William enjoyed killing. He fought without chivalry or compassion, as happy to burn wounded prisoners alive in a barn as to order their women to be raped and then killed, their children spitted on bayonets. Even Englishmen who had feared invasion found the sickening accounts too much to credit.

Lord Gainsford put down Dorothy's lowness of spirits to lack of news from Lyndon. Just before the end of 1745 a torn, stained letter had come, delivered by a pedlar who vanished from the district before any questions could be asked of him. Unmistakably in Lyndon's scrawling hand, it said that they had arrived safely at Carlisle, where the Prince intended to leave a garrison; that he himself was well.

'Not much, but quite enough to hang him,' said Mrs Mercy gloomily. 'I thought gentlemen were cunning in disguising their meaning at such times. And there have I kept as close as a clam about all matters, not a soul in the house allowed to know the why or wherefore of anything.'

Dorothy sighed. 'It was rash, indeed. I suppose he meant to relieve our minds. And so it has, but . . . I wish we knew.'

Against her better judgment, she had appealed to Meliora.

'I know you can see things other people cannot. Won't you try, for me?'

Meliora was downcast. She had discovered, by accident while washing herself, that if she looked into a bowl of clear water and emptied her mind of all but the wish to see a place or a person in it, pictures would appear, sometimes cloudy, sometimes sharply definite. She had seen Lyndon once, on a February night, polishing up a pistol at the door of a tent. He looked worn and shabby, and there was an air of menace about his surroundings which caused her hastily to pour the water away. It was something to reassure Dorothy, but she resolved not to do it again. When Dorothy pressed her, many weeks later, she agreed reluctantly. She would so much rather have been studying her books or improving her needlework than practising this gift which was so uncomfortable and, she felt, dangerous. But, obediently, she filled the bowl and, with Dorothy eagerly looking on, gazed into it.

Beneath her horrified eyes the water turned to smoke and blood, and through it she saw Culloden. She gave a shriek and jumped up, the bowl skimming off the table to send water over Dorothy's lap.

'Never again, madam. Please do not ask me! I can't tell you what I . . .' Her hand over her mouth, she ran from the room.

Now Dorothy knew what she had seen, and blamed herself for forcing Meliora to look on such a sight. So there was no way of finding out what had happened to Lyndon, or to the Prince. One dispatch from Inverness said that at the end of April the Pretender's son and other gentlemen were moving about in the Cameron country; later it was reported that he was in Lewis, or Barra, or Moidart. Wherever he might be hiding, there was a price of thirty thousand pounds on his head; he would be betrayed sooner or later.

On this day of May, the *Intelligencer* announced that the rebel prisoners taken at Carlisle had been brought to the bar at the Old Bailey, then taken back into custody. Dorothy scanned the list of names, and sighed with relief.

'Not among those, thank God. But so many more are coming into London every day, and shootings and hangings all over Scotland. Perhaps we shall never know, Mrs Mercy. And that would be worse than . . .' her voice trailed away. The housekeeper glanced up over her spectacles.

'I've been giving it thought, madam, and to my mind you'd do well to drop a word or two in his lordship's hearing that would prepare him, in case of anything. That way you might spare him the shock – if it came to that.'

'Yes. Yes, I suppose it would be kinder.' She went upstairs to Dove House's second-best chamber, a quiet room hung with silvery-grey curtains and bed-drapes. Her father-in-law was asleep, his big features, so like Lyndon's, calm, his wig laid aside. She had not the heart to disturb him. Whenever he learnt of Culloden it would be soon enough.

In a pleasant castellated mansion by the banks of the River Spey, in Morayshire, the subject of all these anxieties sat at ease, his feet on an embroidered footstool, a decanter of pleasant wine at his side. Lyndon was in the fortunate position of having a relative living in Scotland. Lochachie Lodge was the property of his second cousin, Sir Alexander Drummond, whose father had been one of those to

137

stay at home in the 'Fifteen, and who had himself kept extremely quiet in the 'Forty-five. Eton-educated, he had made the Grand Tour, had sampled Paris and London, and had finally decided that the life of a country squire in the Highlands was the one for him. His wife had died, leaving him childless, so there were no sons to send the Prince. His household consisted mainly of ghillies, with an old woman called Mhairi who had no objection to cooking a daily menu limited to venison and grouse.

'So,' said Alexander, taking another pull at his pipe and surveying his younger cousin with amusement, 'you think you can guarantee not to get me into trouble with the authorities?'

'I can't see how it's possible,' Lyndon replied. 'If they find me here, I am your English relation paying a visit. I have no retainers; I wear no tartan. Elcho's lifeguards were so abominably run that I doubt if even he knew who served in 'em. I never signed a paper to any effect. Of all that army I knew only one or two men to drink with. Unless His Highness kept private records, there's no evidence that I ever bore arms. And while, my dear Alexander, I want nothing more than to join him wherever he is, God bless him, and fight for the Cause again, I see no earthly point in moving from here until the coast's clear.'

Alexander nodded. 'A very good, sound viewpoint. Well, be sure I shall not betray you. I'm no Whig, nor no Jacobite either, but if I can keep any man out of Cumberland's bloody clutches I shall not have lived in vain. God, that man! It will be like a battue in London when all the captives are herded together to be slaughtered.'

Lyndon stared into the fire. 'And he, the Prince, was mercy itself. Even when they caught Weir, Cumberland's valet and spy, he would not hang him, saying such an action was beneath him. He would have stayed the night on a battlefield to comfort a wounded soldier of the Elector's.'

'Folly,' said Alexander. ' "Mercy but murders, pardoning those that kill." An't that Shakespeare?'

'I expect so. Doll would know. I wish I could get word to her, Sandy. It troubles me that she may think me dead. But far better not to risk it.' He knocked out the ash from his pipe. 'I wonder sometimes if she . . . I used to think, in those weeks before Derby, that there was something wrong between us. She didn't seem so fond of me; or maybe I was not fond enough of her. I was never much of a one for women before we married, only I thought 'twas the thing to do, to settle and get an heir.' His eyes brightened. 'Colonel Anne Mackintosh, now *she* was a woman! If they took her after Culloden, I warrant they're sorry for it.'

'Women are kittle cattle,' Alexander said. 'Will I ring for Mhairi to bring in supper?'

'If it's ready for me, I'm ready for it. I shan't forget your Highland hospitality in a hurry, Sandy.'

'May you long enjoy it,' returned his relative politely. As he moved towards the bellrope, a great jangling broke out downstairs, and a storm of knocking began on the stout front door of the Lodge.

'What the devil . . .' Alexander went to the window. 'Three, no, four horses. More fugitives, do you suppose?'

But when his manservant admitted the callers, they proved to be a captain and a sergeant in the scarlet and white of the English Government.

'Sit still,' said Alexander out of the corner of his mouth. Himself rising courteously, he bade the visitors welcome. The captain produced a thick, crumpled document from his pocket.

'Sir Alexander Drummond?'

'The same.'

'And yon gentleman?'

They had agreed to use no false names if challenged. 'Mr Beaumont, an English relative who is staying with me.'

'Mr *Lyndon* Beaumont?'

Lyndon raised his eyebrows. 'That's my name, though I don't know how it came into your hands.'

The captain showed yellow teeth in a hearty laugh. 'Oh, there's more know Tom Fool than Tom Fool knows, sir. If you'll pardon me the expression. It so happens that your name, Mr Lyndon Beaumont, is here on this list of persons wanted for examination, in the name of His Majesty King George.'

The cousins exchanged swift glances, Sandy's assuring Lyndon that he would do the talking. 'Pray sit down, gentlemen,' he said affably. 'I'm sure you are dry from travelling. Won't you take a stoup of wine with us?'

Somewhat cautiously the officers approached, and perched themselves on the edges of ancient chairs, glancing about at the hunting trophies on the walls and the fine swords and targes which had obviously not been used during recent events. Plying them with wine, Alexander chatted lightly to them of his cousin's long stay with him, following a journey to Switzerland which had failed to restore his health; of the remarkable recuperation worked on him by the air of the Highlands, and of his intention to return home before the winter. The captain consulted his document.

'That would be the town of Richmond in Surrey.'

'Yes, yes,' Lyndon broke in impatiently, 'but my cousin will tell you I . . .'

'I'll warrant he'll tell me a lot I don't know, sir. But I'd rather you told us yourself, on the way to London.'

'*London?* I've no intention of going to London with you!'

From another capacious pocket the captain produced a substantial length of rope, neatly coiled.

'Then I'll needs have to persuade you, sir.' He dangled it invitingly.

Alexander was on his feet, grim-faced, his hand on the bell-pull he had not reached for before. Two or three old men about the Lodge, the ghillies and the grooms out on the moors or working in the stables: how could they be reached? His eye caught the great broadsword over the mantelshelf, and for an instant he toyed with the idea of seizing it, murdering the officers and disposing of their bodies in the loch. Then he remembered the other two horses outside. They had brought reinforcements, who were doubtless in the hall below. He drew Lyndon aside.

'There's no point in resisting. Lyn, there can be nothing in this charge, from what you tell me. When you get to London there'll be plenty of friends to speak for you.'

'It would seem one of them's spoken against me.'

Alexander was thinking fast. 'What tale will Dorothy tell any who come enquiring for you?'

'That I'm travelling abroad. We agreed on that.'

'Then stick to it, even with these fellows. If they call on me for evidence I shall tell them the same. God, if only I'd had time to hide you, but it's too late now.'

'I hope you mayn't suffer for this as well.'

'Never fear. I'm too grey a fox to be caught with questions.' He turned to the waiting officers. 'You'll be good enough to give my kinsman time to collect his possessions.'

He'll not be needing many, where he's going,' said the sergeant with a snigger.

'And where may that be?'

'Tae the convict ship at Aberdeen. Did ye think we'd be sae hard-hearted as to make ye ride tae London?'

Lyndon glanced out of the window. 'On one of those nags? I should hope not.'

But it was on one of the skinny horses that Alexander watched his cousin ride away between the redcoats, his head held high.

Mr Fowler knocked discreetly at the door of the Blue Parlour, wishing he need not do so. He spoke of his employers' affairs to no one, not even Mrs Mercy, but he knew only too well that the visitor was not one Mrs Beaumont would welcome.

'An – officer to see you, madam.'

Dorothy looked up from her sewing, startled, to see a figure in Hanoverian uniform looming behind him, impassive of face. Even before the man spoke she felt the blood drain from her cheeks.

'Mrs Beaumont? I have to tell you that your husband, the Honourable Lyndon Beaumont, has been arrested on a charge of bearing arms against the forces of His Majesty's Government in the late rebellion.'

The words seemed to mean nothing. Then she realised what the man had said. Was it a bluff, a trick? On the chance, she tried out the story they had prepared at Derby.

'My husband is abroad, travelling.'

He gave her a token smile. 'I think you're mistaken, madam. Your husband is in the New Gaol at Southwark, along with many other Jacobite prisoners awaiting trial. I have further to inform you that you must hold yourself ready to be arrested on a charge of abetting treason, and that a guard will be placed upon the house day and night. All persons entering or leaving must report on doing so. Your servant, madam.'

With a sketch of a salute he was gone; Mr Fowler, who had been hovering outside, pounced on him and escorted him swiftly downstairs. Dorothy leant back in her chair, shaking uncontrollably, icy cold and sick. Thus Meliora found her a few 'minutes later.

'His lordship is much better, madam. He asked to be sat up, then for a cup of tea. He – oh, madam! What is it?'

Dorothy's teeth were chattering too much for her to answer. Meliora ran to her and clasped her shivering body. Somewhere in the room there was a vinaigrette filled with aromatic salts. She found it, by a workbox, and held it to her mistress's nostrils, watching with relief a faint colour come back to her cheeks.

'There, that's better. I thought you was took with a fever, madam.'

'No . . . no . . .' Dorothy sniffed the vinaigrette again, and began to stammer out the news she had just heard, in incoherent sentences. 'I never thought . . . of this. I thought he might have . . . have died at Culloden. At the worst. But . . . oh, Meliora, what will they do to him?'

Meliora shook her head.

Dorothy's voice was stronger and the shivering was only intermittent. 'I must go to him. Tell Leach to bring the coach to the door. If their guard is here already, tell him I am going to London. And pack plenty of food and wine, and some brandy – as much as you can get into the coach. Oh, and a change of clothes for Mr Beaumont; he's sure to need them. And, Meliora, nobody is to know of this who might drop a word in his lordship's hearing. It would kill him outright.'

'Yes, madam.'

Southwark Gaol was worse than she had imagined. 'New' it might be called, but it was old in stink, slime and misery, imbued with the sweat of fear. Lyndon was in a small damp room with a high barred slit of window, playing cards with three other men. She recognised two of them as officers with whom he had served, Sir John Wedderburn and James Bradshaw. All stood up when the guard showed her in, Lyndon with an oath.

'Dorothy! My God, they haven't taken you, too?'

'No, no, my dear. Not yet.' She went into his arms, to be held only briefly.

'There, don't come too close. I'm filthy, as you can see, and stink, I dare say. How the devil can one talk in this confounded cramped place? Come over here.' With a nod of apology to the others, he drew her into a corner. In low tones she told him of the guard's visit. 'I tried to put him off, but it was no use.'

'No. That story won't wash. I was recognised here, you see.' He gestured towards Bradshaw. 'No good saying I'd been abroad, then. And they have something else to go on, though what it is I shan't know till the trial.'

'Trial? Oh, Lyndon, when?'

'On the sixteenth. We're all to be called up then. The date was put off so that men from a distance might get friends to testify for them. They offered to fetch my cousin Alexander – he hid me for weeks at Lochachie – but I told them not to trouble him. In any case I'm glad it's out. The lie stuck in my throat. I'd never have told it, but I thought perhaps I'd been spared at Culloden so that I could fight again, go overseas, anything . . . It would have been better than this.'

Leaning against the damp-glistening wall, he told her of his flight over piles of bloody corpses after the battle, of his journey over long mountainous miles, living off water from the burns and raw fish caught with his hands, all the time travelling in the direction of Lochachie, where he knew Alexander lived, asking the way from shepherds and herd-girls, from anyone who could be persuaded to approach him. 'They thought I was a Hanover man because I was not wearing the tartan, I suppose. One man tried to kill me with his dirk, till I said "God save King James and Prince Charles" in as near to the Gaelic as I could get. An old woman gave me a wing of fowl and some bread, and a sort of gipsy-fellow let me share a bowl

143

of broth. Then I came to Spey, and so to Lochachie. It was like a miracle; and all for nothing.'

'Oh, my dear.' There was no comfort for the bitterness in his eyes. She braced herself to ask the question she hardly dared to voice. 'The Prince?'

'Safe, I hope and pray. At least he was a month ago, just before they took me – in Corradale, on South Uist, under Clanranald's protection. God knows how he got away so far, with Cumberland's devils after him. Someone brought word to Lochachie that he was well and cheerful, living like the roughest peasant but never complaining. If they do catch him, they'll kill him on sight, for the pleasure of it, and be damned to the thirty thousand pounds.'

Dorothy shut out of her mind the picture of a cheerful, ragged, half-starved, hunted Charles. She must think only of Lyndon now.

That evening at Dove House, with a cockney sentry whistling outside the front door, she made herself go and sit with her father-in-law and behave as though nothing had happened. He certainly looked better; propped up with pillows, wearing his wig, and trying to read a book. As she came in he snatched off his spectacles and impatiently tossed them on the bed.

'Infernal small print – infernal spectacles – 'f a man can't pass time reading, how can he pass time?'

Dorothy smiled. 'Dear me. You *are* better, my lord. I came to see if you would like a game of two-handed whist before supper.'

'Whist. Yes. Very nice. And supper – bottle of wine.'

'Is that wise, do you think?'

'Damn it, girl, not – old grandam.'

'No, but you must take care. Half a bottle.'

He looked mutinous, then smiled and patted her hand. His performance at whist was commendable for a man so out of practice, but Dorothy could tell that his mind was straying, as though the tension in the house had wormed its way through the stout door and walls of the room and sat whispering on his pillow. She was not surprised when he glanced up at her, hesitated. and said, 'No – news?'

Though she had expected the question, it was hard to answer calmly.

'Nothing yet. We must hope for the best, my lord.'

'Won't let me have newspaper. Why not?'

'You shall have one when you are better able to read. And there is really nothing of interest reported just now.'

When the rubber was over (she let him win) he leaned back and practised his hesitating speech by talking to her of King James and the Court, and of Charles as a child, a bright affectionate little boy full of energy, not allowed to jump or make a noise too near the delicate neurotic mother whom he adored. He and Prince Henry had played so pleasantly together, the younger boy always looking up to the elder one. It was a sad thing that the Queen's disapproval of Charles's Protestant tutor caused so much trouble between herself and the King, and there was the quarrel over Lady Hay . . . poor boys, they knew not what it was to have a fond mother and father living in amity. Amazing they had both grown up of a sweet disposition, particularly Charles, on whom everyone doted, yet he never became spoiled and wilful . . .

Oh, stop, stop, Dorothy cried in her heart. How I would have loved to hear all this once, before today. 'I was not easy, neither had I any rest; yet the trouble came,' said the Scriptures. Days and days to wait until the trial.

12

The courtroom of the Town Hall, St Margaret's Hill, Southwark, was painfully small for the number of people crushed into it. On a dais at one end of the room sat Lord Chief Justice Willes, flanked by Mr Justice Abney and Mr Justice Foster, robed and bewigged, under a carved canopy painted with the Royal Arms, the Sword of Justice suspended point upwards above the judge's head. Below them were ranged the counsel, Mr Attorney-General, Mr Solicitor-General, and Mr Yorke for the King, the less awesome figures of Mr Serjeant Wynne, Mr Clayton and Mr Parrot for the prisoners. A row of witnesses sat below, and in the body of the hall the Grand Jury of twenty-three knights and gentlemen of London, trying to see over the mitred hats of a ring of armed guards round the cluster of prisoners in the dock which faced the judge. The general public disposed itself along the sides of the hall and in the gallery, where Dorothy and Meliora were crammed into the front row between a huge woman eating oranges and a toothless old man who occupied any interludes of boredom by pinching Meliora's thigh.

Through the tall, dirty windows the summer sun streamed in, adding to the body-heat given off by the crowd. Everybody seemed to be in a sweat; and the poor prisoners were noticeably unwashed. Flies and bluebottles crawled up and down the windows, occasionally sallying into the hall to be brushed away or squashed. Dorothy kept her smelling-salts in her hand, sniffing them so often that the sharp aroma ceased to revive her. Meliora had brought a lavender sachet, thoughtfully made by Mrs Mercy, to cover her mouth and nose. She was back in the Nightmare that had begun at Jamestown; Dorothy in a Nightmare that was only just beginning.

The man in the dock, young and fresh-faced, in plain clothes, was James Dawson, a captain in the Manchester Regiment. He answered questions in a soft voice with a slight Lancashire accent; he had been a rich young man at Cambridge when a sudden fear of his father's finding out about his debts had driven him to join the rebel army. He was followed by Thomas Deacon, son of an eminent Manchester doctor, and the sturdy, upstanding John Berwick, a linen-draper. There was very little to be said for them, it appeared – and everything to be said against them, by the King's Evidence witnesses. A man named Samuel Maddox, on being called and sworn, denounced Deacon.

'You saw the prisoner at Manchester?' asked counsel.

'Yes, your honour. I saw him sit at a table in the Bull's Head, and take down the names of such as enlisted in the Pretender's service, and gave a shilling to each. And when he was not so writing, he employed himself in making blue and white ribbons into favours, which he gave to the men who enlisted.'

'Thank you. You may stand down. Prisoners at the bar, do you offer any defence to the charges made against you?'

Dawson, Deacon and Berwick exchanged glances. None of them had anything to say. They had been seen to be with the Prince, taking an active part in the affairs of the army. That was enough, they knew. Stoically they allowed themselves to be jostled out by the guards, and it was seen and heard that they wore leg-irons. Dorothy felt her eyes fill as they vanished through the door behind the dock. On the opposite side of the hall, in the spectators' ranks, a young woman was weeping hysterically, being comforted by an older woman. Dorothy's neighbour dug her in the ribs.

' 'Is sweet'art, that is. Young Jemmy Dawson's sweet'art. Come all the way from Manchester to see the hend of 'im, pore young thing.'

There was only one man left in the dock. 'Do you suppose they won't bring Mr Beaumont on today?' Dorothy whispered to Meliora.

'They said he was to be tried with the Manchesters,' the maid whispered back. 'Captain Towneley and the others have already been in the dock.'

Dorothy sighed. 'Oh God, this is interminable. Three days of trials, and still . . .'

The remaining prisoner was being questioned. He was John

Hunter, an ensign. None of the King's Evidence witnesses knew anything about him, surprisingly, for their knowledge of all the other prisoners had been extensive, helped out lavishly by their imagination. A Captain Vere spoke up for him.

'To my knowledge, your honour, the prisoner ran eleven miles in order to escape from the rebels, but was overtaken and made to return.'

Mr Serjeant Wynne brightened up. He was a man of merciful inclinations, and in any case it was not good for the Crown's image for every prisoner to be found guilty.

'Have you any evidence to give us of this?' he asked Vere, who had been prepared for the question. It gave him a chance to put in a good word for himself.

'Why, yes indeed, your honour. I myself was also caught, and the prisoner and I tied together with a rope to a horse's tail, and obliged to run many miles without shoes, in great torment.'

The counsel conferred in mutters for a moment, then requested that the jury deliberate without leaving the courtroom, if possible. They did so, and the foreman rose to declare their verdict.

'Not guilty, m'lud.'

A ripple ran round the court, the guards, the spectators: was it relief or disappointment? The King's Evidence witnesses were filing out, John Hunter was having his irons struck off; he could walk out into the sunlight a free man. Dorothy saw the judge look at the clock, and wipe his perspiring brow. He was going to dismiss the court, she knew.

But as the door was opened to let out Hunter, two guards appeared from the street, escorting another prisoner. She clutched Meliora's arm. It was Lyndon.

He looked shabbier than when she had seen him last, and she noticed that he had several days' growth of beard. He stalked up into the dock looking neither to right nor left, but straight at the judge, who was now yawning.

'You are Lyndon James Ellslie Beaumont of Grosvenor Square in the County of Middlesex and Richmond in the County of Surrey?'

148

Listening to his curt reply, and the questions that followed, Dorothy's attention was distracted by the appearance of a man being ushered into the witnesses' stand. He seemed to be the only one. Evidently the rogues who had spoken against the other prisoners knew nothing against Lyndon. Her heart began to rise, until the man turned, and was summoned.

'Call Nicholas Crowley.'

Master and ex-valet stared across the courtroom at each other. Dorothy, her senses numbed by shock, heard counsel telling the judge that the man was a prisoner who had been in Newgate under sentence of death for stealing, until his offer to turn King's Evidence against the Jacobites procured his release.

'Being apprehended by an Edinburgh shopkeeper, m'lud, and turned over to the Watch, he was proved to have on his person a piece of silver plate engraved with a blazon. This he claimed was given by his late master, who had turned him off wrongfully, and said that his master's name was Mr Lyndon Beaumont, son of the disaffected Lord Gainsford, now in exile.'

For the judge's inspection an usher produced the mate to the silver goblet Dorothy had seen in the Prince's hand at Holyrood.

'Prisoner at the bar,' said Mr Solicitor-General, 'do you recognise the object?'

Lyndon's face was stony. 'I do.'

'Are the arms thereon engraved those of your family?'

'They are.'

'Did you give the same to the witness?'

'No. It was stolen by him at some time. He left my service of his own will, with a number of stolen articles.'

'I see. Witness, what have you to say further?'

Nicholas swallowed. 'Please your worship, I was indeed turned off without notice, and the cup was given me from the collection of silver my master gave for the Pretender's coffers. He no longer wanted my services because he had 'listed in the rebel army. He was often at the Pretender's court and in his company, and I see him ride away with the lifeguards.'

The counsel conferred, and Mr Parrot rose.

'I would wish to proffer, m'lud, that the witness's evidence is biased against his master, and that as he is a man of no character. I think his word untrustworthy. Also, the testimony of one witness is not sufficient for an indictment.'

As he sat down Mr Yorke bounced up like the other end of a seasaw.

'M'lud, I can produce evidence from the prisoner's gaoler that other rebel prisoners appeared to recognise him when he was thrown into confinement.'

'Yes, yes.' Lord Chief Justice Willes was irritable, his attention being taken from the cup of small ale which had just been brought to him. 'I think we have enough. Obviously he . . .' There was some whispering.

'Prisoner at the bar, do you plead guilty or not guilty to the charge of bearing arms against our Sovereign Lord the King in unlawful rebellion?'

The courtroom was very still as Lyndon spoke.

'I plead guilty.'

Dorothy covered her face with her hands. It was unbearable to look at him, or at the jury whom she could hear talking together. It was only a few moments before she heard the foreman saying, 'We see no necessity to retire, m'lud. We find the prisoner guilty.'

The judge nodded. His wig was beginning to slip sideways from the excess of perspiration rising from his head. 'The prisoner will appear before us with the rest of the rebel convicts on the, er, the twenty-second instant, to receive sentence. The court is dismissed.'

Dorothy had no recollection of reaching the street. She was conscious of leaning against a hot wall, smelling the riverside smells of tar and rotting boats, and the land smells of beer and dust and unwashed people. Meliora was speaking to her.

'No use to stay here, madam. We must go back to the inn.'

Seeing that her mistress was not taking in her words, she took her arm and began to guide her back to the tavern where Leach awaited them with the coach. People were staring at them and their fine clothes; there were a few jeers and insults. But Dorothy was not aware of them.

'He never looked for me, Meliora. He never once looked round for me, though he knew I would be there.'

She was in court again on 22 June, when the officers of the Manchester Regiment, and one officer of the life-guards, were herded together in the dock to hear sentence against them. This time Lord Chief Justice Lee presided, a hard man by reputation, hard of feature and voice. Dirty, bedraggled, silent, they stood to hear him.

'The crime you stand convicted of,' he told them, 'is the most atrocious that mankind can commit. So greatly have you offended the Government by which you are protected that you can expect no protection of clemency from that Government, which you have endeavoured to subvert and overturn. You have murdered many of His Majesty's liege subjects, who lately stood up in defence of their lawful sovereign and the laws and constitution of their country, whose blood cries, I say *cries*, for vengeance against you. I exhort you most solemnly to repent your crimes in this world, for if you do not so, you must inevitably be doomed to everlasting torments in the next. I now pronounce the sentence of the court. The following persons are attainted of High Treason, in levying war against our Sovereign Lord the King, within this realm, viz. Alexander Abernethy, James Gadd . . .' The list of names seemed interminable, with its tedious alternative spellings of names which had been taken down wrongly. Lyndon's was among them. Then came the sentence.

'Let the several prisoners above named return to the gaol of the county of Surrey, from whence they came; and from whence they must be drawn to the place of execution; and when they are come there, they must be severally hanged by the neck; but not till they be dead, for they must be cut down alive. Then their bowels must be taken out, and burnt before their faces; then their heads must be severed from their bodies and their bodies severally divided into four quarters; and these must be at the King's disposal.'

The terrible sentence was no news to anyone. It had been the standard punishment for High Treason for centuries. Yet to hear it was a shock, even to those who would not be affected. Some spectators cried out, and a few women fainted. Among the huddled prisoners many faces were pale and sweating with fear, and young Jemmy Dawson was seen to turn his face against Francis Towneley's shoulder. The thin sunlight washed over them, full of dancing motes of dust which gave them a cloudy unreal look, as though they were ghosts already.

'I have a week,' Dorothy said when they were back at Dove House in the afternoon. 'The clerk of the court said that the first executions would certainly be within a week, to make gaol-space for more. So you see I must act soon.'

Mrs Mercy poured cordial into the teacup which her young lady held with a shaking hand. It was dreadful to see her in such distress, and there seemed more to it than met the eye. In her fifty years of life Mrs Mercy had acquired a useful knowledge of human nature, and her powers of perception had informed her that the marriage of Mr Lyndon and Mrs Dorothy was not the most rapturously romantical one she had ever seen, though they were pleasant enough together, to be sure. It seemed a trifle odd that she should take on so very much, in the circumstances. As to little Meliora, any fool could see that she was near out of her wits with the whole shocking business, good though she had been in accompanying madam to that godforsaken trial and sentencing.

Meliora herself could not have described the tortures she had endured. Her senses were so sharply and finely attuned to receive impressions from the minds of others that she had sat wedged in that crowded gallery with her mind bombarded by violent sensations: from the prisoners, fear, anxiety, regret, anger, every sort of feeling; and from the justices a callous disregard of human life and compassion. She had seen, somewhere, a picture of Saint Sebastian tied to a stake and agonised with the piercing of many arrows. It was so with her. Sharpest and nearest were the arrows of Dorothy's divided loves and self-mutilating remorse. She had tried hard not to 'see', even without the aid of the scrying-bowl, the punishment waiting for the prisoners, but it had intruded itself on her inward eye in all its full ghastliness.

She sipped from the cup Mrs Mercy offered, quietly bade good night, and slipped away. Dorothy, intent, did not see her go.

'And how will you act, madam?' the housekeeper asked.

'On Sunday,' Dorothy said. 'It will be Sunday in two days.'

White Lodge stood on the East Sheen road, concealed from the world at the end of a drive flanked with trees. It was easy for an agile person to slip through the gates and hide in the bushes at the side of the columns that formed the Lodge's ground-floor entrance. From the roof a flag flew: King George was coming.

As he stepped goutily from his carriage a figure all in black rushed out in front of him. Guards darted to intercept any danger to His Majesty, but drew back as they saw it was only a female, unarmed, on her knees at His Majesty's chubby legs.

'Get up, get up! Vat is it?' he cried testily. It had been a long dusty drive from London and he wanted his dinner.

'For pity's sake, Your Majesty! She handed him a scroll of paper. 'A wife pleads to you for her husband, condemned to a felon's death.'

He squinted short-sightedly at the paper, then threw it to the lord-in-waiting behind him.

'Vat has your husband done?' He threw up a hand as she began to speak. 'No, no, don't vex me with it; he is von of these damned Papistical rebels. I am sick and tired, I tell you, of the matter. We have 'em and that's an end on't.'

The hood had fallen back from Dorothy's face.

'Mr Lyndon Beaumont is my husband, Your Majesty, the son of a peer of the realm, condemned to die by the hangman's hand on false evidence. I beg you of your clemency, spare him.'

George II studied the upturned heartshaped face. It did not attract him; he liked his women ugly and preferably German. But he had an excellent memory, which recalled to him another Sunday, many months before. A slow, unlovely smile spread across his countenance.

'Your husband,' he said. 'I remember him vell. The gentleman who would not unbonnet to his King. And you, madam, I remember you. I seem to think you did not curtsey. Oho! And now you are on your knees. So this fine husband of yours is a traitor, is he? Vell, traitors must die, *nicht wahr?*' He turned to his courtiers, who murmured.

'I am sorry. He did not mean to insult you,' she said, lying bravely. 'But if he must die, oh, please, Your Majesty, let it be like a gentleman . . . without the . . . the knife.'

'Is this *gentleman* a prisoner in the Tower?'

'No, sire. He lies in the gaol at Southwark.'

'Vy, then he is no gentleman!' The King laughed heartily. 'I knew of him, and of his father, and both are damned traitors, God knows. He has not even a title, this husband of yours, madam.'

'He is a viscount's son, sire,' she pleaded.

'If he were a viscount himself I might give it thought.' The bolting little blue eyes mocked hers. 'But he is not. So, he dies by the knife. Thus perish all traitors, *hein?*'

His courtiers murmured again. Some of them were a little shocked, but it did not do to appear so. The King strutted on, through the open front door of White Lodge, leaving the black figure kneeling on the ground. Her hair had come out of its combs, and lay about her shoulders. She felt faint and sick, but nobody came to help her to her feet or comfort her.

'I did what I could,' she said to Lyndon in the gaol, on the night before the day appointed for his execution. 'Indeed, indeed, I did. I thought he would . . . even he. But he's a brute beast, I see that now. Oh, Lyndon.'

He patted her shoulder, absent-mindedly. 'There, I'm sure you did your best, but you should not have kneeled to that pig. I hope nobody ever hears of it. Doll, for God's sake cheer up, for *I* am not uncheerful. We can die but once, and life is uncertain enough at the best. Don't you see, I am glad rather than sorry that I can speak out at last for my King and the Cause? It's not good for a man to have to keep silence and pretend something he don't feel. Now I shall be remembered for loyalty. What could be better than that?'

'Aye, true enough,' said John Berwick, the sturdy linen-draper, who had strolled over from the corner of the room where he had been tactfully meditating. 'Tha should be proud o' thi mon, lass. He's noan afeared, art tha, Lyn? We none of us are, come to that. I declare, death don't shock me in the least; there's a merciful God above.'

Young Dawson was quietly weeping, his head on the table. His father had just left, almost insensible with grief.

'Come now, Jemmy,' said Berwick. 'Don't shame us, lad.'

'Is there anything I can *do*?' asked Dorothy desperately. 'Any – oh, how should I know? Any drink or drug, that will help . . .'

'There's one thing,' Lyndon said. 'Have you any money about you?'

She drew out her purse, and counted ten guineas into his hand.

'That'll do,' he said, and she thought she saw relief cross his face. 'With that we need fear nothing, lads.' Berwick nodded, smiling. Dorothy looked from one to the other.

'The hangman, lass,' said Berwick gently. 'He's got his price for a quick despatch.'

The gaoler was ringing a bell for all visitors to leave. She clung silently to Lyndon, who tilted up her face and gave her a swift kiss.

'There, go on, my dear. It was a good match between us, but there'll be a better for you, I'll warrant. As for me, I'm as happy as ever I was, believe me.'

As she went out of the door, her handkerchief stifling her sobs, she heard him call after her.

'By the way, that young surgeon who was so sweet on you – what'shisname? I saw him get away at Culloden.'

'But I promised him,' Dorothy said, over and over again. 'I promised him I would be there.'

Mrs Mercy raised her eyebrows. 'And how did he take that, madam?'

'He said I must not, of course. He said he would not see me, for I would be lost in the crowds, and it . . . it would be better for me if I did not see him. But I must be there, for I promised. It's the very last thing I can do for him.'

'But to be at Kennington Common by nine o'clock in the morning. How can you think of it, madam? Besides, there's Leach's feelings to consider. He was very fond of Mr Lyndon, and he's had to drive you there and back many times lately when I dare say he would rather not have had to do so. How can you force him to see such a sight? And Meliora, she will have to go. Look at her. Poor girl, she's far from well.' Meliora was huddled by the side of the small fire, wrapped in a heavy shawl though the night was warm, a cat on her knee for comfort. Her face was grey and monkey-like with suffering.

'Well, then, I'll take Alice, or Dorcas, or Sarah, or anybody. And one of the stable-lads can drive, I suppose. But I must be there. Will you have me called at seven? And I'll take my caudle in bed tonight. Don't trouble to come up, Meliora, for I can undress myself.'

She lay on the bed she had shared with Lyndon, motionless, staring out at the velvet-blue night sky spangled with stars. It had been a star which had begun the tragedy that would end tomorrow. The star of the Stuarts, hanging bright over Rome on a winter night twenty-five years ago, had lured Lyndon to death and herself to dishonour; for what was it less than dishonour to love a man, even a prince, more than the husband to whom God had joined her? She had betrayed Lyndon in her heart, and for that she must endure with him to the end.

Downstairs Mrs Mercy was busy. In the still-room, by candle-light, she was blending powdered herbs with something from a small opal-white bottle. The mixture being to her satisfaction, she returned to the servants' hall and filled two cups with the steaming caudle of milk and arrowroot which Dorothy liked to drink as a nightcap. Having done so, she paused, surveying them and then the contents of the mixing-bowl. Somewhere in the house a door slammed – Alice coming home from a neighbour's. And the bell connected with his lordship's bedroom began to jangle.

'Come, better do it than wish it done,' she said to herself, and tipped the draught into the two cups, half to each. 'May I be forgiven.' One cup she set down by the side of the dozing Meliora, the other she bore upstairs to her mistress's bedroom.

A thrush was singing triumphantly outside the bedroom window when Dorothy awoke, throwing limpid notes into the air in competition with one of the gardeners who was whistling raucously as he went about his work. She felt as though she were climbing out of a deep pit of unconsciousness, dreamless, without memory. Her mouth was very dry and her head ached. With a sudden lurch of the heart she remembered what was to happen that day. She got out of bed, dizzy, and walked over to the mantelpiece. Of late she had found herself growing slightly short-sighted, unable to see the clock from some paces distant.

The hands pointed to half-past eleven.

Minutes later Mrs Mercy, her hands clasped decorously on her apron, stood in front of her furious mistress, who was still in a bed-gown with her hair about her shoulders, and listened to a tirade.

'How *dare* you! I ought to dismiss you at once. You had no right whatever to take matters of life and death into your own hands. I gave an order that I should be called, and you chose to ignore it. Not to speak of giving me and my maid what may have been a dangerous draught, for all I know. Do you realise what you've done?'

As she paused for breath, the housekeeper said calmly, 'Yes, I do realise, madam. I've saved you from something so bad you'd never forget it, did you live to ninety.'

'It was for me to choose.'

'We don't always know what's best for us, madam. As for poor Mr Lyndon, well, it's one thing to be faithful unto death by a decent bedside, but quite another when it comes to such cruel wickedness as this morning's work. I think it would have killed your poor Indian, that feels things so much.' Her placid face was reddening. 'And if you think Anne Mercy would go about to poison anybody, least of all the lady of the house, then little you know her. What I gave you was my own receipt for a sound and a deep sleep that will bridge night and day, and *such* you must own you had.'

Dorothy was beginning to feel repentant under the impact of more words than she had ever heard Mrs Mercy speak before. To feel, also, a growing relief that she had been spared a terrible ordeal which might well have been all for nothing. Lyndon had not looked for her in the courtroom; he would not have looked for her on Kennington Common. She was confirmed in her relief, and Mrs Mercy's action was vindicated when they read in the *Intelligencer* that young Jemmy Dawson's betrothed, the girl who had wept so at the trial, had died suddenly after witnessing his execution against all the advice of her friends – ' 'tis said, of a broken heart', observed the writer.

'Of a seizure from shock, more like,' said Mrs Mercy. 'One day you'll thank me, madam.'

Dorothy remained quietly in the house for almost a week after the day of Lyndon's death. Meliora, who had lost weight and seemed listless and sad, was kept in bed, with a supply of study-books. Her bright mind could shake off the weight of others' sorrows only in learning, which she did with astonishing speed. She had found an old Latin primer left over from Lyndon's schoolroom days, which she studied to the bafflement of the other servants. Since her return from travelling they had almost ceased to regard her as one of themselves; more as a lady in an unnatural dark skin. Her manners were so gentle that even Sarah found it hard to gibe at her, as she would have done at a girl like herself. Mr Fowler served her at table without protest, a compliment indeed.

It was astonishing how soon Lyndon's influence faded from the house. Dorothy was still grieved to come across things he had owned, his gloves, his ivory brushes, his cricket-bat, his silver-topped cane. The horror of his death would never be forgotten; but would he not rather have things so? He had said it himself, in Southwark Gaol. *'Un je serverai'* ran the motto of the family. Well, he had served one race faithfully, and had died for it. Dorothy wondered if the Prince would ever know, and hoped he would – if he still lived.

In the streets of Richmond there was a notable avoidance of

members of the Beaumont household. Shopkeepers served Mrs Mercy hurriedly and swiftly, then turned away to serve someone else; servants who had been friendly with Alice and Sarah ran past them with a sly sideways glance. Tradesmen who had played cricket on the Green with Lyndon hardly looked up as they delivered goods to the house. Luke, the odd-job man who had taken Nicholas's place got a stone full in the small of his back on his way home, not long before a brick sailed through a pane of the drawing-room window with a crude sketch of a gallows on it.

Sarah, her pride injured by many slights, tackled Lettice Peasmarsh about it in her own domain, where she was queen of the hanging flitches, spice-boxes, pale cheeses basking under nets, sweet dried fruits from the Orient, cold meats and fishes. It was, Sarah thought, a beautiful shop. Mr Peasmarsh himself might be a no-account little runt, but to own such a shop one would tolerate much. Sarah's own sweetheart, Joe, was only a butcher's boy; she hoped he had a talent for the trade and would rise in it.

As the shop was empty, she struck the bell on the counter. Lettice appeared from the back, a Lettice apparently two inches taller (in fashionable high-heeled shoes), ornately capped and lavishly shawled, the outline of a future Peasmarsh discreetly veiled by the shawl.

She saw who her customer was and snapped, 'What do *you* want?'

'Same as anybody else who comes in. Serving.'

'I can't obleege you. I'm resting, doctor's orders.'

'Oh, come on, Lettice! *You* know what I come for. What's all this turned-up-nose flummery in the town? We got the plague at Dove House?'

Lettice sniffed and shrugged. 'Might as well. Vengeance is mine, saith the Lord, I will repay. *Romans* twelve, sixteen. Traitors don't merit no friends.'

'*Traitors*? You say that of Mr Lyndon to Mrs Mercy and she'd wallop you proper!'

Lettice gave a high artificial laugh.

'I'd like to see her try, indeed. *I* have a husband to protect me. Not like her, or you, or Madam Beaumont.'

Sarah was half round the counter. 'Don't you talk that way of our missis! Oh, you know what's happened, all right, and so do the rest of us now, though to be sure they kep' us in ignorance and rightly so; but whatever our politics and I'm not sayin' what mine are, we stand up for our missis, right or wrong. So just you be civil!'

But Lettice, fearing a physical attack, had retreated into the back room and bolted the door. Sarah was left breathing fire and fury in the shop.

She thought it her duty to report the conversation, haltingly, to Dorothy, who seemed hardly to take it in, her eyes bleary over a desk covered with papers and account-books. Bills, staff wages, stable costs, the small income from lands, medicines for Lord Gainsford and physician's fees, coal, candles . . . there seemed no end to the paper-work, and she was a poor hand at it.

'I see,' she said on hearing Sarah's indignant account of the conversation. 'How very disagreeable. I never liked that Lettice woman. Well, if the tradesmen feel we are plague-stricken traitors, Sarah, there is nothing we can do to change their minds. They depend on the Elec – on royal patronage a great deal, after all. Go down and tell the others not to worry. There is very little anyone can do to injure us.'

She was reading with Meliora on the following morning when a thunderous knock sounded on the door. A moment later Mr Fowler, looking apprehensive, summoned her to the hall, where stood the same officer who had called on her before.

'Yes?' she asked.

He handed her a scroll of paper. 'Please to read this, madam.'

She unrolled it, peering at the clerkly writing with a few words standing out in bold capitals. Her sight was certainly worsening, with all the poring over figures. 'GEORGE II, by the grace of God . . . a writ of seizure of the house, lands, messuages, and so forth . . .' She let the scroll roll itself up again. 'What is all this rigmarole?'

He coughed importantly. 'A notification of the impending seizure by the Crown of your late husband's domain and property, madam.'

'But *why*? He – he is dead now.'

'A traitor's belongings are forfeit to the State, upon the King's pleasure. An execution will be served on you by five of the clock, madam, before which time His Majesty graciously grants you leave to pack up your personal possessions and dispose yourself and your servants under some other roof.'

'If this is a joke, I think it in monstrous bad taste.'

'His Majesty does not make a practice of joking, madam.'

No, she thought, remembering that red ireful face; I warrant he doesn't, the vindictive German pig. She remembered something else: Lyndon's telling her of the impeachment of the Duke of Ormonde in '15, and the annexation of his house, Ormonde Lodge. So it could be done. The soldier was waiting, insolently studying her figure and her face.

A sudden wave of rage swept over her, and she heard herself shouting.

'This is monstrous! I'll not be treated so. Tell your masters they may come and put me out with their own hands, and my servants too, for we'll not budge of our own accord. This house is mine – left to me in my husband's will that he made in prison.'

He smiled thinly. 'Since you talk of prison, madam, perhaps you'll enjoy a taste of it before you're much older.'

'For what crime, pray? I'm not aware of having committed any.'

'No? Then I have to remind you that the man Nicholas Crowley, who gave evidence against your husband, also testified to your presence at the Pretender's court, and to your travelling with the rebel army. Only His Majesty's well-known leniency has preserved you so far.'

She stared at him. There had been no news of the other Jacobite ladies involved in the march. What had happened to them: imprisonment, even execution? Before she could answer, a movement on the stairs caught her eye. She turned to see Lord Gainsford, bed-gowned, his bald head in a turban, wavering at the bend of the staircase, holding the banister with one frail hand. Dorothy ran to him.

'Oh, sir, go back! You should not be out of your room. Come with me, now.'

He waved her away. 'What's – amiss? Heard shouting.'

She turned to the officer. 'This gentleman is an old relative of mine who has been very ill. Please leave me to get him back to bed, and I'll talk to you later, if I must. He will be very distressed if . . .'

'I'm well aware what relative of yours he is, madam. Do you think King George's informants too stupid to know that Lord Gainsford has been in England some time? As I said just now, you have been very mercifully treated.'

The old man had moved down another step, and was struggling to speak.

'Soldier. Brought – news? My son. News of him? Waited – so long.'

The redcoat ignored Dorothy's warning gesture and terrified face. He approached and stared aggressively up at the trembling figure.

'The news of your son, my lord, is that he was hanged, drawn and quartered some weeks since, for the crime of treason. If you doubt me – as it seems you do – you have but to take coach to London, and you'll see his head on Temple Bar, though the family likeness may be a little less striking now.'

For a long moment they looked at each other, the soldier pleased with his own wit and its effect on the old man, whose face had begun to twitch violently. He was trying to speak, breathing in great gasps and puffs, a high flush rising from his neck to his brow. Dorothy had her arms tightly round him, but her strength was unequal to the force of his movement as he pulled himself free and fell forwards, rolling down the stairs to lie like a felled tree on the marble floor, his eyes staring sightlessly at the ceiling, his mouth gaping open.

13

As though to justify the redcoat's boast of his king's clemency, a document bearing the royal arms arrived at Dove House, graciously permitting Mrs Beaumont to remain there until such time as the remains of Lord Gainsford might be decently interred, but no longer. They buried him beneath the stones of the chancel in the same church where – how short a time ago – a memorial service for Lyndon had been held. The Vicar was unsympathetic to Jacobites, dead or alive, but he considered it his Christian duty to bury any who had been proven Protestants. It was, in any case, his last year of the twenty he had spent at Richmond; he had therefore no fear of getting into trouble, but he saw to it that both services were short and simple.

Dorothy was glad of it. As she stood by the graveside with Meliora, Mrs Mercy and Mr Fowler, she reflected bitterly on the aptness of the solemn words to the fate of her father-in-law.

'We brought nothing into this world, and it is certain we can carry nothing out. The Lord gave, and the Lord hath taken away; blessed be the Name of the Lord.

'The days of our age are threescore years and ten; and though men be so strong, that they come to fourscore years, yet is their strength then but labour and sorrow; so soon passeth it away, and we are gone.'

Gone with nothing. Yet there had been titles, honours, courage, the tedium of exile, the hope that ever buoyed him of a Stuart restoration, the knowledge that his son followed him in loyalty. And I, she thought, who remain in the world, what have I to show for my one score years and one? Neither husband, child, house nor possessions, nor money enough to pay my servants, or a place to lay my head. And all for what? Unheeding of the Vicar's drone, her mind went back to the lighted gallery at Holyrood where she had first seen the Prince; then to the little music-pavilion at Lancaster. All for a smile, a kiss, for the love of a pair of handsome eyes and a princely presence. What will these things do for me now?

She was recalled by the thud of earth thrown on to the plain deal coffin. The Vicar was pronouncing the Blessing; it was time to go. As they filed out of the church, she noticed that two other people had stood with them: Colonel Duncombe, their neighbour, and his lawyer son Paul. The Colonel, a genial, military-moustachioed man in his fifties who had lost a leg in the ludicrous War of Jenkins' Ear some seven years earlier, had been a particular friend of Lyndon's, who had overlooked the Colonel's undoubted allegiance to Hanover in order to enjoy the pleasure of his company; there had been almost a father-and-son relationship between them. The dark, serious young man Paul had been too much of a sober-sides for Lyndon; besides he was for much of the time at his chambers in Gray's Inn. Both of them had called on Dorothy to pay their respects since her return from Derby, and she was grateful to them.

The Colonel took her arm as they walked.

'Come back with us, my dear child. My wife is something of an invalid, as you know, and entertains little, but we can find some supper for you. After such a sad occasion . . .'

Dorothy shook her head. 'Thank you, but I have no spirits for eating.'

'A glass of wine or brandy, then, and a chat with Mrs Duncombe. It would do her good to see you, going out so seldom. Come, now.'

There was consolation in the warmth of his arm, and his kind voice. She managed a smile. 'You're very right, sir. One can mope alone too long.'

'Bravely said. And Paul shall escort your maid.' He looked back. 'All's well, he has her in tow already.'

Behind them two black-cloaked figures were linked, Paul several inches taller than Meliora.

His voice was urgent, hers small and remote.

'Won't you reconsider?'

'There is nothing to reconsider.'

'I know your feelings. But I can offer you so much.'

'And I cannot take it.'

He held her close to him. 'All these weeks. Since I first saw you, I knew you were my only . . . oh God, Meliora, I was taught to plead in court, not to make pretty speeches. I'm not wearing my wig and gown; I'm simply a lover begging you . . . there's so little time . . .'

She looked round, and drew him under the shade of a tree. 'The others have gone on; they will not notice. Paul, I esteem it so much that you wish to marry me, but I have told you so many times why it cannot be.' She stopped his mouth as he began to speak. 'I am coloured, Indian and Negro. How could your parents accept such a daughter?'

'I've told you, they are easy, neither snobs nor place-seekers. If I choose you – if they know your superior qualities of mind and body – they would say nothing to us but "Be happy". I *know* my mother and father, Meliora.'

'And so do I, a little, and I still say it would not do. Have you thought of our children – brown children with black fuzzy hair?'

He shook his head. 'I should love them if they were yours.'

'So you say now. So you say now. And then there is my poor mistress. No, say nothing. Soon she is to have no home. The others have places. Mrs Mercy can go to her daughter, Mr Fowler is already bespoken for a house in the town, the others will be placed at the next hiring-fair. But Mrs Beaumont has nobody in the world. I owe her everything, my education, even my life, Paul. And I am clever – oh, I'm not ashamed to boast. I can work, I can help her, I will do anything for her so long as she needs me. Now do you see why I could not marry you, even if . . .' She touched the dark skin of her cheek.

'My father and mother are willing to take her in, I know.'

'On what agreement? As a charity-girl, or a companion, which your mother does not in any case need, whatever your father may say? Do you think she is humble enough to accept that? *I* would not be, and I am nobody.'

'That's not true.'

'Very well, I *would* be nobody if I accepted your offer; a slave still, in new gold chains. I tell you, Paul, the only way I can be free in my spirit is to work out my freedom until my mistress releases me herself. Cannot you see?'

He smiled, painfully. 'Yes. You are a fine logician, my dear. But can I make my last plea, just before we must go in and talk platitudes?' They strolled on, and were near the Duncombes' house, where lights showed in the hall and voices came through the open door. She leaned against him.

'Yes, Paul.'

'Very well. This is no light proposal of mine, Meliora. I've always been a sober sort of fellow, as your mistress's lamented husband used to say. I never had the time or the patience for simpering misses, with their fans and small talk. One or two girls, yes, in London, like all students. But no thought of marriage, until I met with you.'

'A mulatto, in service.'

'A jewel of a girl, good, clever and beautiful. Like a rare bird in a tree of sparrows. I never set eyes on anything like you, nor heard such either. I don't care a fig whether your skin is black or brown or yellow – it might be of tartan, like the unfortunate Highlanders' kilts, for all I care.'

She giggled. 'That might be very striking. I must see what the cosmetic art can do for me.'

'Don't make a joke of it!'

'Forgive me. One must laugh sometimes.'

Paul's father appeared at the door, calling his name. She drew the boy into the shadows and caught hold of his cloak with both hands, looking up earnestly into his face.

'Paul, believe me, I treasure your love for me, and I know it to be a true love, for I'm not to be deceived in that way. Will you trust me if I say that I *know* there can be no happiness for us, as our life is now?'

His voice was hardly audible. 'Yes.'

'And will you kiss me now, and say good night to me?'

'Not good bye?'

'No; good night.'

The two shadows merged for a moment under the bare hawthorn tree, before they broke apart, to enter the house separately.

Dorothy firmly refused the Duncombes' repeated offer to give her house-room. It was impossible to make herself dependent on people who kept up a large house on half-pay, and had spent much on the education of their children; Paul, the youngest, had cost them for Eton, Oxford and his legal training. She resolved to take cheap rooms for herself and Meliora, who seemed determined to accompany her wherever she went. As she packed, heavily guarded by the sentry from the front door, it became obvious that she would not leave with anything beyond her personal possessions. Anything heavier than a trinket-box or a mirror was declared to be 'Property o' the Crahn'. Her final plea for a small satin-wood table and a little chair which she had herself embroidered was grudgingly given, on condition that a guinea changed hands, and the proffer of another guinea led to the yielding of some bed-linen and what the sentry considered to be a trumpery set of wine-glasses. His porter-reddened eyes were oblivious to the face engraved on the glasses' sides, the armour and the flowing hair, the Thistle and the Rose. He picked one up in stubby fingers without noticing that the stem contained a bubble full of water, for the drinking of the loyal toast. Dorothy wrapped them in a silk petti-coat and sealed them up in a box.

Even though she knew she could take only a few small things with her, it was a shock when a baggage-waggon rolled up to the door and its driver, helped by a burly lad, began to remove furniture from the drawing-room and to load it on to the cart.

'Where are you taking that?' she demanded. 'I was told everything was to remain in the house.'

The driver spat as he passed her with a wing-chair on his shoulders.

' 'S Majesty's equerry's orders. Goin' to White Lodge.'

To the Elector's own country house. Not only cruel and vindictive, but greedy. She clenched and unclenched her hands, watching one fine piece after another go through the door.

Behind the driver's assistant, carrying a firescreen of silver wrought like a peacock, there appeared the figure of a girl child, aproned and grubby. Seeing Dorothy, she advanced, holding out a letter.

'F'r Missus Bowman.'

Dorothy, recognising this local version of her name, took it. The writing was shaky and sprawling, the seal that of her Uncle Petworth.

'My good Neice, Hearing as you was fallen on poor times, even though it be your own doing, I can't but offer you a roof over your head for the time being. Your Uncle and me is one in this. Neether of us gets younger and their is sumthing to be said for one's own Blood in the house, lacking prodginy. Wright me at oonce by Betty that you will come and bring with you not more than 1 servant. No more now my Hand bein tired,

Yr affte. Aunt
SYBIL PETWORTH.'

Slowly Dorothy folded the note. She was oddly touched to be remembered, even by relatives who had never shown much family feeling before. And it would be a refuge, a place in which to gather together the threads of her life. She had a little money and one or two treasures which could be sold. If the society of her uncle and aunt became too unpleasant, she would take lodgings as she had planned. Meliora would not like going back, of course . . .

Meliora shivered when Dorothy broke the news to her. Cold with apprehension she went about the house, making sure that nothing was left which they could have taken, conscious of the sentry's eyes on her as he lounged on a chair in the hall with a mug beside him. The rooms echoed, for only Mrs Mercy remained in the kitchen, with some sticks of furniture His Majesty's equerry had presumably rejected. At the drawing-room door Meliora turned and looked back.

Had no time passed at all since she had stood there before they left for Scotland, and had imagined that she saw an empty room, bare walls, curtainless windows; the rose-cheeked cupids on the Venus clock flown, the grate empty of logs?

It was no illusion now.

Dove House stood forlorn in the moonlight, between its two inhabited neighbours. Behind the dark windows of the despoiled rooms only ghosts moved. The long-dead Viscountess, Lyndon's mother; the newly dead Viscount. Lyndon, an uneasy spirit arisen from a savagely mutilated body, seeking the possessions he had loved; the engraved silver which had helped to betray him, the glasses engraved with the image of the White Rose prince. The smothered child in the remote attic, still scrabbling with phantom baby fingers at the chest-lid that held it down.

Or so, at least, passers-by would say. It had brought no luck to anyone, they said; that was why the King was in no hurry to put one of his courtiers in it. This was what came of treason and Popish plot. Let it be a warning to all.

It took Dorothy less than the space of her first evening at the Petworths' to realise what lay behind her aunt's apparently compassionate invitation. She was shocked to see the change in Sybil Petworth. The cruel winter of 1745 had brought an onset of arthritis, crippling her hands and feet so that she could only move from her chair with assistance. Her face was seamed with lines of pain, and was no longer rouged, though the blonde wig still sat incongruously above it. She met Dorothy's shocked look with a grimace.

'And if I *am* sorely changed, niece, there's no call to gape at me like a hooked fish.'

'I beg your pardon, Aunt. I am very sorry to see you so.'

'No thanks to you she an't worse,' broke in Ozias Petworth from his chair on the other side of the fireplace, one gouty leg up on a stool and a bottle of port beside him. ' 'Tis well known that disgrace and shame in the family increases the humours in the blood and bring on disease. I hope you're content with what you've wrought.'

Dorothy opened her mouth to argue, then shut it again. Whoever had suffered by her actions, it was not Uncle Petworth, who, despite his swollen leg, was more rubicund than ever. 'Dadblast me,' he went on, 'if ever woman suffered as your aunt has since you went trolloping off with that pack of swinish rebels.'

'Aye,' said his wife, 'not a minute free of pain do I enjoy, night or day, and no more use to me limbs than a swaddled baby. The sooner they carry me off to the graveyard the better for all.' She sighed gustily, and her husband leaned forward and patted her twisted hand with unusual solicitousness.

'We've tried all remedies: vomits, purges and sweats, Dr Ward's pills and potions, mint-water and blisters a-many.'

Mrs Petworth chimed in, a doleful counterpoint. 'Every night I must take Daffy's Elixir at full strength or I get not a wink of sleep, nor your uncle neither.'

'Why not try a season at Bath?' Dorothy suggested. 'I believe the hot springs are wonderfully restorative to persons with rheumatic limbs, and the city very pleasant. They say the company is elegant, and the diversions most varied under the care of Mr Nash. Even so late in the year I'm sure you would profit . . .'

He snorted. 'And what sort of money d'ye think my pockets hold, wench, to go jauncing off to Bath, paying out here and paying out there for what after all may do my poor Syb not a ha'porth of good? Bath's for folk with plenty of the chinks, let me tell you, not for a man in low water, for all his scrimping and saving.'

'Nay, not saving, Mr Petworth,' put in his wife rather quickly, 'for hasn't it all gone on keeping up this house and a pack of lazy idle servants, eating their heads off and giving our goods away to their friends, as well I know they have?'

'True, wife, true.' He fixed Dorothy with a challenging glare. 'Not a penny to bless ourselves with, and only that slut of a Betty to look after us in our old age, besides a lad to scamble and carry coals.' His popping eyes wandered to Dorothy's companion, standing cloaked and silent by the door. 'Who's that ye've got with ye?'

Meliora put the hood back from her face and met his stare calmly.

'By the Lord, it's the black bitch!'

'Uncle! I won't hear you speak so!'

'Eh, eh, eh? I'll speak as I like in me own house, damme, and I'll have that besom of a nigra out of it this minute, blast my liver if I don't!'

He pulled violently at the bell-cord which hung by the fireplace, but his wife shook her head and tut-tutted.

'Nay, not so hasty, Mr Petworth. I told Dorothy she might bring a servant, and the wench seems much improved since we took pity on her. Might she not serve usefully in our household, since we're so hard put to it?'

'Aunt,' Dorothy said. 'Meliora is my personal maid, and my friend, and is not used to rough tasks. I hope you don't expect her to turn her hand to anything menial, for it would not do at all.'

'And I hope *you* don't expect to live the life of a lady, my girl, after the ruin you've brought upon yourself! Personal maid, hoity-toity, we'll have no personal maids here, poor as we are, nor no airs and graces and fal-lals neither. A roof over your head you was promised, and that you shall have, in return for some care of us which I hope you're sensible you owe the only kith and kin you've left in the world. Little enough to ask, en't it?'

'Little enough, by God,' Uncle Petworth echoed. A sly look passed between him and his wife as they waited for their niece's answer. At last she spoke.

'I will help you all I can, Aunt. As for Meliora, I depend on you to treat her well.'

In the dark, stuffy chamber they had allotted her, lit by only two candles and the glow of a few ashes in the grate, Dorothy undressed with Meliora's help.

'They mean to make slaves of us. I won't stand for it. Oh, I'm sorry enough for Aunt, who would not be? But I sense a kind of conspiracy to punish me – us – for what happened.'

Meliora slipped a nightgown over her head and, sitting her upon the dressing-stool, began to brush her hair with long smooth strokes.

'You took a cup of wine with them tonight, and it has inflamed you. You were right to say you would help them. I too. They are old and she is sick. There is nothing else we can do.'

'Colonel Duncombe offered. I would like to go back to him. Or there are lodgings. Mrs Mercy told me of a place at Kew. We could walk there tonight. Or we could go to Dilys Watkins in London, who was at school with me. We could take coach there and ask her for a lodging until . . .' She faltered.

'Until what, madam? London is a great cold place, and you are under a shadow. Let us stay and make the best of it. For me, if they put tasks on me I shall not mind.'

It became increasingly clear that they had only been invited to perform tasks. Meliora found herself relegated to the dirty, beetle-ridden kitchen, helped only by the runny-nosed Betty and the half-witted boy Jack to prepare meals from scraps: knuckle-bones and poor cuts of bacon, thin sour ale and potatoes with eyes in them. It was not in her to give orders, but she was forced to tell Jack outright that he must deal with the heavy work of the house. Betty, who lived out with her family in Friars' Stile Lane, took orders obediently enough but with total lack of imagination, so that money was wasted on shopping and the household. A small line of worry appeared on Meliora's brow, and she grew thin through under-nourishment.

Dorothy had pushed her own sorrows into the background in order to live life as she found it, and a dreary discovery the finding proved. Uncle Petworth, despite his declared poverty, mysteriously disappeared up to London on 'business' for several days in the week, leaving Dorothy the entire care of her aunt. Not only were there medicines to administer, but she had the work of a nurse to perform. Aunt would only permit the sponging of her hands and face for cleansing operations, leaving the rest of her person malodorous. In her bedroom Dorothy had to half carry her to the close-stool, and to deal with the results; while downstairs she found herself expected to serve Aunt's bodily needs with the jeremiah kept in the sideboard. Her stomach turned and her soul sickened at these duties, feeling them to be at least partly activated by malice. Yet she felt that in some way she expiated by doing so whatever wrong she had done to Lyndon.

On the right side of Richmond Hill, within pleasant grounds, were the waters of Richmond Wells, found some sixty years earlier. They were chiefly noted as a place of assignation, raffling and gaming, but the tide of magnesium sulphate still flowed, and Dorothy braved the ogling and pinching of the beaux who came to play quadrille, ombre, whist and wench-sampling in order to bear bottles of the water back to her aunt.

'I suppose one of them might take me up,' she reflected, 'and make me more comfortable than I am, but how then should I settle with my conscience? Uncle must be poor or they would not live so, and

Aunt is pitifully crippled. Perhaps I was meant to have one bright time in my life, which is gone, and now I must be nothing.'

Every night she counted the few guineas in her store, and the handful of jewels she had kept: the price of freedom. But it was winter now. News had come of more executions, Scottish lords and noblemen, Sir Archibald Primrose of Dunipace among them. So Lady Primrose had lost her cousin-in-law. At times the impulse had come to Dorothy to go to that good-natured lady and ask for shelter, but now grief stood between them.

It was not as though gratitude rewarded her, for Aunt Petworth grew steadily more cantankerous. Dorothy seemed to be able to do nothing right for her. It was hard to read aloud hour after hour by the light of one candle, without her sight blurring and her voice hoarsening, and then the cry was, 'What ails the creature? I was told she was learned. How has my poor brother brought her up, to stumble so over the words? God a' mercy, I might as well have Betty upstairs to read out of a hornbook.' Sometimes, with Aunt's not inconsiderable weight leaning fully on her, she would lose balance, and was berated for it as a clumsy fool. The only refuge was her bed, where she would lie dog-tired, hungry and heart-weary. There was no use in going about Richmond, to see her old home or the people who once bowed or curtsied to her. The swans on the river were free spirits compared to her, and the children who played and fished by Thames' edge, and the drinkers lurching away from the Star and Garter. She began to feel the blackness of melancholia stealing over her.

Meliora saw it, and sorrowed for it. There was little she could do for her loved mistress – and for herself nothing. When she looked in the mirror she saw the coming shadow of an old woman of her race, gaunt-faced, grey and toothless. She dared not practice her faculty of seeing, for fear of what might be revealed. Only, one night, Dorothy turned to her with a wild look.

'Meliora, *see* him for me. There's no news and I fear he may be dead. Give me that comfort at least.'

Meliora's face said, 'Must I?' but she had no heart to refuse. She filled a cup from the pitcher that stood on Dorothy's dressing-chest.

'I see mist and mountains. A dark cleft, between rocks. A woman.'

'What kind of woman?'

'Short, with brown hair. Not a beauty, but good, virtuous. And – a man. Himself.'

'Oh, yes, yes, hurry. How does he look?'

'In rags. Very thin, unwashed. There is a beard on his chin. He wears the – the – Scots dress. Not breeches, the . . .'

'Kilt. Go on.'

'Now they are in a boat. She is asleep, and he guards her with his cloak. He sings – not in English, I think. There is a storm; the water rises over the boat.' She stopped. 'It has clouded over. I think that was in the past.'

'What now, what now?'

'I can see no more.'

Dorothy clutched her wrist. 'Try, oh do try.'

Meliora shook her head. 'Smoke. A room. The same woman, and another. A meal on the table . . . it has gone. Now there is a ship. The deck of a ship. He is there, looking back at mountains, and the sky is all storm-clouds. His face is very sad . . . not as he used to look. There are sea-birds wheeling in the air, I can almost hear them cry.' Her eyes opened. 'Nothing more.'

'I see. Thank you. So he has escaped.'

'I pray God so, madam.'

They sat so wrapt in reflection that neither heard the door, which had been open a crack, close very softly. Dorothy sighed.

'Perhaps I had better not make you look any more. Will you brush my hair, please?'

Drawing the brush rhythmically through the long strands, Meliora saw that a few flecks of grey had appeared above the temples. Greying, at twenty-two, and a faint line between the brows that had been so smooth.

The room was icy cold, one candle burnt down. In a few minutes there would be the thumping of Mrs Petworth's stick against the ceiling, an indication that they should put out the second candle and go to bed.

.   .   .   .   .

Next morning, at early light, Meliora went quietly down to the kitchen to make the tea which Mrs Petworth had grudgingly allowed Dorothy to have once a day only, because of the expense. Jack was snoring in the wash-house where he slept. A mouse scuttled out of sight as Meliora opened the door, and in a corner a cluster of black-beetles scattered from the food-scrap they had been dissecting. She brewed the tea over the embers which were never allowed to go out (for that was wasteful) and went back upstairs with it. Dorothy lay unmoving, even when the curtains were drawn wide. As Meliora touched her gently she rolled over, to lie on her back, showing a face puffed and tear-stained.

'Madam. It's near rising-time.'

Dorothy's eyelids flickered, and she half raised herself on the pillow.

'No. Still dark.'

'Madam, my dear, it will be seven o'clock soon, and your aunt's bell.'

Dorothy sat up, and scrubbed at her face with her knuckles.

'You must be wrong. It is night.'

She was threshing from side to side, her eyes now wide open, blank and staring. A thin streak of sunlight crossed her face before it was dimmed behind a cloud, but her eyelids did not flutter.

'I tell you it's dark, Meliora. I can see nothing, not even you. Where are you? Is there a candle?'

Meliora took her hand. 'I'm here, madam. Indeed, indeed it is morning. The sun is up – don't you see it?'

She watched, horrified, as Dorothy covered her face with her hands, then slowly took them away.

'God help me,' she said. 'I am blind.'

Book Two

The Darkness

14

A drift of blossom came down from the apple-tree on a little breeze, petals settling like butterflies on Dorothy's face and hair. In the tree a blackbird was singing powerfully its hymn of self-praise: I'm a pretty birdie, I'm a pretty birdie. The knitting-wool in Dorothy's hands was warm from the May sun. She let it fall into her lap, turning her face up to the light. It came through her closed eyelids as a kind of greenness, a brightening of the greyish dark. Her nose would freckle and her cheeks brown from the rays, but that mattered little now that a mirror was useless to her.

From the schoolhouse in the middle of Wylde's Almshouses came the regular chant of twelve childish voices reciting their nine-times table. She smiled, remembering the terrified ignorant slave-girl without a name. Now she was the respected, learned 'Dame' Meliora who, for all her youth and her outlandish complexion, had been considered by the magistrates and governors suitable to teach twelve poor girls of the parish their letters and numbers.

The authorities had, indeed, been uncommonly benevolent in allotting to Dorothy and Meliora one of the almshouses that flanked the school. Founded in the reign of Anne, they were maintained by a charity of two hundred and fifty pounds a year, enough when divided up to keep their occupants housed, clothed in one new dress a year, and fed as adequately as could be expected. Meliora even received a small fee for her teaching, once the parson had sat in on her lessons long enough to be satisfied that she was not imparting sedition or Romanism to the pupils. A suggestion from her that she might teach the rudiments of Latin had been sternly refused. Young women of the poor classes had no need of Latin, and who could tell that it would not be used for Jacobite propaganda? The Young Pretender was said to be still active in France, his father still hopeful in Rome.

Sitting in the courtyard, warmed by the sun, Dorothy was almost happy. The black times of 1746 seemed an age ago, though only four years had passed. It was difficult to remember the shock and fear of waking to blindness, the commotion made by Aunt Petworth, the unexpected, embarrassed sympathy of her uncle.

'Poor gel, poor gel. Know you en't been all you should, but 'tis a hard visitation of Providence.'

He even put his hand in his pocket to the extent of feeing a doctor to examine Dorothy's eyes. It was a wasted expense, for the doctor merely shook his head and murmured of optic obstructions. He prescribed daily blood-letting and the bathing of the patient's eyes in a decoction of boiled earthworms, beer, and the small white flower called eyebright pulped and strained through a muslin bag. After a few applications of this Dorothy asked that it should be discontinued, for it did no good and smelled and felt loathsome.

She knew what awaited her when, a week after she had been stricken, she was summoned to the parlour. Meliora guided her, for she was still lost in a dark world, stumbling and hurting herself, blundering into doors and over furniture. It made her feel helpless, stupid, degraded. In her mind's eye she saw blind beggars in the streets, with white sticks and begging caps, hawking lavender from baskets or offering things of basket-work they had plaited.

The atmosphere in the stuffy parlour was one of strain. Her aunt was sighing noisily, tearing at a loose piece of lace on her fichu. Uncle Petworth was humming an irritable wordless tune, chinking coins in his pocket. It was amazing how sharp the ears became when the eyes were blind.

'Sit down, Niece,' Uncle Petworth hrmphed loudly; she heard him subside into his wing chair, as Meliora steered her into an upright one.

'Ye know how grieved we are at yer misfortune.'

'Yes, Uncle; thank you.'

'Do anything to sustain you, lend a hand. But it can't be, can't be at all.'

'No, no, not at all,' his wife put in.

'Yer Aunt's an invalid, must have constant care. Now, stands to reason a blind party can't do what's to be done for her. I'd engage a nurse for both of ye, if I'd the wherewithal, but it's not to be. Time was when I was a comfortable man, pockets lined, money in the bank, but things are otherwise now. All this muttering against the slave trade, dangblasted Quaker fellers takin' up arms against honest men . . .' Dorothy felt Meliora move, and knew that her uncle's eyes had met a condemnatory look. Hastily he changed the subject.

'Well, as I say, times are hard. It'll be all your Aunt and I can do to keep our heads above water. So to a hospital or some such institution you must go, Niece, I fear, and soon.'

She bent her head. He cleared his throat again.

'If . . . if your nig – er, Meliora needs work, why then she may stay with us and do a hand's turn about the place.' In other words, Dorothy thought, supply you with free service for the rest of her natural life. Meliora spoke up loudly and clearly.

'My place is with my lady, sir, wherever she may be.'

'Oh. Well, suit yourself.' He was floundering, wretched, glancing at his wife for some kind of assistance, which was not forthcoming. She was sunk in a gloomy reverie, seeing herself reproached by the shade of her dead brother for the turning away of his daughter in her need. It would not be the same, with the stupid slut Betty to help her instead of Dorothy. But it was all they could afford, being poor as they were.

'One maid and a footboy, that's all we can keep. So, Niece, the sooner . . .'

'Yes, Uncle. I understand your difficulty. But where must I go?' Rump Hall, she wondered, with the paupers? Some filthy hospital full of people dying of every kind of disease? A madhouse?

'You, er, you haven't a bit put by? A few guineas, something to pawn?' She knew that he was regarding her with his head on one side, a fat thrush in hope of a lingering worm.

'Nothing at all.' In the worst extremity she would not admit to the presence of certain treasures in a padlocked box under her bed.

'Ah, to be sure. Then I fear it must be the workhouse. No other choice.'

'I think there is, sir.' Meliora stepped forward. 'Mrs Beaumont has friends who can surely procure her interest with the authorities.

I will go to them, if you won't, for I can't see my mistress sent to the place you would put her in.' Dorothy knew by her breathing that she was on the verge of breaking out into such a rage as nobody had yet seen in her.

'Hoity-toity! Here's an uppish madam.' Mrs Petworth thumped on the floor with her stick and waved it at Meliora. 'Speak more respectful to your betters, chit, or I'll have you soundly whipped, that I promise you.'

'If you are my betters, ma'am, that's news to me,' said Meliora. 'I am now nobody's slave nor servant neither, only my mistress's companion, and I will do for her as I think best.' She put her hand under Dorothy's elbow and gently raised her from the chair. 'Come, madam.'

As they left the room Ozias Petworth was saying, not without admiration, 'Well, 'pon my soul and body!'

And so it was that, in spite of Dorothy's protests, Meliora went to Colonel Duncombe and told him the situation. In vain he and his wife offered a room and an attendant for Dorothy. She had already impressed on Meliora that she would not impose herself on any private person, particularly a family whose reputation she might damage by being with them. If only the Colonel would use his influence for her to live in some place where she would be a charge to nobody, and yet not humiliated by low surroundings, they would both be eternally grateful.

Colonel Duncombe pulled at his pipe. He had always regarded Meliora as some kind of fantastical creature, a phoenix or a manatee or talking cat, perhaps. Here she stood on his hearth-rug, a grave enough young lady in a neat dark-blue gown and a simple chip-hat hiding most of her hair. But for the hue of her skin, and a certain proud grace which he knew from her history had not come to her by way of dancing-masters and tutors in deportment, she might have been the daughter of any of his friends. He knew that his liberal-minded son Paul admired her; perhaps something more, if he cared to let himself dwell on the matter. But it was neither here nor there now, for she had come to him for help.

'I will speak to Sir William Richardson, the magistrate,' he said, 'and to the Reverend Comer. He's not so set in his ways as our late man. Trust me, miss, I'll be at the utmost pains to help Mrs Beaumont.'

Meliora left him with a confident step. It had been easier because Paul had been away in London. She touched the little cross of rowan-wood that she had made long ago, wearing away now and apt to leave splinters in her fingers. It would bring her luck one day, she knew.

When Dorothy had been resident for two years at Wylde's, her first visitor was announced. His herald was Prudie, Meliora's youngest and most inattentive pupil, whose dislike of learning was such that with all the guile of five years old she snatched at the least opportunity to miss a lesson. It was summer, the schoolroom door open. Through it Prudie came running, red of face, late for class as usual.

'If you please, miss, here's a person asking for Mrs Dorothy, I do believe.' Earnestly she pointed towards the garden-courtyard. 'Shall us show him where she be?'

Meliora sighed at the child's grammar. It was to be hoped Prudie grew up to be a good housewife and mother, for a scholar she would never become.

'Very well. But you must first report to me who the gentleman is, and what he wants.'

Prudie was gone like a swallow, and with the same speed returned.

'If you please, miss, 'tain't no gentleman. 'Tis a great ole giant. And I think he be a beggar, all clarty and his shirt tore.'

The class giggled. Meliora frowned.

'I doubt if Mrs Dorothy can be expecting such a person. Did he give a name?'

Prudie smirked triumphantly. 'Said 'twere Johnson, miss.'

In Meliora's mind a picture formed of a man who had come to Dove House in her early days, an unlikely visitor for her mistress's family, and she had remembered his name. There had been a great deal of excitement after his arrival, and the beginnings of their fateful departure for Scotland.

'Very well, Prudie. But don't linger about chattering, mind.'

183

Dorothy was half asleep on her bed when Prudie burst into the cramped cottage she shared with Meliora. The day was hot, her hands too sticky to knit. Sometimes sleep was an insidious temptation. She hardly took in the child's words, but sat up sharply at the sound of the man's deep, grating voice.

'Who's that?'

' 'Tis I, madam. Sam Johnson, your most humble servant.' The small room was filled with the effluvia of him, a blend of dust, sweat, snuff, stale food and wine. But she smiled in the direction of his voice, pleased to be visited.

'Mr Johnson. I remember you very well. It's kind of you to call on me.'

He choked, and she realised that he was weeping. 'Kind? Oh, ma'am . . .'

'Pray don't be disturbed, sir. Oh, pray don't, or you'll spoil my happiness in seeing you. That is, in having the pleasure of your company.'

He was, she inferred, wiping his eyes and possibly his nose on his wristbands. 'I am a child, a foolish child. But when I recall you last, so fair, so fine, it breaks my heart.'

'Yes, well,' Dorothy said briskly, 'I'm neither fair nor fine now, and as I am quite reconciled to my circumstances, so must my friends be.'

She felt her hand grasped two huge ones. 'Indeed you wrong yourself, ma'am. Your outward and visible surroundings are not fine, 'tis true, but you yourself are as fair as when last I was happy enough to see you. Fairer, I think. "Beauty's ensign yet Is crimson in her lips and in her cheeks" . . . I had feared so much worse.'

What he had feared, she knew, was the look of so many blind people: sunken sockets, or staring white orbs which would have been better hidden behind dark spectacles. At least her eyes were decently veiled by their lids, fringed with the long lashes that lay quietly on her cheeks as though she were dreaming. She was glad of that.

'Let me make you tea,' she said, to lighten the tone of the conversation, and, getting up, she went to put the kettle on the fire which burnt night and day to offset the dampness of the almshouse. He lumbered after her.

'Tea! What a heavenly thing is tea! You could not offer me anything better, ma'am, even an emperor's ransom, but I beg you'll let me have the making of it. How could I allow you to wait on me, even if . . .'

'If I were not blind? But I am perfectly capable of finding my own way about by now, believe me, and it's my pride to do so.'

He said no more, but sat heavily on the one chair, watching her deftly lay out cups and saucers on the table, fetch milk and the sugar-bowl from the corner cupboard, listen, head tilted, for the singing of the kettle.

When the tea was made and set before him she heard him shovel spoonful after spoonful of sugar into his cup and gulp down the resulting draught like a thirsty elephant. When she had refilled his cup four times she asked him demurely to step outside and refill the kettle at the pump in the yard, a request which delighted him as much as a stick tossed to a great amiable dog. Truly Mr Johnson was a menagerie in himself.

'I wonder how you found me, sir,' she said at length, when his thirst seemed to be appeased.

He coughed evasively. 'Why, I . . . the matter came up in conversation. I am at present, and for some time to come, lost in lexicography. That is to say, I am commissioned by a number of eminent booksellers to compile a Dictionary of the English language – now is that not a worthy aim?'

'Most worthy, but I fail to see how it helped you to discover me.'

'Why, how badly I explain myself. I should tell you that in this work, impossible for one man alone, I am aided by a body of clerks, five of whom are Scotsmen. Now, though I confess I am no lover of their speech, I am so great an idler that I cannot resist any opportunity to put my legs under the table and have out my talk. Thus I hear news I might otherwise have missed, and such are the rewards of idleness.'

She decided not to ask him any more about his informant. There was a curious comfort in knowing that somebody from the days of glory and tragedy was aware that she still lived, and how.

'And news of . . . the Young Gentleman? My companion goes to the reading-room for me and copies anything I would wish to know, but there is little in the papers these days.'

'Ah, the Noble Exile! You had heard, of course, that King Louis has been negotiating a peace treaty with England, the Treaty of Aix-la-Chapelle. Now, one article of this infamous document, contravening every promise of good faith made by Louis to our Adventurer, stipulates that no member of the House of Stuart may reside within French territory.'

'But that is treachery – a sentence of banishment. King Louis and King James are allies.'

'Were, madam, were. Now the scene is changed. Nothing loses a man friends like failure, and in Louis's eyes our Prince has failed in his enterprise and is no longer worthy to be helped. Yet, such is his great soul, he behaves as though he knew nothing of this villainous treaty, goes about Paris as though he were a native of it, and has even rented a fine house at the heart of the city.'

'It is like him,' Dorothy said feelingly.

'Had Fortune only been kind enough to allot him the bride he once sued for . . .'

'*Bride?*'

'One of the young daughters of King Louis. Princess Henriette. 'Twas said he drank her health, with the toast of the Black Eye, even in his worst extremity while hiding in Glenmoriston. It would seem the lady is dark and of singular beauty.'

Dorothy sighed. If one princess attracted him there must be others. Mr Johnson took it as a sigh of regret at his news of the treaty, and hastened to change the subject.

'But why do I vex you with this sad gossip? It was of yourself I came to talk to you, madam. Hearing of your fallen fortunes and infirmity, I beg most respectfully that you'll accept the hospitality of my humble household for as long as it shall please you – for all time, if you wish. 'Tis a quiet enough house agreeably near to Fleet Street, where you may have a comfortable room and a servant to wait on you. I am not yet in possession of it, I own, but soon hope to be. You will find a good garden to walk in, and as much society, I dare say, as will please you. Besides, I have a very fine and charming cat – I hope you like cats, ma'am?'

She struggled between laughter and affection for this great, unpredictable man.

'Exceedingly. But Mr Johnson, you must see that I can't possibly accept such a generous offer. What would your wife say?'

He pondered. It really had not occurred to him to wonder what his dearest Tetty would say. She had been sharpish in the past about one or two of his fancies among the female sex, had been known to fall into excessive tears when he had paid a lady some compliment. However, he consoled himself, she was at present recuperating in Hampstead's reviving air from an illness brought on by her fondness for port; no doubt when she returned she would be in the most amiable of humours, and would perfectly understand his purity of motive in presenting her with a female house-guest.

'My dear wife will welcome you, I can promise.'

Dorothy privately doubted it. 'Even so, I could not possibly saddle her and you with such a helpless person as myself. You do understand that I am quite, quite blind, and that the doctors hold out no hope of my recovering my sight?'

'I understand that, too well.'

'Then how can you contemplate such an action?'

She felt the gentlest of touches on her wrist. 'Because I have the utmost compassion for the blind, madam. I am almost so myself, you know. They have warned me that too much indulgence in the printed word may render me totally so, in time. Then we should be good companions for each other.'

Dorothy shook her head. 'It would be impossible. How can I thank you for your great kindness? But it would not do, indeed. I am very well here, besides.'

There was enormous regret, even sorrow, in his voice. 'Then I must be answered. But I wish with all my heart you would give me such happiness, even in prospect. In a year, say?'

'No, sir.'

He seemed to be winding himself up, like a long-case clock, to say something weighty and difficult. At last it came out.

'You will think the worse of me for this. But I must confess to you a thought for which God Almighty will rightly punish me . . . and yet it must be said. My dear wife is many years older than myself, and in rapidly failing health.'

'I remember she was not well, when we entertained you.'

'I have been warned that only with the utmost care can she survive for more than a few years. That care she shall have in every particular so far as I can give it to her, for I will dress her neat, measure out her medicine, pray nightly for her recovery. And yet . . . the time must come when I shall be alone.'

'Mr Johnson . . .'

'No, let me speak. Then I shall be inconsolate indeed, for I adore, idolise your sex . . .' She could not see his helpless, self-baffled look. 'I would never rudely burst the bonds of matrimony, yet . . . the company of a pretty woman is something without which my life is the poorer. I would marry you, Mrs Dorothy, believe me, if my poor dear wife were to die. It may be in very coarse style to come out with it, but indeed it is meant sincerely. I . . . think myself right to say so.'

'I know it.' She spoke with a frankness to match his. 'Some might misunderstand you, but I know your mind. I'm very moved by your offer. But I must still say no.'

A new thought had struck him. 'Your heart is perhaps given already?'

There was a silence, suddenly broken by the outpouring of Meliora's pupils into the courtyard, romping and shouting.

'Yes,' she said. 'Yes, my heart is given.' How foolishly, how hopelessly, you will never know, kind fellow.

'Then I am glad. I envy the man. I shall look to hear that he has raised you from your present condition to a higher one, and made himself a happy man by so doing.' She felt his lips on her hand, and heard him shuffling heavily to the door. He paused there.

'Remember me, Sam Johnson,' he said. 'Farewell.'

Going away from her, up the road between Petersham and Richmond, he recited to himself the lines he had guiltily penned after the second visit he had made to her and Lyndon at Dove House. So fair, so pleasant, so full of good sense. His own, had he been comely enough to deserve her and free to claim her.

> 'Let DOLLY no more my fond bosom possess,
> Nor I in her charms e'er imagine my bliss;
> No more let my eyes on her beauty e'er stray,
> But banish all thoughts of her graces away.
> Since she is so cruel to forbid my repose,
> To damp all my joys, and to heighten my woes.
> But in vain do I strive her charms to forget,
> Her cheerful good humour, and sweet flowing wit.
> She has breath'd in my soul the soft pleasures of love,
> And kindled a flame that no time can remove.'

There was, however, some consolation even in disappointment. Jolting along in the coach to London, he found himself composing with unaccustomed ease the opening stanzas of a poem in imitation of the Tenth Satire of Juvenal. He would call it, 'On the Vanity of Human Wishes'.

15

The worst part of blindness, Dorothy thought, was its boredom. One could not possibly expect even the most faithful of companions to read aloud to one for all of her leisure time. Meliora's own eyes were often sore after her day in the schoolroom, and they could afford few candles. Knitting and crocheting were worthy skills, bringing in a little money, but undoubtedly dull. If only Dorothy had been able to keep the spinet. There would just have been room for it in the cottage, and she could have entertained herself with playing, for she had been taught her Do-Re-Mi at school. Tunes lived on in her head: the shrieking voices of the pipes; gavottes and minuets she and Lyndon had danced to; silly street ballads, hurdy-gurdy tunes, playing themselves over and over, trying to drive her mad.

It would have been quite easy to go mad, if one had been a poor old person instead of a healthy young one. Indeed, when charitable ladies and their families came round to inspect the almshouses and their occupants, they would talk to each other about Dorothy as though she were either an idiot or deaf as well as blind. She found it hard not to fly out at them for their rudeness, as they rustled about in their silk petticoats, filling the air with perfumes of musk, rose-water and eau-de-Cologne.

'An't it a satisfactory thing, Mama, that these poor creatures are so well housed.'

'Indeed, Georgiana, it does the town great credit.'

'And only think what they're saved from!' twittered another voice. 'This young woman, now, is quite well-looking. How shocking to think of how she *might* be earning a livelihood even with such an affliction.'

They all tut-tutted. Then there was a flurry of whispering, and Dorothy heard the words '. . . Jacobite rebel'. A silence fell, before the older lady pronounced coldly, 'It is time we visited the other inmates. Come, gels.'

At one time Dorothy had tried to get the exercise she so much missed, by walking in the paths and lanes nearby, guided by Meliora, learning their twists and turns and individual dangers. But it was too trying a hazard. She knew herself stared at, commented upon. More than once, out on her own, she felt an insulting arm round her waist and heard a coarse invitation. On another day a stone hit her between the shoulder-blades. What hurt even more than the blow was to recognise the voice of the thrower, a child in Meliora's class.

> 'Blindy, Blindy, Blindy,
> Can't look behind ye!'

After that she gave up trying to take walks alone.

'I suppose I shall grow fat,' she said cheerfully to Meliora. 'But they say it makes for contentment. At least I can walk in the gardens.'

Meliora said nothing, tightening her lips. Sometimes she longed to rail against the world and Fate.

Dorothy was most at peace on Sundays, when they were at church. Not the parish church of Richmond, with its memories of Lyndon's memorial service and his father's, but the little cross-shaped church at Petersham. There were Scottish names on tombs here: Dysart, Lauderdale, Bute, Douglas. In the church, it was said, Prince Rupert had married Lady Frances Bard, who bore him a son. Hidden in the high pew, letting the familiar words of the service wash over her, Dorothy liked to fancy that Lyndon was not far away; a hovering, casual spirit, free now as the air. Her closed eyes held an image of him as he had been at Dove House before the rebellion. He was practising strokes with his cricket-bat. He looked up and smiled, and she smiled back. He would know that whatever wrong she had done him in her heart was being fully visited on her, and he would pray for her forgiveness and help.

' "We have erred and strayed from Thy ways like lost sheep; we have followed too much the devices and desires of our own hearts . . ." '

The clergyman's voice chanted on, punctuated by the murmur of the responses. Outside, birds shouted and trilled in the churchyard.

A gust of summer wind blew a branch across the window nearest to their pew, and Dorothy knew how it would look, green leaves suddenly pressing themselves against the clear diamond panes. It was pleasant to be able to visualise such things. How unfortunate were those *born* blind. She began to picture the people who had worshipped in the church: the formidable Elizabeth, Lauderdale's Duchess, who had been a beauty at Charles II's court and whose ghost was said to walk Ham House, nearby. She had been a Murray, some kin to Lord George. And Prince Rupert, of the lovelocks and haughty Stuart features, striding up the aisle with his secret lady on his arm . . .

' "O Lord, save Thy people, and bless Thine heritage. Govern them, and lift them up for ever." '

It was extraordinary how everything seemed to lead back to the same point. She was still in a reverie when the blessing was pronounced. Leaving the church, her arm in Meliora's, she felt her other arm taken in a stronger grip.

'Mistress Beaumont, allow me. I think we walk in the same direction?'

Dutifully the two women greeted Alderman Israel Plumptree. He had shown more interest in their welfare than other gentlemen on the Board of the charity administration. Several times he had called in at their cottage to enquire into their arrangements and comfort. They were grateful for any such concern, but Dorothy had never encouraged the Alderman's visits.

'I suppose it is that blindness sharpens the hearing,' she had said to Meliora, 'because I truly seem to know the person by the voice nowadays, and I don't care at all for that man's voice. What is he like?'

Meliora paused before answering. 'Some persons are hard to describe. Neither short nor tall, neither fat nor thin. Forty or more years old, I guess. I heard he married above his station and sets great store by rank.'

'Indeed. Then it is not my charms, nor yours, my dear, that make him so assiduous. No doubt he's heard that I'm the daughter-in-law of a lord, even though dead and Jacobite. Perhaps he hopes I will get him some introductions into good society. Well, hope is a good breakfast but a bad supper – I trust his wife feeds him well.'

And there their discussion of Israel Plumptree had rested. Looking at him now, as he bent solicitously down to Dorothy (though he had not far to go, being only an inch or two taller), Meliora was pleased to see someone taking pains to be civil to her poor friend. In her prayers Meliora asked for Dorothy to meet either a good, devoted second husband or a man old and kind who would care for her as ward or adopted daughter. Mr Plumptree did not seem to fit into either category. He was unprepossessing, pale-eyed, steel-spectacled and with undistinguished features and bad teeth, noticeable because he showed them so much in frequent ingratiating smiles. These were obviously wasted on Dorothy, but Meliora found that she was being treated to one.

'I han't the pleasure of knowing your name, my dear,' he was saying. 'I've heard the scholars call you Dame Mel, but what else is there to it?'

Meliora replied stiffly. 'My mistress gave me the name of Beaumont, sir, when I joined the family.'

'Indeed? So? Well, well. Quite an elevation for a damsel from – Barbados, may I guess?'

'I am from Jamestown in Virginia.'

Dorothy put in, 'It's quite customary for the family name to be given by way of adoption, when the party concerned has no relatives.'

'Yes, indeed. My wife's nurse was just such a case. She was a Tresham, of course – my wife, I mean. Very highly connected.'

'So one hears,' murmured Dorothy.

Israel Plumptree looked askance at the two women he escorted. He looked with keen interest, for he had only just acquired spectacles, and they had shown him this morning for the first time, when his eyes strayed from his prayer-book, that the two objects of charity were more than worth a second glance. The rebel's widow was a charmer even in her modest dark-green gown, and though her eyes were not to be seen he was prepared to warrant they were handsome ones. There was a quirk to her pretty mouth, too, which suggested that she had a wit to match it.

193

And then the brown girl: well, there was a beauty, a pocket Venus, with those great eyes, the proud little nose and full pink lips. Israel licked his own. It was a pity that neither young woman was of high breeding, for his otherwise unexciting marriage had given him a taste for pedigree. But it would make them all the easier. A compliment here, a gift there, a new gown, a brace of fowls . . . a week of attentions, he reckoned, would bring one of them within his grasp.

Or why not both? They were in no position to be particular. The widow and the schoolma'am in turn, just as the dice fell. What could be more agreeable? Silently he thanked the optician who had made him this pair of spectacles, so heavy on his nose, so ageing to his appearance he had feared. Not so, it seemed. These two young females were conversing with him amiably enough (though to be sure *one* could not see him, and he detected a certain sharpish tone in the other's voice). Jovially he urged Meliora on to his other arm, and proceeded proudly through the homegoing worshippers.

Dorothy heard the whispers. Some of the congregation were their neighbours from adjoining almshouses. Old Mrs Pryce the Welshwoman, who had once kept her own carriage and could have been My Lady, she said, had she accepted several good offers after Pryce had been taken. Miss Anna Semple, a fanatical Whig, who would not speak to Dorothy; in her opinion the creature should have been executed with her traitor of a husband. Poor little mumbling Miss Chalk, who was frightened of Meliora because she had never seen a dark foreign face before and cowered away when they met. The women were sidling along the churchyard path, pausing among the tombs to point and whisper, hissing like geese that the Alderman favoured those two disreputables. It was disgraceful. Sir William Richardson ought to be informed.

Israel Plumptree was also aware of the whispers. Because of them, his siege of Dorothy and Meliora was a slow one, discretion itself. A weekly courtesy call, sometimes not even that, but a gift borne by a servant. So restrained was his wooing that it aroused no suspicion in his prey.

'I believe I misjudged the man, madam,' Meliora said. 'He has a real kindness for you, I believe.'

'And the gifts are more than welcome. 'Tis like the Twelve Days of Christmas. I swear the eggs are from a speckled hen; they have a most particular flavour. And the tea is the best Bohea. How fortunate we are, my dear.'

'I think it admirable in you not to be too proud to take them.'

'Proud? What did pride ever do for a female in my situation? No, I'm glad to be the object of what I'm sure is pure benevolence.'

A few days later the weekly gift was an enormous bunch of roses, bound with ladslove and spikes of lavender. The scent of them filled the tiny room, and Dorothy could almost tell their colours: the heady richness of the deep red rose, the scent of honey from the yellow, the delicate fragrance of the white. It recalled to her the white roses in the silver bowl, on the day Sam Johnson had first brought his wife to Dove House, and Lady Primrose had sung of the Royal Rose.

She pushed the memories back, for the giver of the bouquet had arrived in person with his usual discreet knock. She let him in, and he glanced round with satisfaction. There was no sign of Meliora.

'Our learned young friend is not with you tonight, ma'am?'

'No, she is gone to a neighbour of Sir William's, to teach Latin to her young daughter. Or rather to try to, for I hear the child is not very bright in the head, poor thing.' She hesitated. 'I beg you'll not stay long, sir, for I don't think it wise for me to entertain a gentleman alone.'

'My dear lady, as though I should dream of compromising you! No, I merely called to enquire whether my servant . . . ah, he did deliver the posy, I see.'

'Posy! I never saw . . . I never had a more magnificent bouquet, and I thank you kindly. The perfume is quite ravishing.'

Indeed, she was glad it was, for the Alderman's was not. His breath left much to be desired, nor had his hair-powder been changed for some time. He had drawn up a chair close to hers, with an exaggerated sigh of relief.

'Ah! Monstrous hot outside. I walked from my house to get a breath of air, but there was none to be had, so close and overcast. I believe we shall have thunder later.'

'I hope so. It would clear the atmosphere.' She edged slightly away from him, wondering if she ought to offer him refreshment, in spite of the impropriety of his being there with her alone. He solved the difficulty for her.

'If you have such a thing as a glass of cool wine, ma'am, I'd be mighty grateful for it. The dust . . .' He coughed theatrically.

'Of course. Why, you sent me a fine bottle of claret only last week. Don't you remember?'

He did indeed, having sent it with just such an occasion as the present one in mind. He had also breathed a word in Sir William Richardson's ear, that his neighbour's backward child might benefit from some tutelage from Dame Meliora. Gratified, he watched Dorothy produce the bottle, unopened, from the corner cupboard, and gallantly he opened it for her, with much placing of his hand above hers. She poured two glasses, hoping that he would betake himself to the small table where the bottle stood. But he remained on the chair beside her, only getting up to refill his glass. She refused a second one. His leg was uncomfortably close to her skirts, and she fancied she could feel it pressing against her own. Embarrassed, she began to chat of the weather, of the talk about poor crops this year, of the death of old Mrs Creed in the sixth almshouse. As he responded, the pressure of his knee became quite unmistakable. She edged away, followed by the pursuing knee.

'Sir, you force me to speak. I wish you would not sit so close. It . . . it is very warm.'

'*I* am very warm, Mrs Dorothy. I burn, I smoke, I seethe with admiration – with desire! How could a man remain in the presence of such charms and not be inflamed?' His arm had arrived round her waist, the hand questing upwards towards the swell of her bodice. She tried to tug it loose, but it held her relentlessly.

'Enchanting, cruel creature! Such a pretty play she makes of resisting, but she'll relent, she'll yield to her adorer, she'll see the folly of being coy.'

'Mr Plumptree! Let me go at once!'

He was nibbling her neck and ear, while she tried to turn her face away from the rank breath.

'Israel is my name, lovely nymph, a good name for a man who means you nothing but good. Come now, yield, have pity.'

Dorothy fought with his hands, alternately up her skirts and down her bodice, gasping and panting, her fear and distaste warring with an extraordinary impulse to laugh at the ridiculous situation. Winning the advantage for a moment, she pulled herself away.

'I am very sorry to seem ungrateful, indeed, indeed I am, but I can't accede to what you wish. I have no will to it. Pray do go away and tomorrow it will be as if nothing had happened. Pray do . . .'

Unheeding, he clasped her in an octopus embrace and bore her to the ground, her head striking painfully against the fender and her arm bent under her. Now she was really afraid of his strength and determination. As they struggled, the kettle fell off the hob into the fireplace with a deafening clatter. The noise released something in her, and she screamed at the top of her voice.

Running steps on the path outside, and the door burst open. Meliora took in the scene.

'Madam! Mr Plumptree! what has happened?'

The weight on top of Dorothy lifted. She scrambled up from her awkward position, hearing, as she got to her feet, Meliora's voice railing at the Alderman in high shrill tones quite unlike her usual ones. He stumbled and muttered under the impact of the tirade, recognising the savage in it and fearing bodily attack. Dorothy heard him clattering his way towards the door, followed by his assailant.

'You lay a finger on my mistress and I will see you disgraced. I will see you put out of office, thrown in the street. But by then you will not care about that, because I will have blinded you as she is blinded. I will have cut out your tongue so that you cannot tell vile lies about her. Now, dirty, crawling villain, get out of our house.'

The door slammed, leaving them alone. Dorothy, sitting on the floor with a knob of the fender sticking painfully into the small of her back, began to laugh and then to cry. Meliora, a gentle English young lady again, she said, 'I think it would do us good to have a cup of tea.'

Israel Plumptree picked himself up from the flagstone outside the door. The impact of its slam had sent him reeling to the ground; he was sore, dizzy, and furious. Silently mouthing, he shook his fist at the door with its horseshoe knocker.

Hellion, he said, but to himself. One never knew who might be passing. Termagant, daughter of Satan, spoilsport. Now you shall have no favours from me, and you might have had many. Trollops, paupers, ungrateful whores. Well, we shall see who laughs last.

Old Mrs Pryce, leaning on her ebony stick, drew Miss Chalk under the shade of an ancient fig-tree with a seat built round its trunk.

'What a strange story is this I hear, ma'am, of our neighbours.'

Miss Chalk was slightly deaf. 'Who?'

'Why, the Jack and the Black, look you. It seems there has been bad doings there. Oh, you'd not believe the half, indeed. Spell-bindings, makings of images, fortune-tellings and traffickings with the devil. I always said, now didn't I, there was wickedness in those two. Now it seems 'tis much worse than I supposed, and we are none of us safe in our beds, ma'am.'

Miss Chalk's nutcracker face, enclosed in the yellowing lace frill of her cap, began to twitch with fright as she took in some of these alarming tidings. Nervously she pulled at Mrs Pryce's sleeve, trying to get out words.

'Wha' . . . who . . . t-told . . .'

'Oh, 'tis all round, spoken of everywhere. Now perhaps we shall be rid of these law-defiers, these ill-wishers . . .'

In the handsome library of Doughty House Sir William Richardson impatiently shut the ledger-book on which he had been working, and pushed back his desk-chair. He was annoyed to be interrupted by Israel Plumptree, a man for whom he had no great liking at the best of times and who had come bothering him with a most unlikely story.

'I don't fully understand you, Alderman. Witchcraft? We are living in the eighteenth century, you know. I had not thought you so gullible as to believe kitchenmaids' tales.'

Israel stood his ground. He had not, in any case, been invited to sit down.

'No fable, I do assure you, Sir William. I had it from the servant Betty, from her own lips, and she swore the truth of it on the Bible. She was going to bed one night at Mr Petworth's house when she saw it through the open door of the room where Mrs Dorothy Beaumont slept.'

'Saw what? I did not take in clearly what you said the first time.'

'Saw Mrs Beaumont and her companion, the Indian girl. They were bent over a basin of water in which the girl appeared to be seeing pictures, muttering incantations as she looked. Betty thought she was putting a spell . . .'

'Never mind what Betty thought. How did this story come to you, in the first place?'

'Servants will gossip, sir. Betty told one of my wife's maids, Deborah, who, knowing the two women to be living now in our Almshouses, thought my wife should know of it, and she in turn told me.'

'I see. Well, it sounds to me great nonsense. Either the wench Betty had been at her master's ale, or Mrs Beaumont and her maid were engaged in some perfectly innocent occupation, some beauty-trick of the toilette. If I were you I should forget the whole silly matter.'

'I cannot do that, Sir William. I am one of those responsible for the women dwelling in the Almshouses, and I cannot see unright-eousness in their midst without making some protest. I know the girl Meliora to be of a violent disposition. On one occasion she attacked *me*, sir.'

The magistrate's eyebrows rose, a smile twitching at his lips as he visualised the possible provocation.

'That was bad,' he said, 'but I feel sure you dealt with her sternly, and she will not repeat the offence. As for Mrs Beaumont, I fail to imagine her taking part in any unholy rites or indeed in anything unseemly at all, gentle and charming as she is.'

'She took part in sedition, sir. In vile rebellion.'

'She followed her husband's politics, as any good wife does, regardless of right or wrong. I am sure mine would have gone with me had I supported the Pretender.' Sir William was getting impatient. 'Now, Alderman, as there's nothing I can do in this matter . . .'

'You are a magistrate, sir. She could be arrested and examined, and Mrs Beaumont as well.'

'I think you overlook the fact that over twenty years ago an Act of Parliament was passed prohibiting the prosecutions of alleged witches; and not before time. Enough innocent blood was spilt in our grandfathers' times through silly superstition, and through spite. And now if you'll excuse me, I must be in court by ten o'clock.'

Spite, he thought, as the door shut behind the disappointed Alderman. That was the key to it. Servants *would* gossip, as the man had said; and word had come to Sir William's ears of certain friendly visits and lavish gifts to Mrs Beaumont. Only the week before, had Plumptree not recommended young Dame Meliora as tutor to his neighbour's child, praising her as a most remarkable and accomplished female? Something had happened in the interim to set the man against her. He shook his head at the weakness of humanity, collected his papers, wig and robe, and set out for the courtroom.

I am not a bad man, Lord, said Israel Plumptree to his Maker on his way home. I confess to You freely that I have lusted in my heart after strange flesh these many years, have indeed lain with light women, to my great shame. And I thank You, he added hastily, for not visiting the pox on me for it. Had Agnes been a warmer wife to me it would have been otherwise, but it was as it was, and she brought me good connections. I have not been a bad husband, have I? I flatter myself I've lived a Christian life, apart from the women. And when I find evil in my path – as I have done, whatever Sir William may say – is it not my Christian duty to destroy it? The ungodly are froward, even from their mother's womb; let them consume away like a snail, and be like the untimely fruit of a woman; and let them not see the sun.

As Meliora approached the schoolroom a stone struck her on the shoulder, knocking the breath out of her. She turned, and was hit on the cheek by a smaller, sharper one that broke the skin. The thrower was invisible. Only a scurry of running footsteps from the corner of the courtyard showed where he or she had hidden.

Meliora leant for a moment against the wall, to get her breath back, then opened the schoolroom door. A babel of noise was going on, the children scrambling all over their desks and benches, banging each other with their slates, crawling on the floor, flinging chalk and books about. She clapped her hands loudly, shouting, 'Children!'

As they saw her, the confusion quietened. But, instead of returning to their seats, they stood about, staring at her. She looked into one sullen face after another.

'What is the matter with you?' she demanded. 'Maria, you're the eldest. Tell me what all this disgraceful noise means?'

Maria shook her head, biting the end of her pigtail and staring at the ground. Meliora turned to Prudie.

'Prudie? You tell me.'

Prudie stared her out defiantly. 'I'm not to say nothing to you,' she said. 'None of us is to say nothing.' As Meliora, exasperated, advanced towards her, she threw up her hand in a gesture nobody could fail to recognise, the thumb between the first and second fingers to ward off evil.

'Witch!' shrieked Prudie. 'Witch!'

As though the word had been a signal, the children rushed through the open door, tumbling over each other like puppies, leaving Meliora standing among the wreckage, bewildered, her shoulder aching from the blow.

So began the time of persecution which neither Meliora nor Dorothy could understand. Nobody would give them any explanation, for nobody would speak to them. Their neighbours kept behind closed curtains, or rushed indoors whenever one of them appeared. Dorothy, sitting at her door with her face turned to the sun, had a dead kitten flung into her lap, which Meliora cried over and buried. The window was smashed by a brick. The geranium-pot on the sill was knocked off, soil and the broken plant scattered about the room. Through the gaping hole in the pane, during that night, two toads were inserted, to sit huddled until their chirpings woke Meliora. Whoever had put them there doubtless intended them to fill her with guilt or fear, or perhaps to adopt them as familiars. Instead she wrapped them carefully in a wet cloth and carried them at early light down to Warde's Pond. As she was kneeling on the brink, placing the two baffled creatures among the stones, a hand came savagely behind her and pushed her in.

Choking and floundering among pond-weed and debris from the trees above, she managed to catch hold of a root and drag herself out. Standing dripping on the bank, shocked and chilled, she heard a gleeful voice chanting, 'The witch swims, the witch swims!' and echoing laughter from the bushes, before her tormentors ran off.

Now Dorothy, too, was afraid, though she was less open to attack because she stayed indoors. After days of confinement, longing for exercise, she set out on her once familiar walk along the little path that began at the gate of the Almshouse gardens, along the field at the back, round the side of the buildings to the front again. She knew every step of it, though she had not ventured on it lately.

Somewhere about the second turn of the path, the thread which had been tied between the hedges caught her below the knees, sending her flat on her face on the stones. Trying to clamber up, she caught hold of the prickles of the hawthorn hedge, tearing her hands and making her fall again. There, with the larks singing in the sky above her and no evil to be observed anywhere in that smiling scene, Meliora found her.

She was helpless, shocked, her face scratched and dirt-smeared. Meliora lifted her, wiped away the blood, exclaimed furiously at the unbroken thread that had tripped her.

'This is the end of it,' she said grimly as they stumbled home,

Dorothy leaning on her arm. 'I shall find out from somebody what devil is doing these things to us.'

'How, since nobody will speak a word? The children stay away from school; the neighbours behave as if we had the plague. Either we are mad or they are.'

'There are those who will speak because their tongues hang on a loose string. Lie down and compose yourself. I am going shopping.'

She went further than usual, along the Richmond road, up the hill to the shop which now had the coveted sign *By Royal Appointment* on its fascia. There was very little money in her pocket, for the cash-box at the Almshouse was almost empty. But it would serve as an excuse. The shop was deserted. Repeated ringing of the bell on the counter produced Lettice Peasmarsh herself, hastily adjusting her fichu over her now ample bosom, a baby of a few months old under her arm and a small child at her skirts. She bridled at the sight of Meliora.

'Yes?'

'An ounce of red cheese and two pennyworth of flour, if you please, Mrs Peasmarsh.'

Lettice tossed her head, expensively capped. 'I don't know why I should trouble myself to serve you. But as the girl's out . . .'

She went into the back room and returned without the children. As she stood weighing the cheese, her back turned and every line of her body expressing disapproval, Meliora asked her, 'Why do people avoid and torment us, ma'am?'

Startled, Lettice seemed stuck for words. Then she said, 'Why do you ask me?'

'Because you are so well informed and respected, I thought you would know.'

Lettice considered her across the polished counter. It was years now since they had both served in Dove House. Prosperity and motherhood had put a barrier between that time and this, and she was faintly surprised to find that she had, after all, forgotten her malice towards the Beaumont family and its servants.

'I'll tell you why,' she said after a moment. With a certain enjoyment in the telling of a good tale, she gave Meliora a colourful account of what Betty had said to Deborah and Deborah to Mrs Plumptree. 'And so you see, the word got around.'

Meliora was thoughtful. 'From Mrs Plumptree? I understood she was a lady too grand for gossip with inferiors.'

'That's true enough. 'Tis not her style at all, now I come to think of it. The rumour came to me through Miss Polly Mason, but how she came by it I don't know. Not that I believe such a cock-and-bull story, for though we may not have been the best of friends in the past, Meliora, that's long over now, and I never thought you bad, only misguided in joining the King's enemies. I can't think you would practise the black arts.'

Meliora felt in her pocket and produced from it the little rowan cross, much worn and chipped away, no more than two frail twigs and a fragment of wire. She held it up, the light from the doorway behind outlining its shape.

'Would I carry this if I did?' she asked.

Lettice shook her head slowly. 'No. No. A witch wouldn't dare.' She made a sudden resolution. 'Won't you step into the parlour and take tea? The girl will be back any minute to serve, not that customers aren't few and far between today.' The invitation was issued partly from curiosity but quite as much from good-will, Meliora sensed.

'Thank you, Lettice, I'd be pleased. It's dry and hot walking.'

Going back towards Petersham, refreshed and much relieved by conversation unexpectedly amiable, she went over in her mind the story Lettice had told her. Combined with Alderman Plumptree's behaviour, it could mean only one thing. She heard a clock strike five. Dorothy had been alone only two hours or so, and could be left a little longer. Instead of going home, she would go straight to Plumptree's house.

16

To Dorothy it seemed that she had been alone much longer than two hours. She was still shaken from her fall, still heartsick with disgust that such a trick should be played upon a blind woman. Her face and hands were sore from scratches, though Meliora had bathed them with witch-hazel, and her knee had been badly cut on a stone.

She threw herself on the bed and lay there sunk in unhappiness and apathy. There had been a moment, after the fall, of utter panic as she realised that she was trapped in a world of darkness, hopelessly caged behind her own eyelids. That realisation was still with her, and she felt her heart as heavy as when she had heard Lyndon's death sentence. Only then she had had her health and strength, and some sort of hope for the future. Now there was nothing: neither house, property, health, love; only Meliora's friendship.

Meliora was a long time gone. Perhaps she had grown tired of the wretched life they led together, and had run off to seek her own fortunes. It seemed unlike her, but Fate appeared to be capable of any sour jest these days. Or perhaps their enemies had taken Meliora and drowned or burned her.

This dismal train of thought was interrupted by a soft knock. Not Meliora, for she had a key. Her signal to be let in was to rattle it in the lock, then Dorothy would draw back the bolt from inside. Now her heart began to race at the knocking of the stranger, who would surely be no friend. She got up and crept to the door. The knocking was repeated.

'Who's there?' she called at last.

'Alderman Plumptree, ma'am. Won't you let me in?'

Was he a friend, or not? He had not been near since the night Meliora had given him such a dressing down. Why should he come now? Yet his voice sounded amicable, and company of almost any kind might lift her out of her slough of despond. She drew back the bolt.

The concern in his greeting was quite unfeigned.

'My dear Mrs Dorothy! You have had some shocking accident, I fear.'

'I had a fall, and got some scratches.'

'So I see. Yes, so I see. You must be very careful, in your sad condition. Falls can be serious to a blind person.'

'It is somewhat difficult to be careful when traps are laid for one,' said Dorothy drily. Briefly she told him what had happened, and added, 'It is not the first "accident" we have had lately.'

His voice was grave. 'I heard something of this, and came to warn you. But, dear lady, I came also to try to make some amends for my conduct last time I was happy enough to visit you. What can I say, but that my passions carried me away? How can I blame myself enough for distressing you so? I behaved like a beast rather than a man.'

'Pray say no more about it, sir. It is over and done with, and I know you will not do so again. What is this warning you have for me?'

She heard him walk over to the window and pause there, as if thinking. Then he said, 'You will hardly credit this, ma'am, and I'm loath to impart it to your innocent ears. But – a charge of witchcraft has been trumped up against you and Dame Meliora, which has led to sundry annoyances being inflicted on you both. It is most reprehensible, but ignorant folk can't be measured in these things.'

'Witchcraft. So that is it. Yes, they called out "witch" to Meliora . . . But I can't understand it. What has either of us ever done to deserve such an accusation? I know Meliora has . . .' She stopped, aware of the danger of mentioning Meliora's supernormal powers. 'Do *you* know what began it?'

He cleared his throat. 'Nothing at all. That is – I heard some rumour about an occurence at Mr Petworth's house.'

So long ago; yet she knew at once what the occurrence must have been, summoning up the picture Meliora's words had created in her mind, the mist and the mountains, the hunted man, the brown-haired woman, the stormy sea and the ship. She decided to say nothing about it, not even a hint that any scrying had happened.

Instead she asked him, 'Why did you not come to me earlier with this story, Mr Plumptree?'

He had the answer ready. 'I'd no wish to distress you needlessly. And I hoped you would forgive me for my discourtesy to you here if I stayed away from your presence, especially if I could work on the minds of these people and persuade them to leave you alone. But, alas...'

'Alas what? Is there worse to come?'

He seemed scarcely able to speak for emotion. 'How can I say it? They – the Board – feel you and Dame Meliora are undesirable residents. You are to be turned out.'

She could feel the colour drain from her face. 'But, even if we – if this wicked story were true, witchcraft is not a criminal offence.'

' 'Tis a case of no smoke without fire. For your own sakes you must be removed from here, or the consequences might be fatal. Supposed witches are still ducked in village ponds, or stoned to death.'

'And where are we to go, then? What charitable provision have these generous gentlemen made for us displaced ladies?' His silence gave her the answer. 'The poorhouse. Rump Hall. Oh no, they can't be so cruel.'

He saw her beginning to tremble and with difficulty kept his hand from touching her shoulder. 'It may be that Dame Meliora could find employment easily enough, being skilled in teaching.'

'So we should be parted. And I...'

Now he did touch her, one hand benevolently on her arm. 'I know, I know, a sad, dreadful prospect. Believe me, I feel for you. But there is one way...' How cold her skin was; how much depended on what he said. 'I have a little house. Not here, some distance away, on the far edge of Kingston. It was rented to an old lady, who has just died. Now I am in possession again I can re-let it. If you – and pray don't misunderstand me – if you would condescend to be my tenant there, you should stay as long as you pleased, without rent. I would allow you food, fire, anything you wished.'

Her head was turned away from him. It was hard to tell the expression of a face when the eyes were closed; as hard for him as it was impossible for her to read his own eyes. At last she said, 'What do you want for it?'

'Your company. Your kindness.'

'I see. A bargain.'

'Pray don't put it so hardly. It would mean much to me to have such a fair guest under my roof.'

She pulled away from him. 'I think we understand each other, sir. How long may I have to decide?'

'Why . . .' He had seen Meliora on her way to his house, and had guessed her errand. A stable-boy was under orders to wait for her leaving, and to keep her prisoner until his master gave the word to free her. The lad knew he would be in for a beating if he shirked his duty; such tasks had come his way before. Israel Plumptree calculated carefully.

'Shall we say noon tomorrow? I have others interested in the house . . .'

'Very well. Noon tomorrow.' He was surprised how cool she could be, this blind girl with no cards left in her hand, the whole pack stacked against her. Perhaps he would be wise to point out the fact.

'You see,' he said, apparently with difficulty, 'the prospect for you is poor if you stay until you are ignominiously evicted. There is little sympathy for those who are a burden on the parish. That is what they call it. And the work is hard . . . even supposing you could do it, with your affliction . . .'

He saw her shiver and clasp her delicate scratched hands one over the other as if to comfort them, or to prepare them for what they would have to do. It was a gamble, depending on how long his boy could detain Meliora. He suspected that young woman of digging, enquiring, and if she had spoken with his wife, as he feared, then the fat was in the fire and his game was lost, unless he could persuade Mrs Dorothy out of her nest beforehand. He went on: 'You would vanish from here quietly, in a covered carriage. I would not be with you; nobody would know. The Justices would be glad to have you out of the way. All would be solved easily and pleasantly. I do beg of you to reflect carefully. And as to arrangements . . . can you walk to the courtyard gate without assistance?'

'Easily.' She tossed her head, and he admired the play of the evening light on her hair, the soft powdering of freckles on the tilted nose, the generous curve of her mouth now proudly set. It would cost him more than a little to keep up the house outside Kingston, even without the brown-skinned besom to bribe, and he was sure he would have to do that, but it would be worth every penny.

'Then if you will be there just before noon, a carriage will call for you. Bring little with you, so that your departure will not be noticed, and nobody will know what has become of you.'

'Spirited away by fiends?' she suggested. He wondered fleetingly whether she was going to be quite the dove-like concubine he had envisaged, but put the thought from him. Her nerves were on edge now; time would tame her.

'So,' he said cheerfully, 'I leave it to your good sense to decide, ma'am, and I think I know what your answer will be. Sleep well on it, and I look to see you tomorrow.' Without venturing the lightest caress, though his hands itched to stroke the curve of her neck, the bent head, the pretty face disfigured by scratch-marks. Better not alarm the game before getting it in one's sights.

'Good night, ma'am,' he said at the door. 'I think the weather's on the turn.'

After he had gone she poured herself a glass of wine, drank it, and hesitated before pouring another. No, better to stay unfuddled and detached with such a decision to make. She washed her face in the luke-warm water from the rainbut in the yard, drank a cupful of souring milk, and sat down to think.

Then the storm broke. The hot weather had been closing in all day, bringing clouds of tiny black thunderbugs to bite and irritate. As the sun went down, dark clouds marched up the sky, purple-grey massings which seemed to shut the earth in like a tent. The air turned to warm vapour, hardly breathable; birds that would have sung their evening songs were silent. The first rattle of window-panes, shaken by far thunder, came as a relief, followed soon by approaching peals and dazzling shafts of lightning, the spear-heads of the army that was coming. Soon the battalions met and massed in the sky, and the great slashing rains came, making a shining mirror of the land below, flooding gutter and road, beating down standing crops, washing tiles from old roof-tops to crash on the ground.

Dorothy sat listening to the wild noise, exulting in its violence, so much grander than the battle going on in her own head.

Meliora crouched in a hut at the end of the Plumptrees' kitchen garden. She had been flung into it by the boy, who had come up behind her as she left the house, had pinioned her wrists and carried her to this unpleasant, dark, damp place smelling of hens and compost. For all its rusticity it had a stout door, secured from outside by bolts and hasps. She had tried throwing herself against it and prising at the crack between door and wall, in vain. Whoever had put her there had chosen her prison well.

As the rains grew stronger they leaked into the hut, making a mud-pudding of the floor. Huddled on some mildewed sacks in the corner, she wondered whether the lightning would strike the hut. If so, Dorothy would never know what had happened to her. Dorothy, alone in the Almshouse, with who could guess what fresh mischief brewing. Meliora beat on the wall with her fists in her frustration. She had had a brief and unpleasant interview with Mrs Plumptree, once Agnes Tresham, a high-nosed, dessicated lady who seemed to speak through a mouthful of prunes. Mrs Plumptree had had the greatest difficulty in understanding why a coloured person to whom she had not been introduced was in her house at all, or why she should be asking about some foolish gossip of the servants which had gone in at one of her high-bred ears and out at the other. Meliora persisted.

'I only wish to know if you mentioned this story to anyone outside your household, ma'am. I must ask you to tell me, since it concerns my reputation and Mrs Beaumont's. Did you speak of it to anyone?'

Mrs Plumptree tried to stare her out, but failing, shrugged.

'If you are trying to imply that I'm a common gossip, I must give you the lie. I told my husband, that was all. Good day to you.'

So the rumours could only have been spread by Plumptree himself, for his own purposes, and Meliora now guessed what those might be. Frantically she tried again to break down the door. The storm was growing fiercer, thunder directly overhead and blue flashes of lightning piercing the windowless hut through gaps in the wood. One of them, Meliora saw, was fairly large. Large enough to be widened by the handle of a garden rake she had seen lit by one of the flashes leaning up against a wall. She began to work at it with the energy of desperation.

All night Dorothy sat in the chair by the grate. It was impossible to sleep for the raging of the storm, and she had the most important decision of her life to make. To keep her thoughts clear she spoke them aloud.

'I detest Mr Plumptree. He is odious to me. But what choice have I? To be turned on the parish, live on the women's side of Rump Hall, beat hemp and eat porridge twice daily? I think I should die of it. Now, though Plumptree is odious, he is a way out. One may be in a room that is afire and not be too dainty to escape through an ugly, grimy door. Lyndon is gone. My Prince is far away and has forgotten me, if he ever gave me a thought. What then? I must help myself. I shall go to Kingston, and once there we'll see what the next step is to be.'

Having made her decision, she let her head droop against the high back of the chair, and slept.

She woke to a fusillade of knocks and bangs on the door. The storm had died down. Suddenly her ear recognised the familiar rattle of the key in the lock. She ran to the door and drew the bolt, to be clasped in Meliora's wet embrace.

'Oh, thank God!' Meliora cried. 'I thought you were dead, or gone away.'

'I thought the same of you. But what a state you're in, my dear! Where can you have been? Take off those wet clothes immediately while I make tea . . .'

Wrapped in a blanket, Meliora told Dorothy of her capture and imprisonment. 'Fortunate for me that I had not broken out of the hut before I did, an hour ago, for the rain was dying down then, and I was only half drowned instead of drowned altogether. But why should that boy have shut me in?'

'I haven't the least notion. Unless . . .' A suspicion grew in her mind. She told Meliora of Plumptree's visit. 'I had made up my mind to go with him. But now you're here . . .'

'You must *not* go, Dorothy! Can you not see what a villain the man is? When I talked with Lettice Peasmarsh yesterday I began to suspect the truth, and Plumptree's wife confirmed it, though she was loath to see me at all. It was he who spread the witchcraft story, after I found him with you that night. He wanted to put you in such a case that you wouldn't refuse him a second time, and he almost succeeded.'

'Oh, God, could anyone be so wicked? Yes, you're right, I know it. I suppose he saw you at his house and ordered the gardener's boy to shut you up so that you would not be able to tell me of your discovery. And to think I was simple enough to believe him last night! He must be laughing-mad, thinking what a fool he made of me.'

'I doubt whether he is laughing at all,' said Meliora grimly. 'I saw his lady wife putting two and two together in her mind, and I fancy he will have had a few questions to answer. I shall be very surprised if he comes to carry out this romantical elopement.'

'I hope his wife deals with him as he deserves, the wretch! We'll stay here, and they may turn us out by force if they choose.'

But nobody came to turn them out that day, or next morning. They waited apprehensively, Meliora hardly venturing further than the farm where they bought milk and eggs. The village was battered by the storm, the lanes rivulets of mud, fallen trees lying across them so that no carriage or horse could pass. Flooded fields appeared like lakes, seabirds swimming on the waves, and cattle had been herded into farmyards. One ancient cottage had collapsed, and many more lacked roofs. Men, women and children had left their usual occupations to repair the damage; nobody glanced at Meliora.

They sat through the afternoon, starting at every noise and step outside.

As the church clock struck four Dorothy said, 'Nobody will come today.'

A knock contradicted her. For a moment they froze, as the same thought came to them: this is the time we are to be turned out. Then, without a word, Meliora opened the door. Dorothy heard her gasp.

'Paul! Mr Duncombe.'

'May I come in?' asked the grave, soft voice of their one-time neighbour. He followed Meliora into the cottage and bowed over Dorothy's hand, with the courteous greeting she had heard so often at Dove House.

'I bring you news, ladies,' he said. 'It was thought better I should bear it than any other.'

'Oh, pray don't hesitate,' said Dorothy with a pretence at airiness, though her knees were trembling. 'We know already that we're to be evicted.'

'Evicted? I don't take your meaning, ma'am.'

'They have sent word by you, being a lawyer.'

He glanced at Meliora and saw that she, too, thought this was the case.

'Then I must disabuse you both,' he said gently. 'I know nothing about eviction. I am come to tell you, Mrs Beaumont, that your uncle Mr Petworth and his wife are both dead, since the night before last.'

'*Dead?* Both of them? How?'

'I will tell you that presently. The upshot is, however, that I have a coach in waiting to carry you to their house, to attend the funeral, and to take possession.'

'To – take . . .'

'The house is yours, left to you by Mrs Petworth's will.'

17

The parlour of the house on Richmond Hill was very quiet now that Paul had finished speaking. A clock, which Dorothy remembered as being of ebony and tarnished gilt, ticked slowly. Her late aunt's old cockatoo talked to itself, in short bursts, on its perch in a corner. There was a smell of dust, unswept carpets, medicine and snuff.

Her mind could not yet fully take in Paul's words.

'It seems that when the fury of the storm was past, Mr Petworth came out to see what damage had been done. At the moment when he looked up at the roof a chimney-pot must have collapsed, for the servant found him lying under it, in his night attire, quite dead. The girl being distracted, she ran up to Mrs Petworth's bedroom and awoke her with the tidings, at which Mrs Petworth took a seizure and died some half-hour later.

'The servant then ran into the town to get help. It happened that I had gone in search of a builder's man, for we had some tiles blown off and a roof-leak. I spoke to the girl, Betty Payne, and at her request went back to the house with her, after summoning a doctor and an undertaker. Everything was done that had to be done. There will be an inquest, but natural causes are sure to be brought.'

He paused. 'You will say it was meddlesome of me to concern myself with the business. But, no one else coming forward, I thought it my duty. Besides, I hoped I might further your interests.' His smile took in Meliora, who bent her head, not meeting his eyes.

'Betty Payne told me repeatedly that her master and mistress had no kin except Mrs Beaumont, on either side, but that Mrs Petworth had said to her at the worst of her rheumatic illness that she had left a will in the family Bible. Betty had looked at this, but it was sealed up. She was disappointed, hoping to find her name in it – that is all she can read, her name. She showed me the Bible and, with Dr Woodforde as witness, I opened the will.'

He unfolded the paper, and read its contents.

'I SYBIL ELIZABETH PETWORTH, being of sound mind, do bequeath all of which I stand possessed to my beloved husband OZIAS PETWORTH, and in the event of his death it shall pass to my niece DOROTHY BEAUMONT, of Dove House in the town of RICHMOND, Surrey. Etc.'

'This will was made in 1745, Mrs Dorothy, before your connection with, er, with the Jacobite cause was known.'

'I cannot think why she let it stand,' Dorothy said. 'She was very hot against the Cause.'

'Let's be thankful that she did. I wonder who drew it up? I made enquiries of other lawyers in the town, who all swear ignorance. The witnesses are two servants, a man and woman.'

Dorothy had been thinking. 'But, even supposing the house is mine, I have no money to keep it up. And Uncle Petworth told me they were nearly penniless.'

Paul raised his eyebrows. 'Strange, for a retired African trader.' He looked round the room, handsome in its proportions, but pitifully shabby and neglected. He thought of Betty, a poor slut who had done all the tasks of the house and nursed her mistress for a yearly wage which was less than a man like Ozias Petworth ought to put in the church alms-box. She had sobbed out her story to him, sensing in him a kindness her employers had never shown. Paul had already encountered several clients who were neither more nor less than misers; he thought he detected the signs here.

'I will ask Mama to send up some of the servants,' he said, 'and the house shall be properly cleaned and swept after the funeral tomorrow.'

'Who is to pay the expenses?' Dorothy asked, remembering the cost of her father-in-law's burial.

'Oh, I dare say they will get paid, one time or another,' said Paul cheerfully.

The day after the coffins of the Petworths had been laid in the churchyard, the cleaning up of the house began. A sturdy man and maid of Colonel Duncombe's arrived with dusters, ladders, scouring-powder, brooms and buckets, none of which could be found in the

Petworths' kitchen. While Dorothy sat with Meliora in the garden, Kitty and Peter, with Betty's help, turned the place inside out – with astonishing results. Bedding and upholstered furniture which had acquired a life of their own were burnt at the end of the garden, carpets were ripped up and beaten soundly, china and glass washed in foaming suds; mice, bugs and moths fled in terror, unhoused. When the servants had finished their first day's work the place looked bare but relieved, like a patient recovering from a bad illness.

Paul surveyed it with satisfaction. He and his father had walked up before supper to see what had been done. In the scoured parlour, with its polished furniture and shining windows, Colonel Duncombe congratulated Kitty and Peter. Kitty gave Peter a nudge in the ribs and, when he said nothing but only grinned, she spoke up herself.

'If you please, Colonel, I think the lady should take a look round. There's things what maybe ought to be seen.'

'The lady can see nothing,' said Dorothy gently, 'but the Colonel and Mr Paul will look at anything you want to show them.'

'Where are these things, Kitty?' asked Paul.

'Upstairs, if you please, sir.'

Upstairs; that was where they usually were, thought Paul. He followed his father up what was now revealed as a noble staircase to the big room where Dorothy's aunt had died. The room was as composed as a corpse itself; every personal belonging of the dead lady neatly tidied, the medicines poured away and the bedclothes removed. Only the ineffable smell of old age and illness remained to tell of her presence. Kitty pointed to the stripped four-poster.

'Underneath, sir. Peter and I thought you ought to look.'

Beneath the bed, covering the floor from foot to head, were metal boxes. Some were locked, others half-open, as if the person who had occupied the bed had clambered out sometimes to look in them, and had been too feeble to close them again. Paul drew one out and, at a nod from his father, opened it. His expression unbelieving, he probed the box with one hand, a metallic clinking following its stirrings.

'Fetch Mrs Beaumont and Dame Meliora, Kitty,' he said. 'We must have as many witnesses to this as possible.'

'A hundred and fifty thousand pounds!' Dorothy laughed. 'There's not so much money in the world, in private hands.'

'There is in yours, fortunate Mrs D.,' said Paul. 'In coins, bank securities and jewels. And that only so far as we can judge, none of us being experts in the value of gems. A lifetime's fortune, and none to contest it.'

'But that is very wrong. What must I do with so much money? How can I spend it, being as I am? I shall give it away. Oh, poor Aunt Petworth, living so miserably, and all this stowed under her bed! She could have had so many comforts.'

'In my opinion,' Paul said, 'she knew all about it and abetted your uncle in living like a pauper for the sake of hoarding it. There is a sort of mind which enjoys sitting on wealth like a hen on eggs; only the wealth hatches for the heirs, not for the owner – and you must make yours strut and crow.'

'For one item,' Colonel Duncombe put in, 'you must have a hom and what better than this fine house? It needs some hundreds of pounds spending on it to make it what it should be. The roof is bad, there is woodrot and worm, and new furnishings are wanted. Then it could be the handsomest house in Richmond.'

'Yes, it's a pretty house, I remember. Perhaps it would forget its past if we gave it new clothes. But, Colonel, I can't accept this wealth without at least trying to find those who might have a claim to share it. We must advertise in London, or wherever you think fit.'

The advertisements produced no sign of any relative of the Petworths. If any of Dr Vyner's few relations had survived, none of them came forward. Willingly or not, she was an heiress on a scale beyond her dreams. Fortunate in having kindly and disinterested advisers in the Duncombes, she invested much of the money, banked the rest, and kept a floating sum for the repairs to the house, which were put in hand at once. While she, Meliora and Betty lived in the smallest possible area of it, an army of builders and decorators dealt noisily with the rest, smells of plaster, size and paint filling the rooms, the clatter of hammers and the chopping of axes deafening from morning to the autumn dusk.

'If I could only see to choose!' Dorothy said wistfully to Meliora. 'I had no choice in Dove House. Now I would like to make something which was like it, yet all myself as well. What a plague it is to be blind!'

Meliora looked speculatively at her friend, so much more blooming than she had previously been, well fed and rested, bright-faced with the pleasure of being once more her own mistress and being able to do good. For a handsome gift of money had gone to their old neighbours in the Almshouses, another to the Board for general distribution among the poor. Servants had been engaged, among them the pretty girl who had once been little Dorcas, unwilling lender of her red dress to the ragged Meliora. Betty had been handed over to Mrs Duncombe's staff for training, and had returned a different girl, polite and self-confident and accomplished in the use of a handkerchief rather than her sleeve or apron. And, most delightful of all, Meliora's announcement of a visitor to Dorothy one afternoon at teatime.

'An old friend to see you, Dorothy.'

The visitor said nothing, but brought into the room a fragrance of starch and lavender and a rustle of crisp cottons as she subsided in a curtsey. Dorothy sat upright with a start.

'This is . . . oh, I can't believe it. Mrs Mercy!'

She felt her hand taken and held between two warm plump ones.

'And so it is, my dear, if I may take the liberty of calling you so, for I never thought to see . . .' Mrs Mercy's voice lacked its usual calm measure. 'Meliora came to my daughter's to fetch me, saying you might be pleased with a visit. Of course, I'd heard something, and why for pity's sake did you not send for me when things was at the worst? As if I'd have let you live among paupers and endure so much.'

'But now, dear Mrs Mercy, you see I am very far from living among paupers, and am very happy, especially for your coming to me.'

Meliora spoke. 'Knowing you would be in want of a housekeeper, I took upon myself to ask Mrs Mercy if she would be willing to return.'

It seemed that Mrs Mercy was more than willing. Her daughter's cottage was small, her grandchildren unruly and demanding, her own domestic skills rusting unused. The thought of once again serving her mistress, in this beautiful newly fettled house, with every modern improvement in its kitchens, still-room, bakery and wash-house, transported her with joy. The odd-job boy was sent to her daughter's for her belongings, while Meliora showed her the house in all its glory. That evening, as they sewed together, Meliora said, 'Mrs Mercy asked what the house was called, having only heard of it as Mr Ozias Petworth's. Should you not give it a name?'

Dorothy raised her head. After only an instant's thought she said: 'Carola House. That is its name.'

'Carola? But that is the . . .' Only a very little Latin, less than Meliora had, was needed to know that Carola was the feminine form of Charles. 'Do you not think that is just a little dangerous – with White Lodge so near?'

'Not in the least. When one has as much money as I have, one is not regarded as a dangerous character. Besides, I choose to call it so. And I have had another thought – I shall get Mr Baynes to make me a coat of arms to put above the doorway, and it shall say *'Un je serverai'* very plainly in gold letters.' She resumed her stitching at the raised leaf she could not see.

One morning in late autumn Meliora said to Dorothy at breakfast, 'I have had such a powerful dream. It is with me yet in every parti-cular. I dreamed Mr Sam Johnson came to me and begged to speak with you, saying that he was now known as Doctor Johnson, and might do you some good. I saw him and heard him so clearly. It was as though he were standing by my bed.'

'How extremely indiscreet,' Dorothy said. 'Dear Sam Johnson. Well, I can't conceive what good he could do me, except to flatter me, but I think on reflection it would be very pleasant to pay him a visit. After all, I was invited as a permanent guest. I'm sure a courtesy call would not come amiss, and a breath of London would make a change, after so long. I know your dreams and portents, my dear; you are the sage of Carola House. But it seems to me that this dream portends some good I may do to Mr Johnson, rather than the other way round.'

The house in Gough Square, behind the noise of Fleet Street, was large and untidy, like its occupant. The panelled rooms called out for the sort of beautifying treatment Carola House had received; bare and shabby, they assailed the nose with fustiness. But Sam Johnson's huge delight in seeing Dorothy made a palace of the place. Seating her on a creaking sofa, one of its legs broken and propped up on a book, he danced attendance on her and Meliora with Falstaffian zest, urging on them pastries, sweetmeats, and quantities of tea equal to those he consumed himself, drunk from delicate cups of Dresden china.

'It is indeed a pleasure past words to see you here, my beloved Mrs Dorothy. And in such happy circumstances! When I heard of your good fortune I danced.' He sketched a few bear-like steps. 'Who is to say there's no justice in the world? If a fleet were to sail up London River bringing me the wealth of the Indies, it would not make me more happy than to know of your legacy.' He kissed her hand. 'If my dear wife were only well enough to greet you! But she's abed and in no state for company.'

They talked of the Dictionary brewing upstairs in the garret at the hands of the Scottish clerks; of the new comic novel *Tom Jones*, which Meliora was reading to Dorothy; of Handel's 'Music for the Royal Fireworks' – wasted, Sam declared violently, on a dull dog of an Elector with no more fire in him than a bag-pudding, and a Court composed of whores and knaves. Dorothy asked whether Lady Primrose was still in London and campaigning for the Cause.

'As briskly as ever, ma'am, and still queening it in Essex Street.'

Dorothy sighed. 'I should like to see her again. That is, to meet her again. It is so much a habit to talk of seeing . . .'

Peering admiringly at her, and extremely aware of the elegant ankles set off by pale-green silk stockings, he thought how strange and melancholy a thing it was that so pretty a creature should suffer blindness. He would make it the subject of a set of verses presently.

> How come it, Muses, that on these fair eyes
> The cruel hand of Stygian darkness lies?

Something on those lines. 'I would give what remains of my own poor sight to restore yours, madam,' he said.

'I believe you would. But not even your kindness could avail me that, since the doctors have denied me hope.'

The dawn of a recollection broke up his rugged features into a network of lines. He struck his thigh a violent blow.

'What a dolt I am, to be sure! My brain is so bewildered with words that mere fact is banished to its furthermost recesses, and chaos reigns supreme.'

'I beg your pardon, sir? Is something the matter?'

'Only that the enchantment of your company distracted me from the very thought that made me most wish a visit from you. It is this, then: some months ago, in great anxiety for my eyes, which suffered through an excess of writing and study, I was advised to consult a physician who had lately set up a practice in Frith Street, Soho. He had studied in France and Vienna, I was told; not that that necessarily rendered him less of a blockhead than our native quacks, but in other lands there are other skills, I believe. I consulted him, this Doctor Gambier.'

Dorothy's face had brightened. 'Indeed, with success?'

'Alas, no madam. He told me that the vile condition of my eyes was one for which no cure was known, and which only the excessive use of candles could assist. Though cast down both by his verdict and his fee, yet I felt the man to have a skill above the rest of his trade. I urge you to call on him, for a lady of your young years surely may entertain more hope of a cure than an old monument of mine. I would not desire the phantom of Hope to lead you to take hands with the spectre of Disappointment; yet it is worth the trying, surely.'

'Meliora? Shall I, do you think?'

'It can do no harm. You can afford the fee, whatever it is, and at the worst he can only tell you what has been told you already.'

Slowly Dorothy nodded her head, at which Sam Johnson fell into transports of joy and shouted downstairs for another brewing of tea. Before it arrived, borne by a slovenly servant, he had scrawled a note which he gave the servant with orders to convey it at once to Dr Gambier, and to wait for a reply. With astonishing speed for a messenger of such unmercurial appearance, the girl came back in little more than an hour. Johnson unfolded the doctor's note with fumbling fingers.

'Why, this is famous! He asks you to call on him tomorrow morning at ten o'clock, when he will be at your disposal for a lengthy consultation.'

The questions then arose of where Dorothy and Meliora should pass the night. Johnson eagerly offered them hospitality, but Dorothy declined on the grounds that it would put his household to too much trouble. She was, in fact, not anxious to sleep in what she suspected would be an uncleaned bedchamber, if the condition of the drawing-room was any guide. His recommendation of the Crown and Anchor inn, on the south side of the Strand, appealed to her, for he described it as 'a large house with good rooms, good food and good talk', where only respectable company was kept. It was his pleasure to escort them there, sitting opposite them in the coach with an enormous smile on his face, patting Dorothy's hand from time to time.

'We must put our trust in God, dearest lady. Then, whatever befalls, we cannot lose.'

The hall of the house in Frith Street was dark, narrow and cool, but it was not from cold that Dorothy shivered. As the elderly Frenchwoman who had answered the door ushered them into a small waiting-parlour, Dorothy said, catching Meliora's arm, 'I wish we had not come. It would be better not to know.'

'Everything is meant. If he confirms what others have said, then you must learn resignation. Remember what Dr Johnson said.'

'Do they indeed call him Doctor?' Dorothy was chattering nervously. 'Even though he has no university degree? So your dream was right.'

'We shall see. Dreams go by opposites, sometimes.'

A clock in the hall ticked loudly. Dorothy's acutely sensitive nose picked up a faint scent of medicines or herbs. 'What is this room like?' she asked.

'Quiet, peaceful,' said Meliora. 'A very few pieces of furniture. A painting of a scene: a lake and mountains. I think it is a good sort of room.'

Dorothy started as the door opened and the Frenchwoman entered.

'Mrs Beaumont, please to come in,' she said. 'It is better that your companion wait here. Dr Gambier say I am your chaperone, should you have fear.'

'Thank you. Please lead me.'

She was led into the next room, which she sensed to be larger. The doctor was there already, she could tell. Perhaps he too was nervous, for she heard him take a deep breath, rather like a gasp, as she entered. Then a hand touched her shoulder, gently propelling her into a chair.

'Mrs Beaumont.' The voice was soft, gentle, the voice of a healer. 'My friend Dr Johnson feels that I might help you.'

'If you can . . . But I have little hope.'

'How long have you been blind?'

'Four years.'

'And how did the blindness evince itself?'

What a curious accent the doctor had, for a Frenchman. She was glad to have a puzzle to occupy her mind, as well as the exercise of answering his questions.

'Quite suddenly. I had had some trouble with seeing things in the distance, for a little time. Then one night I went to sleep, and woke up – so.'

He said nothing, but she felt him position himself behind her chair, and knew by the warmth on her face that he was shining a candle on to it. He tilted her head back and slid a small cushion beneath her neck.

'Now you are very comfortable. Try to think of that only.'

Long cool fingers settled her head, moved over her temples, touched her eyelids with the softness of butterflies' wings. His breath was sweet and pleasant, unusual in a world of decayed teeth and tobacco-taking. Suddenly she felt an almost sensual delight in sitting thus, touched by the gentle hands, feeling a goodness and dedication in the man. A strange freedom came over her, as though certain bonds had dropped away.

'Have you any pain in your eyes?'

'No.'

He was pressing the eyelids now, feeling the orbit, from lashes to brow, yet never hurting.

'The eyes are quite full, not fallen away,' he said. She heard him move to a chair next to hers. 'What happened, before you lost your sight?' he asked. 'Some bad experience, was there not?'

'Yes. My husband's death.'

'Suddenly?'

'By the rope and the knife.'

Again she heard him draw his breath sharply, before he said, 'This shortness of sight, when did it first come on? Soon after his death?'

She thought. 'I remember it first on the same day.' The clock on the bedroom mantelpiece, the bright light of late morning, Mrs Mercy's draught. 'Or perhaps it was a little before. But not much. I have always read a great deal, but never needed spectacles.'

'And you are otherwise healthy?' He asked her more detailed questions. When she had answered them he rose from the chair and again stood behind her, his cool hands over her eyes and brow like a mask.

'Now,' he said, 'you will think only of this minute and this hour, and of my hands. Nothing else has ever happened. You understand?'

'Yes.' She knew she was smiling. The voice was so pleasant, so strangely familiar, as though her father had come back to speak to her. Her whole body was resting, relaxed, in the comfortable chair, her whole attention concentrated on the fingers that lightly touched her. Perhaps he was speaking again, perhaps not; her mind floated, unaware of anything except his touch, his power. Time ceased for whole minutes, perhaps for half an hour, or much less. Then, quite loudly and in a different dimension, she heard him say, 'Now I am going to take my hands from your face, and after that you will see.'

The cool fingers, warmer from contact with her skin, were gently withdrawn. Like shutters suddenly opened her eyelids lifted, a flood of light breaking in on her. The window-panes printed a pattern on her brain, the ivy outside them was a dazzle of green, the subdued colours of the room hit her like blows. She gave a loud cry, turning her head from side to side, dazed and shocked with joy.

'A dream, a dream!' she heard herself saying.

'No dream,' replied the man who stood with his back to her, drawing the curtains to lessen the glare of the new light. 'No dream, my dear.'

Slowly the room came into focus, the dark hangings of the window, the square shoulders and dark tie-wig; and, as he slowly turned, the familiarity of the voice was a mystery no longer. 'Dr Gambier' was Allan Carr.

18

Some moments of a lifetime can never be recaptured, so poignant they are: the first cry of a first child; the last breath of a beloved; the ring slipped on the finger. What Dorothy would remember most clearly about the regaining of her sight was the moment in which she thought she had lost it again, as her eyes clouded over and she sobbed and felt the air with her hands; and then Allan was saying, 'It is nothing, only tears.' He wiped them away with her handkerchief, and once again he and the room were there, blessedly visible, incontestably real. She began to laugh as well as cry, and he gently put her back in her chair. Wonderingly she looked at it, seeing that the arms ended in tiny lions' heads. So little did touch tell one; now she need never rely so totally on it again.

He poured some liquid from a vial into a glass and gave it to her.

'Drink this. It will calm the excitement.'

It was pungent, fumes from it rising into her head, and instantly she began to breathe naturally, her heart quietening. He was sitting opposite her, regarding her with a kind of serious happiness; still the Allan of the 'Forty-five, though grey hairs showed at the join of the wig and there were lines on the dark face that had not been there before.

'You are a magician, Allan Carr,' she said.

'No. Only a doctor, of the mind as well as the body.'

'It was my mind at fault, then?'

'As is often the case. Your mind is a valiant soldier. He tried to protect you from the sight of what had happened to Mr Beaumont and to yourself, and so he shut your eyes. The condition is called hysteria.'

She tried to take in what he was saying. 'Then how . . . what did you do to cure me? I remember nothing.'

'You would not. I spoke to your mind, not to you yourself. I can't tell you what I said or did. It must be the doctor's secret.'

She was staring at him, sipping the last of the cordial in the glass.

'Then all the medicine we know is nonsense, all the cuppings and leeches and horrid draughts. Is that true?'

'Some of it, aye. For the rest . . . I think we nave much to learn. I knew nothing of healing when I left in '46; only what any army surgeon knows. I began to learn in Vienna, where I went first. There was a master who taught me things I had never believed possible. They would have burnt him once for sorcery, but, thank God, folk are wiser now. I lodged with a family who took in students; there was a boy, barely fourteen, who led me into the way I follow now, treating the mind with the mind. The world will hear of Anton one day.'

'Yet you had no cure for Sam Johnson.'

'He has an organic disease of the eye, beyond my power to mend, poor man.'

The old Frenchwoman had entered and was murmuring to him. He rose and took Dorothy's hand.

'My next patient has arrived. I must return you to your companion. For the rest of the day you'll be quiet, will you not – take plenty of rest and food, no great excitement.' He hesitated. 'May I – I would like to call upon you later, to hear how you are, if that would not be too much for you.'

'Oh, dear Allan, how can you ask? I don't know what to say or how to thank you. Will you come to the Crown and Anchor in the Strand tonight, and dine with me? Then perhaps I can begin to tell you.'

She was gone, treading uncertainly as the ground wavered beneath her new sight, the Frenchwoman guiding her by the arm. She had not looked back at him, but when his next patient was shown in he had to drag his gaze back from where she had been, framed in the doorway. The handkerchief with which he had dried her tears had fallen on the floor. He picked it up and put it in the inside pocket of his waistcoat, safe from loss.

They were sitting in the coffee-room of the Crown and Anchor, in a small booth winged like a porter's chair, half hiding them from the rest of the busy room. They had dined on roast beef and claret, and Dorothy was flushed with excitement, gleaming with happiness. It had been a far from quiet day, in spite of his instructions. There had first been Meliora's overjoyed reception of the news, which had caused her to faint; then Sam Johnson's – for he must be the next to know, after themselves. Mrs Johnson had come down in a dirty bed-gown, rejoicing in time with her husband, and they had all taken wine after Sam had praised and thanked his God for his friend's deliverance. The cat Minikin had been brought up from the kitchen, with a basket of kittens, so that Dorothy could see their beauty, and the servant who had taken the message to Allan presented herself for once clean and tidy with a red ribbon in her hair, grinning at her own fineness; so much respect was due to sight restored.

Everything was new and wonderful; the blue, swirling tobacco smoke in the coffee-room, the painted patterns on the china they ate from, the hurrying figures of the serving-girls in their print dresses, the leaping of the flames in the hearth. They were now alone, Meliora having slipped away on the excuse of tiredness. She had been quick to sense Allan's mood, eager to give him time and oppor-tunity to express it.

'If only I could think of some fitting reward!' Dorothy said. 'To be given a new life, and to be able to say nothing but thank you, sir. I know what I shall do – you shall have a house of your own, where you will pay no rent, and whatever you need in the way of medicines and instruments. And we will advertise you . . . what made you call yourself Gambier, by the way?'

'Prudence. My name was known in fairly high places – after Culloden. I took the name of an associate in Paris. It seemed as good as any other. Times are quiet now, but it does no harm to ca' canny.'

He was studying her face, watching the play of candle-light in the eyes as widely opened now as they had been shut before, catching and holding his own gaze. She was flirting with him, he knew, how-ever unconsciously. Flirtation is a difficult art without the use of sight, and she was losing no time in practising it again.

Allan wondered why he had fallen in love with her. He had seen many women more beautiful, and lived with a few during his Continental travels. Yet the image of this one had been always with him. Perhaps because of a sort of innocence in her looks that had nothing to do with coyness, seeming to show an absolute childlike trust in this wicked world and its inhabitants. She was no fool, though. Yes, to have kept that clear look through her misfortunes was a sign of some quality within her that had not been in the other women in his life. Perhaps, he thought wryly, it is that she and I are both romantics, always following in the train of hope, however stony the path. Or perhaps it is something that can never be solved, either by logic or arithmetic.

> 'All Love is mystery from first to last;
> His years still young, his childhood never past.'

Dorothy was looking at him quizzically. 'You're far away,' she said.

'No, very near home. I was thinking that we Scots are poets at heart, under our rough exteriors.'

'I would not call your exterior particularly rough. But I suppose you are right, or the Rising would never have gone so far.' She was looking up at a large, dark oil-painting above the mantelpiece, its lower half lit by two candle-branches beneath. 'What a curious picture to find in a coffee-room. It seems to be religious.'

'It is, madam.' The voice came from an elderly man at the next table. 'Forgive my interruption of your talk, but I can tell you the history of this very strange painting. If I may illuminate it for you . . .'

He left his table and held up one of the candelabra to light the picture fully. Dorothy, with an apologetic smile to Allan, rose and stood with him. Now the figures were clear; a winged angel seated at an organ, a smaller one reading at her knee, others playing harps and lutes, a sky full of disembodied cherubs' heads. The figures were ungraceful, to say the least, with disproportionately long, heavily muscled limbs, fatuous expressions, and a general air about them of unskilled rustics rehearsing for matins.

'You are struck by the earthiness of these heavenly bodies, I see, ma'am,' said her mentor.

'A little, yes.'

'The very reason why you see them here, in an inn and not a church, for the thing is an altar-piece. It was painted in 1725 by the artist Kent, for the church of St Clement Danes, and aroused such unseemly mirth among the parishioners that the Bishop of London, to secure the solemnity of the place and worship, very prudently ordered the churchwardens to take it down.'

'Very prudently indeed,' said Dorothy, who had been trying not to laugh.

'Yet *some* said,' he lowered his voice, 'that that was not the true reason, but that the picture represented the Pretender's wife, the Princess Sobieski, and her children, Charles Edward and Henry. If that were the case, it was not at all a proper thing to be placed in a Protestant church.'

'No, not at all,' she agreed, moving nearer to examine the faces of the angelic consort; they certainly bore no traces of Stuart connections.

'An interesting and remarkable story, is it not? I thought you would like to know it, ma'am.' Dorothy stole a covert glance to decide whether or not he was the kind to expect a tip for his pains, but he bowed courteously to her and sat down as she thanked him warmly.

And thank you, too, sir, on my behalf, Allan growled inwardly, for bringing up the one subject I hoped to avoid, and turning her thoughts that way again, just as I was beginning to believe I might speak for her myself. Or rather, sir, damn and curse you!

He could see a new brightness in her face when she came back to the table, a warmth and excitement roused, he noted jealously, by even the casual mention of a certain name. At once she broke into eager questioning.

'Have you seen him, the Prince, lately? I suppose you must have done, being in exile with him so long. I would have asked you before, but I thought it might be more polite to talk of you.'

He acknowledged the naïve compliment with a grim smile. 'I

have not seen him very lately, having been in London over a year. When I last saw him he was in Paris, just before he was arrested at the Opera and banished from France.'

'Arrested? Banished? I know King Louis signed that infamous treaty, but surely a royal personage could not be arrested?'

'It was a very unpopular move, aye. The Dauphin, who is a particular friend of His Highness, condemned his father in public for ordering it, and the other princes and princesses took his part also.'

Including Black-eyes, thought Dorothy, and bit back a question as Allan went on.

'King Louis was not amused, it seems, but said that it might console the Dauphin to know that his friend had only been bound by silk ribbons, not by ropes.'

'They *bound* him?'

'In case he should fire on the guard, or turn his pistols on himself. He was well enough treated at the Château de Vincennes, it seems, and released after a few days.'

'And where is he now?'

'Nobody knows. He went from Vincennes to Avignon, where he upset the archbishop by arranging prize-fights. There was such a to-do about it that the news got back to England, and the Elector's lackeys insisted on his being turned out. Since then he has vanished.'

She was silent, looking down at the glass in her hand as though its contents would show her the beloved face Meliora had seen in her scrying-bowl. 'How was he when you saw him in Paris?'

'Very cheerful, to the outward view. He talked and laughed a great deal. I attended a banquet he gave – it was very splendid, the food served on gold plates.'

He had only been invited to it because of meeting the Prince's valet, Morrison, in the street. Morrison had mentioned the meeting to his master, who had sent him out again to Allan's lodging with the message that all who had served with him in the Rising were welcome. Allan had not enjoyed the evening. French gabble was not agreeable to him, or the reckless extravagance which had provided so much food and wine for what seemed to him a pack of idle, frivolous wastrels, only too pleased to batten on the Prince.

'How did he look? What was he wearing?'

Allan sighed, smiling. 'How can one man say how another looks? Much as he used to, perhaps a little older, which indeed he is. I took small note of his clothes, but I mind he was in full court dress, with much lace and velvet about him, and the George on his breast. I never saw him so fine in Scotland.'

'What did he say to you?'

'Only a few words – there were so many waiting on his attention. He greeted me kindly and asked how I was living. I was astonished that he knew me in all that great company, but he never forgets a face.'

Dorothy was visualising the gathering, the glittering figure at its centre, the musicians and scurrying servants, the painted, bejewelled guests. 'There would be many fine ladies about him, I've no doubt,' she said, half afraid of the answer.

Allan hesitated. Self-interest prompted him to tell her bluntly of the women who clustered round the Prince everywhere he went, fought over him, dazzled him with wit and beauty, and never failed to advertise their triumphs over him to all Paris. The woman who had sat by him at table was Marie Jablonowska, Princess de Talmond; forty years old to Charles's twenty-eight, a flashing dark Juno whose complaisant husband nodded and smiled as she all but embraced Charles in public as ardently as she no doubt did in private. She was Polish, as his mother had been, first cousin to the Queen of France, as influential as she was brilliant; one could not really blame the Prince for succumbing to her charms, but Allan had thought her a rather unpleasant lady. She had made a loud, viciously stinging remark about Madame de Montbazon, who sat within hearing distance on the opposite side of the table, and whose large blue eyes had dwelt fixedly on the royal person throughout the meal. As the sting went home madam's fair face turned deep red. She would clearly have exulted in plunging the diamond arrow that sparkled in her hair into the Princesse de Talmond's expansively displayed white bosom. And there had been other ladies who raised their glasses to Charles, as he to them, with significant smiles and languishing looks. Charles the Chaste had travelled a long way since

232

L'Heureux had carried him away from the shores of Loch Arkaig on a September night.

Allan's better nature prevailed. It was impossible to hurt his lady, even for her own sake. 'There were many, indeed,' he said. 'They were braw enough in their attire, but I would not say they were as ravishing as I'd heard Parisiennes to be.'

He heard Dorothy let out the breath she had been holding, and again longed to say to her: he is out of your reach, out of your star; forget him. Suddenly she began to yawn uncontrollably.

'Forgive me,' she said, 'but I am so tired, and my eyes ache. I fear I must go to bed. It has been such a day – such a day.'

At the foot of the staircase she turned and put her hands into his.

'I owe you my eyes, Allan. You shall have everything I promised – a house, and whatever else you need.'

'I need nothing for myself,' he said stiffly, trying not to let his hands close too tightly round the small warm ones they held. 'But my poorer patients are in need. For them, I would be grateful for a little money to buy instruments, books and medicines. And I'll take it only so that you shall not feel in my debt or I in yours.'

'You're a proud Scot,' she said. 'But I respect that. And for the sake of your patients you'll take my fee. How can I pay you otherwise?'

He watched her go up the stairs, the candlestick she carried throwing a pool of light before her, until she vanished round the curve of the divided staircase.

The bank draft she gave him next morning took his breath away. Some words of Johnson's note had told him she was rich, but the amount was more than he could have earned in a lifetime. He stared at it, angry, resentful and shamed. Now that he knew the extent of her wealth it was impossible for him to speak for her hand; that would look like unblushing fortune-hunting. He dropped the paper abruptly.

' 'Tis far too much. I cannot take it. With such money you could endow a hospital or a charity. For one doctor to have it would be laughable.'

Her face showed disappointment. 'I thought you'd be pleased.

233

And . . . it was the first time I've written my name since I got back my sight. I wanted it to be for you.'

'Oh, Dorothy! Can you not see that over-generosity is not kind to its object? How can you force such a responsibility on me? It will make me unhappy, not happy, believe me. Now, rather than weep, which I perceive you're about to do, why not tear up this and write me another, for a great deal less? Then I shall feel I have real money to spend, not some kind of pirate's hoard, and I can be truly grateful to you.'

Unsmiling, she tore up the draft from corner to corner, and tossed it into the fire. 'Whatever you wish – Doctor Gambier. It's a pity when one can't do what one likes with one's own. I'll write you another.'

He knew he had lost the warmth she had felt for him the night before, and cursed himself for being too stiff-necked to indulge the innocent pleasure of a girl who was still a child in wealth. But it was for her own good, he told himself. She would be glad of his firmness one day.

Still discontented with him and herself, she stared out of the coach window, only half seeing the pageant of the Strand. That so small a thing, the rejection of her offering by a man she liked and admired, should outweigh the glorious miracle of the previous day! The little boats on the river bobbed cheerfully along on their journeys, carts and coaches jostled in the narrow Strand, life surged in the tall old houses that flanked it. As they came round the side of St Clement Danes church Dorothy saw ahead of them, where the Strand met Fleet Street, something that chilled her heart: the familiar arch of Temple Bar, and, above its curved top, tall spikes topped by round dark objects. They must soon drive under the last dreadful relic of Lyndon. She jerked down the window, and leaned out, calling to the coachman to stop. Remarkably enough in the street din, he heard her and drew the horses to a halt. Meliora, dozing, sat up. 'Where are we? Why have we stopped?'

The coachman had come round to the window, none too pleased to be held up in one of the least navigable of London's streets. 'Ma'am?'

Dorothy glanced about her for any excuse but the truth. 'Essex Street,' she said. 'Turn down Essex Street. I wish to visit a friend.'

Ten minutes later she was in the arms of Lady Primrose, who was laughing, sobbing and chattering all at once.

'My dear girl, 'tis the most charming pleasure to see you, when one thought you must be dead or gone abroad – and looking so handsome and prosperous! I can't credit my eyes. It was very naughty of you, most remiss, to stay away from me so long, and I shan't hear a word of excuse – but tell me just the same, there's a dear creature. Is that your coach in the street – and who is that in it? Well, if she'll not come in, you and I shall take sherry together, for no time's too early for drinking when one sees a long-lost friend again.'

Her bubbling enthusiasm was exactly the tonic Dorothy needed. Eagerly the little woman listened to her story, sometimes nodding, sometimes clasping her hands in agitation, expressions chasing each other like scudding clouds across her lively Irish features.

'Ah, now,' she said when Dorothy stopped, 'never did I hear a tale to beat that. And to think that only yesterday you were blind as a bat! I've heard tell of Doctor Gambier, but never a whisper of who he really was. I wonder . . . yes, now I come to think, I believe Sam Johnson has known all the time. He knows more than he gives out, the sly old fox. How very romantic and altogether satisfactory that you should be cured by an old friend, and one from the time of the March.'

'I have behaved badly to him,' Dorothy said. 'Even while I was talking to you it came to me that I had behaved in a vulgar fashion by offering him so much money.' Something else had dawned on her at the same time : the look in Allan's eyes which had told her his heart, if she had had the wit to read it. Hastily she put the thought behind her. Lady Primrose was rattling on.

'You heard I lost my poor cousin-in-law in '46 at Carlisle, a few months after your own loss. Oh my dear, how terrible it was! Yet had I been a man I'd have risked the same fate for Him.'

'Have you recent news of – His Highness?'

Her mouth full of ratafia biscuit, Lady Primrose nodded vigorously, then launched into a flood of gossip and anecdote which was music to her audience's ears. None of it concerned the Princess de Talmond or any other of the Prince's female friends, for the loyalty of Lady Primrose was so fervent as to prevent her even crediting any derogatory story about him, much less passing it on. But one member of the Stuart family came in for her severe censure.

'I never shall find it in me to forgive the Duke of York. Everyone knew he was as pious as his father, but to accept a Cardinal's hat! What a blow to deal his poor brother. He must have seen that it would dismay every good Jacobite, for wasn't His Highness's papacy the bugbear that frightened England? You know, child, my father was an Irish Protestant clergyman of Huguenot blood, Dr Drelincourt, so I've little cause to praise the Pope, but I never for one moment feared the stake and the rack, should the Stuarts come into their own again.'

'*Will* they?' Dorothy leaned forward earnestly. 'Is there any real hope of a restoration, Lady Primrose? Because, if so, and if money would do anything to aid it, then my money is yours.'

Her hostess, for once, forebore to plunge into further discourse, but tapped her fan thoughtfully against her cheek. She lived on the fringe of the shabby-genteel world, straining her purse to give the parties she adored and to buy the clothes to wear for them. It was very odd to hear a lady inviting her to make free with her coffers; quite outside her own experience. She studied Dorothy's rich dress and fur-edged cloak, with a muff to match it, and noted the green silk stockings and the real silver buckles on well-polished shoes. There was certainly money here. A less scrupulous woman might have considered feathering her own nest, with the excuse of spending money lavishly for the Cause, but that was unthinkable to her. It would be like taking the bread out of the mouths of children.

'It's uncommonly generous in you, my dear. I don't know what use could be made at present, though, with no new attempt immediately planned, but be sure I'll apply to you if occasion arises. I pray God it may.' She jumped up and ran to a marquetry escritoire, from the top drawer of which she produced a miniature enclosed in a gilt case.

'There,' she said with pride. 'I got it of a gentleman that had been in France. Did you ever see anything so charming? They say he much resembles his dear mother, and for that the Queen of France adores him, having grown up in Poland with her.'

Dorothy studied the miniature. Its setting was certainly attractive, a pinchbeck frame of oakleaves entwined with thistles and roses, but the portrait itself was far from charming, to her eyes. A distant resemblance to the original came through, as it did in even the worst portrayal of him, but as a likeness it was a dismal failure, showing a long, weak-featured face with a double chin, surmounted by an unflattering periwig. She had no wish to dampen Lady Primrose's pride in her possession, but truth was truth. 'It does him less than justice,' she said, handing it back. 'Do you not think so, now?'

Lady Primrose opened her eyes very wide. 'Why, child, I never saw him in my life. How could I but by going where he is, and I've no means for gadding abroad, with this house to keep up and prices so high. La, what an agreeable idea, a trip to Paris.' She stood tiptoe to coquet with her image in a mirror, primping up the lappets of her cap and straightening the velvet band about her throat. 'Forty-four years old, my dear, but not absolutely ill-looking, would you say? Who knows, I might catch another husband at the French court.'

Dorothy smiled with her, but her mind was all wonder that so great a devotion could be inspired by a collection of inadequate portraits. Yet was it only the face she herself had fallen in love with at first sight? Surely it had been more than that; some radiance that shone in him so brightly as to make all other men dim by comparison. Lady Primrose's sharp wits followed her thoughts.

'When I had Miss Flory Macdonald in my house, after the Government set her free, she told me many things about the days after Culloden. Oh, I could keep you here all day and all night, telling them . . . but I say this because I perceive you're much in wonder that I should love our Prince without having met with him. Now, Miss Flory told me a thing one Malcolm Macleod said of His Highness. It was that "There is not a person that knows what the air of a noble or great man is, but upon seeing the Prince in any disguise he could put on would see something about him that was not ordinary, something of the stately and the grand". And this one feels even through the reports of those happy enough to know him. Don't we love Our Lord by the same token, if it an't profane to say so?'

This long speech from the usually flighty lady impressed Dorothy greatly, making her ashamed of her own superficial judgment.

'Indeed,' she said, 'you're very right. He has such powers.'

'Mark me,' said her hostess. 'There will be those after our time, a hundred or maybe two hundred years after, who will feel those powers and fall victim to 'em.' She kissed the portrait and put it away.

The clock on the other side of the drawing-room suddenly announced the hour of twelve. 'Mercy!' exclaimed Dorothy. 'I was on my way to take a few presents to the Johnsons. They'll be at dinner by the time I get there. And I must be at Richmond this afternoon, or my housekeeper will have the Watch out hunting for me.'

'Let me take your gifts to Gough Square. Then you'll not be delayed, though I'd delay you myself if I might. Will you not bring your friend in and take a bite and sup with me, then go on your way?'

Dorothy shook her head. 'She is not well. My restoration to sight was a shock to her, though a joyful one, and she is delicate. The doctor says it may be months before she is better.

At the door Lady Primrose touched her arm wistfully. 'You'll write to me, or come to visit when you're in town? I'm often lonely, and 'tis a great pleasure to talk with one who feels as I do, and is monstrous agreeable with it.'

Dorothy kissed her. 'Dear Lady Primrose, you shall hear from me often.'

But it was she who heard first.

Essex Street

ye 5th September 1750.

My deere Mrs Dorothie,

Hasten as soon as you get this to my Howse. A Personage is

coming to visit mee. No more now in great haste but pray do make all spede.

The signature was a wild scrawl. Dorothy folded the note and went to the window, where she stood, breathing hard. The garden was a riot of early autumn roses in honey-gold sunshine. The window-sash was pushed up to its full height. She leant out into the warm air and pulled a climbing rose, ivory-white, flawless, and perfumed to charm the senses.

Book Three

The Rose

19

The room seemed full of people, though there were perhaps no more than a dozen. Heads turned as the maid announced Dorothy, and admiring masculine glances rested on the picture she made, standing in the doorway.

She wore a gown of rich damask the colour ' of ripe apricots, gathered into panniers over a petticoat of a deeper shade, heavily wrought with raised embroidery. Her bodice was cut low and square, a border of lace framing her bosom, white silk bow-knots diminishing in size from the top of the velvet stomacher to the point, which emphasised the slenderness of her waist and the becoming swell of her skirts. Ruffles of delicate French lace fell from ribbons knotted above her elbows, and the widow's cap on her high-piled hair was an aerial confection of the same lace, its streamers of cobweb fineness dancing on her neck. She might have stood for an allegorical figure of Plenty on a painted screen, or a Chelsea figurine of an Arcadian shepherdess standing in an arbour of leafy *bocage*, a docile lamb at her feet.

The hands clasped round the stem of her spangled fan were damp-palmed, and the knuckles showed white. She managed to smile and greet Lady Primrose, who came fluttering up to her pink-faced and breathless.

'My dear, dear Mrs Dorothy, what a happy occasion! How glad I am to see you and how did you get here so fast, and looking quite ravishing too? I beg you'll take some wine, and, la, my dear, you'll think I've taken too much already, but indeed 'twas only a glass and the rest is pure agitation. Susan! the wine over here, if you please . . .'

A darting pain, born of shock and joy, struck Dorothy in the small of the back so sharply that she gasped aloud, as she saw him again at last, and five years dropped away into the chasm of forgotten things. He was not difficult to see, the six foot two of him topping the rest of the company by inches. He stood at the fireplace, leaning against the mantelshelf, profile towards her, in earnest conversation with an oldish man in black, wearing clerical bands, whom she remembered having seen at one of her father's Tory gatherings. Charles was far from being the glittering figure she had carried in her imagination since Allan's description of the banquet in Paris. His coat and breeches were of sober brown, his waistcoat of a dull gold colour, his neckband plainly tied, a dark ribbon holding back the long curls of his wig. Directly above him, over the mantel, hung a painting made from the miniature Lady Primrose had shown Dorothy with such pride; but the artist had taken painter's licence and something of the living man who stood below it looked out from the canvas.

As she moved into the room, nearer to him, she thought: I am walking into the fire, I know it, yet it draws me as the lovely perilous candle-flame draws the moth. There was no hesitation in her gait, even a quiet boldness that drew surprised looks and whispers from those of the company who stood reverently aloof from the conversation between the Prince and Dr William King, the noted Oxford Jacobite. The little groups parted to let her through, until she was only a foot or two away, and he turned his head and saw her.

Their eyes met and locked, and for a terrible moment she saw complete blankness on his face.

Confound it, Charles was thinking. Here was a young dame who obviously expected him to recognise her, yet nothing was more damnably difficult than to know one woman from another after a lapse of time. Men were easy enough to register in the memory, with their craggy individual faces, scars, beards, bushy brows and the like – but women! All painted to look alike and none of the slightest political significance. Yet he noted that this woman was not painted, and something in the pleading look of her face brought back a damp room and the scent of wood-smoke, and a curious incident that had amused and touched him at the time, though it had quite vanished from his mind later.

And so he was able to say, as though he had known it from the first, 'Mrs Beaumont. I'm very happy to see you again.'

She sank down in a deep, floor-touching curtsey, rising from it with her face of the same warm flush as her gown. He gave her the smile for which so much blood had been shed, and raised her with a hand which held her hers for a moment. Dr King raised brindled brows and turned away, annoyed. The company stared and murmured; Lady Primrose's eyes were like saucers.

'So you remembered me, sir,' Dorothy said. 'I'm more than honoured.'

'How could I do otherwise?' asked Charles mendaciously, rapidly summoning all possible information about her to the forefront of his mind. But suddenly he found it impossible to condole with her on the fate of Lyndon. Always he would shy away from any mention of those who had died martyrs for him. 'I heard,' was all he could say. 'I am very sorry.'

She bent her head, then lifted her glowing face again. 'My husband was glad to suffer for the Cause. I hope that your presence here means new hope for it, sir.'

He handed her to a chair, not really aware of what he was doing; glasses of wine were placed before them both by hands as unseen by them as the wings of Ariel's harpies. He thought how comely she was, how kind, with a sort of honest warmth to her that reminded him of his dear Miss Flory the night he had met with her in the hut at Rushness, the shieling of Arisary, when she had modestly offered her lousy, unshaven Prince a bowl of cream to drink. This girl had the same wide-eyed look, but with something to it that Charles had learned to recognise on the faces of Parisian demoiselles of all ages. He tossed back the wine and began to enjoy himself.

He was five years older than the lad who had come to take Scotland by storm. With tender concern Dorothy saw the hair-thin frown-lines between his brows, and the marks that time and disappointment had drawn at the corners of his mouth. He was paler, the healthy brown of Scotland gone from his complexion; as the strong light from the windows touched his face, the dark eyes were illuminated to a golden-brown agate. As he talked lightly about his wanderings since the end of the campaign, Dorothy noticed a foreignness in his speech, the odd French word or intonation overlaying the strange, endearing pseudo-Scots accent she remembered. He saw her baffled look at something he had said.

'You don't follow me, ma'am.'

She flushed. 'It was only a foreign word Your Highness used. I am quite untravelled.'

His chin came up with a sharp, proud tilt. 'I am only a poor Highlander. I speak French badly. You'll be kind enough to excuse me.'

Instead of apologising, she shook her head and laughed at him. A strange, exhilarating feeling was upon her, as though she and not he were in charge of the interview which was the envy of the whole room. Even Lady Primrose appeared a trifle hipped. Edging up besides Dorothy, she gave her shoulder a gentle tweak.

'His Highness is very much in demand, my love.'

Obediently Dorothy rose, but the Prince was on his feet first, and, still at her side with a hand proprietorially under her elbow, was drifting from person to person, chit-chatting with one and another. Dr King had reasserted himself.

'I believe I may be able to add another name or two to the list of loyal gentlemen I gave Your Highness – now that you're known to be in England.'

'Good, good.' He was listening patiently to a small elderly woman with the face of a worried squirrel, bending down to catch her words.

'Don't Your Highness run a great risk of discovery, being at large so near the Elector's court? I fear for you, indeed.'

He laughed. 'Why, as I'm well disguised, ma'am, I don't think you need have too great an apprehension. Who will connect the Chevalier Douglas with a certain wanted prince?'

Dorothy wondered just how heavily he supposed himself to be disguised. He was unmistakable to anyone who had ever set eyes on him. But then few in London had done so. He still had the massive self-confidence which had drawn reluctant chiefs to his Standard in the 'Forty-five, though Dorothy thought she could detect a look of something else: defiance, desperation? He had turned away from her and was talking to an elderly man of military appearance, who,

Lady Primrose whispered to her, was the Earl of Westmorland, Lieutenant-General of Britain's forces, under which cloak he hid a warm Jacobitism. With a splendid disregard for any less devoted ears that might be listening, Charles was telling him that he had lately been in Antwerp negotiating the purchase of twenty-six thousand muskets. The Earl was visibly taken aback.

'For what purpose, sir – since you don't propose to invade Scotland a second time?'

'To attack the Tower, of course. Once that bastion is ours, St James's will surrender and the Elector take boat for Hanover. As he would have done when we reached Derby,' he added bitterly, 'but for bad counsellors and secret traitors. *He*, the infamous Murray, had the insolence to come to Paris, begging to see me. I sent him away with a flea in his ear.'

Westmorland tactfully changed the subject. 'And brave Lochiel, sir?'

'Dead. Two years ago, in France. Of a melancholy fever.' Charles's tone did not encourage the Earl to pursue the fates of those other followers whose lives would be dragged out in shabby exile unless their leader's strange new enterprise succeeded, as, with such panache as his, it well might do.

'I wish to meet with you and the Duke of Beaufort at the first possible moment to discuss plans,' he was saying. 'Colonel Brett here,' waving to a man who had remained silently near him since Dorothy's arrival, 'has travelled with me as my aide-de-camp. To-morrow we intend an inspection of the targets.'

'Then I'll send to Beaufort tonight, sir. And now, if you'll kindly forgive me . . .' He was going, and other guests began to take their leave. They had had enough excitement for one afternoon; Dorothy hoped it would not be too much for any of them, for none could be called youthful and most appeared more than middle-aged. Where, she wondered, were Charles's young supporters? With creaky bows and quavering curtseys the company departed, one by one, until only Dorothy remained. She knew that etiquette demanded that she, too, must go, though the very thought was almost unbearable. The Prince and Colonel Brett were staying at Lady Primrose's house.

She began to make an excuse for departure, but Lady Primrose seized her by the hand.

'I beg of you, don't go, my dear creature! Now they're all gone I have something very particular to say to you, in front of His Highness, who, I'm sure, will be much taken with what I have to suggest.'

Charles looked from one woman to the other, politely concealing his puzzlement. Surely Lady Primrose was not turned bawd? The idea was too ridiculous to entertain, but his curiosity was roused.

'I shall be vastly happy to have Mrs Beaumont's company as long as she'll oblige me with it,' he said, not entirely out of gallantry, for such a fresh and seemingly fond beauty made a pleasant change from the dagger-tongued belles of Paris of whom he was becoming extremely weary. If one might not spend an evening with a pretty woman, even with a new campaign to wage, it was a pity.

They dined at the fashionable hour of five. The servants had folded down the two end-leaves of the mahogany dining-table so that the small party of four might be intimate and comfortable, which seemed much to the Prince's taste.

'Not,' he said, 'but what I flatter myself my voice carries as well across a battlefield as any other man's, but the Court of France makes conversation not so much difficult as impossible. Do you know, ladies, when King Louis first received me at Fontainbleau after my return in '46, we had to shout at each other to be heard at all across a monstrous great Salle du Trône, and between my bad French and his bad hearing it was no wonder I got no help from him – then or at any time.' Again Dorothy noticed the cynical note in his voice. The banishment from Paris had become iron lodged in his soul, and it was to his credit that he would not willingly talk of anything painful to him but, aided by Lady Primrose's excited chatter, kept the conversation on a light level. Dorothy, seated opposite to him with Colonel Brett discouragingly silent at her side, at first found herself miserably tongue-tied, since she must not mention anything that might lead back to Culloden or the executions of '46. But between the wine, the Prince's increasing gaiety and wit, and the fund of comical Irish stories which Lady Primrose reeled off one after another, she lost all her shyness and began to chatter as happily as her hostess.

She would never be able to remember precisely what they had to eat, except that there seemed to be a great deal of wine accompanying the fairly modest courses of fish, meat and fowl. The Prince drank glass after glass without appearing in the least affected by it; only his colour rose a little, so that one could see he might become rubicund with age. Disposing briskly of the boiled mutton, he made them laugh with accounts of his own cooking skill in the Highlands.

'I promise you, ma'am, I became as neat a hand at turning the spit as any poor dog in the Elector's kitchens. I'll warrant not many chefs can boast of having not only cooked their meat, but killed and dressed it first, as I and my seven men did in Glenmoriston.'

Lady Primrose shuddered. 'Lord! how horrible, sir.'

'One had to be horrible to survive, ma'am. And I swear a dish of near-raw cow's liver makes as fine a feast as your royal sturgeon or your stuffed peacock, to a parcel of starving outlaws.'

'Better is a dinner of herbs where Love is,' Dorothy pronounced solemnly, then blushed from brow to bosom, putting her hands to her neck to conceal the tide of colour. But Charles had seen it, and was eyeing her quizzically over the rim of his glass. What was Lady Primrose up to? Was he, he wondered, supposed to play Troilus to this Cressida? He was not given to classical comparisons, but in early youth his tutors had introduced him forcibly to the volume of Shakespeare's plays which had been treasured by his martyred ancestor, Charles I, and, as boys will, he had devoted most of his attention to the racier ones. 'Prince Troilus, I have loved you night and day For many weary months . . .' If that was not the sentiment expressed by the looks of Mrs Beaumont, he would be vastly surprised. 'Come, come, what need you blush? Shame's a baby,' old Pandarus had said.

Lady Primrose's intentions made themselves clear when the meal was ended, and they retired to her boudoir for tea, which to Dorothy at least was more than welcome. Her ladyship's ebullient high spirits were, as she had said, more due to the pure exuberance she felt in the company of the royal being she had worshipped from afar so long than to wine. Dainty cup in hand, she sat between them on a flowered French sofa. Colonel Brett had betaken himself into a corner, evincing little interest in tea. A disinterested observer would have pronounced him to be asleep if he had not occasionally murmured a reply to remarks addressed to him.

'He's an Irishman,' the Prince remarked. 'Takes his drinking seriously. Did ye ever hear the tale of the pig and the priest of Derry, now, my lady?'

Lady Primrose shrieked and rocked, and all but gave him a playful push, recovering her gravity in time to save her cup and its contents.

'Faith, yes, I did, Your Highness, but I beg you to be quiet a moment and listen to what I have to say. Mrs Dorothy, you were good enough a while since to offer me moneys for the sake of the Cause.'

Dorothy sat up, startled. 'Yes, and I meant it, truly.'

'Then will you now make me that offer again, but this time to His Highness for his own uses? I am sure he needs all he can get – isn't that so, sir?'

Charles looked surprised, and as embarrassed as it was possible for him to look. 'Why, my lady, I have a few private funds. The sum King Louis gave me I put to the support of my poor Highlanders in France; I have not kept one livre of it. But I don't wish for charity.' Nobody would have dared offer it to him, at that arrogant toss of the head. 'Besides,' he went on, 'I don't think it kind to ask anything of madam here, a private person.'

'But rich, Your Highness, rich! May I tell your story, dearest Mrs Dorothy?' Taking a nod for approval, she launched into the tale of Dorothy's decline and ultimate fortune, the recovery of sight and wealth all at once. The royal eyes widened, reflecting the newly lit candle flames, and even Colonel Brett stirred in his corner.

'A marvellous tale,' said the Prince at last. 'Allan Carr – who would have thought it? I always liked him, and Thriepland said he would go far if – if he was spared. But this fortune is Mrs Dorothy's. I have no claim to any part of it, and she should keep it for herself. I'm happy with her goodwill alone.'

'And that you have!' Dorothy broke in. 'You know that, sir. But

I'd wish you to let me give you any funds you need for the Cause. I heard you speak to Lord Westmorland of muskets. And there must be many other things. Pray don't think it wrong to take anything from me because I'm a woman. I own it, I am but a woman, yet does that make me less hot for the Cause, or for Your Highness?'

'No,' said Charles thoughtfully. 'No.' He doubted if the pretty creature altogether knew what she was saying, but he was altogether touched and charmed by the double offer she had unconsciously made him.

'I'll take counsel on it and speak with you again,' he said. 'I'm truly grateful, believe me.'

There was a silence, in which it seemed that Lady Primrose and Colonel Brett receded on some fortunate cloud to another region, leaving the two of them together in the small, pink-shaded boudoir, with the September sky darkening outside, the fragrance of pot-pourri heavy in the room, only a foot or two of flower-besprinkled carpet between them. He leant forward and said, very quietly, 'Do you lie in London tonight?'

She met his gaze. 'Yes, sir. In Red Lion Square. I was brought up there, and had a fancy to see it again.'

'Very well. I'll escort you there.' He rose swiftly and slapped Brett on the shoulder. 'I'm going out, Brett. Don't wait for me. I may be late. Lady Primrose, you'll forgive me if I escort Mrs Dorothy back to her lodging? I've heard poorly of your London footpads and rascally chairmen. Will you send your servant to procure us a coach?'

Lady Primrose got up, reeling slightly. 'How very kind. As Your Highness wishes. Certainly.' She left the room and returned with a servant bearing Dorothy's cloak. There were bows and farewells, and they were out in the warm, exhilarating autumn air, the dust of the day laid and the Surrey hills darkly clear across the river. He handed her up the steps of the waiting coach, and when they were within it his arm went round her shoulders, and she lay against him as though she had always lain so, utterly content.

The old house where Dr Alured Vyner and his daughter had lived was changed for the better. Years before, in 1737, an Act had been passed for the beautifying of the decaying glories of Red Lion

251

Square, which, like most Acts, had taken years to operate. Now the ancient frontages had been restored, the pavements mended, new houses put in place of those too far gone to save, the obelisk in the centre cleaned. The Vyners' old lodging leaned a little more heavily askew than it had once done; but it had been sliding sideways since the Great Fire and would last many more years yet. The ground floor, where their crabby landlady had lived and cooked endless fish, had become the shop of an engraver and statua-maker, whose works filled his window with imposing profiles and busts. Mr Roberti, who rented the shop and the building, had been surprised by the arrival that morning of a fine lady requesting to lease his first floor; but delighted at the chance of letting it to anyone so personable and, it seemed, rich.

He emerged from his living-room at Dorothy's knock, weighted stick in hand (for one never knew who was abroad in the streets at night). But seeing only his charming lodger, and behind her a tall gentleman, he smiled and bowed and showed them to the foot of the staircase, bidding them good night.

'*Buona notte, signore,*' said the gentleman, taking him by surprise.

As they went up the staircase, lit by the flickering candle Dorothy carried, she said, 'There were mice in our time. And beetles, enormous ones. Papa used to throw books at them.'

Charles laughed softly. Her voice was shaking, just enough to notice. They entered the living-room of the lodging, now trim and bookless, fashionably furnished, the curtains already drawn. She went to light the candle-branch on the table, and felt his arms come round her from behind, his hands on her breasts and his lips against her neck. Then she was lying on the wide bed in the room that had once been her father's study, quite naked, while Charles composedly stood untying his neckcloth, graceful and handsome in breeches and shirt. He met her adoring look with an affectionate smile.

'*Ma belle,*' he said, then wished he had not, for it had been said to so many others. She moved to make room for him, her arms held wide. The kingdoms of the world would never have more to offer her than this moment.

About dawn she stirred. Enough light was coming through the

curtains for her to see him, still fast asleep, breathing softly and evenly. Afraid to wake him, she sat up with caution, and looked her fill. Asleep, he might have been fifteen again, the age when his mother had looked on him last. The frown-lines had gone, the mouth that could twist bitterly was soft and relaxed; the ageing wig was laid aside and his own short fair curls became him a hundred times better. The lashes that lay against his cheek were as long as a woman's, gilt-tipped. She bent to kiss the cheek but drew back, afraid to disturb his sleep.

She sat, her arms round her knees, in a happy, incredulous reverie. All dreams, all fairy tales, had come true for her, and so much more perfectly than imagination could ever have conceived. Now she knew that the lure he had held for her in Edinburgh was no false magic; she and he were mates, not merely Prince and subject. She saw the union of herself and Lyndon as of no significance; if it was not unkind to the dead to say so. She was Juliet, Imogen, Rosalind, all ladies of legend who had loved and won their loves.

'Did my heart love till now? Forswear it, sight;
For I ne'er saw true beauty till this night,'

Her murmur was enough. He woke in a flash. A quick turn of the head as if to see where he was, and a movement of his right hand beneath the pillow, to grasp what lay there, then he saw her, and smiled.

'Good morning, my dear,' he said. 'I am most confoundedly hungry. Do you think the people downstairs could find us some meat, or eggs, anything of that kind?'

Dorothy looked down at her own nudity, laughing. 'If Your Highness would give me time to make myself decent . . .'

He lay back, lazily regarding her.

'On second thoughts,' he said, 'there are some hungers more urgent than others.' He turned to her, and again she was lost in a joy even more wonderful than that of the night before, when she had been a little mazed with wine. He was young, ardent, experienced; she starved for five years of love. He looked down at her with

253

satisfaction, reflecting on Marie de Talmond, who chattered, scolded and enthused continually throughout an act which he felt required a certain amount of concentration, and who was old enough to be his mother; and of poor Lucie Ferrand, attractive in her fair, soft way, and intellectual to a degree – he admired intellect in women – but too frail in health to be anything but a platonic *amie*.

'And now,' he said, 'I am hungry again. But I see from the clock that it's too early to rouse them below.' He drew a hand raspingly across his chin. 'I am most fearsomely bearded, and poor Morrison will be in fits by now, thinking me murdered at the least. I shall go back to Essex Street and let him console himself by shaving me.' As he dressed, he whistled a tune that brought back Dorothy's childhood. Softly she sang it

> 'Greensleeves is all my joy,
> Greensleeves is my delight,
> Greensleeves is my heart of gold . . .'

He emerged from his half-donned shirt with a surprised face.

'What words are those? I know a vastly different set.'

'Were you then brought up with our old English songs in Rome, sir?'

'Not I. Poor Papa knew little of them beyond 'Lilliburlero', the tune that drubbed his father out of Britain. No, I had this song from old Macdonald of Kingsburgh the night I lay at his house. Miss Flory and the others were gone to bed, and we two sat up over a pipe and a punch-bowl. Kingsburgh told me he always sang it when in liquor.'

'Well? Was it so dreadful that you won't regale me with it, sir?'

He laughed, adjusting his neckcloth with the aid of the wall-mirror. Then, with a mischievous glance back at her, he sang Kingsburgh's song.

> 'Greensleeves and pudding pies,
> Tell me where my mistress lies,
> And I'll be with her ere she rise—
> Fiddle an' a' together.'

Though she knew he expected her to laugh, she felt a slight shocked surprise at this unexpected version. But then he was altogether unexpected. An ordinary man might have made gallant speeches, expressed overwhelming gratitude for her favours, even voiced the fear that he might have ruined her reputation – as in fact he probably had, though with her more than willing assistance. Though their association was so new, she was instinctively aware that he would never lower himself to flattery, never apologise, and that even in these circumstances any over-familiarity on her part would be less than well received. When he said, with his hand on the door-knob, 'I must be away,' as though he had merely been paying a casual call on her, she restrained herself from any pretty protests or requests for a last kiss. But she got one, for he suddenly returned to the bedside and took from under the pillow a small, wicked-looking knife which he carefully fitted into its sheath, produced from an inner pocket of his coat. At Dorothy's startled exclamation he said calmly, 'My skean-dhu. John Mackinnon gave it to me in Borrodale. I always carry it.' He bent to give her a light kiss, and she held him for a moment, daring to say, 'Will you come back, sir?'

'When I can. Tonight, perhaps, or tomorrow night. I have great business today in this London of mine. Adieu, keep safe.'

The door shut behind him and she heard him running down the stairs, astonishingly light-footed for so large a man. For more than two hours she lay, looking round the familiar yet unfamiliar room, in a sweet sensuous apathy, remembering. He was all she had ever dreamed of, all she would ever want.

20

The most ardent romantic, embarking upon the most high-spirited of adventures, does not always take into account the discomforts that may lie along the way. When Dorothy came down to earth sufficiently to dress and go out, she found herself with nothing to do and nowhere to go. Impossible to visit Essex Street, where Lady Primrose would without doubt be entertaining a very poor idea of her young friend's behaviour. She regretted now not having brought her maid, Harriet, the girl who had replaced Meliora following her collapse in health. Even in the modest gown she had packed as well as yesterday's *grande toilette*, it would not be very agreeable for her to go on foot about the streets unattended.

She surveyed herself in the cheval-glass, the cloak and chip hat clearly of good quality, and the shoes of dark red leather quite obviously not made for walking far in London dirt. Something was needed to make her appear less of a fine lady. Suddenly inspired, she went downstairs, knocked at Mr Roberti's door, and asked for the loan of a basket.

The little monkey-faced man stared. He had married an English wife, but he would never entirely understand the complexities of the English female character after the simple dames of Italy. This lady, patently well-to-do, yet with no servant, and of questionable morals: he had heard the bang of the street-door at an early hour. Still, she was pretty, amiable, *gentile*; it was not for a Neapolitan to be ungallant.

'A basket, madam? With great pleasure. Just as madam wishes.'

He disappeared into the back regions and returned with a shopping basket. As he gave it to her, its possible use occurred to him.

'Forgive me, but madam does not propose to buy food . . .' He struggled for a word. 'Madam does not sup with friends?'

She shook her head. 'I have no great appetite, Mr Roberti. A little fruit will be enough.'

'Absurd, absurd!' He waved his hands in the air. 'My wife will be happy to prepare a meal for madam. It will be what we eat ourselves, if that is not too humble. No, no, I will not hear of a denial. It shall appear.'

And appear it did, borne in by the comely, ludicrously cockney Mrs Roberti, a stout and cheerful person who had taken the trouble to learn the cookery of her husband's native land. She whipped off the covers of the various dishes on a large tray, to reveal a steaming bowl of soup garnished with cheese, a savoury dish which Dorothy did not recognise as superb pasta, and a bowl of fruit sliced and steeped in a pungent liqueur; the whole accompanied by a flask of red wine.

'There you are then, my dear,' she said, 'and I'm in hopes it ain't too outlandish for yer, but the quality generally seems to like such stuff, and I must say it grows on the palate. Mr Roberti says as you was brought up in this house.'

'Yes,' said Dorothy. 'I lived all my life here till I was twenty.'

'Must seem uncommon odd, stayin' as a lodger.'

'It does.' Dorothy imagined Mrs Roberti's intriguement if she could but know how uncommon odd her circumstances were.

A day and half an evening passed before Charles came to her again. She heard his loud, incisive knock, and the murmur of Mr Roberti's voice in conversation with him, before he bounded up the stairs and she was in his arms again.

'Do you know, my dear,' he said, 'that curious little landlord of yours has a fancy for making a bust of me. According to him I have an unusual face. Now what do you think of that?'

'I agree, sir. As to your face, that is. But a bust . . . would that be altogether wise? People would recognise it – you might be traced.'

'If our plans succeed I'll have no need to hide. I'm hopeful, very hopeful. Brett and I reconnoitred the Tower today – it should be an easy nut to crack, I believe, a very different matter from Edinburgh Castle. There's a gate we could blow in with a petard – that would give us the entry, and then . . . Geordie should not sleep sound in his bed *that* night. Have you some wine? Good.'

As he drank, his face dreaming with plans and secrets, she said: 'But where will you find troops, sir? Unless from Scotland—'

'No, no. This time my army will be recruited in England. I'll have no more of my brave Highlanders butchered . . .' He broke off, shaking his head angrily. 'Though I never could believe my cousin William could have committed such atrocities as they said. There must have been exaggerations – don't you think so?'

Dorothy knew that he was pleading with her to agree, to preserve his peace of mind.

'I only know what the reports said, sir. I 'think it better if you forget the past and look only to a happier future.'

He brightened. 'You're very right. And I have such promises . . . tomorrow I meet Westmorland and Beaufort and others for a conference. After that I shall have great news for you, I swear it.' He seized her hand and pulled her to her feet. 'Come, let's see what your landlord can make of my royal features.'

She was dismayed. 'You didn't promise him, surely, sir? I really think it very rash.'

'Nonsense. It will please the little man and do no harm.'

Mr Roberti was indeed pleased. Obsequiously he ushered his handsome sitter and his lodger into the small studio, up a few stairs at the back of the shop; Dorothy remembered that in her childhood it had been used as a storeroom. Now it contained an easel, a work-bench, artists' properties and an array of tools, and smelt agreeably of plaster, wax, and the numerous candles which Roberti had lit, declaring that daylight was quite unnecessary for his art, and that he preferred the chiaroscuro, the flickering play of light and shadow, to the flat illumination from the window. Carefully he positioned his subject in the model's chair, a high-backed piece with arms, calculated to provide the maximum support and relaxation for the nervous. It was perfectly obvious, however, that, far from being nervous, Charles delighted in being modelled. His soldierly straight back, the correct, proud poise of his head, needed no adjustments by the artist, who exclaimed rapturously on the gentleman's aptitude for posing. Dorothy, looking round the studio at the stiff beaux and belles and hard-featured ladies in high caps whose images awaited collection, understood his feelings.

As the little man worked at incredible speed, his sitter chatted amiably, since Roberti had said that conversation helped his art by showing him the face in animation; which was just as well, for Charles in his elated mood found silence difficult to maintain. He asked where Roberti came from, and discoursed knowledgeably of Naples, Vesuvio and Posilippo, of vineyards and wines and local legends of saints. Gradually he dropped into Italian, and a rapid crossfire of conversation assailed Dorothy's ears.

With horror she heard 'Roma' mentioned, and then what sounded like a torrent of description of that city, which Roberti had apparently not visited. Surely now he would realise the identity of his sitter? She moved her chair unobtrusively into Charles's line of sight, and very slightly shook her head at him – a gesture of which he took not the least notice. Then, to her relief, the door creaked open to admit Mrs Roberti with a flask of wine and glasses.

'I thought yer might fancy a morsel of refreshment. Lor! what a fine 'andsome model you're makin' of the gentleman, Tony. I'll stay and watch a minute, if it's all the same to you, sir.'

Sir bestowed on her a radiant smile and a gracious word, reducing her to the state of awestruck bedazzlement he was so used to seeing in females. The minute turned into ten, then into twenty as she sat gazing at the noble features as raptly as though an archangel had taken the place of the average sitter. A waste of Tony's art, mostly they were, and she often longed to ask them right out why they wanted busts of themselves at all. Dorothy feared to see recognition in her eyes too; there had been so many cartoons published in '45, some of them not too inaccurate portraits of the Bonnie Prince. Though Roberti was obviously Catholic, that was no guarantee that his lady was not a Whig. Dorothy began to devise ways of bringing the sitting to an end; a sudden attack of vapours, an upset candle?

She was saved from either of these measures by the entry of a small girl of about five or six, who sidled up to her mother's skirts and clung there, finger in mouth, watching.

'Antonia!' said Mrs Roberti sternly. 'Didn't I say you was to stay out of yer pa's studio? Besides which it's long past bedtime.' She gave the child a push, but Charles was beckoning, and when he beckoned, no woman, however young, resisted. Antonia ran to him before her mother could pull her back, and stood looking up into his face.

'There!' Mrs Roberti was truly vexed. 'What a naughty, impudent, disobedient wench, that shall get the flat of my hand in no time at all. Come here this minute.' But Charles, with an expression Dorothy had never seen him wear before, had gathered the child up and set her on his knee. She leaned confidently against his breast, smiling and fingering one of the silver buttons of his coat, while he stroked her long black hair.

'Miss Antonia,' he said gently. 'Do you, too, speak Italian like your papa?'

She shook her head and murmured something; he bent to catch the words.

'So, only a little? Then say something, only to please me.'

Antonia looked up and, with a purely flirtatious grin, said, *'Bello signore.'*

Her mother gasped, and her father, straightening up from his work, laughed outright. 'She is so shy, so quiet, sir. You have bewitched her.'

' *"Bello signore"* ' repeated Charles. 'I'm most flattered to be called a beautiful gentleman by so beautiful a lady. She will slay many hearts in her time, your daughter, Mr Roberti.' He laid his hand over the small fingers still playing with the button.

'Would you like it, to remember me by, Miss Antonia? Here, then.' He wrenched it off and closed her hand round it, then, with a kiss on her cheek, set her gently down. 'To bed now.' He watched her to the door, past her still speechless mama, with a tenderness that transformed his face. A stab of pain went through Dorothy. To be able to see him look so at her own child, their child!

The sitting was over, a completely recognisable reproduction of his head and shoulders in miniature, some five inches high. He exclaimed on its excellent likeness, turning it from side to side.

'Please not to touch it too closely, sir,' Roberti warned. 'I am happy it proves so good. But with such a striking physiognomy it could not be otherwise.'

He bowed them out, Mrs Roberti having gone after her daughter. At the door Charles said casually, 'By the bye, when you complete the busto I'd be obliged if you'd clothe it in Scottish dress.' At Roberti's baffled look he produced from an inside coat pocket (the one, Dorothy presumed, that held the skean-dhu) an unframed coloured print of himself, in a tartan jacket with the Garter ribbon and star. Dorothy pulled at his arm in agitation.

'Not the star, sir, for God's sake! Oh, do have a care . . .'

He shrugged. 'Very well. Perhaps you'll leave out this small ornament, *signore*!' They discussed the fee and the day on which the bust would be ready, and with another bow Roberti showed his visitors into the hall from which the staircase led up to Dorothy's rooms. But Charles turned towards the street-door, ignoring her pleading look.

'I've much to attend to tomorrow, my dear.'

'Then when will you . . . when shall we meet?'

'Oh, very soon, I dare say.' He kissed her firmly but briefly, and disappeared into the night. With a heart leaden with disappointment she went slowly upstairs and threw herself on the bed.

It was two days before she saw him again, except for a glimpse in the street. She had taken coach to Bond Street, and there, having satisfied her craving for silks, laces and perfumes, returned by way of St James's Street and the Mall, the press of traffic in Piccadilly being heavy. He was there, gazing at St James's Palace from the opposite side of the road, a tall conspicuous figure among small scurrying people, an eagle among sparrows, gesticulating in his foreign way to the impassive Colonel Brett. Heads turned to stare at him. Dorothy would not have been surprised to see scarlet-uniformed guards cross the road to arrest him; surely somebody would have recognised him from a window – perhaps the Elector himself. Her coach moved away sharply, and he was lost from sight.

When he had not come to her by the end of the second day she steeled herself to face Lady Primrose. It was not easy to stand at the Essex Street house-door, hearing the jangle of the bell within and the measured steps of the approaching footman, or, having been admitted, to follow him to the boudoir where his lady was writing letters.

Lady Primrose raised her head as Dorothy was announced. There was no coldness or censure in her look as she rose to embrace the visitor with her old eager warmth.

'My dear! I knew you would come.'

Dorothy held back from her. 'First tell me what you think of me.'

'Think of you? Why, that you're brave, and clever. And much to be envied. Wouldn't I give the world to be you, now?'

Dorothy hugged her. 'I didn't expect such generosity. Yet I might have done, from you.'

'You must be happy beyond belief. I'd be in the skies, in your place.'

'Not so happy as I was, alas. Is he – here?'

Lady Primrose nodded. 'Yes, and in very melancholy case. His hopes have been dashed by those big-talking, little-doing leaders of the Party, or whatever they call themselves.' She snorted. 'A wonder 'twould be if they could lead a flock of sheep up a mountain, or down one, come to that, Beaufort and Westmorland and the rest. As for Doctor King, I thought better of him, but it seems I flattered the man. He had His Highness to tea yesterday, and told him flatly there'd be no support for a rising. Then at night some fifty of 'em daunted him further. Pie-crust promises made at race-meetings and card-tables, if you ask my opinion. These are what brought him to London, and better if he had stayed away.'

'Do you think he would see me?'

'As to that . . .' Lady Primrose hesitated. 'I don't know for sure whether he'd welcome visitors at all. Since this morning he's been shut up in his room, taking no food, and answering but shortly when I called to ask how he did. I could send a servant to enquire . . .'

'No. I'll venture myself – he can but be angry with me. Where is his room?'

Lady Primrose led her upstairs to the first landing, and a door at the end of a small corridor.

'I wish you well,' she said. 'Anything to do him good.

Dorothy's first hesitating knock was unanswered. She knocked again, then tried the handle. The door was locked. From inside the room a voice demanded to know who the devil was that.

''Tis I, Dorothy, sir. Will you let me in, please?'

After a pause the key turned. She opened the door and entered, shutting it behind her. He returned to his chair and sat much in the attitude of the discontented young husband in Hogarth's *Marriage à la Mode*, his wig thrown aside and his cravat discarded. He may have taken no food that day, but it was obvious that he had taken a good deal of drink. An overturned empty bottle lay in the hearth, another stood on the table beside him; and at Dorothy's entrance he filled his empty glass from a vine-engraved decanter and drank it off defiantly.

'Well? To what do I owe the honour of this visit, ma'am?'

Dorothy seated herself – though it was unheard of to do so without invitation in the presence of royalty. She resolved to be as calm and composed as though he were his usual self, and to give him no grounds for adding her to the list of people he thought his enemies.

'Will you not offer me a glass of wine, sir?' she asked pleasantly. 'I see you have some by you.'

He looked impatiently round him. 'I don't see another glass.'

'Then I'll share yours, sir, if I may.'

The hand with which he poured shook, she noted, and as he handed it to her drops fell on the polished surface of the table, drying into white marks. She took a sip, and shuddered.

'But this is brandy. It's too strong for me, I fear. And, I should have thought, for you.'

He gave a short, mirthless laugh. 'You sound exactly like my brother Henry. "Less of the eau-de-vie, Charles my dear. Don't you know 'tis the road to ruin?" Ruin. Henry has been my ruin, not the eau-de-vie. I suppose, like the rest of the world, you've heard what my brother did to me?'

He drew the wet base of his glass to and fro across the table-top, making aimless patterns. 'Little Henry. Good, patient, obedient

263

little Henry. We were so close to each other as boys, I don't think we ever fought once. He was never jealous that I was the one to be courted and flattered, the one who would be King. Always Henry was my dearest friend . . . And then, not a year after my return from Scotland, I got a letter from my father telling me that I might be surprised to hear my brother was to become a Cardinal of the Holy Roman Church.' He banged the glass down, snapping its slender stem.

'A Cardinal. A fat, luxurious, pompous, petted Cardinal, to be carried about Rome in satins and gold lace, like the Pope's whore. I had rather he'd become a humble monk. At least one could have respected that. But a Cardinal. It was a dagger to my heart; I wish it had killed me, for I knew it had killed the Cause. What was England to think, England who feared us Stuarts so much for our Papacy? No, no, it was a death-blow and Henry dealt it deliberately. I was never betrayed in Scotland, you know, though I had thirty thousand pounds on this head of mine. It took my own brother to betray me.' He was weeping. Dorothy went to him and drew his head to her breast. He clung to her, and she knew that she was not to be numbered with his enemies. Releasing himself, he reached for the bowl of the broken glass. She took it out of his hand.

'I have been given bitter waters to drink,' he said.

'Yes, sir. But too much brandy will make them no sweeter, and you'll be ill tomorrow. What good will that do you, or the Cause?'

He nodded, and let the glass fall, empty, to the carpet.

'Tomorrow. Tomorrow we will go to church.'

'Church, sir?'

'Yes. To the new church in the Strand. And tonight you'll stay with me. I should not like to be alone tonight.' He led her towards the bed that loomed in the shadows. He was not quite steady on his feet, he reeked of brandy, but she knew that she loved him utterly. As they reached the bed she put her arms round his neck.

'I wish I might call you something other than sir.'

'Call me what you like. What does it matter? Except Carlucchio. That was what my father – and Henry – used to call me. In France they call me *le Prince Edouard*, God knows why. I have a selection of other names, if you care to choose one – Louis Philippe, Casimir, Sobieski . . .'

'I shall call you what your Highlanders called you, to remind you that you still have much love and loyalty.' She raised his hand and kissed it. 'I shall call you Tearlach.'

21

Next morning, to Dorothy's surprise and relief, there remained no trace of the unhappy stranger of the previous night. Bright-eyed and cheerful, Charles ripped open the window-curtains and viewed with satisfaction the September sun breaking through early mists and throwing myriads of dancing diamonds on the river.

'Excellent,' he said. 'A perfect morning. I have the most confounded monstrous appetite – would you be so kind as to warn Lady Primrose's cook, my dear, when you've got your clothes on?' He laughed at her astonished face. 'I see you expected to find me roughish today – is that it? *Eh bien*, now you observe that I can drink three ordinary men under the table and arise as fresh as a lark.' He caught sight of himself in a mirror. '*Dieu!* while you're about it, you might send one of the footmen to valet me.' He sniffed. 'This place smells like a tap-room. Tell them I shall breakfast downstairs – and add that I hope my Chantilly cravat has been properly laundered.'

Fortunately it had, as it was required to provide an elegant contrast to the rest of his costume. He was an impressive sight at breakfast, in a wide-skirted coat of black velvet, breeches of the same, and a dark silver waistcoat wrought with an intricate design of roses and thistles. The effect was one of quiet magnificence, heightened by the stately white wig he wore today. He demolished his breakfast of cold beef and pheasant – an immense one by the measure of the day – with a look that was part abstraction, part a secret excitement. Dorothy did not know him well enough to recognise it as his response to a challenge, the change of breaking out of the inactivity he hated so much.

During the meal a servant entered with a letter. Seated opposite him, Dorothy could not help but see that it was addressed to Le Chevalier Douglas in a spidery foreign handwriting. Charles's face darkened at the sight of it. He opened it with a violence which detached the seal completely, sending it spinning across to land by Dorothy's plate. She picked it up, idly.

'An armed cupid – how charming.'

He muttered something in French which she could only gather was to do with hunting, and, crumpling the letter into a tight ball, hurled it accurately into the fire, where it blazed and died.

The household was alive with excitement. Throughout breakfast the front-door bell was frequently heard to peal, followed by indications that gentlemen were being shown into the drawing-room. Lady Primrose appeared occasionally with her best cap askew, the maids flew in and out. Dorothy, excusing herself from the table, caught her hostess in the hall.

'What is it about? Why are we going to church?'

'He won't say. Some special service. I thought *you* might know! Forgive me, so much to prepare . . .'

It was almost eleven o'clock when they set out for church, a straggling cavalcade led by Charles, the agitated Lady Primrose on his arm. A very short walk brought them to St Mary-le-Strand, a newish church of elegant proportions with a baroque half-domed porch. Inside all was light, golden colours, radiance pouring down on them from the sun's rays through the clear windows, clustered cherub faces eyeing them plumply from the roof, gilt scatterings from the Holy Ghost's wings in the plaster ornaments above the altar. Where the nave met the chancel, the ceiling bore a huge representation of the royal arms: a golden lion and a silver unicorn with the shield between them. Charles glanced up at it as he strode up the aisle towards the altar, where he bent his knee in a ritual genuflexion before standing motionless, not glancing aside as the clergyman passed him and took up a place in front of the communion rail. In the first four pews a scattering of gentlemen stood uncomfortably, none meeting another's eye, some gazing about them, some apparently lost in thought. One Dorothy recognised as the elderly Earl of Westmorland; another proved to be the Duke of Beaufort. She tucked herself away at the end of the last pew, out of sight of the clergyman but with a clear view of the tall black figure and the imperious profile.

It was hard to hear what was being said. The clergyman's words bounced off the walls into the echoing empty church and were lost, but it seemed that some kind of question and answer was being exchanged. Then, as the ear became more accustomed to the acoustic, Charles's voice was heard clearly.

'. . . I do hereby make a solemn abjuration of the Romish religion, and do faithfully embrace that of the Church of England as by Law established, in the Thirty-nine Articles in which I hope to live and die.'

A wave of shock ran through the small congregation. Charles's face was grim and set. This was the challenge he had risen to meet, the hoped-for gate to action. He was kneeling now, the clergyman taking him through the long interrogation of the Catechism, the hearers chiming in at the Creed and murmuring amens to the Commandments. There was an audible ripple of interest as Charles replied to the question regarding his duty to his neighbour.

'To love, honour, and succour my father and mother: to honour and obey the King, and all that are put in authority under him . . .' He had learned it all so carefully; he kept his hands firmly at his sides at all moments when he would automatically have made the sign of the cross. Now it was almost over, the newly received child of the Anglican Church promising to have a lively faith in God's mercy through Christ, with a thankful remembrance of His death; and be in charity with all men. The brilliant light from the east window streamed in upon the bowed, white-scrolled wig; then he rose in one graceful movement and, with a bow to the altar, walked swiftly away down the aisle and vanished through the west door.

At a sign from the clergyman, those left behind knelt in a short prayer, then, with murmurs, straightened stiff knees and began to file out. Dorothy longed to run, to overtake him and cling to his arm, to say how brave she thought him, to comfort him for a renunciation that must have hurt. But he was nowhere to be seen until they straggled back to Essex Street and found him ensconced in the drawing-room, all smiles, with a glass of wine.

'Of course it was necessary,' he was saying loudly to the shocked Dr William King, himself wearing clerical bands. 'I should have done it long ago, before the Rising. It's the only way to convince Britain that a Stuart need not be a Papist.'

'But, sir, your upbringing . . .'

'My upbringing? And what of the upbringing of the other princes of Europe, with not a ha'porth of Christianity between them? Do you suppose my good cousin Louis of France has not broken the Commandments a thousand times over, forsworn himself in the confessional every week? What is religion but a set of words? And that being so, why should a set of Latin words be better than good honest English? I am a Scot, Doctor, not an Italian.' Abruptly he turned to Beaufort, an earnest Royalist and descendant of John of Gaunt.

'Do you not think the church was fitting, your grace? It was built to the order of my Aunt Anne in her blessedly Protestant reign, by one Gibbs, a Scotsman and a Jacobite. Now what could be apter than that? I see your glass is empty.' In an instant it was filled. Beaufort raised it towards Charles. Dorothy watched the black velvet figure, the flowing white curls, moving among the company, and remembered his attendants on the march : the ex-priest O'Sullivan, the pious, rheumy old Sir Thomas Sheridan. Always Irishmen and Papists about him, they had whispered. And in Rome the worried man who was rightful King of England was telling his beads, praying for the beloved son Carlucchio, and the other son, now Cardinal York, who had committed Cain's crime against Abel, but more subtly and with no anger.

In a corner of the room, half hidden by a draped curtain, Allan Carr was watching her with the same obsessive hunger that he saw, too clearly, in her face. He had been at the church, and his heart had sunk when she entered. What he had feared then was confirmed now; not only in her look but in the casual possessive touch Charles had bestowed on her in passing. Without being told, he knew of the curtained bed upstairs, the other bed at her lodgings, the reason for the bloom that shone on her in spite of her momentary sadness. So his prize was lost. He had known it would be so, yet it was hard to accept the reality. He longed to go to her, if only for the flash of kindness he knew she would show him. Perhaps a few more glasses of wine would give him the courage to seize her hand and pull her away from that assembly and the beautiful peril at the heart of it. He drank again, and suddenly ashamed of himself put down the glass and stalked into the hall, where he called for his hat and cloak.

A few minutes later and he would have had Dorothy to himself. Something in the morning's ceremony, with its futile gesture and vain hopes, had tired her. She had lain awake besides the heavily sleeping Charles for much of the previous night, and suddenly she longed to be alone and quiet. Without saying good bye she stole from the room and asked the footman to call her a chair.

Red Lion Square was baking in noon sunshine, some urchins playing whip-and-top by the inn door, a dog sprawled sleeping on the hot cobbles. At the entrance to her lodging she paused, drawn by a new splash of colour in the shop-window. On a shelf in the centre, gaudily conspicuous beside the pallid portraits which had been gathering dust there for weeks, stood a row of six wax busts portraying Charles to the life, habited in tartan of brighter greens and blues and reds than the Highlands ever saw, the royal star which Mr Roberti had been expressly asked to omit blazing in silver on the left breast.

Mr Roberti was in the shop, counting his morning's takings. He looked up, beaming, at his lodger's abrupt entrance.

'The busts,' she began without preamble. Eagerly he interrupted her.

'Ah, you have seen the bustos already. Very fine, are they not, madam? I told the handsome Italian gentleman he would make the perfect subject for me. Perhaps it was not wise to put them in the window on a day so sunny, but I was so proud I could not resist temptation.'

'It was not wise at all,' she said emphatically. 'I . . . how can I explain to you, Mr Roberti? The – gentleman – concerned is in a little trouble with the authorities at the present moment. It would not do for them to know he is in London, and I fear these busts may be all too much of an advertisement.'

The little sculptor looked mystified. 'In trouble? But surely he is some great gentleman, not a *criminale*? No, no, I cannot believe it.'

'Of course not a criminal. 'Tis a – a matter of state. I can't say more, but I do beg you to take the busts out of the window before any of his – his pursuers see them.'

Mr Roberti, whose face had fallen, brightened. 'But I have already sold one. This morning, soon after I put them in.'

Dorothy gasped. 'To whom, pray?'

He shrugged. 'How can I tell you? A large man, very polite. He admired the busts greatly, and asked whether they were done from life. I said that was so, and the mould had been made only a day or two before. At this he seemed very pleased, and paid me well for one. It was all I sold this morning, but for two little profiles of King George and the late Queen.'

'I am so sorry, Mr Roberti. I will buy the others from you myself at the same price, or whatever you like to charge. Only please take them out of the window.'

Obediently he reached into the window and collected them.

'I thought – five shillings each?' he suggested wistfully, and at the sight of the money his eyes widened. 'Madam is so kind. I am sorry to have displeased her. But – I was so proud of them. Will you present one to the gentleman? I said to him they would be ready today.'

'I will, and he is sure to be pleased.' A dreadful thought struck her, turning her cold in the warmth of the little shop.

'Did the man who bought the bust ask any more about the sitter?'

'Ah yes, he seemed very interested. Who was the gentleman, was he known to me, and so on. I told him all I knew, that he was a friend of the amiable lady lodging in my house. Is madam ill, faint perhaps?' He dragged forward a chair.

'No, no, I'm quite well. Only I fear I must leave – very soon, this afternoon.'

His sincere regrets followed her as she hurried upstairs and began to pack her belongings, her heart hammering. The buyer of the bust might just possibly have been a Jacobite, pleased to see his Prince's likeness openly displayed, but he was far more likely to have been someone with memories of the £30,000 offered by Cumberland for Charles's head and hoping to qualify for some reward, even if the

Treasury was now only prepared to pay out a smaller one. The Prince had taken so many chances already; this was too much to risk.

She looked out of the window, standing well behind the curtain. The Square was almost empty, for it was dinner-time. Those people who were about looked harmless enough, a chimney-sweep and his boy, an old woman who was certainly not a disguised officer, two men on their way to the inn. It seemed as good a time to run as any. She pulled the bell and asked the girl who answered it to fetch her a coach from the nearest stand. Then she went to settle her account with Roberti, whose regret at her sudden departure was only exceeded by his mystification. Antonia appeared, finger in mouth, smiling shyly, and Dorothy gave her a shilling. For the last time she looked round the hall, up at the staircase that had known her when she was a child herself. What would her father's shade, if allowed to return to his old home, think of the masquerade in which his daughter was involved, muffled on this hot day in her cloak with her hood pulled almost over her face, glancing to right and left for soldiers or spies? She thought he would give her his blessing, good High Tory that he had been.

On her instructions the coachman took her by a roundabout way to Essex Street, sustained by the promise of double payment. The journey was incredibly tedious and trying to her nerves, as she looked from side to side for any sign of pursuit. The emptiest streets appeared the most dangerous, though the coach could move through them faster. Round those seemingly innocent corners, in the sharp shadows of the afternoon sun, anyone might be lurking. The appearance of a face at the coach window sent her crouching back in her seat; but it was only a flower-seller holding up a drooping bunch of autumn blooms.

They were in Newgate Street now, in sight of the gaol, which looked today even more threatening than usual. She was glad when the coachman turned south towards St Paul's, and so into the little streets that ran between the river and the Strand, and gladder when she alighted at Lady Primrose's door without any vestige of interest from anyone except the coachman. He gazed thoughtfully after the cloaked figure who was being admitted to the house. Some little piece on the run from a husband, he thought, meeting her lover. A pretty enough baggage, what he could see of her. Well, it was no business of his, and for all the rambling distance she'd made him drive, his pockets were better lined than they had been all summer. He decided to take the rest of the day easily, beginning at the Essex's Head.

Dorothy's royal lover was, in fact, drawing up lists of names with the help of Colonel Brett. He looked up with an absent-minded smile as she appeared.

'Ah, good,' he said. 'Now you can help us. We have two hundred and more letters to write, think of it, to gentlemen who will spread the word of my becoming a Protestant. A tedious job, but it must be done. Give Mrs Beaumont half your list, Brett. You can begin with the Welsh ones, for *I* can't spell 'em . . .'

She ventured to interrupt him, a thing not many people did.

'Your Highness, I think you must leave here.'

'*Leave?* In God's name, why?'

'Because of this.' From a reticule she produced one of the busts. Charles stared, then laughed.

'Your little landlord's work. A very pretty likeness. Is it for me?'

'Please listen, sir.' She told them hurriedly of the events of the day. Brett frowned and nodded agreement as she insisted on the seriousness of the incident, but Charles looked mutinous.

'This may be nothing but a storm in a teacup. Haven't I walked openly about London, showing my face to all, without once being recognised?'

'Yes, sir, but not clad in tartan and wearing the star.'

'There are plenty of print-shops and model-makers' windows. Why should the Elector send his spy to that one in particular, pray?'

'We don't know that it *was* a spy – only that whoever it was took a great interest in Your Highness's features, and wanted to know as much about you as he could learn. If he had been an honest man and a sympathiser, don't you think he would have left his carte-de-visite, with a request to call on me? I think he saw the busts by accident, and went off to report at St James's. They have my name in their records – that alone would be enough to tell them they were on the scent.'

'Mrs Beaumont is very right, sir,' said Brett. 'I believe she would be in custody now if she hadn't taken swift flight. Too dangerous to ignore, this bust-buyer.'

'And I,' Charles said bitterly, 'am I dangerous? All I can do is plot and plan, most like to no end. They know very well that even if I got Geordie and all his relatives under guard, I would not have one hair of their heads harmed. I always held firm to that, even in time of war.'

'They would find out about the muskets,' Brett pointed out. 'That would not look very like peaceable intentions. And I take leave to doubt that such men as Cumberland have the least comprehension of a merciful victor. If they did believe such a person could be, no doubt they'd laugh heartily at him. Your existence is still a threat to them, and your capture would put them in very good case with King Louis, who would then be spared the embarrassment of your presence in France. For the sake of the Cause you must not risk being taken.'

There was a silence, as Charles gloomily drew designs on the list before him. At last he said, 'Very well. I retreated once before, God help me. I suppose I can do it again. Go and see to arrangements for our leaving tonight.'

When the Colonel had gone Dorothy took Charles's hand, glad that it was not snatched away. 'You are so wise to do this, sir. I can sense danger nowadays, and believe me it was there, in that shop. Your life is too precious to be risked.'

He sighed heavily. 'So once again the bird has no nest. Where now? Back to France, to Antwerp, to Sweden? Back to Avignon and the sour-faced Archbishop? I suppose it will go on all my life, this hiding. I may even get a taste for it in time, and only come out of doors at night, like a tom-cat. I wish I had never left Scotland. I wish I had died at Culloden.'

She put her arms round him. 'Take me with you.'

Surprised out of his dramatics, he tilted up her face towards him.

'Take you, child? But you have your fine country house, your friends. Why should you leave so much, to live miserably in exile?'

'It would not be exile. My home is where you are, for ever.'

'Fair and fond,' he said, touching her cheek. 'Are you faithful too?'

She nodded, unable to speak.

'Very well,' he said. 'We will try our fortune together. Go and speak with Lady Primrose.'

Left alone, he folded methodically the lists of his supporters' names and put them into his secret pocket. His hand went out for the little bust that stood on the table; then, suddenly savage, he dashed it against a wall. It splintered into small pieces, meaningless coloured fragments that had once been his own image.

22

The stars over Paris were brilliant; it was going to be a frosty night, which tomorrow would yield a crop of broken limbs on the heights of Ste Geneviève and Montmartre. But that was preferable to the deluges of the past five days, which had turned the narrow streets into swamps of filthy mud and, descending in sudden cascades from sloping roofs and broken gutters beneath the eaves, had drenched from above the unfortunate pedestrian who was already soaked and splashed to the knees.

Even in the best of weather, in which Dorothy had not yet seen it, Paris was a dirtier city than London. It had had no Great Fire to purify it, no new houses to speak of to match the smart pink-bricked dwellings of Bloomsbury and Cavendish and Portman squares. Clusters of leaning twisted medieval dwellings, dark with soot and centuries of weather, had seen François Villon and his *dames du temps jadis*, the red slaughter of St Bartholomew's Day, the swaggering *Vert Galant*, Henry IV, who remained in effigy, a stone rider on a stone horse, on the old Pont Neuf. In the great Place Royale one might with a little imagination meet with the scarlet-robed Richelieu or the lovely shade of the young Marie Stuart in white mourning for her boy-husband.

In order to explore the city, without a maid (for she had left the still ailing Meliora in charge of Carola House), Dorothy had to learn to go about like a bourgeoise, in heavy pattens to keep her feet out of the worst of the mud, and a sensible hooded cloak. In the two months they had lived in Paris her quick ear and training in Latin enabled her to pick up enough French to do the shopping without attracting curiosity; her far from Parisian accent was taken for the speech of some province, and in time she became used to hearing something she had said repeated with apparent bafflement in what sounded to her exactly the same pronunciation.

'Des oignons?'

'*Oui, j'ai dit des oignons.*'

A slow beam of comprehension. '*Ah! des* oignons.'

At first she had been accompanied on shopping and sightseeing expeditions by Charles's footman and general attendant, Duncan Cameron. In his household capacity he was less than efficient, being a born smasher of crockery and spiller of wine, but his personal devotion to Charles was total, and Dorothy thought he was probably employed more as a potential bodyguard than as a servant. He had been a shepherd, speaking only Gaelic, when his chief Lochiel had joined the Standard, and it seemed that some of the characteristics of the sheepdog were his: gentle brown eyes, his shaggy hair wearing powder very oddly, yet in manner steel-sharp with questionable visitors. His French, with its Gaelic inflections and the occasional phrase of argot, was a continual astonishment to Dorothy, the more so because it seemed to be better understood by the Parisians than her own painstaking efforts.

He and Morrison were the only members of the household. How they accommodated themselves in the five rooms that made up the lodging was a mystery. Morrison seemed to inhabit a small window-less room probably intended as a powdering-closet, and Dorothy suspected that Duncan slept on the half-landing, wrapped in the old plaid he had managed to keep. Food was sent up from below, cooked by a hard-faced female concierge who dealt only with Duncan; there was no question of Dorothy giving her orders or taking any active part in the running of the strange ménage.

As to Charles, she was learning to know him a little better than in England, but only a little. As a lover he was accomplished, sophi-sticated, so infinitely desirable to her that she willingly overlooked the very slight abstraction, almost absent-mindedness, which attended his love-making. If I were Britannia in person, she thought with amusement, I might inspire more ardour; but what of it, when I have enough for both? She discovered, with surprise, that he could on occasion be quite violent, leaving her with bruises, and that these occasions were connected with news he had received from one of the visitors who came so stealthily to their door, or a letter brought in by Duncan from some *poste restante* unknown to her. Once she saw a superscription in the same thin hand that had been on the letter he had burned in the Essex Street fireplace, and later she found fragments of it on the floor, where Duncan had overlooked them. She left them where they lay. In this house it did not do to pry or to ask questions.

One did not enquire, for instance, why Charles hardly went out by daylight; he was proscribed from living in Paris at all, and might well have been arrested if recognised. Only when dusk fell he would go, leaving her to pass the long evening reading to improve her French, or fingering haltingly the clavichord he played so brilliantly when the mood took him. She improvised from the tunes that came into her head, for the printed music lying on top of the instrument was far beyond her skill. One evening, when the wind moaned and rattled at the casement, and Duncan was mending the fire, she strayed into a tune she remembered from the days of the Rising, when the men sang in billets and by campfires. Duncan raised his head.

'That iss being "Lewie Gordon", my leddy,' he said.

'Is it? Yes, of course.

> 'O send Lewie Gordon hame,
> And the Lad I daurna name,
> Though his back be at the wa',
> Here's to him that's far awa'.

'It iss about His Highness, my leddy. Sometimes he hass given himself the name of Lord Lewiss Gordon.'

'I remember Lord Lewis – he was brother to the Duke, I think.'

Duncan seemed to be struggling for words. 'If you pleass, my leddy, I would not be singing the Highland songs to His Highness.'

She smiled. 'I'd not dare to, Duncan. He is far too good a musician to bear with my bad playing and singing.'

'No, it iss not that.' He hung his head, murmuring something which was hard to make out, but which Dorothy gathered was to the effect that the songs would make his master sad and drive him to drink too much strong wine. Then, suddenly overcome by his own volubility and daring, Duncan ducked a swift bow and hastened from the room.

If Duncan's inarticulacy sprang from his language difficulties, Morrison's was born of a natural taciturnity. In her first days in France Dorothy felt the valet must have taken a dislike to her on sight, for she could barely get the time of day out of him. When it became apparent that she was not going to put on airs, bother his master with trivialities, or behave like certain other ladies who had in the past been violently unpopular with Morrison, his manner improved somewhat. A thin, middle-aged man with a careworn face, he treated her at first as though she had dropped in for a cup of tea and might be expected to leave at any moment. When her continued presence became an undeniable fact, she received at first the occasional grim smile, then a surprising offer to clean and press her mud-soiled skirt, followed by a burst of confidence in which he disclosed to her his disapproval of the Prince's other valet, Daniel, left behind at Avignon. Their friendship was sealed on the day when she struggled in vain with a new bodice, cursed by a row of small buttons fastening up the back. Half dressed and feeling ridiculous, she rang the bell. Charles was out, and in any case she was still too much in awe of him to ask him to perform such a task for her.

Morrison took in the situation at a glance. 'If I may assist, mem.' Firm fingers subdued the rebel buttons. 'It's no' fitting, if I may make the observation, that a leddy should have nae maid of her own.'

'But I'm quite accustomed to maid myself, Morrison. It was only these stupid buttons . . . thank you.'

He was surveying her hair speculatively. 'I could gie ye a guid fashionable coiffure, if ye'd allow it, mem.'

'Heavens, am I as behind the times as all that? Yes, I suppose I *do* look a fright. But then I don't go much into society here, so it hardly matters. And yet – yes, pray do. It will be so luxurious.'

The result was something that would not have disgraced the charming head of La Pompadour herself. Morrison was pleased with it. He decided, after further cogitation, that the English lass would do very well, and made an agreeable change from French besoms and hizzies. He approved, too, of the additions she made to their diet from her own pocket, for he knew all about her withdrawals from the Paris branch of her English bank, to which she trudged weekly over the Pont Royal. The concierge's cookery was not bad, in his grudging opinion, but he suspected her of keeping back some of the better supplies and substituting rubbish eked out with sauces. His Highness, who neither noticed nor cared what he ate, would never have complained, and only a few months earlier had suffered a bad attack of food poisoning. Now, when Mrs Beaumont bought meat, meat was what she expected to see appear at the table, as it did with agreeable frequency.

It was a trouble to Dorothy that Charles would not let her contribute openly to his expenses. The only time she had asked him outright they had come near to a quarrel. She had reminded him that he had made no strong objection when Lady Primrose suggested that her money might be of assistance to him. He turned on her furiously.

'They may call me the Beggar-boy of Europe, but I've not yet sunk to being kept by a woman, madam!'

'I never meant any such thing. How could I? Only that I could perhaps help you . . .'

'Help *me*? Am I shabby? Am I starving? And if I were I'd not take a sou from you. What my father chooses to send me I take – God knows, Rome owes me enough, one way and another. But any other sum that comes my way must be for the Cause.'

'Well, then, for the Cause. Fees for your messengers – the Antwerp muskets . . .'

'Shall we agree not to discuss the Antwerp muskets, since my whole expedition to England was a ludicrous failure? And shall we also agree not to discuss money any further? The topic sickens me.'
He turned his back on her and began to scribble away at one of the letters he was always writing, some plea or diplomatic suggestion to the English Ambassador in Paris, the King of Sweden, anybody who might be of use. How many of those eager epistles, in his large, bold, dashing hand, had arrived on royal or ministerial desks, to be sneered

at and tossed into the fire? Dorothy crept out of the room, rebuked. She would finance him so discreetly that he would never guess where the good meat came from, the pair of fine partridges, the extra coals, the apparently inexhaustible supply of candles. They were a curious ménage, indeed.

And yet she had a strong idea that even stranger ones might hide behind the windows of the rue St Dominique. It was a long, narrow street, winding its way behind Les Invalides; a secret-keeping street, the tall houses leaning conspiratorially towards each other. Neighbourly gossip no doubt there was, but foreigners were not included in it, even though England and France had been allies since the treaty of Aix-la-Chapelle. In the narrow tunnel of the street scents congregated, a blend of cheeses, wines, fresh bread, herbs, garbage, and the inevitable onion. It was pleasant, one soon became accustomed to it, but it was not the smell of England any more than the smell of the Seine could have been mistaken for that of Thames-side. Every other person seemed to be a nun or a priest, strange apparitions to Protestant eyes as they glided past, black-robed, white-faced, their beads and crucifixes swinging. Dorothy could never quite grow used to them, or conquer her feeling of slight revulson; slight, and quite illogical in a Jacobite. There had been so many cartoons in the London print-shops at the time of the 'Forty-five showing the Pope in various sinister situations, leading a procession of torturers, the devil at his side, or hanging the Elector on a common gallows.

She tried to overcome the feeling, for what was the use of living abroad if one could not tolerate its religion? At the opposite end of their street was the small Convent of St Joseph, whose bell was one of those that shattered the peace of early Sunday morning with its monotonous summons to Mass. One day, studying the statuary group outside it, a representation of the Marriage of the Virgin, she was taken by an impulse to go inside.

It was dark, gloomy, lit only by the ranks of candles surrounding various statues. Everywhere there were kneeling figures, muttered prayers; occasionally one of the figures would rise, light a candle, and leave. A nun passed Dorothy, who was standing aimlessly near the door, with no obvious intention of worship, and shot her a reproving glance. Embarrassed, she left, glad to get out into the air away from the smell of incense.

When she told Charles, thinking to amuse him, he looked first startled, then angry.

'Have I done wrong?' she asked. 'Is there some rule about Protestants entering churches?'

'No, no, of course not. It is merely that – these places can be dangerous for a stranger.'

'Dangerous? Why, what could happen to me in a holy place?'

'The Convent of St Joseph, my dear,' he said grimly, 'is about as holy as a brothel, and if you were to be stabbed to death in its porch I should not be in the least surprised, but very sorry. I beg you'll not go there again.'

'No, Tearlach. I won't go anywhere against your wishes.'

The next day he left, abruptly, for Lunéville, where the exiled King Stanislaus of Poland kept court. Stanislaus was the Queen of France's father, and she had always had a kindness for Charles; it was worth trying.

Dorothy watched him ride away, Morrison following him laden with baggage like a mule. Somewhere perhaps they would pick up a coach, or perhaps Charles would insist on riding all the way to Lorraine to keep himself in trim. He might not return for weeks, he said, and the longer he was away the more hopeful she might be of the outcome. But it was what Morrison would have called gey dreich without him.

Now her only companion was Duncan, who at present was cleaning the stairs and humming what sounded like a particularly gloomy hymn, or possibly a clan dirge. Steely November rain trickled relentlessly down the window-panes; the fire was smoking. For the third time that morning Dorothy picked up *The History of Mr Joseph Andrews*, and for the third time put it down again. Comic novels fell very flat when one lived in a legend. Determined not to mope, she began to write a long letter to Meliora.

The thin sunshine of an English December threw a gold veil over Meliora as she lay on the sofa where most of her day was spent, in the bay of her favourite window. It belonged to the oldest part of Carola House, and projected over the garden, so that in summer one might lean out and touch the boughs of the apple-tree below. She wore her warmest woollen wrapper, and a furry rug covered her, but the fingers that held Dorothy's letter were blue with cold. She handed the letter to Paul, smiling.

'So she has got her heart's desire.'

Paul shook his head in wonderment. 'It puzzles me to know how such a thing could have come about. In a romance, perhaps, but in life . . . when I think of all the misfortunes that befell her, and now to be the mistress of a prince.'

'Romances need not be between the covers of a book. And she was born to follow his Star. I told her so, in Edinburgh, before she met him. There was no other way for her to take, or for him to escape her.'

Paul studied his love's face, so much thinner than it had been, the eyes enormous in contrast to the delicately hollowed cheeks and pointed chin. She looked, he thought, like a little wild creature out of its element, a pretty squirrel in a cage. Since Dorothy had left her as chatelaine of Carola House and himself in charge of business affairs, he had seen her every day, unchaperoned as they were now. Mrs Mercy never intruded on them, but let events take their course. It was plainly to be a match between them, whatever folk might say, and they had said a good deal at first. Betty had brought her a tale from the Duncombes' Kitty about Mrs Duncombe coming weeping to the Colonel because Mr Paul would do no more than be polite to Miss Arabella Fisher, that eminently eligible young lady, having his mind set on the foreign girl who had been a slave; and how the Colonel had patted her shoulder and said that Paul was a sober young man who could be trusted to make his own life.

After that Mrs Duncombe had called formally, as Meliora was not well enough to visit, and had sat on the edge of a chair, very stiff and very nervous, weighing up the young woman her son had declared his intention of marrying, if she would have him. Meliora's simplicity and gentleness put her at her ease on one count – at least the girl was civilised and well-mannered – but she feared, she greatly feared, that she was not going to get the bouncing fair-haired grand-children she had pictured clustering about her knees. It was extra-ordinary that the girl had not yet consented to Paul's frequent proposals; one would have thought she would have jumped at an honourable offer.

Paul finished reading Dorothy's letter.

'So,' he said, 'it seems that she'll follow the Prince wherever he goes. And what will that mean to you, my dear, I wonder?' He took her hand. 'Meliora, I have not liked to speak of your powers, any more than I like to think of your dabbling in such matters. But will you tell me – can you *see*, by any means, what will become of Dorothy, and the Prince, and ourselves?'

She turned her head away, gazing out of the window. The bare apple-boughs melted before her eyes into a series of pictures, flashing one after the other like the pages of a book rapidly turned. She closed her eyes to shut them out, and a shudder went through her. Alarmed, Paul knelt beside her and put his arms round her.

'My dearest, what is it? Are you ill? Shall I call Mrs Mercy?'

She opened her eyes.

'No. It was only that – I saw – without intending it – so many things . . .'

'Bad things?'

'Not bad, no. Only one thing very sad. It was the suddenness . . . I am not quite strong yet, and it shakes one. I must not try to see again until I am better.'

'Never again!' he said vehemently. 'You are not to wear yourself out with it, and I was a fool to ask you. Won't you tell me, share it with me, whatever it was?'

She shook her head. The vision was still there, and she was trying hard to blot it out.

'It is better not to put some things into words,' she said. 'If you tell a bad dream at breakfast it will stay with you.'

'Only tell me this, my dear. Was it of you – of us?'

'No.'

He kissed her forehead, damp with sweat, and stroked back her hair.

'Then everything is well, and I shall ring for Mrs Mercy to bring you a cordial, or tea, whichever will do you the most good.'

She put out a hand to restrain him.

'Not for a moment. Paul, I will marry you.'

Hardly daring to believe his ears, he stared down at her. 'But – you always refused . . . Marry me? At last? How happy you make me, how happy. But why now?'

She lay content against his shoulder, silent. There was nothing more she could do for Dorothy, and at last she had come into haven.

They were married in Petersham Church, five days before Christmas. Meliora wore white, as befitted a bride, a full-hooped dress of silk and a mantle over it trimmed with white fur, a muff of the same fur keeping her hands warm until the moment came for Paul to put the ring on her finger. The holly-berries decking the pulpit were no brighter than the flush on her cheeks, and the servants wept at the proud tenderness of the bridegroom's look as he led her, his wife, down the aisle and into the snowy churchyard.

23

Eleven days later, on 31 December 1750, Charles came back to Paris. Dorothy saw him dismount in the little courtyard which divided their house from the street, and rushed downstairs to meet him. His cloak and tricorne hat were snow-scattered, his high boots muddy with long riding, and, though he smiled and greeted her affectionately, she sensed at once that his mission had not been a success.

'*Ça marche, belle amie? Dieu!* it's cold. I hope we have fire and food in plenty. Where's Duncan? This poor beast is half frozen; he must be stabled and rubbed down at once. Morrison, get these diabolical boots off me and then help yourself to some brandy, man. Have you missed me, Dorothy? Or have you amused yourself with Jean-Jacques at the boucherie? In which case, have we something good for dinner?'

Dorothy forebore to point out that their dinner would have had a better chance of being good if he had sent notice of his arrival. Instead, she gave Duncan some hasty instructions and set about attending to Charles's wants. With the aid of an excellent bottle of wine he never noticed the delay between Duncan's fetching of the meat and her cooking it, as the concierge was out attending a funeral. When he was warm and well fed, he talked of his visit to Lorraine.

'*Mon oncle* was not very helpful, no. I call him *mon oncle* not, you understand, because he is precisely that. Leszczinskis, Sobieskis, we are all out of the same box. There are things he could do for me . . .' He frowned. 'I suppose exile makes one lazy. It would me, if I allowed it, but I shan't. And what can one expect from a king who willingly gave up his throne for a pair of miserable French duchies? Poor man, at least he is alive, and living more like a human being than Louis does in that great mechanical birdcage at Versailles. Imagine it, a king who must rise when his courtiers expect it, even if he goes to bed again afterwards, and go to bed at the hour appointed, however quickly he may leap up when the door shuts and go on his tom-cat travels! Well, let Louis play the game by his fools' rules of *lever* and *coucher*; I shall make a new pattern when my turn comes.'

So there was some hope from the visit to Stanislaus's court. She wondered if he would tell her, but he said no more. After the meal she went away and came back with something which she put shyly down before him. It was a miniature white rose-tree, growing in a pot, with three tiny perfect blossoms on it. He stared at it in delight, touching it to make sure it was real.

'But what is this, and where did you get it in December?'

'It is your birthday present, and I got it from a *pépiniériste* – isn't that right – a man who grows flowers under glass?'

He was still holding it, turning it round and round, with a look between pleasure and pain.

'Charming. Exquisite. Come and kiss me.'

Against his shoulder, she said, so softly that he did not hear it, still gazing at the little tree, 'I gave you a rose before, in Preston.'

'So,' he said with a self-mocking sigh, 'I am thirty years old. What a terrible age to reach. Tonight we must celebrate; then we shall not feel sad.'

'*I* am not at all sad,' said Dorothy. 'I should like to go out and explore Paris tonight. It will be beautiful in the snow, and I have seen so little of it. Will you not show it to me, Tearlach?'

His face lit with delight. 'Of course! What an excellent suggestion. I shall disguise myself heavily, and you can be *en masque*.' He opened a cupboard and produced a heap of cloaks, hats and wigs, sorting out some for himself before coming to a box of sundries from which he drew a tiny black velvet eye-mask with a diamanté edge. '*Voilà*! the very thing.' He tried it on Dorothy, who laughed at her reflection in the mirror.

'But why do you keep a thing like this? It fits me perfectly, but it most certainly would not fit you. Or did you foresee walking about Paris with a masked lady?'

'I really have no idea,' he said. 'I believe I found it in my pocket – probably after a *bal masqué*. These trifles have a habit of straying, in the heat of the dance and the fight for the refreshments. I wish the lady had left her diamonds as well, but it would be too much to hope.'

They set out in mid-evening, when the fallen snow had crisped with a touch of frost. It lay whitely on the old mansard roofs, on the lovely bridges and the great twin towers of Nôtre Dame, and touched with silver the turrets and spire of la Sainte Chapelle.

'That is where St Louis came each year on Holy Thursday to wash the feet of poor men,' Charles said. 'I doubt if they thanked him for it. I had it done to me in the Highlands, and vastly uncomfortable it was, though kindly meant.' They were walking along the Quai des Théatins, where he pointed to one of the grander houses that looked across the river to the Louvre.

'That was my house in '48. I took it to show Louis how little I cared for his traitorous peace treaty, and set myself up with a staff of servants. What feasting we had there, what entertainments! It cost me more than I had, and did no good.'

They stood before an ornate building in the rue St Honoré.

'The Palais Royal,' he said. 'Where Louis was thoughtful enough to have me bound in black silk ribbons, after arranging for my arrest at l'Opéra. Silk, you note, not common rope. I hear that in England noblemen are hanged only in silk. Then I was carted off to the Châteaux de Vincennes, where Henry V of England died – of cold, I should imagine. I thought I should never leave the place alive, but Louis is no Cumberland, to do him justice . . .' He shivered, whether with memory of that cold fortress or with the chill of the night, Dorothy could not tell. She thought it more tactful to assume the latter.

'Could we not – *mon Prince fait froid, il souffre, n'est-ce pas? Nous buvons, peut-etre?*'

Charles laughed, so cheerfully and loud that a passer-by threw him a frightened look and scuttled away.

'What a good little Frenchwoman you're becoming, *ma chère*. Pray don't. I prefer you in your English habit. Yes, we will drink, and quickly.' He hurried her up a narrow, far-from-fragrant alley, up a little street to an even narrower passage from which light and noise came. They were in a tiny auberge, still garlanded with the leaves and dried grapes of autumn, crammed with drinkers and deafening with the twanging of a guitar played by a gipsy-looking fellow with flashing shining teeth who went from table to table, holding out a flat cap for alms. The wine brought to them was hot and spiced, and they drank it from earthenware cups, not glasses, so that a great deal more was consumed than they noticed. They drew nearer to each other, Charles's arm round Dorothy's shoulders, warm, happy and amorous.

'This, if you wish to know it,' he said, very carefully and distinctly 'is the rue Neuve des Petits Champs. Remember that.'

For some reason Dorothy found this extremely amusing.

'In that case,' she said with equal care, 'it is my opinion that we should have another drink.'

Charles snapped his fingers, and in a moment the smiling landlord had refilled their cups, aware of the handsome tip that had come his way last time.

'*A vos beaux yeux, madame,*' Charles said, and kissed her over the rim of the cup.

A man stood up on a barrel and began to sing in rivalry with the guitarist, while a girl in sabots broke into a maenad dance, accompanied by the rhythmic hand-clapping of the drinkers around her. Someone passing slapped Charles on the shoulder, a liberty which in his euphoric mood he acknowledged only with a smile. Suddenly, drowning the music and clapping, a church bell began to clang, just above their heads it seemed. Then, a little further away, another, and another out of tune with it, until the air was full of metallic jangling. Charles leapt up, his face thunder after sunshine.

'Midnight Mass for the New Year. Let's be out of it – fasten your cloak, hurry.' He flung some money down on the table, pulled her to her feet and pushed his way through the company towards the door. When they were almost there a young woman, painted and common, pulled at his sleeve. Another man might have shaken her off, but Charles, impatient as he was, took her small dirty hand covered with imitation rings.

'*C'est le prince Edouard,*' she was saying breathlessly. '*C'est le plus beau prince du monde.*'

'*Non, ma p'tite, de Grande Bretagne seulement,*' he said lightly, and to Dorothy, 'Quickly, or we shall be here all night.'

The house in the rue St Dominique was cold. The fire in the living-room was out, and Duncan, huddled asleep on the stairs, exuded a strong smell of brandy. Churches were still flinging out their chimes, for it was not yet half-past midnight.

'Let's go to bed,' said Charles, 'as nobody seems to have prepared for our staying up. The damned priests will stop ringing their wretched bells in a few minutes. *Dieu,* these boots, I must buy some more tomorrow if the shops are gracious enough to open and the shopkeepers not too drunk.' Dorothy heard him through the open bedroom door, herself struggling at the hooks and ribbons of her gown. She stopped suddenly as a noise reached her from the stairs, beyond the living-room door; Duncan's voice raised in slurred protest, and the high furious voice of a woman. Dorothy pulled the bedroom door almost closed, én déshabillé as she was. The living-room door opened and was banged shut. The dialogue that followed, in rapid French, escaped Dorothy's understanding except in the sense of it.

'What the devil are *you* doing here?' Charles demanded.

'I might ask the same!' shrieked the visitor. 'I, who innocently think you far away, yet look out of my window to see you pass with a masked woman on your arm. And wearing my mask, *perfide, ingrat*! Now what do I behold, I who have given you all, I who love you more than my life? I behold you unattired for bed, and that *putain* doubtless in the same state on the other side of that door. *Mon Dieu*, do you wish to kill me? I have swooned a dozen times since I saw you from my window.'

'A remarkable performance, as I returned only five minutes since. You should see a doctor, madame.'

'Madame! Is it thus I am called now? And what else have you called me in writing to that other *putain*, Lucie Ferrand? "*Ma tante*" no less. So, I am your aunt – I who was your divine goddess, your Astrea, your Muse? How can you bring yourself to throw my age in my teeth because I am a few pitiful years older than you? Oh, cruel, cruel!'

'For God's sake go home and go to bed, Marie,' said Charles wearily. 'You will wake the whole house and do no good to anyone.'

'Why have you not been near me?' moaned the voice. 'Why have you sent letters only to la Ferrand, not to your Marie who loves you? You have been corrupted, I see it. And now la Ferrand and I are both betrayed, for you have a new "counsellor"; I can smell her perfume from here. Ah, traitor, traitor!'

'I am in no mood for theatre at this time of night.'

'Theatre!' A sharp laugh. 'Since when have *you* ceased to play-act? This disguise, that disguise, now one name and wig, now another. Do you think all Europe does not laugh at you?' She gave a shrill impression of all Europe laughing, ending in a peacock scream. 'And now I will see this new nymph of yours.' There was a struggle, then a thump as the visitor fell against the bedroom door, forcing it wide open. Dorothy, in only her corset and stockings, clutched her discarded dress round her, backing away from the Fury in the doorway. She was conscious of a great deal of black; a black dress, a rich black lace shawl round the woman's shoulders, snapping black eyes and black hair in which any streak of grey had been ruthlessly subdued. Long diamond earrings swung from her ears, there were glints of more diamonds round her neck and on her arms. If she was not old enough to be Charles's aunt, she was perhaps forty-five. In the flickering candle-light it was impossible to tell; only that she had, or had once had, a hawklike beauty, high-nosed, high-cheekboned.

She advanced on Dorothy with a series of little angry shrieks and shrill words. 'Daughter of infamy! Siren! Do you not know on whom you prey? Wretched half-naked creature! Give me back my mask, the mask you stole from me!'

Dorothy cowered away from the long nails that were getting alarmingly close to her eyes. Then, in one stride, Charles was behind the woman, shaking her violently so that at the last shake she fell, hitting a chair and bringing it crashing to the ground, herself with it. She lay there, staring up at him with wild eyes, like a shot bird;

and Dorothy, with the clear-sightedness that sometimes comes with wine, had the impression that it was not the first time she had lain so, and that she did not altogether dislike it.

'Get up,' said Charles. 'You have done whatever mischief you meant to do. Now leave us.'

The woman scrambled to her knees and remained there, with a certain grace, her bodice half off one shoulder and her fine bosom visible somewhat further than decency allowed. Charles stood with his arms folded, not offering to help her up. Dorothy had never seen such a look on his face before, of anger and scorn mingled; the scorn partly for himself. The visitor stood up, and with another venomous glance at Dorothy went back into the living-room, Charles following her. There was a murmur of voices, followed by the slam of the door. High-heeled shoes (they had been scarlet, Dorothy remembered) clicked down the stone stairs.

The wine continued to do its work. Sitting on the bed, Dorothy tried to speak, but her lip trembled uncontrollably and she burst into tears. Charles let her cry, as he moved about the room mechanically tidying it, picking up the fallen chair, laying Dorothy's discarded clothes neatly over it.

'Who – who is she?' Dorothy managed to gasp out at last.

'She is Marie-Louise, born Jablonowska, la Princesse de Talmond, and a cousin of mine – as she is of the Queen of France.'

'*Cousin!* She is your mistress.'

'Was,' corrected Charles. 'She was also my agent, having access to the Court, where I am not allowed. That was her principal function in my life.'

Dorothy relapsed into sobbing. 'I thought – I was your only lady. I see I was a fool. I should never – have come here.'

'As to that, my dear, you may be right. I only know I am glad you came. Oh, pray give over now.' He sat beside her and gently mopped her eyes and nose with his own large laced handkerchief. 'Dorothée, *ma chèrie,* do you think I am made of stone like the statue of *le bon roi Henri,* or of ice-cream like the swan at the end of the banquet? I need women now and then, as any other man does. But I am not a *gaillard* like my great-uncle Charles. If in return for giving up female company for time everlasting I could lead my Highlanders again, and successfully this time, do you think I would hesitate? No. And as to Marie, I must tell you another thing: that she and poor Lucie Ferrand are something I am not, great wits and great brains. They are *philosophes, bas-bleus,* they and others, Madame du Deffand and Madame d'Aiguillon – brilliant women who have no time for old ways and old ideas. Now, you see—' he settled himself more comfortably on the bed. 'To be a good king, it is not enough to be a good soldier. One must rule with one's head, isn't that so? My great-uncle saved his own that way, and poor Queen Mary might not have lost hers if she had had more brains than beauty.'

Dorothy nodded. She was beginning to feel a little less wretched, though she had had to borrow back his handkerchief.

He went on, with his most serious air, 'Marie and other ladies hold salons at which they and men like the great *philosophe* Condillac discuss such matters as freedom, reason, enlightenment, escape from the tyrannies of orthodox religion. Now, while I have been forced to live in hiding, Marie and Lucie have concealed me from time to time in their *appartements* at the Convent of St Joseph. Do you see why I asked you not to go there? I know Marie's temper too well. There I hid in a small antechamber and listened to these discussions, taking notes as well as I could . . . Why are you smiling? But I'm glad to see your tears are dried. *Eh bien,* it was hearing these new, noble ideas so cleverly discussed that impelled me to renounce the Roman faith in London. That in turn may lead to my ascending the British throne. Now do you understand why I have cultivated Marie?'

'Yes. But – you don't love her?'

'Love? What is love? My brother loved me – and took a Cardinal's hat. My father loved me – and has done nothing but reproach me since I forsook his Church . . . I found love in the heather, nowhere else.' He shivered suddenly, and pinched out one of the candles. 'The damned bells have stopped ringing, and one may go to bed.' The 1740s were over, the days of hope and defeat. It was time to begin the new decade; but with what hope?

In the darkness he said abruptly, 'I hate this Paris. Tomorrow I shall go away.'

Fearfully, she asked, 'Where?'

'Anywhere. Anywhere but Rome.'

'And I?'

He sighed. 'I suppose you will go back to England, weary as you are of me.'

'No. Where you go, there I go too.'

24

After all, it was another week before they left Paris. Charles was hardly at home, going out for hours and days on end without explanation. Marie de Talmond had not reappeared, but Dorothy had a strong idea that she was being visited, and that the visits were not entirely amiable, judging by Charles's expression when he returned. She was glad when the time came for them to leave, on a wet, cold January morning, with Paris mud at its thickest and greasiest.

Morrison handed her into the shabby hired coach, on which he and Duncan were stoically to ride outside. As Charles was about to follow her, several small figures appeared from doorways and alleys and clung about him. They were the street-arabs, children who slept by night in passages, churchyards or hovels, and by day earned what they could by running errands, pilfering or begging. They were treated as lepers by respectable folk, spurned and kicked out of the way; the death of one in the gutter was regarded as no more important than the crushing of a stray dog under carriage wheels.

But to Charles they were only pitiable children. Many a sou had left his pockets for their dirty claws; Duncan, disapproving, had been under orders to give them scraps of food saved from the table. Now they were clustering round Charles as he half knelt on the cobbles, his arms round three or four of them. A little girl with matted hair hanging over her eyes had scrambled under his cloak. In the shadow of it she was weeping loudly, in competition with the shrill shrieks of the others.

'*Mes p'tits, mes gamins, non doucement!*' Charles hushed them. 'Yes, Milor is going away, but he will come back, and you shall not starve. M. Moreau, *l'épicier,* has something in charge for you, so that there will be food when you need it. I don't give gold to you, you understand, for it would only get you hanged. When you are very hungry you will go to M. Moreau and demand something from the Chevalier's larder. *Ça marche?*'

He extricated himself from them and quickly entered the coach. As they moved off, the small figures ran after them, until the corner of the street was turned. Dorothy did not shrink away from him, close as he had been to large armies of lice and fleas. This it was in him that had won him the Highland hearts.

'*Eh bien,*' he said, settling back, 'we are for Avignon.'

The journey south through France was bitterly cold and uncomfortable. Avignon gave them no glowing welcome from its rocky perch. Dorothy's heart sank as they approached its skyline of towers and belfries and ancient roofs, dominated by the frown of the battlemented fortress that had been the Palace of the Popes until the last century, making small Avignon the centre of the Catholic world. There was no getting away from that grim building; wherever you were it looked down at you, a relic of medieval terrors. St Bénézet's bridge, broken down centuries before, had a hopeless air, cut off in mid-river, leading nowhere. It offered the perfect invitation to would-be suicides to walk along its length and fall off at the end. Below it the Rhône swirled greyly, and in the town the streets were half empty, for the mistral, that bitter wind of Provence, was blowing, and nobody who could be indoors wanted to be out.

The house rented to Charles by the Pope's Vice-Legate was a sharp contrast to the rue St Dominique. It was of mansion-like proportions, belonged to the Archbishop's nephew, and was hundreds of years old in parts, with great open fireplaces and walls five feet thick.

'Oh, this is nothing,' Charles said when Dorothy exclaimed at its magnificence. 'Every cardinal had his own house once, little palaces for little kings. The difference between them and me is a small matter of money. As you see, half the rooms are shut up. When I came here first at the end of '48 they fêted me like one of their holy images, until I got into hot water with the Archbishop for setting up prize-fights.'

'So I heard,' Dorothy said. 'Why did they object?'

He shrugged. 'How do I know? Possibly they feared the sport was heretical. Here, you see, nothing amuses them if it does not include the torture of animals. At the Camargue aux Arênes, every Easter, you may be entertained by the sight of a mêlée of bulls and horses struggling in a small arena. It is not so bloody as the Spanish sport, of course. I attended one when I was in Madrid, at Ferdinand's court, but it sickened me. I have asked myself why, because as you know, Dorothée, I am not an intellectual person and don't know the answer to every moral question, as a true *philosophe* would.'

'Surely it is because you are naturally merciful?'

'To men, yes. I could never hurt an enemy. And I hunted every day, as a boy in Rome, and long afterwards . . . Yet, when I came back in '46 and stayed with – with Henry at Clichy, we hunted then, and I had less of a stomach for it, though I never let Henry see that. He is such a good Catholic, and they hold that beasts have no souls. Perhaps I was an ordinarily brutal boy and I have changed a little since then – who is to say? Or perhaps it was because I saw my Highlanders cut so many noble horses into collops with their broadswords. It was for my sake, I know, but I found it horrible. Or perhaps it is merely that I was a hunted creature myself once. I know how a stag or a fox feels . . . what a carnival the English cartoonists would make of it, if they were to find out. They would draw the Pretender as an old maid, nursing a lap-dog. And now we will have some dinner.'

There were plenty of staff to provide it. Scottish footmen, in a motley assembly of garments which could not by any stretch of imagination be called uniforms, came to pay their respects to their royal master. Dorothy knew herself to be looked on with wonder, as the first female to be seen in His Highness's company. One strange-looking youth threw himself at her feet and kissed the hem of her gown, muttering rhapsodically in a Provençal dialect of which she could not make out a word.

Morrison, all but kicking him out the way, interpreted: ''Tis Michel's son, a puir daftie. He takes you for the Queen, ma'am, His Highness's bride.'

'Tell him I'm obliged,' Dorothy said, glancing down at her limp, dirty travelling clothes, 'but he must look further and fare better.'

Two highly superior servants – or were they rather major-domos, or agents, or friends? – ran the household. They were John Stafford and Michael Sheridan, one English, the other Irish; quiet men who smiled politely and made light conversation. Another resident was Henry Goring, who had been young in Rome when Charles was a boy, and had served him devotedly ever since as messenger and adviser. He had the worried face of a bloodhound, watched Charles with tireless anxiety, and went to pray daily in Nôtre Dame des Doms, Avignon's great church – an activity which Charles regarded with ill-concealed impatience. There were no resident women servants, only a large female wearing a kind of wimple who was occasionally to be seen leaving the kitchen quarters for her home in the town.

Dorothy was uncomfortable and unsettled. Life in the rue St Dominique had at least been something akin to normal. In Avignon she felt like a woman alone in a monastery or a barracks. Nobody took much notice of her, though she was well looked after. At her request a daily maid was engaged to look after her clothes and the enormous shadowy bedchamber which had been given to her for her own use, but the girl, Barbe, spoke the same dialect as Michel's son, so that communication with her had to be conducted by signs. Morrison and Duncan continued friendly towards her, but from the other men of the household she felt hostility, spiced with the jealousy Charles inspired among those close to him.

She longed suddenly for the peace of Carola House, where the snowdrops would now be thick under the apple-trees, wood-smoke scenting the parlour where Paul and Meliora, newly married, would sit, talking perhaps of her. She longed urgently for her own place, where she would not be alien and suspected; she longed for feminine conversation and idle jokes, the scanning of the newspaper. Looking anxiously at herself in the mirror, she saw a few gleams of grey in the brown hair swept back from her forehead, and a fullness to her throat which had not been there before. Perhaps she was growing old and Charles would tire of her soon.

And he was still kind to her; affectionate as he had ever been, though she saw little of him now that he was often closeted with Goring and messengers from his father. Sometimes they dined alone, and she read to him from one of the English novels Lucie had sent among the heavier works. When he laughed it was as though no time had passed since the night of Holyrood; but, seen in the brightness of the unspared candles, he too seemed older, a shade heavier, the broad shoulders stooping a little with constant writing and lack of exercise. She rejoiced in these signs, for they seemed to make him more hers, less the bright prize of the world. It was impossible not to know that names were being mentioned as potential queens for him; not the poor 'Black Eye', Princess Henriette, who was dying of a broken heart, people said, for love of the Duc de Chartres, but German princesses, even the Czarina of Russia. One night, as they played at chess by the fire, he said, without looking up, 'I wish I could have a small commodious house, not this great ugly barn.'

'Where would you have it, sir?'

'In Scotland, where else? A pretty, turreted place with a round tower and gardens. I would collect portraits and busts for it, and make a good stable for my horses. There would be a hall for fencing and boxing.'

Without looking up from the board, Dorothy asked, 'And what would you build for your Queen, sir?'

Surprised, he glanced at the little chess-piece with the fretted ivory crown. 'My . . .? Oh. Why, she would be – at St James's, I suppose. Where should she be? And why do we talk of her? I'm very comfortable with you.'

'That won't always be possible, sir. When your Queen comes, I shall go.'

It was said as a piece of bravado, half hoping to win a protest from him; more than the sad, sidelong look he gave her.

'They have a legend here in Provence,' he said, 'of a troubadour who sought for years *la princesse lointaine,* the faraway princess. At last he heard that she was to be found in a country across distant seas. He sailed away from Provence in a small boat, always hoping to find that land over the horizon; but before he reached it illness struck him, and as he set eyes on the princess, he died. Perhaps it will be so with me. Shall we continue the game? My move, I think.'

Spring had touched Avignon with beauty, painting old stone with light and throwing blue reflections into the Rhône's waters; tiny jewel-like rock-violets grew out of the crevices of walls, the perfume of early garden flowers was in the streets; even the Palace of the Popes wore a less unrelenting air.

And they were to leave. Charles had decided to set out on his travels again, weary of inaction as he was. Colonel Brett was to report any news from England, where, in March, Frederick, Prince of Wales, had died. Elector George was unpopular, William of Cumberland was cordially disliked by his ungrateful country; the moment might have arrived for the Cause to be triumphant.

Dorothy turned cold with fear when she was told of the departure – not by Charles but by Sheridan. He gave her the news with studied brevity and nonchalance, leaving her in doubt as to her own part in it all. She stared at him; he stared insultingly back.

'And I?' she asked.

'Oh, did I not say? Madam's to accompany His Highness, I hear, at least while 'tis convenient. But Barbe is to be turned off as being too costly. The expenses of this house are terrible without the paying of extra servants.'

'Perhaps,' she said coldly, 'you'll accept fifty guineas or so to furnish us for the journey. His Highness will accept nothing directly, and I don't wish to be a burden on him. I have plenty more if it should be wanted.' She turned and left the room, feeling Sheridan's eyes on her back, jealous and resentful.

Sometimes they travelled for long stretches at a time, jolting in a carriage over stony roads and passes; sometimes they stayed for days at an inn or post-house, waiting for messengers. She and Charles, Morrison and a groom, four oddly assorted pilgrims, crossed France from south-west to north-east, moved into the little states and principalities of Germany and Prussia, till they came within sight of Berlin, a fine town rising on the banks of the blue Spree, growing in splendour under the determined hand of Frederick the Great.

Here Charles left Dorothy at a village inn.

'I must see the King alone, you understand, and I shall be under the wing of James Keith, my father's old friend. It would not do to go in company with a lady.'

He was away a week, coming back silent and preoccupied. Frederick had politely but firmly refused to consider a match between Charles and his sister Wilhelmina. 'He intended her for the Elector's son once, and that was thwarted. Now I suppose he means her for the grandson,' Charles said bitterly to the old soldier, Marshal Keith. 'As the grandson is barely thirteen it would be an unequal match, but better than one with a Stuart in Frederick's eyes. Lord, what liars and hypocrites these rulers are! Well, I shall try for Austria and a daughter of Maria Theresia.'

Keith shook his august powdered head. 'She will have nothing of you, sir. All she wants is a French alliance, and you would not be the way to it. You were turned away once before – why invite it again? Besides, there is – madam, the lady who travels with you. They have all heard of it, believe me, by backstairs talk, and it does you no good. Could you not pay her off?'

Charles shrugged, and turned the conversation. Whatever re-assurance he may have given Dorothy, he had so much hoped to leave Berlin with the promise of a wife, and now it was not to be. He said nothing to Dorothy, or she to him, but she knew very well, as they lay in the stuffy inn-room's painted wooden bed. How far, she wondered, was *la princesse lointaine* now; as far as Vienna, where they were going next?

Here, too, she was left behind, this time at a city inn, at the end of a narrow lowering street. He had allowed her to drive with him to Schönbrunn, the palace outside the city where Maria Theresia, the young Queen of Hungary and Archduchess of Austria, held court in the summer months. Charles surveyed its stately proportions from the road.

'Very much on the plan of Fontainebleau,' he said. 'It might be lucky for me.' She watched him stroll through the gates and into the long courtyard, a gallant figure today in blue and silver, very different from the sober-suited Herr Thomson he had been only a day or two before. In Vienna she walked about the streets; it was a religious holiday, the church doors open, the interiors a cheerful blaze of candles, their portals guarded by saints, archangels, and devils, the Christian equivalents of the great statuary groups of nereids and tritons who posed, massive in stone, outside the Hofburg Palace. In St Stefan's Cathedral, Mass was being held: Dorothy stood at the back of the immense church, breathing incense, watching fascinatedly the piercing flames of the candles, blue at the core, as one after another was lit by worshippers. The congregation was singing a solemn, simple chorale of Bach. She knew little German, but enough to tell that this was a humble prayer for forgiveness and redemption. For what, for whom, she wondered, and, clasping her hands, tried to pray.

Charles came back from Schönbrunn with a light tale of a chamber with a secret staircase and door, all painted with Chinese people, dragons and lotus-blossoms, where after much whispering he had been received by an ample lady in a bedgown who was not Maria Theresia at all, but one of her court, with a message that Her Majesty was engaged in devotions and could not receive Herr Thomson. 'And so,' said Charles, 'I was sent home in disgrace with my begging-bowl empty. Home! Where, in God's name, is home? What shall a bird do that hath no nest? *Ainsi usent les hirondelles.*'

'But swallows have nests, my darling,' she said, 'and you will find one yet. Could you not go to your father? They say he is very ill, and longing to see you. Won't you see him? Rome is not so very far . . .'

His lips set mutinously. 'Too far, until I have some news. No, I shall go to Paris and court the Pompadour for Louis's favours, if that's the only way to his ear. Why should I care? Since Poor Fred of England died he may think better of me as a prospect. Where's the other bottle of wine?'

'You drank it.'

'No. You have it somewhere. Come now, out with it. Morrison would never dare to hide it, so that means you must have done. Or do you think I had enough from the Archduchess's flowing tables? Believe me, I got nothing, not even a cup of tea. Now, where is it?'

He looked half laughing, half dangerous, and she took the missing bottle from the cupboard where she had put it, behind some food.

When she refused to join him he poured out glass after glass for himself, while she looked on helpless, afraid to remonstrate. Suddenly he put down the glass and began to wander restlessly about the room. In the June dusk of the courtyard a late bird was singing, the only sound but for the murmur of voices from the public room two storeys below. Charles had thrown aside his coat and wig because of the heat; in the gloom his white shirt had a ghostly look. Dorothy shivered, and went to light a candle, but he took it from her, saying, 'Leave it.'

'I only thought it would make the room more cheerful . . .'

He was at the table in the window, flicking a pack of playing-cards across its surface. She saw in the dim light the garish colours of the Tarot – reds, whites, greens, the grotesque designs, medieval figures in stiff poses, castles and animals. The cardboard was dog-eared with use, for he played with the pack constantly, telling his own fortune.

'You'll strain your eyes,' she said. He seemed not to hear.

'Cups, wands, and swords. The sun, the moon, the stars. There is everything in the world in these cards. Look, here's the Pope and the Devil; there should be the Pretender somewhere . . . The strange thing is that what looks most sinister, is not – the cards go by contraries, like dreams.' He sat down and shuffled them, laying them out with practised speed. 'There, you see, the Hanged Man. Always I draw the Hanged Man. He is Christ, did you know that? So I am not so unlucky. But sometimes I've been very near to drawing Le Mat, the Fool. What do you suppose it would portend, if I did?'

'I don't know. I was only taught to play whist and ombre. And it probably means nothing whatever. One should not be too credulous of these old games.'

He had picked a card up, staring at it. 'The Empress. She comes up again and again. Who is she? Not you.'

'No, not I. Your Queen, perhaps.'

'I don't think so. I don't think so.' Noisily he banged the cards together and put them back in their box, then flung open the window.

'We should be out in one of the villages of the Wienerwald, not here. They put red and white ribbons outside the inns there to signify the serving of the Heuriger, the new wine; and the people come to sit under the walnut-trees and drink. They are honester than the French, these Austrians. The Archduchess sent her woman to tell me frankly I was not welcome, instead of putting me off with lies.' There was a small spinet in one corner of their parlour, an old instrument from the time of Bach, painted with bucolic red-cheeked German cherubs and defective in several notes. He sat down and began to improvise: snatches of Italianate music, clashing chords and discords; then broke into a sad, simple air that was recognisably Scottish.

'The men used to sing that at night by the camp-fires,' he said over his shoulder. 'I never knew the words. So you think they will make songs about me some day? Yes, for the Scots have long memories. They will be songs of hate for the Stuart who came to ruin Scotland. For I did that, you understand, and I would not be saying so if I were not drunk. I must pretend always, because I am after all the Pretender. You don't find that amusing, *chérie*? Well, perhaps it is not, but don't be sad. I am not at all deterred by today's fiasco, you must know that. I shall fight on, and fight on, until I can go back and free my country.' He played the air again, this time with delicate variations. 'And if I cannot go back, my life will be over.' He lifted his hands from the keyboard.

'It is the end of an old song,' he said, 'the end of an old song.'

Dorothy knew, without reason, that the journey back to Paris would be the last she would ever take with Charles. When they reached the lodging, two visitors were waiting. Dorothy remembered John O'Sullivan, the Irish failed priest, at once. Easy-tongued as ever, he declared himself to be enchanted beyond words by the sight of his master after so long; his rapture at renewing Dorothy's acquaintance was a little more forced, and she fancied he looked at her askance from the corner of his eye.

'And what must be Your Highness's pleasure,' he enthused, 'to meet with Miss again after so long! Sure, she's been sitting here all impatience to see you since five this afternoon, and I telling her it wouldn't be long now. I said, Your Highness would have had my letter, and made all speed to get to her.'

Charles was looking puzzled. 'Letter? I had none from you. And who is come?'

O'Sullivan threw open the door of the main room. Dorothy would never forget, all her life, the room and the person in it, outlined against the dead green of the curtains. 'Why,' said the Irishman, 'who but Miss Clementina Walkinshaw?'

The woman seated stiffly on the high-backed chair swung round, and half rose. She was somewhere around the age of thirty, of middling height, very slim; her face was pointed, the nose as over-large as her forehead was disproportionately high, her mouth tiny and tight-lipped, the severely braided hair sandy, the complexion freckled. Only her eyes, large, brown, and at the moment startled, had any beauty. She was sitting in travelling clothes, drably shabby, her chip hat in her lap. It fell to the floor as she got to her feet.

'Your Royal Highness don't remember me, perhaps?' she asked in a strongly accented Scots voice.

A sudden tide of scarlet swept over Charles's face, then receded, leaving it white.

'Yes,' he said. 'Of course. Very well. At Bannockburn House.'

'That's so,' said the visitor, her eyes never leaving him. 'I'm rejoiced to see Your Highness so well now, after seeing him last but poorly.'

O'Sullivan jumped in to rescue a difficult situation. 'Mrs Beaumont, Miss Walkinshaw. Miss was instrumental in nursing His Highness through a severe bout of fever in '46, when he rested with Sir Hugh Paterson, her uncle.' Dorothy heard him rambling politely on about the extreme devotion of Miss Walkinshaw's family to the House of Stuart, her birth in Rome, the graciousness of the late Queen Clementina in standing godmother to the babe, the charming fact of His Highness and Miss Walkinshaw having played together as children in the Palazzo Muti. During the narrative Miss Walkinshaw kept her gaze steadily on Charles's face, and he seemed unable to speak or to move. As though by a blinding light thrown on the past,

Dorothy saw how it had been between them years ago at Bannock-burn House near Glasgow, the adoring young daughter of a loyal line and the desperate young man at the head of an army on the run.

'Captain O'Sullivan will already have told you, sir,' Miss Walkinshaw was saying in her soft, flat voice, 'that I had fallen on very poor times and was of a mind to enter a convent in the Nether-lands. Then I thought me of Your Highness and your . . . promise.'

'Of course,' he said. 'You were very right.' He had not looked at Dorothy since the first words had been spoken between him and the Scotswoman. Quietly she left the room, and found her way to a bedroom above, where she sank down on the bed and sat staring before her.

Later she heard Charles go out with O'Sullivan. It was mid-morning of the next day before he came home, to find her with her luggage still packed, as it had been on their arrival, waiting for him. He looked haggard and exhausted; she guessed at a scene in the rue St Dominique with Marie de Talmond followed by a night of searching for somewhere to lodge Miss Walkinshaw. He sat down beside her on the sofa, but she made no move towards him. At last he said, 'Dorothy?'

'Yes, sir.'

'You don't understand this, but O'Sullivan will tell you it is true. I owe Miss Walkinshaw my life, perhaps, for her nursing at Bannockburn – and I wish she'd not troubled to save it, for the pain it's been to me and others. So I must do what I can for her now, when she has nothing. I shall not be popular for it, since she has a sister at the Elector's court; but then I've been blamed for not doing enough for my poor followers, and so I am never to do right, it seems.'

'I do understand,' Dorothy said carefully, 'and that is why I must leave Your Highness, today, now, before anything else is said. Morrison will fetch me a coach, and I can be in Boulogne or Calais in a day or two, and in England by the end of the week. So you see I have it all arranged, and it is quite for the best.'

His face was impossible to read, but she thought she saw the look of desperation which was there so often now, and was bitterly sorry to be the cause of it. At last he said, 'You told me you would only go when I married. This is not marriage, or anything like it, merely a befriending.'

'Do you truly believe that, sir? I see you don't. Oh, pray don't make it harder for me, when 'tis so hard already to part from you. I have been awake all night thinking what to say to you. Please listen. My time with you is over, that's all. I have been very, very happy; I could never tell you how much. "For he that is mighty hath magnified me." '

'Mighty!' he said. 'I think you're mocking me; and blaspheming into the bargain.' He turned his back on her sharply and stood looking out of the window, at nothing.

Trying not to lose her own control, she rang the bell. Morrison had been hovering outside the door, to judge by the speed with which he appeared.

'The coach, please, Morrison, and you may take my luggage down.'

Gently she touched Charles's arm, and turned him towards her.

'You were the crown of my life. Must we part in bitterness?'

The beautiful Stuart eyes were shining with tears. He bent and kissed her, a long rueful kiss; then he gave her a little push away from him.

'I never did like partings,' he said thickly.

She tried not to look back, but longing overcame her. He was still at the window, leaning against the wall, his face on his arm, as though he had turned from the sight of a lost battle.

'I shall love you all my life,' she said, and went out of the door and down the stairs, with a smile and a tip for Morrison and a greeting to the driver. It was not until the coach began to lumber away that the agonising knot in her throat dissolved in a passion of weeping.

25

The fire leapt in the grate with the opening of the door, and the two
men sitting by it turned sharply. The lady of the house, so long away,
ran forward to embrace one of them.

'Paul! Oh, I'm so glad to be home. And Dr Carr . . . Allan! What
a delightful surprise.' She looked from one to the other, enjoying
the sight of these friendly and familiar faces after so many days of
strangers.

'I had your letter from Dover,' said Paul. 'It had been so long
since we heard that I was anxious. All the better to see you now,
and in good health.'

'Oh, excellent.' Indeed she looked it, thought Allan, noting with
a doctor's eye the change in her from an ardent girl to an experienced mature woman, much travelled. But it was more than travel
that had wrought the change, he knew. At least she was not heart-
broken, as he had at times feared. And the figure revealed when she
took off her cloak was as neat as ever, he noted with relief.

She was gazing round the room at polished furniture, bowls of
flowers, every sign of loving care bestowed on the house.

'How well you have looked after it, Paul. I saw the windows had
been painted, and there was a gardener working hard when I came
in. The maid is new, too, surely. What a lot of building there has
been in Richmond – and where have so many people come from
since I went away? The river was crowded with pleasure-boats; I
never saw so many before.' She was chattering to ward off the
questions they might ask her; they were silent because of what she
would inevitably ask them.

'But where's Meliora? I thought she would come running out to
meet me – all the way from Dover I imagined it. I long to see her
as Mrs Duncombe.' Their silence halted her. 'Has she gone to bed
early?'

Paul turned away and appeared to be studying the bookshelves in the alcove. Allan took Dorothy's arm.

'Sit down, Mrs Dorothy. I'll ring for some refreshment for you.'

She looked up, startled. 'I need no refreshment, and you have not answered. Is Meliora ill?'

After a pause, he said, 'She has been . . . very ill. We thought her better in the Spring; then in May there came a cold dreich spell.'

'It was warm in High Germany,' Dorothy said, half to herself.

'Aye, but here the winds were cruel. She was too frail to withstand them. Och, I am telling this badly, but it's kindest to be quick when one must use the knife. My dear Mrs Dorothy . . .'

'I know,' she said, quite composedly. 'Meliora is dead.'

With a smothered sound, Paul went out of the room. Allan drew a chair up beside Dorothy's, and quietly told her of those last weeks when the consumption that had Meliora in its grip took possession of her fragile body so strongly that he and Paul knew there could be no hope. He had turned his new flourishing London practice over to a locum and come down to Richmond to tend the dying girl. 'It is sometimes a sad gruesome business. But with her it was swift, for her heart was not strong, and in the end she went out like a candle-flame.'

He paused, remembering the almost unnatural calm and happiness of his patient; she who was a six-months' bride and had everything to live for. It was as though she were a child going on a holiday, treasuring up the anticipation of it, not seeming to find anything sorrowful in her situation. At the end she had asked for one of the kittens to be put beside her, and it had gone to sleep in the crook of her arm. She seemed to be sleeping too, but when her husband bent over her to hear if she breathed she lifted one transparent hand to stroke his face, and in that moment died, with such a blissful smile as Allan had seen on the lips of a marble saint in Rome, Bernini's Santa Teresa.

Never again would she sorrow, never again see the last of her earthly visions: the face of Prince Charles Edward Stuart in the years before his death, ruined with drink and disappointment, infinitely sad, all beauty gone as all hope had gone long before, a man abandoned by the gods.

It was a year after Dorothy's return to England that Allan visited her again. It had been a strange year; of loneliness for Dorothy, of readjustment to everyday life, of longing for a sign or a word of remembrance from Charles. But none came. As with others who had followed him faithfully, it was as though once they were out of his sight he found it too painful to recollect them. From Lady Primrose, who had been in the Netherlands and France, Dorothy heard that a new uprising was planned, organised by one Alexander Murray. Anonymously, she sent money to Charles's banker in Paris, Waters, with the faint hope that he might be curious about the sender and trace it to her. The plot fizzled out; it had been a poor exercise in conspiracy, perfectly well known to the English Government, who made a terrible example of the Jacobite agent Dr Archie Cameron, brother to Lochiel, by condemning him to be hanged, drawn and quartered, ostensibly for his activities in the '45.

Dorothy heard, too, that Clementina Walkinshaw's life with Charles was increasingly unhappy. There were rumours of quarrels and jealousy, allayed for a time by the birth of a daughter.

'He adores the baby,' said Lady Primrose, 'indeed he dotes on her. But I fear the mother rues the day she crossed the water to him. 'Tis said she drinks glass for glass with him; they are destroying each other.'

Dorothy tried to shut out the picture from her mind, and busied herself with charitable works. She was now on the Board controlling Wylde's Almshouses, and had also founded twelve new ones, called by her name and equipped with every comfort; too much, said Mrs Mercy, who disapproved of her mistress flinging good money away on paupers, as she put it.

'What else should I do with it?' Dorothy enquired. 'I have no children to inherit. Shall I hoard it for my old age, and die miserly and miserable as my aunt and uncle did? No, let those have it that need it; there's more than enough left for me.'

To Allan, when he visited her, she renewed the offer she had made him when he restored her sight. 'Though I suppose you'll snub me now as you did then.'

He shook his head, smiling. 'Not at all. If I was short with you, it was out of pride. I am prosperous now, as physicians go. Did you know that I have left Soho for a handsome house in Hanover Square, and call myself Dr Gambier-Carr? The other day I was summoned to the Princess of Wales herself: is not that an irony?'

She looked apprehensive. 'I hope you are not being too daring. After the fate of Dr Cameron . . .'

'Poor Archie. That was a wicked business. Did you know that the Elector had Jeannie Cameron put in prison, for pleading to him for her husband's life? No, Archie was the scapegoat – they killed him to show that the hatred at Culloden was not dead. There'll be no more risings in the North.'

Dorothy sighed. 'I suppose one should not hope for any more. Indeed, I wonder if – if he came back, it would be the same . . .'

'I have heard things, too. No, it would not be the same at all. He is much changed, and for the worse.' He was watching her carefully, sitting staidly, her needlework in her hands, a little heavier of figure, a little sadder of face; with a look of youth about her still, yet matronly, the dresses of rose and silver put aside for a quiet grey, the cobweb caps for a sober plain thing that tied under the chin, hiding her hair. Here was Andromeda in sore need of rescue, and Perseus must go cannily about it.

'I had another patient known to you recently,' he said. 'Mrs Johnson, the Doctor's lady. Poor thing, she was too far gone for me to pull back to life, and heavily that good man grieves for her.'

'Oh, I'm sorry to hear of it! She was so much to him, for all her odd little ways. How lonely he will be now . . . And that reminds me – I think that our Paul will marry again. There is a young lady in Twickenham very set on him, and I believe he doesn't altogether mislike her. Now that would be a good thing, don't you agree, Allan? 'Tis not healthy for a man to live alone.'

'Or a woman?'

She looked up. 'A woman? I . . . suppose not. Though the two cases are not the same, are they?'

'Are they not? Are you happy in your single life, Dorothy? Is it enough for you, this world of good works with a card-party now and then for enlivenment? Is there nothing else you would wish for?'

Her face was turned away from him, hidden by the edge of the hideous cap. 'What a number of questions . . . I suppose I am happy enough – as happy as I may expect to be. I *have* been happy above the luck of most women.'

'But that's over and done with now. There's no use in clinging to a dream, my dear – for that's what you have been doing, is it not? The Prince is gone out of your ken for ever. He will never be yours again, nor can you do him any more good. Forget him, Dorothy!'

Her face flamed. 'How can I? You don't know what you say.'

'Maybe not. But I know a starved heart when I meet with one, just as I know a starved body. Dorothy, look at me. I am not your Prince, nor anything like him. I served him too, you remember, and I felt the magic of him – who could not, when it touched them? I think he will go on capturing hearts long after we are dead and gone, he and you and I. But here and now we're alive, I in my lonely state and you in yours. Shall we be wise, my dear, and live our lives out together? I've loved you since I first set eyes on you.'

'Yes,' she said wonderingly. 'I think I knew. It was the night at Holyrood. That was the night of our fate – mine to love him, and you to love me. But – marry me, Allan? Would you do that – now?'

'Now, more than ever.' He took her hands. 'I was too proud to ask you before, when you were rich and I was poor, but now I believe I can match you, shilling for shilling, since much of your wealth has been given away. Will you have me, Dorothy? For I'll never marry any but you.'

She looked up into the dark, kindly face of the man who had waited so patiently for her, and knew him worthy of all the trust and all the love she could give him, though the first dayspring glory was gone from her heart; for it comes but once in a life.

'Yes, Allan, gladly I will,' she said, and went into his arms. He held her as though he would never let her go – then, 'For Guid's sake, take off yon beldam's mutch!' he said, and snatched the offending cap from her head, so that her hair fell down about her shoulders in a brown riot, and she seemed a girl again.

L'Envoi

And after all, against great odds, they were happy. Allan was firm
that from the day of their marriage they should live in his house in
Hanover Square, both for the sake of his London practice and his
appointment as physician to the newly founded Middlesex Hospital,
and because he wished Dorothy away from Carola House and its
memories. Paul and his second wife, who had been pretty Miss
Sophia Templeton, bought it out of the bride's handsome dowry,
and lived there many years in great comfort among their large
family.

Four children were born to Dorothy: an infant who died at birth,
and two more boys and a girl, James, Edward and Mary, the last
two being twins. They were all healthy, thanks to the watchfulness
of a father with advanced ideas of medicine, and their looks were
striking. To Dorothy they were a constant joy and cause for deep
gratitude when she thought of the barren existence to which she had
been drifting when Allan rescued her. The daily round of a famous
physician's wife was busy and social; her old dreaminess fell away
from her, and it seemed almost as though there had never been a
time when she and Allan had not been together. Only when she was
quite alone, Allan out and the children asleep, and the watchman
called the hours in Hanover Square, did she allow her mind back to
the past, and another companion.

She had heard of him, over the years. English Jacobites had rejoiced in his separation from Clementina Walkinshaw, whom they
had unjustly suspected of being a Government spy. She had run
away from him, taking their daughter, the little Charlotte who was
the only creature he cared for deeply in the world. Then, years later,
Jacobite hopes revived with his marriage to a pretty, shallow German
princess thirty-two years younger than himself. The marriage had
been fruitless and disastrous; 'Queen' Louise, too, had left him and
gone to a young lover.

Old George II was gone. His grandson George III was English-born and amiable, restoring the Hanoverian line to popularity. In England the Jacobite Cause was finished and dead. But in Scotland, that poor penalised country, still suffering from the harsh laws that had come in after Culloden, they remembered Prince Tearlach, prayed for him, made songs of love and longing, told their children and their grandchildren of his beauty, his bravery, his power to charm hearts. The least scraps of clothing he had worn in the Highlands – tattered brogues, a fragment of plaid – were treasured like the holy relics of saints, to be handed down the generations or buried in the owner's coffin.

Dorothy had nothing. Neither miniature, brooch, letter or lock of hair was hers to cherish. The Star had blazed across her life and gone into the darkness, leaving nothing behind. And she cared not at all, for her memories of him were alive and enduring as no frail ribbon or flower or curl could be, her secret joy and pride.

On a February day in 1788 Dorothy sat by a bed in the night-nursery at the top of the tall house, reading to her first grandchild, five-year-old Robert – James's son. Now sixty-three, she was the very picture of a plump, contented, comfortable matron, grey-haired, but elegant and still, Allan was kind enough to say, beautiful. She glanced from the pages of *Goody-Two-Shoes* to Robert's chubby flushed face, now burrowed into the pillow, his long dark lashes sweeping his cheek, his mouth a pouting cherub's. She closed the book and was about to leave the nursery quietly (for Robert had a feverish cold and must sleep as much as he could) when a copy of the *Monthly Chronicle* caught her eye. Mary had brought it up to her earlier, but she had not had time to glance at it. She opened the paper, wincing at the loud crackling it made, and saw the notice.

DIED. On the 31st ult. at Rome, about half past nine o'clock, Prince Charles Edward Lewis Casimir Stuart. Since the death of his father in the year 1765, he assumed the title of King of England. He was just sixty-seven years and one month old on the day of his

315

death. It is reported that Prince Charles had for some weeks
previous lain in a stupor, rousing only to caress a small dog which
never left his side, after having suffered a stroke brought on by the
incautious remarks of a visitor who had spoken to him of the
lamentable events of 1745. He died in the arms of his natural
daughter by Miss Clementina Walkinshaw, Charlotte, styled
Countess of Albany, and was interred in the Cathedral Church of
Frascati; of which see the Cardinal Duke of York, his brother, is
bishop. The Cardinal had scarcely begun to chant the Office
appointed by the church for the dead, when it was observed that
his voice faltered, the tears trickled down his cheeks, so that it was
feared he would not have been able to proceed; however . . .

The paper slipped to the floor as Dorothy covered her face with
her hands.

Robert's eyes were open, wonderingly staring at her. 'Grandmama?' Adults, in his experience, did not weep; that was the
privilege of the nursery. But Grandmama's handkerchief had
already swept briskly across her face, and she was smiling quite as
usual.

'Nothing, my dear – I think I have caught a little cold, like you.
Shall we have some more of Goody Two-Shoes?'

Robert pondered. 'No. A song, if you please.'

'Oh dear! I am in very bad voice, I fear.' But after a moment she
began to sing, very softly.

'If you had seen my Charlie at the head of his army,
  He was a gallant sight to behold,
  With his fine tartan hose on his bonnie round leg,
  And his buckles of pure shining gold.

'My love was six foot two without stocking or shoe,
  In proportion my true love was built,
  'Tis no wonder for sure, upon Culloden Moor,
  For his sake the brave Highlanders were killed.

'Prince Charlie Stuart was my true love's name,
And he was the flower of Scotland and a pride unto her fame.
And now they have banished him over the main,
And sae dear was my Charlie to me.'

Robert had been listening raptly. 'More, Grandmama, more.'
She shook her head, a voice now stilled echoing in her heart.
'There is no more, my dear. It is the end of an old song.'